NIGHTWING

THE STARCHASER SAGA
BOOK III

R. DUGAN

WAVE WALKER
press

NIGHTWING
Copyright © 2020 by R. Dugan

For information contact:
R. Dugan
PO Box 1265
Martinsville, IN 46151
reneeduganwriting.com

Cover design by Maja Kopunovic
Map by Jessica Khoury
ISBN: 978-1-7339255-2-5

First Edition: December 2020

10 9 8 7 6 5 4 3 2 1

CONTENT WARNING:

This book contains scenes of verbal badgering, emotional and physical abuse, intense confinement, and sexual harassment and mentions of assault.

Discretion is advised for readers sensitive to these themes.

DEDICATION

To Danny
With my whole heart. For my whole life.

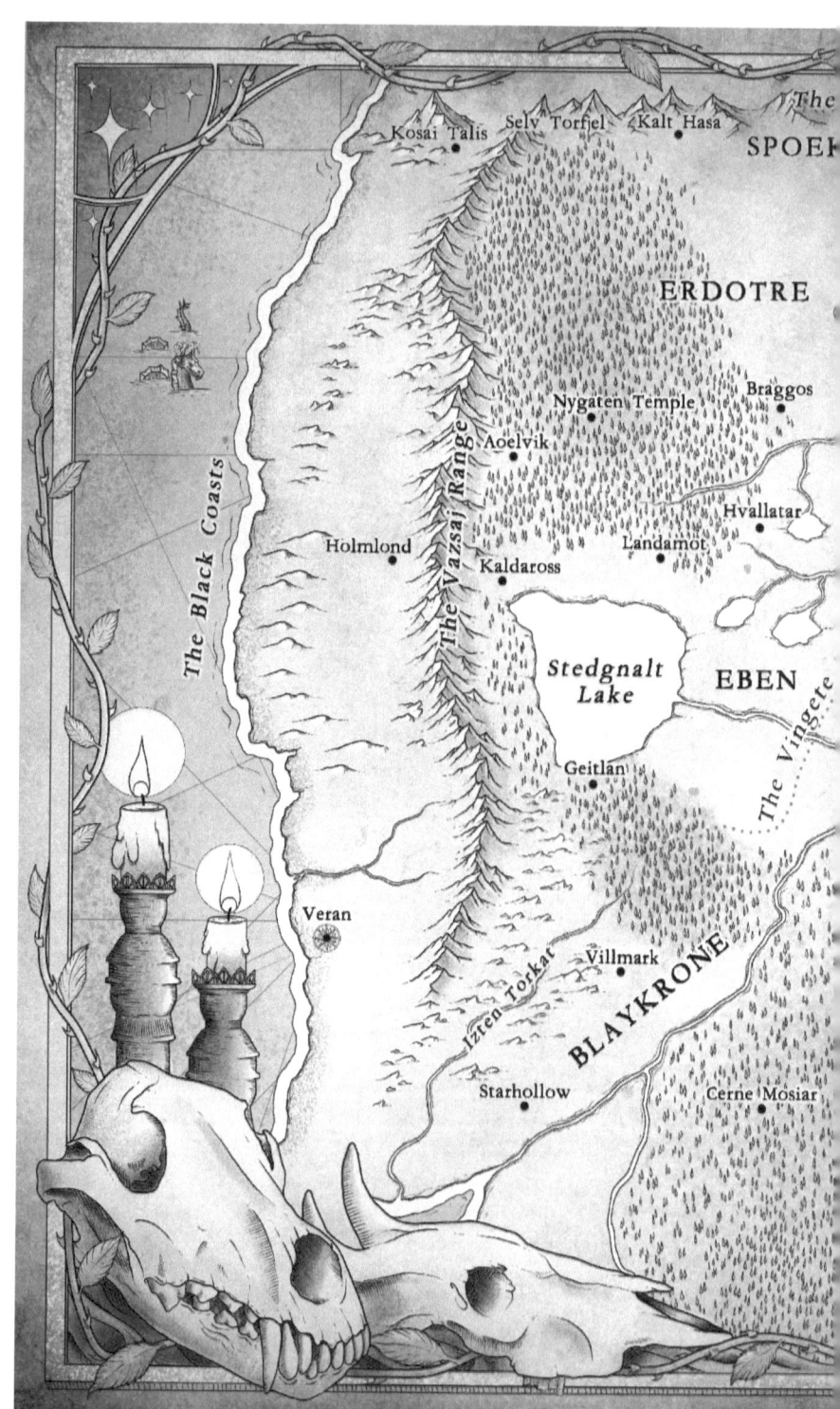

The

Kosai Talis • Selv Torfjel • Kalt Hasa

SPOEK

ERDOTRE

Nygaten Temple •
Aoelvik •
Braggos

Holmlond •
Kaldaross •
Landamot •
Hvallatar

The Black Coasts

The Vazsai Range

Stedgnalt
Lake

EBEN

The Vingete

Geitlan •

Veran •

Izten Torkar
Villmark •

BLAYKRONE

Starhollow •
Cerne Mosiar •

ek

ORDBRAN

Azkai Temple

KROAKEN

Felstrond

Hatcheries

Detlyse Halet

Keltei Temple

Niort River

LATAUS

ERD

The Wildwood

Soratt Temple

copr. 2020 Jessica Khoury

THE QUEEN

OF

ICE AND
STONE

CHAPTER ONE

Six names hovered like a vapor in the darkness above Princess Cistine Novacek of Talheim, pushed from her mouth in whispers while she rose and fell in steady curls from the floor.

"Thorne. Ashe. Quill. Tatiana. Maleck. Ariadne."

Her stomach throbbed when she raised herself up with her core and touched her elbows to her bent knees for the thirtieth time. The thirty-fifth. The fortieth. She kept her gaze on the ceiling bathed in freckles of ghostlight, pale like forks of lightning, like—

Cistine slammed down on her back and squeezed her eyes shut, but not quickly enough to dispel the image of Julian Bartos racing toward her, sword upraised, before the augmented lightning pierced straight into his body, pocked and blistered his skin, and melted his midnight eyes from their sockets.

Muscles burning, pulse pounding in the base of her skull, Cistine slowly sat up and peered around the cold chamber's dark hollows, mineral-licked roof, locked door, and the lonely bed where she'd huddled for the first several days of her captivity, rocked with grief-stricken dreams of Julian and the cabal. Then she'd started to hear them, whispers of their presence reminding her what they would have done if *they* were captured.

Tatiana would recite names and places to keep her mind focused. Quill would hone his muscles, preparing for a fight. Maleck would internalize the quiet and make it an ally rather than an enemy. Ariadne and Ashe would map the room and choose where to make a stand. Julian would tell her not to let them make a fool of Talheim's sole heir; to do her crown and parents proud. And Thorne would hold his head high, like a Valgardan High Tribune should, and make his captors feel they were trapped with *him*.

These thoughts had finally goaded her into core-tightening exercises and push-ups, then to drawing maps of Valgard's eight territories—Spoek, Nordbran, Kroaken, Lataus, Unsverd, Blaykrone, Eben, and Erdotre—with water from the drinking cup waiting on the steps every morning when she woke. While she did these things, the same gnawing reminder always lingered.

She should not be able to do any of them. She should have died on Eben's plains when she confronted Chancellor Salvotor of Kanslar Court. But she'd survived the unsurvivable because she was the Key.

She shuddered and shut her eyes, hugging her sore middle. All the excuses she made when augments didn't destroy her before were worthless that day on the plains; somehow, when the Doors to the Gods were sealed shut at the end of the war between the Middle Kingdom and the North, her destiny was forged—a Key to the lids that sealed the wells of gods-given power. So Salvotor had captured her and locked her away in this small room for *weeks*, waiting to discover the mystery of her.

Iron clattered as the chain on the other side of her door loosened. Cistine scrambled onto the bed, fighting to slow her breathing as a burly man descended the short flight of steps into the room. He was old enough to be her father, and as well-groomed as a King's Cadre Warden, silver-fletched hair, beard, and mustache meticulously trimmed, warm brown skin freckled with old scars, and slate-gray eyes solemn in the rosy light of the crushed ghostplants in his lamp.

He'd been here when Cistine first woke in this place, leaving a pair of muslin pajamas on the bed and taking away her shredded nightgown. He hadn't spoken a single unkind word to her, but there was a shadow on his brow Cistine didn't recall seeing whenever he left food and water while she watched through her lashes, pretending to be asleep. This time, he carried only a simple wooden box.

Unease curled in her stomach. "You're...Kristoff, aren't you? The head of the Vassora here?"

His brow creased. "In practice, if not in title." His voice was slow, warm, and husky—things she wished she could trust. "You've been summoned for supper."

"I thought I wasn't allowed to leave this room."

"You have a...guest."

She folded her arms. "I'm not feeling well enough for supper tonight."

Kristoff sighed. "You aren't being given a choice. Neither of us are."

"Will you drag me out?"

"No, but I will absolutely throw you over my shoulder. If you behave like a child, that's how you'll be treated."

Cistine almost jutted her tongue at him, almost reminded him she was not a child, but a prisoner.

The thought made her grow still.

A princess imprisoned. Like her own mother, Solene, and Julian's mother Eboni, abducted by Jad of Mahasar to goad Prince Cyril into starting a war more than twenty years ago. The clever women had plunged Mahasar's capital into disarray with manipulative words and playacting, turning Prince Jad against his father.

That was the legacy she came from.

The memory lifted Cistine's head high and drew her shoulders back. "I suppose I can make time for a guest."

Kristoff's mouth twitched, then firmed again when he opened the box. The dress inside was artfully-tailored lace and silk, floor-length, with long, sheer sleeves. It was also pale purple—the color inside a stroke of lightning.

Her heart jumped into her throat, and she shook her head.

"I don't like this any more than you," Kristoff grunted. "But things will be far worse if you don't do as you're told."

Bristling with more than just indignation, Cistine snatched up the dress and stalked to the small relief alcove at the foot of the bed. She loathed the clash of pale lavender against skin that had begun to lose its sun-kissed tan, as if the hours spent training on the rock top in Hellidom and tending her garden behind the Den had never happened. "Where did this come from? Should I assume this place has shops?"

"That gown belonged to my sister."

Tears pricked Cistine's eyes at the terrible heaviness in Kristoff's voice. When Baba Kallah died, she struggled to fathom the cabal's grief; yet now that she'd lost her and Julian both, she not only fathomed this man's agony, she *felt* it like a blow to the ribs.

For the first time, it occurred to her that the Vassora who often thwarted the cabal's plans might have their own griefs to carry.

She stuffed her feet back into her dirty slippers and stepped out to find that even while she took pains to hide herself, Kristoff had also turned his back, giving her all the privacy he could.

Cistine's fury softened. He was obeying his orders; that was not something she could fault him for. After all, why would he defy his superiors for her? She was only a tool of his kingdom.

"Should I twirl?" she asked.

Kristoff faced her, a strange emotion guttering across his face. "Come. We're short of time."

They stepped out into an arched stone corridor, the ghostlamp in Kristoff's hand bringing the only light for many paces. Cistine tried to decipher anything about her prison from the dark, heavy rock, which opened into a larger chamber at the corridor's end, the walls hewn in articulate lines and inlaid statues. Kristoff led her down another hall to the right, shorter than the last one and lit with a string of smaller ghostlit bulbs paving the way into a broad stone dining hall. Her so-called guest sat at the table, and at the sight of his face Cistine's knees turned to water.

Chancellor Salvotor.

CHAPTER TWO

L IMBS LOCKED, HEAD reeling, heart slamming against her ribs like a caged animal, Cistine didn't know whether to retreat or catapult across the polished stone table to wrap her hands around Salvotor's diamond-hard, armored throat.

Kanslar's leader. Thorne's father. The man who murdered Julian Bartos in cold blood.

As if he sensed her pain and grossed pleasure from it, the Chancellor smiled up from his meal of pork and asparagus. Cistine's empty stomach snarled at the smell of food, and Salvotor's brows leaped. "Kristoff, I didn't realize you resorted to starving children. That seems so *unlike* you."

"She's been given her meals every morning and evening," Kristoff replied stiffly.

"Far be it from me to a question a fellow father's routines, of course, but hasn't it been some time since you had children to feed?"

Kristoff's breath audibly hitched.

"She'll dine with me each night from now on," Salvotor continued, "so I can ensure she's being *properly* looked after. Out you go."

When Kristoff retreated, hands in fists, Salvotor dabbed his scaled face and gestured down the table. "Sit. I insist."

Slowly, Cistine lowered herself onto the throne-like chair opposing his.

"Eat."

She would not.

Salvotor smiled, dark and humorless, folding his napkin and then his hands on the table. "I understand you've been quite lonely these last weeks, so I'm prepared to sit with you until you finish your supper."

Cistine looked down at the meal before her, the same as his. Her mouth watered against her will. "First, tell me where I am."

Salvotor's brow cocked. "One of the old temples...the place where you were created."

Her spine tingled. Over two decades ago, her father had stood somewhere in these same halls with the *visnprests* of that time—cruel masters of augmentation now called Bloodwights—and forged the lock over the lids. Salvotor had suggested the keying came from her father's bloodline straight to her...that she could reopen the wells. Yet he'd done nothing about it for weeks.

There was something more to this. Something he wasn't telling her.

Salvotor delicately sliced his portion of meat. "You know, I've considered lately that you and I aren't so different." A scoff bubbled up in Cistine's throat, and he smiled. "Really! My father crafted me into a sword at Valgard's neck, guiding the Courts back to unity under one King. And you...born or made, however it was done, your father saw *you*, and he said, *Now, here is the perfect vessel to harness augmentation's potential.*" He popped the bite into his mouth, hungry gaze fixed on her while he chewed. "I will give purpose to your suffering, a call higher than your throne. You will be the salvation of Valgard when I spill your blood on the Doors...all of it, I gather."

Underneath the gray haze of terror, a spark ignited at his questing tone.

"You gather?" Cistine echoed, raising her eyes to him.

Brushing aside his platter, Salvotor studied her. "I understand that when you first came to the Northern Kingdom, my son struck a truce with you. I'm prepared to do the same."

Cistine curved her fingers over her kneecap until her unpared nails bit into her skin. Make a truce with the man who *slayed* Julian—

"There is information I require from you," Salvotor said, "which none of the *visnprests* I've brought here possess. They do suspect there are other items which must be gathered to open the Doors. And as much as I would like to think the former Order wasn't foolish enough to spread the Key's power among tangible objects...well, nothing was beneath your father's cunning. So, rather than risk spilling all your blood only to find I sullied everything, I'm prepared to strike a bargain with you. Talheim's knowledge of the ritual in exchange for one solemn act from me."

The offer woke no more than a flutter of hope in her. This was Chancellor Salvotor, who beat his wife and son and broke his own mother's leg out of sheer rage and spite. He would give her *nothing*, no matter what she gave him. So she told him the truth: "I don't know about any ritual."

"I see." Salvotor studied her a long moment, then rose. "Come. I want to show you something."

Kristoff awaited them in the hewn antechamber, his gaze latching onto Cistine when Salvotor beckoned to him. They marched her between them across the room, through a row of high stone arches, into the temple's interior—a broad gulch that dropped away to nothing, its halves laced together by stone bridges.

"This is where the keying took place," Salvotor said. "Before, it was undivided. But with that ritual..."

Cistine stared into the foul darkness below, her stomach clenching. Her father's choices had brought about so many wounds she never fathomed, even to the North's very flesh.

A pair of Vassora guarded a staircase across the gulch, and Salvotor led Cistine and Kristoff up the steep vault to a landing high above that cratered wound, then left into a tunnel hollowed from the temple wall. They walked for what seemed like a full mile in darkness; sweating despite the cold, Cistine almost gasped with relief when hints of light prodded around a pair of half-doors ahead.

For the first time in weeks, she stepped outside—and slid to a halt.

They stood on a crescent balcony jutting from the face of a mountain. A dark sky stretched above, its cloudy face shredded by great gales of wind and blinding snow lifted from the peaks all around. Miles and miles of great heights and deep chasms enclosed this fortress, clearly not one of the four temples on Tatiana's map. The cabal might not even know this place existed.

So they might never find her here.

Cistine ran to the railing and flung herself against it, peering down. The plunge was straight and far, down into bottomless shadows even deeper than the Wound. No handholds to climb like Quill taught her.

She was truly trapped.

Salvotor slammed his hands against the railing on either side of hers, and Cistine tasted bile at his lewd heat. "This is all that's left of the world. I am more than glad to take my time with you, so ask yourself just how quickly you would like this to *end*—Wildheart."

She stiffened at the sound of that Name, spoken by Thorne in a pain-and-panic-stricken daze on Eben's plains. It was meant to belong only to them; she'd never even gotten to ask him about it, when he chose it, what it meant for them. And already Salvotor wielded it as a weapon to break her.

"Consider it deeply." He tucked a thread of Cistine's hair behind her ear. "This all ends the moment you tell me the truth about that ritual."

He left her leaning against the railing, knees quaking, staring across the void, windswept landscape.

Heat and heaviness descended on Cistine's shoulders, and she flinched; but it was only Kristoff, shedding his coat for her. Wrapping her fingers in the collar and inhaling the comforting smell of leaves and smoke from its folds, she stared up at his blazing eyes. "What *is* this place?"

"Kalt Hasa. One of the oldest of all the temples, now a prison for Kanslar's most valuable informants," Kristoff sighed. "Salvotor is like a raven who stashes his treasures here where no other thief can find them. He's been doing this since the war ended."

Notions of ravens punched into Cistine's throat, awakening a brush of cinnamon sticks and dangerous smiles. "Why are *you* here?"

He swept snow from the railing. "You'll have enough nightmares to contend with from now on. You don't need my stories adding to them."

Cistine's bowels clenched. "What's going to happen to me?"

"Salvotor will find a way to break you. He's exceptional at that...he perfected the craft on his own *valenar* and son."

The words struck through her body like a blade, snapping her back to awareness of the cold stone against her slippered feet and the wind kissing her brow. The abuse Thorne suffered at Salvotor's hands, scripted both in tangible whipmarks and shame invisible to most, was the reason he never wanted her to confront his father. But she was here now, and there was no escape in sight. Not yet.

Cistine shut her eyes, and for a moment she was on the balcony outside her room in the Den, with Thorne beside her. The moan of the wind became the roar of the Nior River. If she looked to her right, he would be leaning there, arms folded, dark sleeves pushed to his elbows, augment-shocked silver hair falling into his eyes, staring across the garden he gave her.

She let the memory shift, imagined his chest against her back, sheltering and strengthening her, letting her lean into his might—blended hearts becoming one between every breath.

Selvenar.

The impossible word beat through her blood, a truth she'd wrestled with and finally made sense of after days lying in her chamber, sorting through every memory she and Thorne shared. He was her blended heart, and somewhere out there in the wild lands beyond these mountains, he was fighting to find her. She knew it. As long as he drew breath, as long as anyone in the cabal did, she was not forgotten in this desolate place.

She was not alone

Returning to him, to those six names whispered in the darkness, would not be easy. Salvotor had allowed her this glimpse of freedom only to break her. But if he wanted her broken so desperately, it was because he feared what she would become if left to flourish.

The cabal had trained her to face Salvotor, not only with weapons, but with an adamant mind. They'd taken a princess hiding behind her Warden and yanked her through a crucible so she could stand on this battlefield and not be cut down.

I'm not going to die here.

She would sleep tonight a captive and rise a warrior. Tomorrow, the battle began—not just for herself, but for everyone Salvotor sought to make victim with his fist tightening around Valgard's vulnerable throat.

She would not be a prisoner, a victim, a tool of Valgard's designs. She was a princess. A warrior of the cabal.

She was the Wild Heart of Fire. And she would burn this mountain of ice and stone to the ground.

CHAPTER THREE

T HE MOMENT ASHEILA Kovar entered the Den, she knew something was wrong.

The gush of the Nior River down Lataus's plains into Unsverd, the throaty churn of the watermills, and the quiet hum of night life in Hellidom were all exactly as she remembered from before her captivity in the desert prison of Siralek. But when she stepped into the Den, haunches smarting from weeks of hard horseback riding, all illusions of peace dispelled.

The entry room was unnervingly empty. Rarely had Ashe ever entered this house without being accosted by at least one of the warriors who lived here, but all that greeted them now was silence and a dark sort of anticipation.

Judging by her companions' faces, they found the pause as unsettling as she did. On her left, Maleck grazed his hands over Starfall and Stormfury, the twin sabers harnessed to his back. Dim ghostlight from the hallway painted the contours of his face, a battle of youth and age framed by warrior braids, his right eye rived by a gnarled scar. On her right, Aden tensed, the sharp lines of his muscles bulging against his shirt. "Where are they?"

Maleck stepped forward, sliding Starfall a bare inch from its sheath. "Thorne?"

The answer echoed down the hall ahead: "Here, Maleck."

With a punctuated breath of relief, Maleck clicked Starfall back into its sheath and led the way down the dark hall, past the empty doorframes of Ashe and Julian's rooms, to the kitchen where the cabal gathered amid a cluster of tawny ghostlamps.

Cistine must be asleep—it was well past the usual hour she retired—but all the others were there. Thorne, wearing his swords and usual dark shirt and pants, bent with his hands spread on the maps covering the tabletop, silver hair knotted at the nape of his neck and threads hanging loose around his unshaven cheeks. To his right was Ariadne, mouth set fiercely, upturned eyes charting strategy from the maps.

To Thorne's left stood Tatiana, dark skin limned in licks of amber, curls tamed in a short, frazzled braid down her back, and wearing battle armor rather than her usual fashionable threads. Perpetually at her side was Quill, tall and muscled, his thumbs hooked in his belt and his white topcoat of hair turned over the shaved half of his head, revealing the scar that turned the roots as pale as Thorne's.

They all looked up from the maps when Maleck joined them, completing the intimate image of the small band of trusted warriors and leaving Ashe and Aden exposed in the doorway.

Tatiana straightened up, eyes wide. Quill swore colorfully, his gaze flashing to Thorne, who slowly slid his hands from the table. Ariadne pressed her hand to her mouth, staring at Aden like a specter. None of them paid Ashe any mind, much to her relief.

Thorne pushed against the table's edge as if to round it, then halted, trembling. "*Aden.* You're—I thought Noaam—"

"Tortured your location from me?" Cautious softness edged Aden's voice, a tone Ashe had never heard before. "Not on pain of death, Thorne. Not even then."

Thorne blew out a hoarse breath and fell on his heels, sweeping the loose threads of hair from his face and looking from Aden to Ashe. A jolt of shock coursed through his eyes. "You were in *Siralek?*"

Ashe mustered a nod. There was no telling what he would do once he discovered the whole truth.

"Thorne," Maleck cut in suddenly. "Why do all these maps lead from Jovadalsa?"

Ashe's muscles strummed with warning. Jovadalsa was the city where Tribune Sander, her sponsor and tentative ally in Siralek, had instructed them to bring Thorne in exchange for setting Ashe and Aden free.

Thorne slowly settled his fingertips over the maps, broad fingers trembling. "There was...an incident."

Ashe's hair rose, her gaze darting around the table, then toward the hall leading from the kitchen. "Where is Cistine?"

The way Thorne looked at her...Ashe would've rather been trampled by a rampaging Dahadt or had a knife shoved into her gut again. *Anything* to escape that life-shattering collision of anger, sorrow, and ferocity in his gaze. "That's what I'm trying to find out."

Ashe grabbed the back of the nearest chair to keep from buckling to the floor. Maleck rasped, "What happened?"

"Salvotor brought all of Kanslar's Tribunes to Eben's plains outside Jovadalsa. I made a mistake...I went to confront him. Cistine and Julian followed me."

"You confronted him?" Aden's voice dripped shock. "You can't kill him, Thorne! To put a blade to *any* of the Chancellors would mean your head, or have you forgotten that after ten years of running?"

"I thought it was worth my life to end his before he hurt someone else!"

Guilt ripped through Ashe at the break in his tone. People were already hurt because of her mistakes. Thorne's grandmother was dead on her account. No wonder he'd been reckless, even desperate enough to face Salvotor himself. Just like Nimea and her Tumult devised from Siralek's catacombs.

Just like Ashe had once hoped and helped bring to pass.

Softly, Thorne added, "Cistine did not agree. She confronted my father...her blade against his augments."

Horror stole Ashe's breath. She'd earned a place in the Cadre running from a life of confections and bakeries to fight in the war that took augments away. During those battles, she'd seen Cistine's grandfather fall and her father become King on the battlefield. She'd seen what augmentation could do. "Tell me you gave her something more than those pitiful training threads to stand against him."

Thorne's face darkened. "She had no armor. She didn't need it."

Maleck's eyes snapped to his High Tribune's face. "What?"

The next words harshened, torn from Thorne's throat. "She's the Key."

CHAPTER FOUR

"THAT ISN'T POSSIBLE." Ashe's voice clattered into dead quiet around the table. King Cyril had mentioned the Key's existence, but never what it was—only that it could open the Doors to the Gods, and as part of the truce with the northern kingdom, he'd taken it with him when they left Valgard as conquerors. But Cistine had been born nearly a year after the war.

Only when Ariadne nodded did Ashe realize she breathed those words aloud. "It's possible the Doors were keyed, not to an object, but to the Novacek bloodline. Cyril and all his heirs would be Keys."

"How can you know that?" Ashe snapped.

Ariadne's eyes cut away. "I know a great deal about augmentation."

Augmentation. Which Cistine needed no armor to guard against.

Gods, Ashe hated that it made *sense*. The way Cistine yearned to go to the north long before her father ever suggested alliance with them, and after they came, how enraptured she seemed with this place....

"What happened when they fought?" Maleck demanded.

Thorne turned his face away, but not quickly enough to hide the cut of a tear down his stubbled jaw. "Salvotor killed Julian and captured Cistine."

Ashe broke down to her knees, ears full of a dull, endless whine, vision straying with sparks and dapples. Julian...*dead*. And Cistine, the *Key*, her own princess—

"I know that look," Tatiana said. "Mal, catch!"

Maleck barely snatched a bowl from the counter and hurled it to her before Ashe's stomach spewed out the day's rations of dried fruit and jerky.

Quill grimaced. "That's how we felt when Thorne told us."

"I am going to find her." Thorne held Ashe's gaze unflinchingly. "And anything my father had done to her, I'll repay him tenfold. A hundredfold. I will do anything—*anything*—to bring her home."

"What do you have so far?" Aden asked.

Thorne drew a dagger from his hip and traced paths from Jovadalsa with its edge. "We've searched almost as far as Eben's borders in every direction. There's no sign of which way my father went when he fled like a stars-damned *coward*."

"But there are other places we can search," Ariadne added. "Salvotor wants to unlock the Doors and gather as many augments for himself as possible. With spies in two of the four other Courts, he's in good position to take power when Kanslar's constellation sets in just over a month."

"All he needs is a crippling blow that would force Traisende and Yager to submit." Quill turned his hair across his head, covering his scar. "Killing Cistine and taking control of a whole well would do it, but for that, he needs a *visnprest's* touch."

Maleck paled. "The temples."

Thorne dug the knife lightly into separate parts of the map: "Keltei, Sorrat, Nygaten, and Azkai."

Cleaning her mouth on her wrist, Ashe hauled herself shakily up against the table to follow his plan. "Dividing your forces?"

Thorne nodded. "He'll bring her to a temple sooner or later. When he does, we'll intercept him. It's good you're back, Maleck. We rely on your swords."

"And you have them." Maleck's voice was steady, but when he glanced at the knife sunk into Azkai Temple, his face turned the color of sour milk. "But first, there's a price we still must pay for stopping the assassins and bringing Aden and Ashe home. I received aid from Tribune Sander in exchange for securing a meeting between you and him, Thorne."

Wary recognition flashed in Thorne's eyes. "Interesting, since I watched him tackle my father to the plains and buy us time to run." His gaze flicked to Ashe. "Where and when?"

Maleck tapped the map. "Jovadalsa. As soon as we're able."

"Tomorrow, then."

"Faer's not back from Starhollow yet," Quill protested.

"He'll have to fend for himself when he returns. I'm sorry, Quill. I'd rather keep a raven waiting than a Tribune with tenuous loyalties."

Frowning, Quill took his leave from the kitchen without further argument. The others trailed after him, even Aden, until only Thorne and Ashe remained.

Thorne ripped the knife from the table's surface and gestured to Ashe with the tip. "So. It was you who told Nimea about Hellidom."

That name blasted through Ashe like a foul wind—the leader of the Tumult, a part of Thorne's secret Court until she was caught, condemned, and sent to Siralek because of Aden's betrayal. One of many injustices she and Ashe accounted to Thorne and tried to retribute from the Hive, killing Baba Kallah in the process.

When she didn't deny her guilt, Thorne's eyes brightened with grief. "Why, Ashe?"

"I blamed you," she said, "for breaking Cistine's heart, for trying to use her against your father. I hated Valgard with everything in me after what you did, and I thought she hated you, too. I was doing it for both of us."

Thorne grimaced. "You aren't the first to try to kill me. What I want to know is how you justified attacking my cabal. My *grandmother*. And putting Cistine in that kind of danger."

"I didn't—"

Thorne stabbed the knife point into the tabletop, the dull crunch silencing Ashe like a slap to the mouth. "This is where she sat with Baba Kallah and our witness against Salvotor. Both of them drank poisoned tea meant for me. Both died within minutes. Thank the stars Cistine didn't touch her cup."

Her cup. Ashe's knees wobbled again. "I thought she and Julian left

Valgard like I told them to. I didn't know she was ever in danger."

"But you knew my cabal might be."

"Nimea gave me her word no one else would die."

But she'd never truly believed that. She'd listened to them make bets about which warriors might fall on a sword to keep Thorne alive. She'd thought of Maleck dodging assassins, fighting to stay alive, and every time wrestled her guilt in the dark. And still she'd followed hate over sense.

"You took her word because her fury fed yours." Thorne shook his head. "It's one thing to be honest about your deeds. It's another to be clear about the motivations behind them. You were selfish, and that endangered my cabal, *your* princess, and Julian. It cost my grandmother her *life*."

"I didn't mean for her to be caught up in this. My quarrel was with you."

Thorne's eyes gleamed. "The lies I told Cistine were reprehensible, but I confessed to them and begged for her forgiveness...and she gave it. I would have begged for yours if you hadn't struck back from under the desert sand like a scorpion." He shook his head. "But my apologies would've gone unheard, anyway. You were determined to repay my deception with anger, even if it put innocent people in danger. That kind of self-justification is dangerous, and so is the hatred it shields. I can't trust my back to you...or the backs of my cabal. Your knife is already buried in them." He left his place at the head of the table and rounded its edge at last, shadows gathering in his gaze. "You are banished from Hellidom, from this Den, and from my cabal. If you're seen in the city after dawn tomorrow, you'll be run out at the tip of a sword."

Ashe crooked her fingers into fists, a fight building inside her; but what good would it do? There was no reason to stay except to spite him, and that would only delay their search for Cistine. Still, she couldn't resist a final jab. "As you wish, *Chancellor*."

Thorne's sharp intake of breath was the closest to a reaction she would win. But all he said was, "Your things remain as they were. Take them and as much food as you need when you go."

Once he was gone, the Den's front door whispering shut behind him,

Ashe returned to her room.

It looked almost untouched. Her last change of clothes was still folded on the bedside table, with her soap of choice for the bath she never took the night Cistine dragged her and Julian off to Villmark. Only the pillow had moved from where she left it, taking up the middle of the bed now.

"Cistine grieved for you here."

Ashe glanced over her shoulder at the doorway, taken up with Maleck's dark presence.

"Baba Kallah told her to fall a princess," he added, "and rise a queen. And she did. She's become mightier than any of us could've fathomed. I have no doubt we will see her again."

Ashe nodded, clinging to that desperate hope, dangerous though it was. Maleck stepped into the room, brandishing a cloth-wrapped parcel between his hands.

"I have something of yours." He cast back the wrap, and Ashe cursed with relief. Echelon—her prized sword, gifted to her by Lord Rion himself—was still honed as fiercely as when she dropped it down the sewer shaft into Maleck's hands. Its polish reflected her face when she drew it gently from Maleck's flat, open palms. "I hope its quality remains to your standard. Valgardan swordkeeping differs from Talheim's."

"She's flawless." The snag in Ashe's voice surprised even her; the sword's familiar weight was like a handshake from an old friend.

"Then may she serve you well as you journey home." Maleck let the armored cloth flutter to the floor between them, lifted her sheath from his back, and offered it. "In spite of what you've done, I only want your freedom and happiness, Asheila. And to see you walk from this kingdom without pain in your stride."

"If I can do that, it's mostly thanks to you." She slipped on the sheath and spun Echelon into it. "Thank you for looking after my sword. And my princess."

Maleck tousled a hand through his braids. "What happened in Siralek, with Nimea's Tumult—"

Scowling, she turned away, snatching up her rucksack and piling her change of clothes into it. "We're not discussing that."

"I want you to know I harbor no hate in my heart."

Ashe yanked her pack shut and snapped back around to face him. "Are you blind?"

His gaze bored into her, seeing clearly. Seeing too much. "I too have been desperate. Fought with shadows...and surrendered to them."

"You've never betrayed the people you love."

"You know I have. I told you how Quill came by his scar."

Ashe grimaced, yanking a hand through her own hair. "Not like this. Not this badly."

"If I did, would you scorn me forever?"

Her breath caught. Even when she scorned every other Valgardan, had she hated him?

"Just stop," she muttered. "You don't get to do this."

"What am I doing? Understanding you? Seeking a way to forgive you?"

Ashe tossed her pack over her shoulder. "I don't need your pity, Maleck."

"I don't pity you." He bent his shoulder away as she brushed past him. "But my heart breaks for you."

Ashe's heels snagged on the threshold.

"I know what it is to feel friendless in the world," Maleck spoke into the room, not facing her though they stood nearly shoulder-to-shoulder. "To believe no one will ever welcome you back after what you've done. I hope you can find forgiveness for yourself...for those around you. And know that I will do everything in my power to find Cistine, as I did everything I could to find you. I'm sorry I didn't come sooner."

"Don't apologize for that." She picked up his scarf and thrust it back to him. "I didn't ask you to look for me. I just gave you my sword."

Shaking his head, Maleck gently pushed the scarf back. "Keep it. The southern woods are cold this time of year." He offered the barest flicker of a smile, the same one he gave her the first time she slipped and told him her full name, back in Starhollow while they waited for Thorne and Cistine to find their way back from the Izten Torkat. Then he brushed past her and strode down the hall. "If you ever need aid, go to the *Tavern of Six Thieves* in Jovadalsa. You'll find it there."

He vanished, one shadow slipping into the many shrouding the Den.

Binding the armored scarf around her throat, Ashe glanced at the vacant sleeping room across from hers. Pain rooted deep in her chest, pushing heat to her eyes.

Julian had been so young, cocky, loyal, and Ashe didn't need the entire account to know he perished protecting Cistine. If he were still here—if she had the minds of two Wardens on this task, rather than her own, muddled and alone—they wouldn't have to rely on the cabal. That would be enough.

All at once, a notion slid into her mind. Risky. Desperate. But it might be Cistine's best hope.

It wasn't Julian she needed. It was his father.

CHAPTER FIVE

I T WAS A pity Quill didn't take her bet and make her five mynts richer. Tatiana insisted it wouldn't be ten minutes before Aden joined them on the Den's porch, and it was barely a blink shorter than that when the door opened and he slipped outside.

But Quill wasn't in a betting mood, like he hadn't been ever since they learned Julian was dead and Cistine was gone. He leaned silent and brooding against the other side of the post where Tatiana reclined, and that alone made her too tense to even muster a smirk when Aden flicked her ear in passing. She'd hated that greeting as a child fallen under his care with Thorne and Quill, but tonight it made her feel melancholy, not furious.

She could still barely believe he was even alive.

Sinking lower against the porch's support column, she watched Aden join Thorne at the railing. Ariadne and Maleck took up the other half across the wide steps down from the Den to Hellidom's footpaths. After five years, they were finally all together again—but still in danger, and about to go looking for more.

Even under normal circumstances, trying to steal from Salvotor was as good as begging for a poisoned arrow to the shoulder or a broken leg. Trying to steal the Key that could ensure his conquest...Tatiana might as well choose her own clothes to be burned in.

She was contemplating that—which clothes she'd bring with her to Cenowyn, or more likely Nimmus, given her penchant for overindulgence in alcohol and slitting throats—when Thorne swung his head toward Aden. "Did you know Ashe was involved with Nimea and the Tumult?"

"On my orders, yes," he admitted. "I didn't realize she shared their beliefs until it was too late."

"It was Ashe who betrayed Hellidom to the assassins?" Ariadne growled.

"I'm afraid so. But I set her on that path to protect Thorne. I knew he was in danger...Devitrius was stirring up trouble in the catacombs. It was only a matter of what sort and who was involved. And how far it reached."

"Too far," Quill muttered.

"After all this time." Thorne straightened up to grip the railing with both hands. "Nimea was beyond saving."

"Yes," Aden said. "That place made her cruel. She was almost a better strategist than Ariadne. In the end, she would've gladly cleaved anyone aside to reach you, no matter what vows she swore to Ashe. She even aligned herself with Devitrius, and through him, with Salvotor. There was no place her hatred of you didn't reach."

"Imprisonment can change anyone's perspective. So can loss." Thorne balanced his elbow on the railing, facing Aden sideways. "Sending you to that Nimmus-pit to redeem yourself was no better than what my father did to Nimea. What he's done to Cistine."

"You didn't send me. I volunteered to go."

"After I put the thought in your head. And I'm sorry for that." Thorne dragged a hand down his face. "I understand why you did it. Why you would've sacrificed everything to see *Nahdar* again."

At the Old Valgardan word for his uncle—a term he rarely spoke in the decades since Aden's father died—Maleck took in his breath swiftly. Aden's gaze flashed with pain. "I'm sorry about Kallah. She was the best of us all." His thumb smoothed the chipped wooden railing. "But I'm not certain I deserve your forgiveness yet. My crime against all of you was greater than the cost I paid in the Blood Hive."

"Then you can repay the rest of it by helping us find Cistine."

"Offering me a hunt on the night of my return?" Aden scoffed. "You're losing your edge, Thorne. My actions led to Kallah's *death*."

"And mine led to Julian's. And to Cistine's capture. If we're going to fall into my father's trap of blaming ourselves for *his* crimes, I'll tally more blows than any of us."

Aden didn't argue, but doubt still burned in his eyes.

"If you aren't ready for this hunt, I won't force it on you," Thorne added. "Finding Cistine is...personal. For all of us."

"Define personal."

Thorne's face whitened in the strong late-autumn moonlight. "I Named her. Though not officially."

Aden's whole body sagged with a sigh. "You *Named* Talheim's princess. The daughter of our fiercest enemy."

"She's more than that. She's stood against Chancellors and swordsmen and augmentation itself for Talheim and this cabal. She came for me when she should've left me to die for my choices, and forgave me when I deserved her hate. She's seen my heart when I've tried to show her my back." He curled his fist against the railing. "To be her friend has been my privilege. To die searching for her would be a worthy end."

Aden folded his arms. "And if I say no, *mavbrat?*"

Tatiana held in a snort. *Little cousin* hadn't quite fit Thorne since he passed six feet tall, but it was a good attempt to lift the mood.

Still, Thorne didn't laugh. "I trust you'll follow your instincts, as you've always done. As I'm doing now."

After a long pause, Aden dipped his head. "I'm with you. For now."

Though Tatiana hated it, *for now* was all any of them could promise. They were looking to steal from Salvotor, to find the Key. No tomorrows were guaranteed.

Tatiana's arm swung boneless and heavy at her side, scraping the column. Around the side, Quill took her hand, laced their fingers together, and held on. She clung to him like an anchor while the moon slipped away behind thick stormclouds rolling in from the south.

CHAPTER SIX

THERE WAS A vent in Cistine's roof, siphoning air to and from the outdoors. And not just here, she suspected, but throughout the whole mountain. Even prisoners and Vassoran guards had to breathe, so each chamber needed a pocket through which stale air could flow in and out.

That was one way she could escape; and if those vents proved too narrow for her, then there was likely a door somewhere besides the one to the balcony. Salvotor received his prisoners somewhere, after all.

After a particularly wearying dinner full of questions about the keying ritual which she couldn't answer, Cistine begged Kristoff for a pen and paper to help pass the time; to her surprise and relief, he brought them with her nightly cup of water, his glare warning her not to do anything rash.

Just as she once filled a journal with Old Valgardan words, now she wrote strategies of escape in a Talheimic cipher: the hole in the roof. A hidden door. The balcony.

She had no sense of day or night when her eyes grew weary rereading those words. She tucked the paper beneath her pillow and curled on her side to sleep.

When she woke, she knew it had not been a natural slumber. There was a gritty taste in her mouth, a harsh floral waft in her nostrils. A drug in her water.

Head throbbing, she floundered upright, clutching her throat with a gasp and then wishing she hadn't breathed so deeply. A stench raked her sinuses, so dry and cloying she gagged.

Dozens of red roses lined the floor and walls, spilling from baskets and twine trappings, from a trellis over the relief alcove. And there at the door, pressing a scarlet bouquet to his face and inhaling their scent, was Salvotor.

"Judging by your scarred hands, I suspect you're a horticulturist unafraid of thorns," he greeted slyly. "I'm a bit of one myself. Yet I find it much more rewarding when the fruit owes its growth to augmentation. You're always guaranteed a harvest then."

Cistine clamped down on a spurt of panic that he'd managed to do all this without waking her. "I shouldn't be surprised you'd cheat even nature. You don't know how to gain anything without manipulating it."

He set the bundle of roses aside and paced to the trellis, trailing his knuckles along the deep emerald stems. "Augments are a gift to ease the mundane so greater men can aspire to even greater heights."

"Augments don't exist just to make *your* life simpler! The gods gave them to the entire Northern Kingdom." Cistine flung off the covers and lurched to her feet. "The way you treat the augment stores like your own personal armory is against everything the gods intended. It's an abomination!"

"You can sense that, can you—*Key?*"

She bit the inside of her cheek, scowling at him.

Salvotor grazed his fingertips under one flower's delicately-arched petals. "Did you know my *valenar* never wanted a child? It was I who needed a Tribune I could entrust the future to as my father entrusted his to me. I learned to succeed where he failed with me, to tame the mind as well as the body. I succeeded on the woman, and I would succeed again with my son."

He plucked a rose from the arch and passed it slowly under his nose.

"A thorn in her side—that was what she called him during her pregnancy. Always under her skin, but never deep enough to pierce her heart. So that was what she named him...Thorne." He tossed the rose, and Cistine caught it by reflex, wincing as the barbs nipped her palm. "He failed to live up to his potential. I wonder if your father feels the same about you."

Cistine hurled the rose down. "Why don't you kill me, and when I see you in Nimmus you can tell me what my father said when he caught up to you and ripped out your throat, *bandayo*."

Salvotor whipped forward, slamming her back on the bed and yanking her face up by her chin. "Oh, this *is* death, Key...by a thousand slices, one piece at a time. Until you give up every detail of that ritual and beg for the final blow. It's in your hands how long this goes on. Remember that."

With a harsh kiss to her brow, he swaggered out. The door clattered shut on his heels, and she dragged herself up, breathing out the panic that came from the ache of his reinforced hand against her jaw. She focused on the pain in the backs of her knees where they clipped the bed, weighing and measuring these promises of more pain to come.

She could endure his threats. When she tested the gravity of them against all she had to fight for—to *live* for—her resolve did not waver.

She climbed to her feet, walked to the trellis, and gave it a gentle shove. Heavy, but moveable.

The chain rattled on her door, and she scrambled back to the bed, hurling the roses out of her way so wildly their barbs slashed her palms. She hit the mattress just when the door opened, and Kristoff stepped inside.

His gaze took in everything—roses, trellis, and Princess—then dropped to the cup. Her eyes followed his.

"I didn't know," he said quietly. "I don't drug women."

Her heart raced. "But you serve a man who does."

Kristoff's face twisted in a scowl, and he averted his gaze. Had he been waiting out there for Salvotor to leave so he could look in on her? How could he offer these piecemeal kindnesses, this and the pen and paper, yet still condone her imprisonment?

"*Nadrian!*" A shout floated through the open door so loudly Cistine flinched. Kristoff pivoted as a young man slid into the doorway, disheveled, his nose bleeding. "*Nadrian*, Salvotor's guards won't take their rotation. They're calling it *menial labor*."

"Absolute stars-forsaken children." Kristoff shoved the boy back out into the hall. "Rally the others and wait for me, Dain."

"*Ha, Nadrian.*" The boy's eyes slipped to Cistine, cheeks reddening slightly under the mop of his russet curls; then he strode back down the corridor.

"Did he lay a hand on you?" Kristoff asked Cistine.

"Barely," she answered, though her knees and jaw still smarted.

With a curt nod, he stepped out and slammed the door so hard, it bounced in its fastenings. The latch did not click into place—nor did the chain rattle again.

Bitten with curiosity, Cistine hurried to the door and tested it; to her delight, it eased open soundlessly. She slipped into the hall, which ended in a dark wall immediately to the left. She had nowhere to go but toward the hewn chamber and the echoes of furious shouting.

It seemed Dain's argument had escalated; two Vassora restrained him when Cistine peered around the end of the hall, another four flanking Kristoff. They opposed six more, all standing at the rounded half-moon mouth of a dim doorway across the chamber.

"That is not how we do things in Kalt Hasa," Kristoff snapped. "The patrols at the cellar change their shift every four hours. Since Chancellor Salvotor dispatched more than half the guards to the watchtowers when he arrived, I need every man shouldering his weight."

"Yes, that's what your degenerates said." The leader of the opposition hooked his thumbs in his belt, rocking back on his heels. He might've reminded Cistine of Quill, if not for his smug drawl and his oddly-familiar, unlikeable face. "Now let me say something to *you*: we are part of Chancellor Salvotor's private retinue. We don't take assignments from a disgraced widower going limp in a mountain prison."

"You listen to me, *allotok,*" Kristoff growled, and the man scoffed. "Every Vassora in this place does his share, even the Chancellor's pretentious personal guards."

He stepped chest-to-chest with Kristoff. "Who do you think the Chancellor would side with? A member of his own retinue, or a man so weak he couldn't save his own wife and sons?"

Cistine clapped a hand to her mouth as Kristoff smashed his fist into the man's jaw. He managed to land two more blows to the same spot before his own men towed him backward, and even then, he raged and twisted, swearing.

The infuriating guard only laughed as he wiped his bloodied mouth. "This mountain hold has made you men as soft as your leader. You can't even take a joke."

"My family is not a joke!" Kristoff roared. "And you will not shirk your duties and force my men to carry twice the load!"

"But I will." The man flicked blood from this thumb. "Don't forget why you're here, Kristoff. Your rank means nothing. No one even knows you're still alive. Don't risk making that belief a truth just for these *bandayos.*" He bent an elbow toward Kristoff's men, then swaggered toward the dining room with his entourage in tow.

Cistine stared at the well-guarded cellar they argued so fiercely over, curiosity rubbing sharply against her chest.

"And they call *us* lazy." Dain wiped his bloody nose on his sleeve. "What are our orders, *Nadrian?*"

Kristoff pulled a hand slowly through his short hair. "I'll stand the night watch myself whenever I'm not with the Key. But I won't force any man to take it with me. This shift is only for volunteers."

"For you, *Nadrian?*" one of the men smirked. "I'll stand every watch."

"*Ha, Nadrian!*" the others shouted.

Kristoff shook his head. "Spread the word to the other patrols. I can't have the six of you always running yourselves ragged on my account."

"I thought you said you were accepting volunteers," Dain grinned.

Kristoff slapped him upside the head and turned away—and Cistine withdrew too slowly to dodge his sharp gaze, finding her tucked in the corridor mouth.

A beat of silence; then his footsteps clipped rapidly across the room.

She smacked her head back against the corridor wall, teeth gritted at her own ignorance, but she didn't run; she'd take a tongue lashing if it meant a few more minutes outside that room.

Kristoff stepped into the hall, eyes blazing. "Is this what princesses are taught to do? Listen in on other people's conversations?"

"No." Cistine tucked her hands behind her back and leaned into the wall. "But I'm also Talheim's most famous court gossip. And that's exactly what *I* do."

Kristoff rubbed his bearded mouth, cursing. "Back to your room. Go."

She went; it was pointless to argue with nowhere to run.

To her surprise, Kristoff entered the room with her, shut the door, and leaned against it. "Whatever you overheard, it is not a weakness for you to exploit. Do you understand me? You will not tear this guard apart, you will not report to Salvotor of my...struggles to bring his detachment to heel. Is that clear?"

Cistine scowled. "I wouldn't put *anyone* in the path of Salvotor's rage, not even to save my own life. Not after what he did to...to Julian." Her voice broke, and his name emerged a whisper.

Kristoff's brow creased. "Then you care nothing for your own life?"

"Of course I care for my life! I don't *want* to die on a Door! But if I sacrifice everything I am to survive, that's not really surviving. I won't sacrifice you or your men, either."

Kristoff folded his arms, studying her. "Talheim's royal family has always had more nobility than wits."

"My nobility is the only thing Salvotor has no power over. And I think dying for what you believe in is more important than living just to survive."

He tilted his head. "You are not what I expected of the Key."

"And you're not like any Vassoran guard I've ever met. Do you have any other surprises for me? Because I have plenty more for you."

Kristoff scoffed under his breath and opened the door. "Remember what I told you. Keep what you saw today to yourself."

"*Ha, Nadrian.*"

Kristoff cast a doleful look over his shoulder, and she arched her brows, daring him to make a remark. He banged the door shut instead, and this time the chain slid audibly back into place, sealing her in a rosy tomb.

CHAPTER SEVEN

ASHE WAS BEING followed.

It took her two days to realize it, distracted at first by the shock of Cistine's abduction, the agony of Julian's death, and endless questions of the Key—what Talheim knew of it, whether the King forbade any mention of it for fear Cistine would grow curious and travel north, exactly as she had.

It was dusk of the second day when she noticed the unusual quiet behind her, and that the forest creatures did not resume their chatter after she passed by them. Ahead, silence. Around her, silence. And behind her...dead quiet.

Something stalked her.

Ashe halted before full dark and built a fire with dry leaves and sap-soaked branches giving off a spicy aroma. She slung her sparsely-packed satchel to the ground, unbuckled Echelon, and laid it down as well. Then she went some way into the trees to relieve herself.

Or so she wanted her pursuer to believe.

Instead she circled wide, keeping the fire just within view to her right. It took time to enclose her pursuer, a small, slim shape that halted by her fire, arms akimbo, peering around the undergrowth. Looking for her.

Ashe lunged from cover, snatching a handful of bony shoulder, and the girl wailed—shrill and *familiar*. Ashe whipped her around, snapping the hood from her hair. "*Pippet?*"

Quill's younger sister glared up at her, cheeks dust-smudged, eyes narrowed, scowling furiously. "Let go of me!"

Ashe shook her by the shoulder. "What in God's name are you *doing* out here?"

"I tracked you!"

"*Tracked*...from where? *Hellidom*? Why aren't you in Starhollow?"

"I came with a caravan...some of the sick people who stayed with us after Geitlan. I was looking for Quill, but I couldn't find him. And then I saw you leaving the city, so I followed you."

"Why? What is the *matter* with you? Do you really think this forest is any place for a child? You should have stayed with Helga!"

"Helga is dead!"

The heartbroken shout pulled tears from Pippet's eyes, streaking the grime on her cheeks. Ashe's cold fingers unwrapped, arm falling boneless at her side. "What?"

Pippet wiped her nose on her wrist, dropping her gaze. "Quill sent a letter about...about Baba Kallah. Helga got sick after she read it. Really sick. Cassaida said sometimes people's hearts break and they die." She shrugged miserably. "After Helga went to sleep, I couldn't stay in the cottage anymore, so I went to find Quill."

Shame bathed Ashe's throat. "I'm so sorry, Pippet."

Round eyes flicked to her, tears tracing again from the corners. "Do you have anything to eat?"

Grimacing, Ashe beckoned her to the fire.

They shared tough salted meat and an onion roasted over the flames— sparse rations Ashe bought before leaving Hellidom, dismissing Thorne's offer of food from the Den. She'd only purchased enough to feed herself, but when the meat disappeared into Pippet's hungry mouth, she couldn't bring herself to be irritated about it.

She had plenty of other reasons to be irritated.

Pippet finally paused for a breath between bites. "Why are you traveling south?"

"I have a duty to fulfill." Ashe finished her own skewer and tossed it back into the flames.

"In Unsverd? Where are you going all the way down here?"

"The border forts."

"Why?"

"Because Cistine needs rescuing, and I need help finding her."

Pippet's eyes blew wide, jaw hanging slack. "Cistine was taken?" She sat up sharply toward the flames. "I want to help! You've seen how good I am at tracking."

"Tracking is one thing. Finding a woman who's been stolen by a Chancellor..." Her breath snagged. Valgard was such a large kingdom, and she had so little idea of where to begin looking.

"Why would a Chancellor take her?"

"Because Cistine has something he wants."

"Why don't you ask the cabal for help, then? I thought you were friends."

A harsh laugh tore from Ashe's chest. "I'm afraid not. This is a Talheimic problem, so I'm going to enlist the help of Talheimic Wardens...people I can depend on."

"Wardens." Pippet crinkled her nose. "Like you and Julian?"

Ashe's chest ached at his name. "Just like us."

"That's good! If they're anything like you, we should find her in no time."

"Not *we*, Pippet. You're not coming along."

She scowled, flopping back from the fire. "You sound like Quill. He never lets me help, either."

Nor should he. Girls of eleven belonged in safe places, sheltered from steel and politicking—

Baking cakes and spinning sugar. Girls your age belong in a confectionary, Asheila, not in the yard hitting trees with wooden swords.

She shrugged off the memory of her mother's disdain like an ill-fitting cloak. "You heard what I said."

Pippet raised her chin. "What are you going to do, make me walk all the way back to Hellidom alone? What if I get lost? What if something *eats* me?"

Ashe gritted her teeth. "You should have thought of that before you followed me out here."

Pippet gathered her knees to her chest, shivering. "But everything is so *big*, and I'm so small..."

"Oh, for God's sake, all right!" Ashe groaned. "But you are not part of this. I'm escorting you to the border forts, where the people on your side of the wall will be responsible for you."

She's your problem now, Cyril. You keep that child alive, and the people will follow you forever. King Ivan's cold voice rattled the backs of Ashe's teeth like a blow as Pippet beamed at her. "Go to bed. And stop looking at me that way."

Pippet eased down on the leaf litter, pillowing her head on her arm. "Do you know any good stories?"

"No." Ashe pulled out her pocket whetstone and unsheathed Echelon.

"Oh. Helga always told me a story before bed." Pippet scraped circles in the dirt. "I've been trying to tell them to myself, but I keep forgetting how they go."

Ashe set her teeth against a bitter surge of guilt.

It would be simpler to turn around, drag Pippet back to Hellidom, and throw her to the care of people equipped to handle excitable, angry, grieving children who didn't want to stay where they were told. They didn't have a princess to save or a Chancellor to thwart; time wasn't working against them like it was against Ashe. But that was the very reason she couldn't afford to waste days traveling back to Hellidom and out again.

Cistine was her only responsibility. If she had to drag Pippet to the forts and leave her there to fulfill it, so be it.

A quiet sniffle dragged her focus to Pippet, curled with her back to the flames. Her small shoulders lifted and dropped in quiet, genuine sobs.

Panic lanced through Ashe's chest. "Pippet?"

"I *miss* her!" The words burst out so loudly, Ashe flinched. "I needed her, and she didn't stay for me! She wasn't hurt, she just got *sick*...why wasn't I *enough*?"

Swallowing, Ashe pocketed the whetstone and crawled around the fire to sit by Pippet's back. Useless words of empty comfort flirted with her lips, things she would say to families of Wardens who died in training accidents or bandit scrapes in the Calalun Peaks. Words that wouldn't touch Pippet's loneliness or grief.

Then other words came: the lyrics of a Talheimic lullaby she sang over Cistine's cradle on her fussiest nights, when Ashe didn't how to comfort an infant so small that there was no understanding between them yet—a song of heartache and home, of mountains and faraway lands. She breathed through the melody, every note tugging up long-buried feelings: the skim of a violin's neck beneath her fingers, the articulate lines of the bow in her hand, Cistine and Julian sitting in wide-eyed rapture at her feet while the enchanting notes filled the Citadel's glass music house.

Her stomach clenched when Pippet nestled back against her leg, sobs finally staggering out, but she didn't pull away. The girl's grief was her responsibility, too; and whatever Thorne thought of her, Wardens did not run from responsibility.

So Ashe sang until she was hoarse, until Pippet slept and the words became just another piece of ember, floating up to the cold, distant stars.

CHAPTER EIGHT

J OVADALSA ALWAYS INTRIGUED Tatiana—not just because the threads were cheap or because, in the past, she could drink herself silly at half the cost of Hellidom's only tavern. But it was the clearest advocate for the sort of change Sillakove Court built itself to bring, the neediness found wherever Courts turned a blind eye. The destitutes begging in the gutter; the substance-lovers propped against questionable walls with bottles in fist; the thieves eyeing Thorne and Tatiana as they slipped down the long, arched bridges hemming the city together, following Maleck's directions toward the prearranged meeting place.

Tatiana peered sidelong at Thorne. "You're quieter than usual." His hood was raised, masking his features in shadow, but she had gotten used to hunting her friends' dramatic faces from the darkness of brooding.

Thorne swallowed. "Last night, we camped steps away from where Julian died."

Anger pulsed in Tatiana's fingertips. "You tried, Thorne. You couldn't bring him back with you."

"I know. But there was no body." He rubbed the back of his neck. "Did they throw him in the Ismalete? Sell his body in the Shadow Market?"

Tatiana winced. "It would've been nice to give him a proper burial by Talheimic standards."

"He deserved that and more." Thorne lengthened his stride. "We'll at least ensure his end wasn't in vain."

They ducked into the tavern Maleck had described, broad and laid open with only two doors: one to the cellar, presumably, the other to the street. Ale bottles and fishing paraphernalia, Jovadalsa's two greatest prides, crowded the walls. The tables and chairs were plain enough that Tatiana longed for the comfort of the fainting couch in her room in the Den.

Notes of mead, strong spirits, and mulled wine made her stomach rumble when she followed Thorne to the counter. She'd been sober ever since they sacked the Black Coast mines, but setting foot in a tavern still stirred those old cravings.

Perhaps Thorne had brought her along to test that she could keep her head around strong drink, even with all this madness of the Key and Cistine and Julian and *Aden* crashing around their heads. But what need was there to drown her concerns in alcohol? They were only here to meet privately with one of Stornhaz's elite, the kind of people who turned up their noses at Tatiana when she scraped through schooling with their well-bred heirs. And when she was a rebellious adolescent, sneaking into their expensive parties in a sewn-together opal dress—

The memory of a warm harbor breeze stirred the hairs on Tatiana's arms. She lazily turned back the sleeves of her emerald-and-violet shawl, and a few eyes followed her.

Good. Let them notice some color had come into their world.

Thorne ordered a cup of water and a stein of mead from the barman while Tatiana leaned casually against his back, studying the tavern's patrons. Most were deep in drink, some even asleep in booths along the back wall. None cut the figures of guards in disguise, but one couldn't be too careful. Ever since she'd tricked Ariadne into sharing the knowledge of Thorne's secret yearning to reopen the Doors, Tatiana suspected Salvotor kept him alive from a distance in hopes his far-cleverer son would lead him to the Key. If that was true, then now he had one less reason to stay his cruel hand.

Tatiana licked her lips as Thorne turned and handed her the water. With her back against his chest now, she could feel his heart thudding hard and fast. "The booth in the far corner."

She'd grazed over the man there already, assuming him another unconscious drunk with his head tilted against the wall and his hood drawn up. But when they approached, he sat up, hand resting on a jewel-handled knife on the tabletop.

"Welcome, welcome." His heavy accent was reminiscent of the northern territories, Nordbran and Spoek. "I thought perhaps you were too frightened to show your face after all."

"You've never frightened me, Sander." Thorne slid into the bench across from the Tribune, and Tatiana sat next to him, angled to face the room in case trouble arose.

"No, I suppose not," Sander sighed. "Tatiana. You look absolutely ravishing."

She hefted a brow. She was used to empty flattery from Tribunes who sneered when she turned her back, but that compliment almost sounded genuine. "I assume you look the same. It's difficult to tell with your hood up."

"You'll have to pardon the rudeness. One can't be too careful."

"Naturally." Thorne drummed his fingers on the table. "How close are the Vassora?"

"I convinced them I needed to nurse my wounds in private today, so they've wandered off to gamble away their boredom. You've kept me waiting a long time, so I'm afraid the ruse of lamenting my damaged face wears thin."

"Damaged because you helped us escape from my father."

Asking a question that wasn't a question—one of Thorne's many talents. Tatiana bit back a smile as Sander sat forward, but when the table's dim ghostlamp flared across his features, the urge to laugh vanished. His nose was bent and reset, the rest of his face bruised. The way he moved so gingerly suggested injured ribs. "I'm surprised you remember any of that. You were in a terrible way when we last saw each other, though I suspect it would've been far worse had the Key not been there."

Hand flattening on the table, Thorne inclined toward Sander. "What do you know?"

"Nothing I've repeated to anyone. And fortunately for you, it doesn't seem any other Tribunes were close enough to overhear that exchange."

"Do you know where she is?"

"If I did, I wouldn't have waited for Maleck to deliver my message. I would've done something drastic to draw you from hiding."

"Why?" Tatiana asked. "I thought all you Tribunes wanted the Doors open."

"That generalization is *thoroughly* up for debate. I wouldn't mind, certainly, but I'm not fond of *Salvotor* opening them. We all know what happens if he does. To prevent his conquest, we must accomplish two things: rescue the Key, and unseat the Chancellor."

"We?"

Thorne stared at Sander, bleak comprehension tugging the corners of his mouth. "You were the Tribune who voted for me to retain my title."

Tatiana's gaze darted between them. "*Him?* Really? Why would he stand for your title against Salvotor?"

"Well, certainly not because Thorne is quick on the uptake," Sander scoffed. "I know it may be difficult to comprehend with the likes of my fellow Tribunes in Kroaken and Lataus, but not all of us are in the profession for blood and women. Some of us give a damn about the law as well."

Thorne folded his arms, the only indication that he was reeling—and rallying. "How much do you know?"

"I've been watching you and your cabal for some time, though I didn't realize until recently that it was *you* raiding your father's caravans and thwarting his motions to creep into the other Courts. That was dangerous but effective, passing yourself as a band of common criminals on the Vey."

"Struggle breeds endurance."

"I can see that." Sander sipped from his cup. "The question now is how far that tenacity extends. Because I have information that could bring your father to his knees, but there's plenty of danger in sharing it."

Tatiana met Thorne's eyes, their pale depths smoldering with reserve. Then he swiveled back to his fellow Tribune. "Then why risk it?"

"For the same reason I voted against stripping your title all those years ago. You see, besides the fact that your father is happy to twist or outright defy every law of Valgard as it suits him, there are other aspects of his plan for conquest I don't find particularly exciting."

"Such as?" Tatiana prompted.

"Well, for one thing, there would be no seasons of rest, and I quite enjoy when Kanslar is out of power. Plenty of time to enjoy the company of my twenty-seven lovers and my wolf. Imagine how much less leisure there will be if all my days are consumed with overseeing Nordbran."

"There are worse fates," Thorne deadpanned. Though his old territory had gone to another's care after his banishment, he and the cabal still watched over it. They'd gone to the aid of its citizens personally when Kanslar refused to send relief in the harsh autumn months.

"Be that as it may." Sander folded his hands on the table. "I hope my trust in you all those years ago was not in vain. I believe you have the means of stopping your father's conquest, and I'm prepared to give you the blade to hold against his throat—for a price."

Thorne snorted. "Even in the schools, you never did anything without some sort of repayment. What will it be this time?"

"Nothing particularly difficult. Just that when you become Chancellor, I would very much like to be named High Tribune."

Dead silence descended like a dump of snow over the booth. Tatiana folded her arms and glanced at Thorne. He looked back at her, a question in his narrowed eyes.

She'd never been one for politics, that was always more Thorne and Aden's strength. But she understood posturing and maneuvering were part of the game Tribunes and Chancellors played with the rising and setting of each Court's respective constellation. Sander's movements didn't surprise her, not even that he'd manipulated Aden, Ashe, and Maleck just to reach Thorne, or saved him from his father's wrath to sway his trust.

That was why he had selected her for this mission. He already suspected Sander would have a few cards stowed in his sleeves; and as a card sharp herself, those were odds Tatiana was used to playing.

Everyone at this table was cheating. Thorne trusted her to decide if

Sander's hand was something the cabal, with all their strengths and weaknesses considered, could outplay.

After a long moment's consideration, she nodded.

Thorne swung his head back toward Sander. "If I take my father's place, legally I have no choice but to instate a High Tribune in my stead. It might as well be you."

Sander rubbed his hands together. "*Excellent.* I'll want your word, naturally. A blood oath."

"And I'll strike it, provided your information is worth the risk. What's so damning it could send my father to Nimmus?"

Tatiana shifted away from the room toward them, too intrigued to focus on anything else as Sander laid his flat palms on the table. "I've spent the past decade searching for any means of unseating Salvotor. While rumors are plenty, and most of Kanslar's Tribunes are aware to some extent of the influence he exerts in the other Courts, it always comes back to proof, doesn't it?"

"Always," Thorne echoed softly.

"Well, at last, in a fit of desperation and outright masochism, I went back to the law books and read every last one, cover to cover, starting with the most recent and trawling my way backward." Sander shuddered. "It's taken me many, many years, but I've finally found something I think may be the weapon we need."

Thorne bristled, clasping his hands on the tabletop. "Tell me."

"Do you recall that after the Bloodwight incident, when the former *visnprest* Order fled, the temples were empty for some time? Few wanted to study augments anymore with the wells closed, and then there was that rather nasty rumor started about how joining with a *visnpresta* would grant one godlike powers..."

"I remember."

"Well, there was a law passed, I would say fifteen years ago now...punishment by imprisonment for up to a decade for any man who forced himself onto a *visnpresta* or their acolytes."

Tatiana's pulse throbbed in her ears. Thorne twitched as if he was trying with all his might not to look at her—not to show how personally, how deeply, that notion struck him. "I've never heard of this law."

"Because it was buried...hence why it took me all this time to find any record of it. From what I gather, Yager Court were the greatest supporters." That was no surprise to Tatiana; a Court secretly governed by women and their faithful *valenar* and lovers would certainly advocate a law to defend *visnprestas* from the heinous acts that could end their commission in the Order. "But even then, it was never made as widely public as some other laws...I suppose because its only goal was to encourage repopulation of the temples by casting a net of safety around the *visnprestas*. Once a few joined, the rest began to follow. That law became chatter again only once since it passed. A rumor began just after you and your cabal fled Stornhaz...a young woman claiming our very own Chancellor Salvotor assaulted a *visnpresta* acolyte and nailed her to a door in Stornhaz."

Tatiana's stomach rioted against the small sips of water she'd taken. Thorne pulled a hand backward through his hair, laying it flat to his scalp.

That was Ariadne he was talking about, a dedicated *visnpresta* whose dreams of serving a celibate Order were ripped away when Salvotor, forcefully, made certain she was *not*.

"What happened to the girl who spread that rumor?" Thorne's voice trembled.

"The usual things," Sander said. "Threats and beatings—all accidental and with untraceable perpetrators, naturally. She vanished some time ago, and the rumor with her, but how interesting would that be if she lives? A witness with testimony of your father's misdeeds, a horrific crime against a *visnpresta* that would, by law, require his disbarment...his imprisonment, if convicted..." he balanced his fingers on the rim of his mug and met Thorne's eyes, "and your ascension to the Judgement Seat of Kanslar Court."

A chill capered through Tatiana's body. Thorne's eyes sizzled with frenetic energy.

"All we need," Sander went on, "is for someone to convince the victim and the witness to both come forward, and another Court to try Salvotor. Unfortunately, Kanslar cannot convict its own Chancellor."

Though Tatiana wished it could be Yager who tried Salvotor for breaking a law they passed, Traisende was next in the cycle, and an ally of Sillakove Court as well, though not as courageous as Yager. Not to mention the cabal's standing with Yager was tenuous after their lost witness and failure to bring proof of Salvotor's actions at the Black Costs.

But if they could bring charges against the Chancellor by the time the Court of the four Wayfinders rose...

Tatiana danced her fingers on her thighs, setting her bangles singing, but Thorne's face sobered again. "None of this matters if my father uses the Key to open the Doors before Kanslar sets."

Sander rubbed his brow. "True. The law will go away, along with everything else good and fair in this kingdom."

"And you don't have the slightest notion where he's taken her?"

"I haven't seen him since he left the plains. And that's fortunate, really. I should be in Nordbran, picking up the pieces of the Blood Hive and putting it back in fighting order, tempting the elites back, not lingering in Jovadalsa. Besides, if I saw the Chancellor again after how he cut down that boy..."

Tatiana dragged her thumb slowly down the weeping condensation on her glass and watched his face. "Did you burn his body?"

"Not where anyone could see."

Thorne dipped his head. "You have my gratitude for that. He was a friend. Leaving him behind was one of the hardest things I've ever done."

"I know. I saw how you tried to carry him with you." Sander bobbed his shoulders. "The pyre was the least I could do for the most dishonorable killing I've ever witnessed."

"My father has never shown clemency to children. One of a thousand reasons we're going to unseat him."

Sander's eyes flashed in a slow blink. "What's your strategy, Thorne?"

"I'm going to speak to the *visnpresta* who started the rumor and convince her to testify. And then I'll find the Key, whatever it takes, and ensure Salvotor doesn't lay a hand on her ever again." He nudged Tatiana to slide from the booth. "Go tell the others. Have Maleck secure lodgings for the night. At dawn, we ride."

Tatiana glanced between the men. "Are you sure about this?"

Thorne's steely gaze softened. "I value your wisdom and your caution, Tatiana. And I value your faith in me. I ask for that now."

She held Sander's intrigued gaze. "If you try to cross him, I'll ensure you never have a means of pleasing your *twenty-seven* lovers again."

His brows rose. "Violence is so attractive in a woman. Would you like to become my twenty-eighth?"

Tatiana gestured rudely and swaggered from the tavern. She'd barely crossed the threshold when Quill descended on her from the rooftop, rubbing his hands against the late-season chill. "Where's Thorne?"

"Sealing a blood oath with his future High Tribune." She sighed at his wide-eyed look. "Gather the others. I'll explain everything once we've found shelter for the night. Hopefully somewhere that doesn't leak or crawl with roaches."

The small, two-bed, single-table room at the ramshackle inn was by no means sealed against outside sounds, yet when Tatiana finished recounting everything they learned in the tavern, quiet filled the world.

Quill, sitting on one of the beds beside Maleck, bent forward and rested his hands, palm-to-palm, against his mouth. "Sander. Preening, strutting, twelve-lovers-and-a-trained-wolf, *Sander.*"

"Twenty-seven now," Aden grumbled from his seat across from Tatiana at the table.

"He's been busy, I'll give him that. But *he's* the one who voted against stripping Thorne of his title? That maneuver left Kanslar without a High Tribune for ten years!"

"And somehow he's kept his part in it secret all this time," Maleck mused. "Though Salvotor must have threatened and compelled all the Tribunes through their Names."

Tatiana frowned. "You think someone else Named him, like Baba Kallah did with Thorne?"

Quill shrugged. "She couldn't be the first one to ever think of that, especially if Sander's sharp enough to know how Salvotor is."

"Ariadne?" Aden's eyes flicked to her.

She was the only one standing, back propped to the grimy window between the beds, arms folded at her waist. That posture, which usually exuded a kind of formidable fury, seemed self-protective tonight. "That law. I never knew of it. I never knew he could face legal recourse for what he did to me."

"If Saychelle would stand as witness, will you accuse him publicly?" There was a strange reticence in Aden's tone; he studied the tabletop, not Ariadne's face.

"In a heartbeat," she said. But her voice shook.

The door's rusty hinges creaked and Thorne joined them at last, hands stuffed in his pockets, Faer on his shoulder. Maleck snatched up his satchel and produced a spool of bandages; before he even reached Thorne, the High Tribune had his left palm bared. A shallow slit wept lazily from the center.

"The blood oath is forged," he announced. "Assuming we aren't all dead within a month, Sander will be my High Tribune."

Aden sighed, pinching the bridge of his nose.

"Do you know where Saychelle's gone?" Thorne added to Ariadne while Maleck cleaned, powdered, and wrapped his wound.

"Keltei Temple," she replied without hesitation. "That was where Iri served, where we always talked of taking a commission together."

"Then Keltei it is."

Maleck knotted the bandage on Thorne's hand and stepped away. "I've furnished our supplies and divided the augments as evenly as possible. We have to decide who will carry the last healing augment."

"Cast lots between the rest of you. I don't want it."

"Only you would balk at the power of healing," Tatiana scoffed.

"Your safety is my priority. Not my own." Thorne shucked off his shirt, went to the table, and washed his head, chest, and arms with the stained cloth from the water basin.

Tatiana, Aden, Quill, and Ariadne cast in their lots, and to Tatiana's surprise, they landed on her. Either the gods favored her for once, or they were warning her about something. She tried not to dwell on that as she crammed the healing augment with the rest in her beaded satchel, snatched a pillow from the bed, and stretched out close to the door. The moment she shut her eyes, exhaustion swept over her like a dark curtain, and she was asleep.

She woke hours later, judging by how cold and stiff she was, stirred by a thin blanket drifting around her shoulders. She recognized the feeling of the hand tucking it against her, a hundred memories of naptimes on plush rugs with Quill not far out of reach, already snoring.

Aden.

His footsteps retreated. At the table, a chair scraped out, and he settled himself, coaxing a creak from the weak hinges. A pair of low chuckles suggested Thorne and Maleck were there, too.

"Are you prepared for this, Thorne?" Maleck murmured after a beat. "You and Saychelle haven't laid eyes on one another in nearly a decade, and back then you were all but joined. Now she's taken refuge in a temple, possibly even become a full *visnpresta*..."

"I know," Thorne sighed. "But even before we fled Stornhaz, she hadn't decided for certain she would give up her acolyte training and risk disappointing Ariadne and their parents. I've always respected it was her choice to make. I was not the only future available to her, even if I wished she would choose me."

"Are we discussing Saychelle, or someone else?" Aden prodded.

The silence was long, and too heavy.

Maleck blew out his breath. "Thank the stars you and Saychelle never joined, or you might be standing trial for the same law, Thorne."

"I know." Thorne's callused palm rasped through his hair. "But I can't look back on what might've been or what nearly was. Even when I see her, my gaze must be forward."

"There's more than one path forward," Aden said. "Sander might not know which way Salvotor went, but perhaps someone else in this city did. I'm going to stay here a while...loosen tongues in case things in Keltei don't work out for you."

A familiar creak—Thorne shifting in his chair. "Was this your idea, or Maleck's?"

Twin sighs. "Both."

"You're hoping Ashe will take your offer and come to the tavern here." Thorne's groan was directed at Maleck. "After everything she did…"

"She needs our help. Not our hate." A vein of passion slithered through Maleck's usually-even tone. "Just as you needed Cistine to believe in you again after Stornhaz."

Tatiana cracked an eyelid and found the three men sitting exactly as she envisioned at the room's small table, faces pitted with shadows and exhaustion.

"Is there any way I can convince you to come with us, Aden?" Thorne's tone was steady again, betraying nothing of how desperately he must want him at his back—the last of his true blood family, the cousin he'd ransomed back from Nimmus just days ago.

"I know my talents, where I can serve the mission best. This is for me to do, Thorne."

Maleck dipped his head, studying the tabletop. When Thorne nodded, his shoulders slumped with relief.

"Whatever happens in that temple, send someone to inform me," Aden added. "I'd like to know what your next steps will be."

"Someone will come back for you." Thorne's voice was thick with emotion. "I swear it. Always."

CHAPTER NINE

TRAINING WAS TWICE as difficult amid the stench of rotting roses. Once the headaches from the sensuous fragrance faded, the stomach-churning reek of the white-furred stems set in. Another blow from Salvotor, making Cistine's exercises nearly impossible when every deep breath produced a gag.

In defiance and desperation, she made every session about him. She imagined it was his face, not her pillow, she pummeled with her fists. When her lungs sizzled with the oily reek of blackening petals, she reminded herself that every repetition was another step toward breathing clean, free air after she escaped.

She studied that heavily-manned cellar entrance whenever Kristoff walked her to dinner. Nowhere else in this place was so well-guarded; there had to be a door down there through which Vassora came and went.

A door to freedom.

The thought gnawed her focus while Kristoff led her toward the dining room for yet another meal, silent and scowling. He hadn't brought a dress today, hadn't spoken to her at all in fact, not even his usual brusque greeting. She tried not to fear what that meant, keeping her thoughts on the cellar instead. But when they reached the dark stone hall, empty for once, her focus leaped at once to the dress box waiting on the table.

She should've known.

Kristoff backed from the room, his gaze lingering on that box. In his absence Cistine wandered to the table and tugged out the night's attire. The color, at least, was bearable, a deep wine-red rather than the pale lavender she loathed. But once she ducked behind a high-backed chair to change, she realized why it was so immediately comforting.

This was the color she wore in Veran to the meeting with Traisende and Yager's Chancellors, when she and Thorne stood together as equals.

A throat cleared across the room, and she froze halfway into the dress, gooseflesh sprinkling her arms, her heart slamming into her jaw.

"By all means, don't stop on my account." Salvotor lowered himself into the opposite seat and unfolded his napkin in his lap. His eyes, cool and demure, stabbed into her.

The flame of humiliation burned hotter against her skin than a lightning augment. She yanked the straps over her bare shoulders and found the dress to be little better than nudity after all. The fabric was slit up the sides as high as her waist, and the bodice dipped nearly that low. Shivering, she collapsed into the seat, weak-kneed with shame and anger. When a pair of prisoners brought their platters, Cistine raged in silence and ignored the smell of roasted quail and golden potatoes stroking her nostrils.

"Aren't you going to eat, Cistine?"

The hair rose along her spine, and her gaze snapped to Salvotor. The way he cast his words so *perfectly*, down to the last inflection...

He sounded just like his son.

She hastily carved off a bite, and Salvotor smiled. "There. Much better."

Cistine forced herself to swallow, though she would've sooner drunk spoiled cream. "I know what you're doing. Stop it."

"I'm not doing anything. *Wildheart*."

"*Stop!*" A dull scrape pierced through the roaring in her ears as she shoved back her chair. "Stop talking to me like he does!"

Salvotor tipped his head. "And how does my son speak to you? Gently? Sweetly? Like *this*, Wildheart?" She slammed her hands down so hard, her plate jumped. Salvotor merely chuckled. "I wonder how that Talheimic boy felt, knowing Thorne spoke to you this way."

"Don't," Cistine snarled. "Don't you *dare*—"

"Tell me, did you wait for that passion between you to cool completely before you joined with my son? Or were you just a *prize* for them to pass back and forth?"

She couldn't help it; the way he said the word, throwing his voice like Thorne's...she flinched.

Salvotor smiled silkily. "Well, if how the boy met his end was any proof, the passion had *not* cooled completely. At least not for him."

Cistine's arms shook at the memory of Julian's smoking skin, his empty eye sockets, the brush of his kiss on her knuckles, the roar of his voice as he came back for her—

Smile stretching, Salvotor stood, tossed down his napkin, and sauntered away. Cistine waited for him to vanish down the hall before she sank down and buried her face in her arms. In the darkness she saw Julian fall again and again, her name on his lips turning to an agonized cry.

Her shoulders shook her cheeks damp with silent sobs, until Kristoff fetched her back to her room. But there was no relief even when she entered those dusky, rotting confines; though the sight that greeted them stopped Cistine's tears like the end of one storm, another began to churn.

The bedspread, the platter and cup, and the ghostlight were now all one color: gaudy purple-white.

She leaned back against the wall, knees shaking. Kristoff's attention landed on her from the side. "What is this?"

"Julian," her voice broke. "Salvotor is using him against me. That color..." she swallowed, shaking her head.

Kristoff blew out a long breath. "Come. I'll help you strip the bed."

Another kindness.

Cistine was beginning to like this guard.

CHAPTER TEN

ASHE HAD NO more time for reflection while she traveled with Pippet. Questions about landscapes and birdsong filled the long daylight hours, remarks on trapping game and campfire cooking fading into the same Talheimic lullaby night after night, rocking the world mercifully quiet.

They couldn't reach the border forts quickly enough.

"Pippet, for God's sake!" Ashe snapped one day while they crossed a broad, boggy fen; the stench of putrefaction hung on the air, and Pippet wanted to know what precisely was causing it, what was the difference between bogs and swamps, and what sort of creatures lived here—a bevy of curiosities leveled with hardly a breath between them. "Do you ever stop asking questions?"

"No." She hopped up on a log and walked its length with arms outstretched. "Do *you* ever stop being quiet?"

"Silence is valuable. You might try it sometime."

"I have. It's boring." She bounced down to walk beside Ashe again. "Does Cistine ask questions, or does she like being quiet? She seems like she asks lots of questions. Is that true? What's the strangest question anyone's ever asked you?"

"I don't—"

"Aleida asked me why people kiss." Pippet wrinkled her nose. "I said I don't know. Have you ever kissed anyone? Was it nice? Was it all wet? What does *mouth* taste like?"

Ashe swatted Pippet's backside. "There are some questions you shouldn't ask people."

"Helga always told me if you don't ask questions, you never learn. Then she told me about Nimmus and Cenowyn. Where do you think she is?"

Ashe didn't put much stock into Valgardan myths of what came after death, but she could see by Pippet's wide eyes that the question was important to her. "A woman like Helga—"

She broke off, throwing out an arm to stop them both. A staccato hum rose from the bog like the whip of a thousand flies' wings all at once, swelling and breaking and vaguely, uneasily familiar; she'd heard that sound once on patrol during the war in these same fens.

"What is that?" Pippet asked, turning a full circle.

Three enormous, knobby backs surged up from the bog ahead—horse-sized frogs thudding onto the land shelf, their throat sacs bulging with that grating, rattling call.

Pippet shrieked. "What are *those*?"

"Zabekas!" Ashe drew Echelon, shoving Pippet aside. "Stay back, their hide is poisonous!"

Pippet scrambled back behind the log for shelter, and Ashe raised Echelon high, muscles keening, thrusting her forward into battle.

Light on the shriveled grass, she twirled between the largest and smallest frogs, distracting them with the flashing metal, then gouging their sleek muzzles. The third reeled, lashing out its tongue, and Ashe dodged a hair too slow. The impact against her ribs burned like a whip; she tumbled to her side and rolled back to her feet again, staggering away from another lash—then another, and another.

The pattern of strikes settled in. With the fourth blow, Ashe planted her feet and cleaved that fleshy whip in half. The Zabeka bellowed and toppled backward, blood spewing from its ruined mouth, but the largest sprang before Ashe could turn on it. Its boulder weight knocked her to the grass, the knobs of its pustulated hide shredding her sleeve and rashing her bare arm beneath. She cursed, freeing Echelon from under her body and swinging desperately until steel gouged something that gave.

The creature reared back in agony and fell on her again, and this time something gave out beneath her body. Her satchel shot from below her hip and splashed into the bog, sinking below its peaty surface while the frog bore down on her, driving her deep into the mud.

A shrill scream cut through the air, and the Zabeka lurched backward, guttural hums turning to bleats of agony. Ashe flipped over to find Pippet charging in again, watery daylight flashing along a tiny knife in her fist. She jammed it into the Zabeka's haunch, drawing it in a clumsy circle away from Ashe—buying her enough time to stagger up and plunge her blade into the creature's throat sac. Blood sprayed the grass, and the third frog abandoned its nest in the face of certain death, lunging away into the fen.

Silence descended as swiftly as it first broke. Ashe grabbed Pippet's shoulder, wrenching her away from the dead Zabeka and catching her knife-wielding wrist. "Where did you get this?"

"I...I took it from the cottage." Pippet's eyes were wide and wet. "I didn't want to hurt it, but it was hurting *you*."

"You did well." A wave of dizziness washed over her, soaking into the pain that gnawed her arm. She needed to flush out the stinging welts and bandage the bleeding rash, but all her supplies were sinking to the bottom of the bog—bandages, food, and waterskin among them.

"Ashe, are you all right?" Pippet demanded when she wavered.

"I'm fine," she grunted. "We need to keep moving."

With her first step, another surge of vertigo slammed into her. She might've pitched to her knees if not for Pippet, who pulled her arm across her shoulders with a steady familiarity that made Ashe wonder just how often she saw the cabal do this; how much hurt she noticed even from her sheltered life in Starhollow.

A dull ache pressed into her ribs like a blade seeking to enter, but she didn't know what to say; and for once, Pippet was quiet while they continued on.

A gusting wind found them on the far side of the fen, icier than Ashe was used to for autumn, and with it the shadows gathered early. She dreaded sunset's arrival; no fire would survive this wind, but the night promised to be unseasonably cold. She had no food, no water to offer Pippet, and she was too unsteady to hunt tonight.

When darkness fell, she couldn't put it off any longer. "We need to make camp."

"But—"

"I know it isn't ideal, but I'll show you how to stuff your clothing for insulation, and maybe in the morning we'll find some berries—"

"*Ashe.*" Pippet jostled her lightly. "Look."

Grimacing, Ashe followed the girl's gaze through the trees.

The radiance of ghostlamps revealed itself in the shifting gaps between wind-tossed leaves, an edged glow from shuttered, glassless windows in slope-roofed structures cropping up from the bog ahead. Ashe counted fifteen derelict outlines rising and receding among the thickets.

"What is this place?" Pippet whispered.

A faint strum of displaced recognition moved through Ashe; she shook it away. "I don't know, but we may need to find out."

Pippet's arm tightened around her waist as they wended slowly over stilted, unrailed bridges to the nearest shack and knocked twice. Every fiber of Ashe's Warden's training, every beat of her Talheimic heart warned her to run before the light footsteps within reached the door. But beside her, Pippet shivered, miserable and pale in her unseasonable attire. And the pulse of pain in Ashe's arm begged for relief, too.

She couldn't keep either of them alive in the wilds tonight. She would just have to take this chance and hope she could fight off whoever was inside if they were dangerous.

The door swung open and a woman peered out at them, brown skin painted in silvery ghostlight, eyes wide at the state of her visitors. "Nimmus' teeth! Where did the pair of you come from?"

Pippet rattled through chattering teeth, "H-H-Helli—"

Ashe pinched her shoulder. "*North.* We stumbled into a Zabeka nest crossing the fens. Lost our supplies."

The woman's lips twisted with pity. "You poor things."

"Could we sit by your fire for *just* two minutes?" Pippet begged, teeth gnashing with cold.

"Please. I insist." She widened the door and hurried inside ahead of them, adding logs to the hearth burning brightly on one wall.

Pippet's shivers and chattering teeth stopped, and she winked at Ashe. And despite the pain in her arm, she bit back laughter when she ruffled Pippet's hair and followed her inside.

CHAPTER ELEVEN

"MY NAME IS Pippet. This is Ashe," the girl announced once they settled in front of the modest hearth, sipping hot tea.

"Disa." The reply came from within the cupboard, where the woman rummaged for supplies.

"Are you all alone?"

Disa emerged from the cupboard with a jar in hand and joined them by the fire. "No one in Cerne Mosiar is ever alone."

That name stirred something in Ashe's chest, a faint, nagging memory. "I thought this was the Wildwood."

"It is. Cerne Mosiar is what we call this stretch of the bog. I am its matron." Disa crouched beside Ashe's rickety three-legged chair. "Your arm."

"You don't have—"

"I insist."

Heat coursed up Ashe's neck as she surrendered the burned, blood-crusted limb. Disa opened the salve jar and dabbed the stinging welts, keeping her eyes on the task; Ashe tried not to imagine different calluses on those fingers or another head bent over her wounds.

Are you actually putting a salve on that, or is it poison?

I suspect you'd know if it was the latter. You're a far better poison study than I.

Damned right I am. Don't try anything.

I thought we agreed—

I don't mean poison. Watch your hands, augur.

"What do you mean, you're a *matron?*" Pippet's question pulled Ashe from her memories.

"There are fifteen families in this corridor of the Wildwood," Disa explained. "It's my responsibility to ensure their wellbeing, just as it was my mother's, and hers before her. And it would have been my daughter's, if things had gone differently."

Ashe frowned. "I'm sorry."

Disa's eyes flicked up to her, glazed with an old sadness that hadn't faded with time. "So am I."

Pippet sipped her drink, staring at the fire. Disa swaddled Ashe's arm in loose bandages.

"You'll need to keep that clean." She pressed the jar into Ashe's hand. "Keep this. It will help."

"Are you sending us away?" Pippet blurted out.

Disa turned, tugging the blanket more tightly around Pippet's shoulders. "Do you want to stay?"

She scuffed her toes against the floor. Her boots were wearing thin, the balls of her feet pumping the abraded soles. Why hadn't Ashe noticed that before? Why hadn't Pippet *complained*? "I'd like to sleep on a bed, if that's all right. Just for one night."

"I have just the thing."

Disa relieved Pippet of her cup, and Ashe followed them to the shack's only other room. A bed took up nearly half of it, draped with a handmade quilt, the seams crooked and well-loved. Pippet took a running leap into its folds, burying her face in the pillow with a groan of delight, then flipping over to peer at Disa. "Where do *you* sleep?"

"I'll keep the fire."

Discomfort pricked Ashe's skin. "We can't take your bed."

"Well, one of you can, it seems," Disa chuckled as Pippet rolled among the sheets. "And if one would, you both should." She turned that tired, sincere smile on Ashe across the narrow doorway. "I still have some of my daughter's things, about her size...fresh clothes and boots suited for Wildwood terrain. Would you like them?"

Ashe gritted her teeth, but a heavy sigh still escaped. "I'm sure *she* would. She's used to a better wardrobe than this."

"I'll fetch them while you two rest, then. You're welcome to stay as long as you need."

Your things remain as they were in your room. Take them and as much food as you need when you go.

"Why are you doing this?" Ashe demanded, silencing that echo in her mind. "You don't know us...we could have plans to rob you for everything you have." *Or we'll kill your grandmother or your nanny.*

"If you think I own anything worth stealing, I'll gladly help you search for it!" Disa laughed. "What I do have is a warm hearth and good drink, and the law of the land, which is that we help our own. And we do not leave children in the cold. We never do that." She laid her temple to the doorframe, watching Pippet burrow under the blanket. Shadows of a distant before danced in her eyes—the same shadows that wrapped around Ashe's chest, squeezing tight.

"What happened to this place?" she murmured.

Disa turned away from the room, and Ashe went with her back to the hearth, where she took Pippet's empty chair, staring into the flames. "The stars have shined bright on you if you've not heard the stories. Cerne Mosiar has always been modest, yet mercifully peaceful. But during the war, life was exceptionally difficult. Children disappeared, then reappeared on the battle lines."

A snow-capped world freckled in blood; a blade before her, harsh eyes as dead as the augmented tundra peering from a sunken face. Ashe's ears rang with the tinny memory of her own scream: *I am not afraid of you!* "Did the children attack you?"

Disa's gaze sharpened like a blade. "Attack? No. They came to us for help. We ferried them north, away from the war." She traced a wide, jagged ridge of scar tissue along her wrist. "Though it was at great cost to our own future. When *Meszaros* came, it wielded the Undertaker's scythe, carving a great swath from our numbers, ransacking our dwellings, leaving despair in its wake. So many dead, even the children...especially the children."

"What is *Meszaros*?" Ashe asked.

Disa shook her head. "A creature. I dare not call it a man. Something bred of hate in the war."

Ashe forced another sip of earthy tea through the narrow gap of her throat. "Why did you shelter the children, knowing the danger?"

Disa's smile hung faint with sadness. "Because safety should never be necessary for doing what is right."

The thought of Julian filled Ashe's mind, leaping unabashedly into danger, protecting Cistine even at the risk of certain death. And Aden, a shadow of vengeance going to retribute the men who stabbed her in the Blood Hive, knowing he'd earn the whip for it. And Maleck, his expression impassive at Ashe's brutal threats while he stitched her leg in the back of a merch's wagon, because though they were enemies, he hadn't thought it right to leave her bleeding. And Thorne, offering her rations even when he cast her out for killing the most precious person in his life.

Swallowing became impossible. "I'm not sure we—*I* deserve your help. But I'm...grateful for it."

Disa laid a light hand on Ashe's bandaged arm. "I imagine this wound wasn't taken entirely in your own defense. I don't know what brings that shadow to your stare, but that child trusts you. That is high praise indeed."

Heat crowded Ashe's eyes, blurring the hand on her arm. She didn't deserve Pippet's trust—nor would she keep it if the girl knew about Ashe's part in both Baba Kallah and Helga's deaths. Pippet was in this place, with blistered feet and a broken heart hidden behind childish excitement, because of her. Tonight, Pippet and Disa and Cerne Mosiar and the whole world's burdens felt like her doing.

Ashe set aside her cup. "I give you my word we won't impress on you any longer than necessary."

"It's no trouble. It's good to have a child's laughter in this house again."

That remark seeded and grew when Ashe left Disa by the fire and crept into the bedroom, peeling off her tattered, ruined armor and sitting on the bed, back against the wall.

Pippet fit here, in this house with its generous matron, far better than she fit with Ashe, a warrior with devotion to a different girl. She could thrive here; she and Disa could heal one another. But Ashe couldn't bear to stay a moment longer than she had to. Every passing second filled her with inexplicable panic, like the shadows themselves came alive, reaching from the walls.

Pippet snorted awake, feeling backward with one hand for Ashe's knee. "Why are you breathing like that?"

She sealed her lips against her staggered panting. "I think I've been in Cerne Mosiar before."

Pippet rolled over to look at her with groggy shock. "*Really?*"

Ashe sucked in a harsh breath through her nostrils, and the filaments of memory faded. "I don't...no, I'm probably just imagining it. Every stretch of this forest looks the same." She tucked the blanket up around Pippet's chin. "Go back to sleep."

Pippet rolled over, snuggling back against Ashe's leg, and her stomach clenched and plummeted.

In the morning, she would do it. She had to do it.

But for now, she had to sleep.

Ashe woke to the soft brush of breath on her neck, her heart galloping as the room distilled into focus. She was not on her slab bed in the Hive's catacombs, and the body curled against hers was not some Hive fighter braced for the kill; it was Pippet, her head on Ashe's shoulder, snoring into her hair. Ashe's gut turned over with a fierce protectiveness she hadn't felt since Cistine was still small enough to crawl into her lap and fall asleep listening to the beat of her heart.

Urgency sizzled in her fingertips at the thought of Cistine, bringing the room into sharp clarity: the dark walls, the dark doorway, and two changes of clothes on the floor at the foot of the bed. Slowly, she nudged Pippet aside and went to examine Disa's offering: a sturdy shirt, trousers, and thick boots for Pippet, and Valgardan battle armor, the jar of salve, and a spool of bandages for Ashe.

Heat closed her throat as she fingered the reinforced threads. She did not deserve this after what she'd done to Valgard's people.

Still in semidarkness, but with the waxing daylight strengthening her resolve, Ashe tugged on the armor, belted it tightly around her hips, and pocketed the salve and bandages. With Echelon slung across her back and the dark cloth from Maleck bound over her hair, she stole past Disa stretched out before the hearth and out into the chilly morning air.

Sinewy bridges joined Cerne Mosiar together, and Ashe made dull music with her new boots on their damp wooden planks, crossing the swamp. Judging by the soft daylight glow, she'd be far beyond the last of the two dozen homes by the time anyone stirred.

Striking off on her own again. As it should be.

Dull regret and resignation weighed her chest when she sprang from the last bridge and landed on solid ground. The Wildwood opened up around her again, a straight avenue to the border forts. She coiled to run— then flinched when a rock glanced off her hip. Cursing, she whirled back toward the village.

Pippet sprinted down the last bridge, haphazardly dressed in tunic and trousers, her new boots smacking the planks with every hard step—and another flat rock raised to throw. "What is wrong with you, Ashe? You can't just leave me behind! You're just as bad as Quill!"

Ashe sighed. "Pippet..."

"I know I'm not a warrior like you!" She hurled the rock at Ashe's feet. "And I'm not cabal. But I'm *coming with you*. Stop trying to make my choices for me!"

But that was precisely what Ashe did—she made decisions about what people deserved, and then she acted on it. Like with the Tumult. "You should stay. Disa would give anything to help a Valgardan child. You're good for each other."

Pippet scowled. "I've been nannied my whole life. I'm halfway grown now and I'm not staying behind. If you keep running away, I'll just keep following you."

I'll follow you no matter what, Lord Rion—even if you send me back to the forts. This is Talheim's war, and I'm Talheimic. So let me fight!

Ashe rubbed the memory of her own stubborn voice away. "How are your feet?"

"Don't tell me I have to stay because I can't walk!"

She clapped a hand over Pippet's mouth. "I'm asking if you can keep up."

Pippet's eyes widened. She nodded.

Ashe took her hand back. "If you get tired, tell me. If your feet start to hurt, *tell me*. Otherwise, you stay quiet unless I say you can talk. Agreed?"

"Agreed," Pippet whispered. "You're really letting me stay?"

A smile tugged at Ashe's lips. "You may not believe it, but I've stood exactly where you're standing. And I did exactly what you're doing."

"When? Why?"

The shadows of last night's restless dreams shuddered into memory, fragments of rime ice and darkness and dead eyes whispering a word to quiet the birdsong: *Meszaros.*

Ashe shrugged it away. "Time to walk."

CHAPTER TWELVE

L AVENDER LIGHTNING SEARED across the rain-wrapped sky and thunder tolled like war drums. Cistine screamed until her lungs shattered, screamed without any voice as the augmented bolts slammed into Thorne, warping his body, setting his silver hair aflame—

She woke still shouting, twisting against callused hands wrapped around her shoulders, and slammed her fist into the first inch of flesh she could reach. A gruff, familiar curse shattered the echo of thunder in her ears, and she withdrew with a sharp yank, scrambling up against her pillows. Kristoff crouched with one knee on the bed, clutching his cheek where she hit him.

"Who taught you to throw a punch?" he demanded. "You hit better than half the guards under my command."

Cistine bleated with hysterical laughter, hugging her knees to her chest. "I've only had a few months of practice."

"With a good teacher, by the feeling of it." Kristoff dropped his hand, grimacing. "You were screaming."

Her gaze darted to the door, ajar behind him. "And you came?"

Kristoff straightened, fingers flexing uneasily. "I had a son with night terrors. A thing of habit, I suppose."

Silence lingered between them. The terror of another awful dinner with Salvotor, his voice thrown just like Thorne's when he ordered her to eat and mocked her about Julian's last moments, hung heavy on Cistine's chest; she didn't know what to say, and neither did Kristoff, it seemed. He stood there, hands still curling into fists, staring at her.

Laughter echoed in the hall, and he finally glanced over his shoulder. "I should get back."

Still half-frenzied from bed dreams, Cistine leaped up from the bed when he turned to go. "Kristoff, wait! What are they doing out there?"

He hesitated. "A game of cards."

"I love cards," Cistine said, though she'd only ever played a few easy games. "I'd like to watch."

"You know you're not permitted to leave this room except for suppers."

"I'll keep quiet. You can even bind my hands and feet! But please...*please* give me some time away from this room. I feel like I'm suffocating." The remnants of her nightmare hung in every curl of the light-purple glow dripping from the ghostplants on the wall niches.

She couldn't be alone with the vision of Thorne struck dead by his father. Anything was better, even being subject to Kristoff and his guards. Even being in chains.

He stared at her, pale and still, like he saw someone else entirely in her panicked face. After a long moment, he put out his hand. "Your wrists."

Cistine let him bind her, the knots loose but secure, and trailed after him from the chamber. The hewn room was deserted apart from the six guards at the cellar and six more at a stone table, all looking up at their arrival. Cistine recognized Dain, his nose crooked now, eyes brimming with curiosity. "*Nadrian*, what is the Key doing with you?"

"A short reprieve."

"Is that what you had to check in on?" one man drawled in a great, booming voice. "And here I thought you were just slinking away from a bad hand!"

Kristoff fixed him with a stare so chilling, even Cistine winced. "This overzealous slack-jaw is Baldvin. Beside him, Markvard, and that one to his left is Krusar. Dain, you must recognize." Dain nodded shyly, eyes fixed on his cards and face streaked with color. "To his left are our twins—Selanus and Suandi."

The gnarled guards almost split the seams of their armor as they reclined in their chairs and flashed mirrored smiles full of jaundiced teeth and cracked lips. Baldwin, Krusar, and Markvard were slightly shorter, but hardly narrower—the fittest Vassora Cistine had ever met, as if they too passed the time in this place with training.

"Who are we to deny the presence of a lovely woman at our table?" Baldwin kicked out the chair across from him. "Even if she is the Key."

"Untouchable," Markvard sighed. "A pity."

Kristoff drew the chair out the rest of the way for Cistine—six kindnesses. "Remember what brought you here in the first place, Markvard."

He flashed a wicked smirk. "*Ha, Nadrian.*"

"What does that mean?" Cistine settled herself in the seat between Kristoff and Suandi and tried not to notice the neck-snapping girth of the man's bicep flexing right beside her face.

"Old Valgardan title," Dain muttered, "for a leader."

"The Vassora have rituals as ancient as their roots," Kristoff said. "Now, are we playing, or not?"

The game resumed, freckled now with uneasy silence and glances shot Cistine's way. She ignored them, balancing her bound hands on the table and leaning over Kristoff's elbow to surveil his cards. Julian had taught her some games growing up, and a few more during their nighttime patrols in Hellidom and Starhollow. For a few moments, her memories of him were pleasant again—not lightning and smoke and melted eyes, but his arm around her waist and his chin on her shoulder, his amused voice reminding her which cards to play, and when. He'd been so proud of her the first time she beat Quill, even if he'd done most of the plotting.

"Wait!" she grabbed Kristoff's hand when he reached for a card, and he jumped away from her touch, cursing. "Don't play that one—play this one."

After a beat, he plucked out the card she pointed to and tossed it onto the table. The rest of the Six hurled down their hands, groaning and cursing. Krusar sat forward, red forelock tumbling into his eyes. "Now, this is unfair!

That's five mynts each you've cost us."

"Did you bring her along to help you cheat, *Nadrian?*" Baldvin demanded.

"I didn't realize she had a keen eye for cards." Kristoff's gaze slid to Cistine, pensive and intent.

"There's more to me than the blood in my veins, you know," she said hotly. "Or is the Key still just a tool to all of you?"

They glanced around at one another, the twins blank-faced and Krusar scowling; but Dain looked almost sheepish, and Markvard and Baldvin studied her with newfound interest. Kristoff would not look at her at all.

"My name is Cistine Novacek of Talheim," she said. "I'm twenty years old. I love gardening, and books, and shopping, and I've recently learned I like to climb things when my life's not in peril. I cry too much sometimes, and I make mistakes…plenty of them. I've fallen in love, I've been betrothed, and since I came to this kingdom, I…I've lost people I couldn't bear to lose." Swallowing a surge of tears, she clasped her bound hands until the roots of her knuckles throbbed. "I am a *person*, like all of you. I'm not some weapon your Chancellor just stumbled across out there. I'm *real*."

Kristoff stared at the winning cards in his hand. His men shifted, and at cellar mouth, the Vassora exchanged glances.

Good. Let them *all* see the truth; if Salvotor slit her throat, it would end a life that mattered enough that Ashe had been captured for her, that the cabal had taught and defended her, that Julian had *died* for her. A life Cistine would fight for, as fiercely as she was able, for as long as she could.

Krusar cleared his throat. "Shall we play another round?"

Dain sat up taller, looking her straight in the eyes. "You said your name was Cistine?" She nodded, and his mouth curled slightly. "I didn't know that. It's a pretty name."

"There's no sense in her being anything but the Key," Markvard scoffed. "Nothing good comes from naming a deer before you put an arrow through its heart."

"And how would you feel," Cistine seethed, "if everyone forgot *your* name when you were exiled here?"

"That's enough," Kristoff said. "If you open your mouth again, Cistine, you return to your chamber."

Scowling, she dropped against the seatback again, watching the game resume. It was several moments of mutinous silence before she realized he'd called her by her name.

CHAPTER THIRTEEN

KELTEI TEMPLE PERCHED on a jutting peninsula at the northernmost tip of Lataus territory, the sheer-sided brown cliffs capped with domed wings and alabaster walls sloping down to the glittering hazel-blue Agerios Sea. Tatiana silently recited everything she knew about this temple while the cabal dismounted, lashed their horses to a grove of stunted trees, and approached its gilded front door; every temple excelled in a different kind of augmentation. Keltei's was medicinal, its *visnprests* trained to knit bone and muscle, heal wounds without a scar, cure poisons, mend torn insides, and mop up blood from bodily cavities.

She wondered if her mother ever had a chance to visit this place before her untimely sickness and death.

A pair of braided cords hung on either side of the temple door, and when Quill and Tatiana yanked on them the sweet, glistering music of silver bells iced the sea breeze.

"Imagine being summoned by *that* every day," Tatiana said. "I'd stuff my ears with cotton."

Quill should've bantered back at her—something about how he assumed she already did. But he just stared vacantly past her.

Thorne rolled his shoulders loose and took several deep, steadying breaths. "Maleck, you're on watch. Anyone else?"

Quill glanced at Ariadne. "Do you want this hunt, or should I take it?"

Before she could answer, the temple doors unlatched and slid open. An aging woman, steel-spined in soft gray robes with even softer gray eyes, smiled at them from within. "The stars shine brightly on you. For what reason have you—?"

She broke off. Devastated recognition flickered in her eyes, and Tatiana's heart leaped at the nearly-forgotten memory of her winsome grins and summer-bright laughter. "*Iri.*"

"Stars above!" The *visnpresta* yelped. "Tatiana, Quill, Thorne—" her gaze skipped past them, and she flung a hand to the arched doorway, her knees buckling. "*Ariadne.*"

Her breath tumbled down through her, heavy as stone. "*Kenahri.*"

Teacher. The anguish in Ariadne's voice struck Tatiana like an arrow through the shoulder.

Iri parted their company with arms outswept to grip Ariadne by the shoulders. "I've prayed every day for ten years that I would see your face again."

Ariadne inhaled wetly. "I'm sorry I couldn't come sooner to tell you I was all right. It was never the right time."

"All good things happen when the gods wish it, not a second sooner." Iri pressed a kiss to the top of Ariadne's head. Her gaze flicked to Maleck in silent, reserved recognition; then she swiveled to face Thorne. "Why have you come?"

"We seek an audience with Saychelle. Is she here?"

"Of course she is. And somehow I'm not surprised it's her you came to see." The flicker of dry humor reminded Tatiana that while this woman was head of a temple now, she'd grown up in the mire of Stedgnalt Lake keeping pace with Baba Kallah, Helga, and the mischievous Sigrid. She was more than capable of seeing through the cabal's bluster.

Tatiana had missed that ever since Baba Kallah's passing.

But the moment of happiness, a sense of homecoming, vanished when Iri released Ariadne's shoulder and turned back to Thorne, studying his face. "I remember that look in your eye when your uncle died. What have you lost, Thorne?"

His faced bunched—almost a wince—and the words came through a tight jaw. "Baba Kallah is gone."

Iri's hand flew to her throat. "*No*. Age? Illness?"

"Salvotor. And he isn't finished. I hope Saychelle might be able to help put a stop to his schemes."

Iri beckoned. "She may. Come inside."

Tatiana followed, barely catching a glimpse of the arching entry parlor before Thorne's voice turned her back. "Ariadne."

Eyes tight with distress, mouth trembling, she rested her gloved hand on the doorframe and didn't move. "I can't. Forgive me, Thorne. I can't."

"There's nothing to forgive," he said. "Quill."

Ariadne bowed stiffly to Iri and hurried after Maleck to take watch. Tatiana tried not to think of that look on Ariadne's face—or how she would've felt in her friend's stead, standing on the threshold of a dream so cruelly torn away—when they entered Keltei Temple.

The pearl-white walls flourished with hanging boxes of sea ivy and moss, the smell of sweet herbs and moving water pulsing from a fountain in the parlor's center beneath a dome of pure glass. Hot coals twinkled through iron lattice on the floor, and on a scattering of stone benches, *visnprests* and *prestas* read books and scrolls.

Iri scooped water from the fountain into wooden cups and offered them to the cabal, eyes still wet with grief. "Saychelle came to this place a broken child full of regrets. Now she has learned to heal the hurts of others as well as her own. But tread lightly with her, Thorne."

At his nod, she led them through a broad archway and into a maze of halls swished in sunlight. There were no guards on watch, and every *visnprest* they passed offered amicable nods; still, Tatiana tensed when they ascended their fifth flight of stairs and entered a pair of double doors into a pool chamber. Planters of ferns and orchids skirted the walls, and braziers burned between lofty pillars capped in lichen and ivy. *Visnprests* and *prestas* sat at the poolside, books open in their laps, following along with a woman reading the Old Valgardan script aloud.

Iri coughed, drawing her attention, and she raised her head so sharply her pale hair swung from the beaded shawl across her brow. Tatiana grimaced; the last time she laid eyes on this woman, her hair was as black as her sister's.

Saychelle's eyes locked on Thorne, and his on her. The depth of aching history between them stormed the humid air.

After a moment, Thorne lowered his head and folded his hands in the small of his back. Saychelle rose from her cushion seat. "That's all for today. Be certain to practice your runes. And remember—these augments should be used as a *last* resort in our healing efforts. What is the principle lesson of the old *visnprest* scrolls?"

The answer came from Thorne. "When man is defined by the work of the augments rather than the work of his own hands, he seals himself for Nimmus and condemns his spirit to the Sable Gates."

The acolytes swiveled curiously toward the steps. Saychelle's brows scrunched as she clapped her own book shut. "It seems my visitor thinks himself a master of augmentation. You're all excused."

Tatiana brushed Quill aside, and Thorne bowed out of the acolytes' way. Several looked a bit too long at Thorne, almost with a trace of displaced, uneasy recognition. But when Tatiana nudged one of her knives up with the pad of her thumb, baring a wicked gleam of well-oiled steel to the light, they hastily forgot about the silver-haired man in battle armor.

"You may go as well, Iri." Saychelle stacked the sitting cushions off to one side. "I'm perfectly capable of receiving the sick on my own now, no matter how ill of mind they are."

"Saychelle," Iri chided. "Don't be quick to assume you know the nature of a wound before you examine it."

She scowled, dipping her head. "Yes, *Kenhari*."

Iri backed away, trailing a hand against Thorne's shoulder. "I will say the mourning prayers for your grandmother. She was dear to me. I'm sorry for your loss."

Thorne's throat bobbed roughly, and he swiveled his head without breaking posture, brushing his cheek against his shoulder. "Thank you."

Iri dragged the opalescent doors shut. The moment she was gone, Saychelle said, "Baba Kallah is dead?"

Thorne nodded. "But that's not why we've come."

"Of course not." Saychelle mounted the steps to join them. She'd grown in their years apart—not quite to match Ariadne's willowy height, but enough that she didn't have to crane her head to look into Thorne's eyes anymore when she halted before him.

Tatiana couldn't remember how they'd ever been close enough to touch. There was nothing but frost between them now.

"Your hair," Thorne said after a beat. "That was my father's doing."

"Aren't we quite the matched pair. Now I see you even in the mirror. What do you *want*, Thorne?"

"I have a plan to unseat my father. And I hoped you might help me achieve it."

Saychelle's eyes flashed. She studied his face for a moment, then descended back toward the pool. It was as good an invitation as any for them to follow, so Thorne did, Tatiana and Quill closing rank behind him with a brief glance and their hands on their weapons.

"If you're coming to me with this notion," Saychelle said, "I can only assume you've heard rumors of why I came to Keltei."

"You tried to expose what was done to Ariadne," Thorne said. "How did you know it happened?"

"Because I was there in your family's apartment, creeping out after seeing *you*. When I realized what was happening, I panicked and hid."

Tatiana's throat knotted. Seeing Ariadne after that night had nearly been unbearable; she couldn't imagine witnessing it. Or hiding while it happened.

"I'm sorry I broke my promise," Thorne murmured. "I didn't spare you or your sister from the injustices you helped me fight against."

"I never held *you* accountable."

"I held myself accountable." They reached the poolside, and Saychelle gestured them to sit. "I know you tried to condemn my father in our absence, but there was never any hope you would convict him without

Ariadne there to press charges."

Saychelle scowled. "It's difficult to condemn a man for unhappy joinings besides."

"This is different." Thorne's eyes narrowed. "He buried a law that forbids joining with a *visnpresta* against her will. With Ariadne's charges and your account, we would have enough to place him on trial, and that would cost him the Judgement Seat."

Saychelle's lips parted, but no sound emerged. Tatiana's focus hung on the stillness of Saychelle's chest, the uncommon quiet of her mouth— hoping these were signs of a tide changing in their favor for once.

"Kanslar cannot try its own Chancellor," Saychelle finally said.

"It won't. I can't tell you any more than that, I can only promise if you have the courage to come forward, we have friends in powerful positions who can try Salvotor and bring him to justice."

Saychelle peeled her shoulders up. "You're asking me to testify in a courtroom against the most powerful man to walk Valgard's face since the Elder Kings. Something even *you* wouldn't do without mounds of legal precedent after he beat and humiliated you for eighteen *years*—"

"The beatings were never beyond what's permitted for an irreverent child. He knew that. He was careful about it. As for the rest...a man can't be tried and convicted for the filthy names he calls his son. My word on the matter would not stand in a courtroom, Saychelle, but yours *would*."

"Especially now," Tatiana added. "Wouldn't Keltei's people stand behind you if it came to that?"

"Iri seems to know how things were," Quill said carefully.

Saychelle fixed him with a look so frigid, Tatiana wanted to sidle between them. "Iri is the only reason I'm alive after the threats I endured. This," she tugged down the shawl, exposing her hair, "was done to me with a light augment while I traveled home from the market. My foot was crushed by a cart and only saved by a healing augment, which could *not* reattach the three toes I lost. Expletives were nailed to our front door. My parents' flower shop went to ruin, its customers threatened away. Creatures stalked outside our home night and day. I didn't sleep for weeks, even after Iri brought me here. And you want me to face the man responsible for that suffering? To trust you can stop him *now*, when we've had nothing for ten years?"

"Saychelle," Quill said. "I hear what you suffered trying to bring out the truth, and I know why you did it anyway. They hurt your *sister*. You couldn't let them get away with that."

Thorne peered at Quill over his shoulder. Tatiana was already looking at him, her heart cracking in her chest.

"I know how that felt because they tried to do the same thing to *my* sister. You remember Pippet? Salvotor let slavers take her the day our parents died. I spent weeks finding her. I know that obsession, how you'd give up anything to set it right."

Some of the frostiness melted from Saychelle's gaze. "Is she—?"

"Alive. But I knew Salvotor would never try those slavers because they would just blame *him* for letting them take her to get to me. So I took justice into my own hands."

"Quill." Thorne's tone was quiet but firm.

Quill swept a hand back through his hair. "I'm not suggesting you try to kill him. But making your own justice might mean taking this to the Courts so he pays for burying and breaking a law that destroyed your sister's future."

"A future you carried on," Tatiana added.

"At what cost?" Saychelle snapped. "It seems I have a talent for learning and teaching augmentation, but I only do it because Ariadne is forbidden to, and her dream deserves to live."

"Her pain also deserves to be avenged! You can help with *that*, too. In fact, you're the only one who can."

"Everything is in place," Thorne said. "The connections, the Courts. All that's needed is your testimony to supplement her charges."

"And what will you do if I agree? Take me back to Stornhaz and remand me to the Courts? Trust *them* to keep me safe, since they did such a wonderful job of it before? Or become my personal protector yourself?"

Thorne shook his head. "I can't. My hunt isn't finished."

Saychelle tipped her head. "Hunting for what, exactly?"

"For the Key."

She regarded him shrewdly, the drape of her hair falling over her shoulder. "I'd heard the rumor someone found the Key to the Doors to the Gods. I wondered how long before it awakened your old curiosity."

"Do you know where the Key is?" Quill demanded.

"Do you know *what* it is?" Tatiana added

"No, and no," Saychelle said. "Only hearsay. Why? Do *you* know what it is?"

"Not *what*," Thorne rasped, "*who*. Someone I consider a friend. She's Salvotor's prisoner."

Saychelle leaped up and started to pace beside the pool. "The Key...a person? I suppose...there's nothing to necessitate the Doors be keyed to an *object*. If they used *Gammalkraft*..."

"I know I've heard of that somewhere. What is it?" Quill asked.

Saychelle flicked her fingers at him. "It was a passing mention in school. During the reign of the Elder Kings, the gods spoke with man on far more personal terms. They gave them many sacred gifts, powers time has forgotten. *Gammalkraft* is so old not even we know how it's ritualized now. The Bloodwights were the last to learn, and they took the sacred scrolls when they fled. Those rites were older than the bones of the world, and they were not for the eyes of your usual acolytes. But I can surmise it all ends in death. These things usually do."

Thorne stood, the shift in his height raising his intensity. "Tell me everything you know about the Key."

Saychelle took her hair over her shoulder and began to braid it. "Let's consider if the Doors *were* keyed to a person. We all know Cyril Novacek was present when the Doors were shut—just him and the *visnprests* of the old Order. So, I'm to assume the Key is joined to him somehow?"

"His daughter."

"A direct heir. I suspected as much. It's in the blood, then...Cyril and his daughter, the purest of all the Keys, first and second made. Spill Novacek blood on the rune-slabs over the wells, and it must open the Doors."

"Ari was right," Quill muttered.

Pain flashed in Saychelle's eyes. "Of course she was. And Salvotor is like every man who ever corrupted augments or misused *Gammalkraft*. I'm sure he'll bleed her dry to achieve his ends."

Thorne dragged a hand down his face. "Will he need *Gammalkraft* to do it?"

"He shouldn't. If it's in the blood, spilling it on a Door should be enough. But he can't know that for certain...the Chancellors were forbidden from the ritual, after all. Salvotor could lose the Judgement Seat for dabbling in this, *Gammalkraft* or not, but once he opens a Door it won't matter."

"Tell us how to stop him. Stand with us and bring him to his knees."

Saychelle caught her bottom lip in the corner of her teeth, looking at the door like she might flee, as she'd fled the night they the cabal left Stornhaz. Tatiana felt a twinge of sympathy; she'd chosen life in the city over exile with them, and she'd *still* been exiled to this temple. Salvotor left a trail of anguish and misery across Valgard, and it would require nothing less than his victims banding together to bring him to justice.

"No, Thorne," she said at last. "I won't testify."

Tatiana cursed. "Why *not?*"

"I only have so much luck left after the brushes with death I escaped in Stornhaz. I'm not eager to test that in the courtroom where Salvotor can reach me."

"If there's no one to testify," Thorne said, "he can hurt others the way he hurt Ariadne."

"I'm sure he already *has*," Saychelle snapped. "You can hardly throw a stone in Stornhaz without finding someone your stars-damned father has abused or intimidated or hurt in *some* way. Take your length of rope for his noose from the pocket of someone who hasn't already given *everything* trying to further the cause *you* started."

Thorne turned his back on her and rasped his palms over his stubbled cheeks, eyes fixed sightlessly on the door. That look reminded Tatiana far too much of his despair after Baba Kallah's death. If he started to slip down that slope again, this time without Cistine to tow him back up...

"What about the Key?" he asked. "No witness, no testimony, nothing in this kingdom will be able to destroy him if he uses her as he intends."

"You have some time," Saychelle said. "Because the Chancellors were forbidden from the ritual, they don't know how it's performed. Salvotor might be able to wrestle that truth from the Key, but as long as it hangs in the balance, she will live."

"You're so sure about all of this," Tatiana said, "but you still don't know where she is?"

"No, I don't. But that doesn't mean I don't know *how* to find her."

"Please." Thorne's tone stopped Tatiana's heart. She'd never heard him speak that way before—desperate, half-broken, ragged. *Begging.* "I will do anything. Saychelle, *please.*"

After a torturous pause, she said, "You aren't going to like it."

"Tell me anyway."

"Not with your guards here."

Tatiana favored her with a dry smile and waited for Thorne to tell her this was his cabal, and they had no secrets.

"Quill. Tati," he said. "Wait outside."

Tatiana's jaw dropped. Quill stiffened. "Thorne—"

"You heard me."

Tatiana gritted her teeth against a protest. This hunt was Thorne's, and the cabal had an understanding: where the hunt leader sent you, you went. Even if you disagreed.

She and Quill stalked back out into the hall. Clouds smothered the sun now, blanketing the hallway with fistfuls of shadow. Tatiana shoved her half of the door shut and punched it for good measure. "How can she stand there with the power to destroy Salvotor and *not* use it?"

"Saychelle was never a warrior," Quill said. "Not everyone is carved out for this life. It takes a special kind of strength to stand against that *bandayo.*"

Tatiana flopped with her back to the door, folding her arms. "You would never know she helped forge Sillakove."

"If defying Salvotor was any man's game, we wouldn't be in these straits." Quill reclined beside her, mirroring her posture and resting one foot against the door. "Thorne knew Saychelle back then better than anyone. He has to have a contingency in mind, knowing it might go like this."

"Or he let his feelings blind him."

"No, he hasn't thought about Saychelle that way in years. Especially not since..."

The breeze traveled through the glassless windows, dragging Tatiana's corkscrew curls into her eyes. She pinned them to her scalp with one hand, scowling. "I hope you're right. Because our best hope for thwarting Salvotor just abandoned us."

"We'll find another way. The fight isn't over yet."

"But it's not going to *be* much of a fight," Tatiana argued. "And what if Cistine's not in the temples? You would think Saychelle would've heard *something* if she was."

Worry carved a deep divot between Quill's brows. "That's true."

The door behind him started to bow, and he stepped out of the way so Thorne could escape. He didn't speak to them, only motioned with a jerk of his head; and if Tatiana hated the look on his face when he realized Saychelle wouldn't help them, she absolutely despised the one he wore now. That special blend of despair, resignation, and daring never amounted to anything good.

"What news?" Maleck demanded the moment they emerged. Thorne strode past him, beckoning the cabal to follow.

"Saychelle?" Ariadne murmured as she and Tatiana fell into step behind Quill and Maleck.

"She won't testify. Salvotor hurt her after we left Stornhaz. Badly."

Ariadne's fingers tightened into fists. "I should have found a way to stay. Or convinced her to flee with us."

"You were preoccupied with bleeding to death."

"She is my younger sister. My responsibility."

"I know," Tatiana sighed. "I know how important it is for you to protect her. I just wish she'd return that favor."

"I can't demand that. But thank the stars I do have a sister at my back, always." Ariadne squeezed Tatiana's shoulder and hurried to help Thorne untether the horses.

Even with their mounts unbound, Thorne didn't ride. He wrapped the reins in his fist and looked around at each of their faces, soaking up their stares. "My friends..." he broke off and amended quietly, "my family."

Tatiana groped desperately for something to anchor herself, because whatever was coming, it would not be good. She found Quill's hand, and he grasped hers tightly.

"This is where we part ways. Ariadne, Maleck, you're going to Stornhaz," Thorne said. "Start the search for a different witness who can testify against my father. Start with your family, Ari, if you can find them, and any reports in the Vassoran watch from ten years ago. We *will* find evidence or witnesses to pin him with that law."

Maleck dipped his head. "On our way, *Allet*."

"Tatiana, you'll take Sorrat Temple, Quill, Nygaten. I'll take Azkai. Gather every scrap of information you can, then report to Hellidom. We'll meet there before Kanslar sets and decide which temple to strike."

Ariadne swung onto her horse and looked down at them. "Thank you for trying today, Thorne."

He rested his hand on her horse's flank. "Saychelle asked me to give you her love. And her apology."

"I would prefer action over apology. But I hope she knows I love her, too."

Maleck embraced Thorne, murmured something in his ear, then mounted as well with a parting smile for Quill and Tatiana. "Safety and peace until I see you again."

"Look after yourselves," Quill warned. "That city has claws and teeth."

"True. But its heart is still good." Maleck's gaze lingered on Tatiana. "I'll give your love to your father."

Silence enveloped them as Maleck and Ariadne rode away, its heaviness broken only by the crash of the surf on the cliffs.

"What did she say to you?" Quill demanded.

"Nothing I didn't already suspect." Thorne turned to them. "You should ride together as far as the Nior. You two are always safer together than apart."

"Isn't that true." Tatiana rubbed the crumbled scar on her shoulder from a poisoned Tyve arrow.

"Whatever happens," Thorne added, "we find an accuser and a witness. If Maleck and Ariadne learn what they need, don't wait for me. Bring my father down from the Judgement Seat." He curved a hand around the back of Quill's neck and set their foreheads together, then wrapped an arm around Tatiana and embraced her so tightly her chest nearly caved. "Look after one another and be safe."

"Always," she murmured.

Thorne swung into his saddle, turned his horse northeast, and looked down at them as Ariadne and Maleck had. "Thank you. For this day, and every one before it. You two have never hesitated to walk into danger at my side. Ever since we were children, I've never felt like I walk alone."

"You never will, either," Tatiana said.

Thorne smiled. "I know that."

He snapped the reins and sent his mount into a gallop down the coast. Tatiana watched him vanish, and with every drum of retreating hooves, her chest knotted tighter and tighter.

First worry. Then grief. Then *anger*.

She stalked to her own horse, cinched the saddle, and swung into it, turning north as well.

"Tati," Quill said, "wrong direction. Sorrat is south, remember?"

"I'm not going. There's something Thorne isn't telling us, and that's his choice...his hunt. But I think we're right, Quill, she's not in any of the temples. Saychelle would know."

Quill braced his arm on the saddlehorn. "What are you thinking?"

Conviction tightened her fingers around the reins. "I've done this before...found people Salvotor took. I can find her on my own."

"Where would you even start?"

"That's the bit I'm still working on." She peered at him sideways. "Any help?"

He scratched under his hair, gazing north. "Wherever the Order keyed the Doors, it had to be somewhere they could keep the Chancellors out...somewhere there was no chance of them being seen. And if the Key was made somewhere other than the temples—"

"Maybe that's where she can be unmade," Tatiana finished. "Then we don't need to know where the whispers of the Key are pointing now, we need to know where that rumor first started two decades ago."

"Helga told me once about this woman who trades in secrets, sort of a blend of myth and truth. She started plying that trade not too long before the war with Talheim. Maybe she heard something back then."

"Back then? Maybe she heard something now!" Tatiana snugged the reins gleefully. "Why didn't you mention this to Thorne in the first place?"

Quill shrugged. "Because it's probably nothing, and I didn't want to waste time...or endanger the hunt."

"Endanger it? Since when?" Tatiana smacked her knee against his. "Tell me where we're headed, Featherbrain!"

An odd looked crossed Quill's face, then faded. "Nordbran. According to Helga's story, anyway. But I could be wrong."

"You know I'm always willing to take a chance on you, Featherbrain." Tatiana angled her horse's head. "Nordbran it is."

CHAPTER FOURTEEN

*Y*OU REALLY SHOULD *eat. Look at you, Wildheart. I can't even enjoy you in that dress.*

The echoes of Salvotor's voice, the inflections just like Thorne's, gnawed at her heart while hunger gnawed at her empty stomach and grief and anger clouded her mind. Only her hands obeyed her will this morning, flying over her secret task, desperate to be one step closer to possible escape.

She finally found a use for the lavender quilt and sheets Kristoff helped her strip from the bed: picked apart at the seams and torn into three long hanks, braided into a rope the way Ashe taught her. She'd been thirteen years old when her Warden taught her how to make such a rope and rappel from her balcony window into the garden below.

"I know, it's time-consuming and humiliating and you deserve to do so much more with your afternoon," Ashe had deadpanned. "But you need to know how to escape from your rooms if the Citadel catches fire or if there's a siege."

If she couldn't infiltrate the cellar, she would lash this to the balcony and scale down the mountain. She prayed it wouldn't come to that, but prayer alone wouldn't part the men from the cellar or help her chart the air tunnels.

The chain slithered suddenly from the door, and Cistine dropped her braiding under the bed just as Kristoff stepped inside. His eyes landed on her, sitting with the burgundy dress spread across her lap and her back propped against the pillow. "What are you doing?"

She almost smiled at his cautious, fatherly tone—suspecting mischief. "What are *you* doing? Have you come to fetch me for dinner?"

"No." He jerked his head. "Come with me."

Curiosity stroked, she followed him back out into the hewn chamber—toward the card table with the six guards. Stricken with relief, she laid an unbound hand on his arm. "I didn't think, after last time—"

"I heard the things he said to you last night." Kristoff's curt tone closed the subject, and he drew the chair out for her. Another kindness.

The men were far more relaxed this time, and Dain, sitting on her right, flashed his cards several times in a silent plea for aid. He desperately needed it, far more than she could give; but she tried her best, accepting the jeers when Dain lost anyway.

"I don't think I've ever enjoyed taking you for all you're worth so much." Baldvin raked a pile of mynts toward himself, winking at Cistine. "Why don't you sit beside Selanus next? He's the only one who's a real threat. Perhaps you could bleed him of his talent, too."

Cistine curled her lip. "Maybe I'll come and sit by *you*."

"I wish you would." Markvard patted his thigh. "There's plenty of room in my lap."

"*Plenty*," Krusar repeated. "He's got nothing else there, if you catch my meaning."

Markvard lobbed an empty mead cup at his head. "He knows nothing! Come and sit with me!"

"Don't sit with him," Kristoff said flatly, still looking down at his cards.

Cistine couldn't bite back a smile. This almost felt like a night of cards and tea at the Den's kitchen table; and as she watched cards flash and trade hands, melancholy seized her. She'd accused these men of seeing only the Key, not the girl who *was* the Key, but when did she ever see a Vassoran guard as someone more than an enemy? These men, the Six, were friends and brothers; they weren't just a line of armored bodies to plow through on the way to Salvotor, and they no more deserved an impersonal death at the tip of a sword than she did. If she called the hopeless, imprisoned, and oppressed her cause, then they were her people just as much as the cabal.

"Well, now," a silky voice cleaved into her thoughts. "What a delightful gathering."

The Six threw their cards down on the table, shooting upright. Cistine was much slower to stand, knees watery as her eyes found Chancellor Salvotor entering from a side hall. He held her gaze for a beat, then glanced at the men flanking him: the guard who refused to stand watch at the cellar, and Devitrius, the bald, smug *bandayo* whose whip rived Thorne's back open on Eben's plains.

Cistine didn't realize she'd jerked toward him, seething, until Dain grabbed her under the arm.

"Thank you for your report on the Key's whereabouts, Grimmaul," Salvotor said. "Once again, you prove your value."

The guard smiled gleefully, his expression like a dagger's cut when his gaze fell on Cistine. Just like that first time, a jolt of recognition speared through her, bringing the smell of tree sap and blood, the echoes of battle and terror.

Salvotor linked his hands behind his back. "And today began so well! I just received a most interesting report from Devitrius." His eyes settled on Cistine again, and she took an involuntary step back. "And then I received another...that someone allowed the Key from its chamber to drink and play cards with the men. Whose idea was that, I wonder?"

Cistine drew a deep breath and set her shoulders. She'd asked for that first reprieve—foolish in retrospect, a direct opposition to Salvotor's attempts to wear her down; and opposition, he had already proven, would be met with pain. But though her fingers rattled and her bowels clenched, she would accept the consequences, not hide behind others and force them to pay for her mistake.

"That was my doing." Kristoff brushed her back before she could speak, his words hanging cold and unrepentant on the air.

Salvotor studied Kristoff. "I should have suspected. And to what do we owe the displeasure of your defiance, *Nadrian?*"

Dain tensed and the twins shifted on their feet.

"I thought a bit of time with my men would help loosen her tongue," Kristoff said. "Women tend to respond more favorably to a gentle hand than a harsh one."

Cistine stiffened, glaring at his broad back. Had all those kindnesses been a lie? But Dain cleared his throat quietly, and when her eyes jumped to him, he shook his head.

"I see," Salvotor murmured. "Forgive me if I don't come to *you* for insight into attaining a woman's favor, Kristoff. A dead *valenar* and son—"

"Sons."

"Please. The second one hardly counts. Now, tell me the truth: are you certain the Key played no part in its own release?"

"She did not."

Cistine's heart thrummed in her ears.

"Very well," Salvotor said. "Grimmaul, have your men restrain his. Devitrius, you know what to do. Come and see me in my chambers afterward."

Grimmaul's retinue swarmed them at once—knives at the twins' throats, a man each to Baldvin, Markvard, Krusar, and Dain. Grimmaul himself caught Cistine with a hand over her mouth, silencing her pleas for Kristoff's life before they could escape. Devitrius uncoiled the whip, its merciless barbed tips grazing the floor, and tore the back of Kristoff's uniform open, exposing tan skin almost as scarred as Thorne's. This had happened before; Kristoff knew the cost, and still took the blame.

The Six struggled against their fellow guards, cursing and shouting, but Grimmaul's retinue held them fast. Held *her* fast—but not enough.

Grimmaul didn't fear her. He didn't know what the Wild Heart of Fire was capable of when provoked.

The first lash jerked a wince from everyone in the room, including the six guards at the cellar steps. Kristoff buckled forward, gripping the nearest stone tables to keep from planting face-first on Kalt Hasa's icy floor.

The second strike. Devitrius chuckled at the moan from Kristoff's throat.

The third. Tears of rage blurred Cistine's vision, turning Kristoff's body to the form of a High Tribune on his knees in the mud, his back broken open by the whip in his father's hands.

Wildheart! Close your eyes!

But she had not then. And she would not now—or ever again.

She sank her teeth into Grimmaul's hand so hard, bone scraped between her teeth. He swore, loosening his grip by instinct, and Cistine kicked free and slammed her elbow into his eye socket. He crumbled, and she rushed Devitrius.

She had no sword to pluck up this time. No weapon. Only a shield...only herself. So she lunged between Kristoff and Devitrius, dropping her weight, letting go of her breath, bracing like Quill and Thorne taught her—and catching the whip against her arm.

Blinding white pain seared through her body, and her knees cracked the stone beside Kristoff. The whip had landed wrong, ripping deep, bloody furrows into her forearm, peeps of white showing through. Vomit climbed up Cistine's throat and she wobbled, sagging into Kristoff's side.

The guards at the cellar shouted at Devitrius, a blurred mixture of syllables—something about wasting her blood. He stared at her, the hoods of those lazy eyelids torn wide open; then he ordered Grimmaul's men to get her and Kristoff on their feet and sent someone to retrieve a healing augment.

It seemed they didn't know where her chamber was, so they threw her with Kristoff into his. The moment she landed on the side of his bed, a flagon shattered in the dark. Warm, milky light swarmed her arm, spinning her head into a daydream. She shuddered and sobbed as the pain crested, one long, keening tone at the close of a funeral dirge; then it wilted like a rotting rose, petals dropping one by one in the dark silence.

The pain vanished and the nausea dissipated, but a strange, visceral hunger took their place. Cistine blinked her eyes open and found Grimmaul's men retreating from the small, dim chamber. There was some commotion in the outer hall—Kristoff's men shouting, demanding to see their *Nadrian*.

Kristoff.

He was sprawled face-down beside her on the bed. They hadn't spared any of the healing augment for him; his only movement was to curl his fist around a compass-star pendant hanging from his neck—something he must've kept tucked inside his uniform before, giving Salvotor one less thing to taunt him about. Cistine had seen it sketched in the margins of stories about the Four Wayfinders, one point on the compass for each of the wise women, an instrument that guided lost men home.

She dragged herself up the bed, scooping up the thick blanket as she went and pressing it to the bloody mess of his back. He groaned at her touch, and the sound jerked tears from Cistine's eyes.

"What are you doing?" he rasped.

"Trying to keep you alive." She wanted to tell him he'd been a fool to take this punishment, that she could've endured whatever Salvotor or Devitrius did to her, but she'd be lying. Who knew what they would've done? Spilling her blood was clearly forbidden; they could torture her mind, not her body. Kristoff had likely saved her from an even grimmer fate.

The bleeding slowed under her hands. Cistine peeled back the blanket to observe the nine intersecting slashes from the three barbs and wished she intervened sooner. "Why did you tell him this was your decision?"

"Because it was. I could have denied you if I wasn't a sentimental old fool." Kristoff's back lifted in a deep breath. "Why did *you* intervene?"

"Because you've done me so many kindnesses, and even if I don't understand them, I couldn't let you take that punishment alone. You didn't deserve it."

Kristoff was silent for so long, Cistine feared he'd fallen unconscious from the pain. She strained to hear anything outside, but Grimmaul's men and the Six had taken their conflict elsewhere.

"The Chancellor is a fool." The pain-harshened rasp of Kristoff's voice stopped Cistine's hands. "He doesn't know what to do to anyone around him except break them. It isn't enough he's slated you for death...he must kill you before he ever lays that knife to your throat. What has Valgard become that we blindly follow a man like that?"

"Is that what happened to your family? Did Salvotor break them?"

Again, that deep, throbbing silence.

"Yes," Kristoff murmured at last. "I caught him in his cruelty, and when the Courts would do nothing about it, I took matters into my own hands." His fingers left his pendant at last, grazing a knotted scar above his hip instead. "I thought it was some strange mercy I survived that encounter. That the True God himself intervened on my behalf so I might fulfill some greater purpose, escape someday and be reunited with my sons."

The heavy truth hung between them before he even spoke it.

"My *valenar* died before Salvotor threw me in this Nimmus-pit, and my sons a decade after. Salvotor saw to it himself. A long, slow end for them...he made certain to tell me every grisly detail. I can hear their screams in my sleep. I still wear my shame." Shaking fingers returned to the pendant. "That pain is with me every day, knowing they suffered. Knowing I could do *nothing* for them."

Cistine's throat tightened. "Kristoff, I..."

"Don't tell me you're sorry for me." He caught Cistine's wrist when she tried to press the bedspread down again and slowly turned himself so he was propped on his side, facing her. "Not when I've sat idle and let that *bandayo* do what he's done to you."

Desperate hope stole what remained of her breath. "Then *help* me."

Kristoff's fingers uncoiled from around her wrist. "There's nothing I can do. I have no augments to give you. You would not be able to cleave your way from this place, and even if you did, you would die in these mountains."

"You don't know that!"

"I do. I've tried to escape, and Salvotor brought me back to suffer worse than before." Kristoff laid his head on the pillow, looking away from her. "I couldn't even save my family. I cannot save you."

"Then why take the punishment for me? Why do you *care*?"

"Because I can't save your life, but I don't have to let one more child suffer the way my sons did." His eyes, clouded with pain, fell shut. "You remind me of them. The fire—that tenacity. You fight as strongly as they did. But it will do you no better than it did them in the end."

Cistine had heard that same tone from Thorne after Baba Kallah died; another man broken by Salvotor's schemes.

He would not help her escape. He was too tired, too hopeless from loss and cruel imprisonment. She'd been a fool to hope these kindnesses would amount to an alliance, to let herself imagine he would grant her passage to the cellar or tell her how to escape Kalt Hasa.

Card games and kindnesses meant nothing, and after today she suspected there'd be no more of either. She was still alone in Kalt Hasa.

CHAPTER FIFTEEN

THE NORDBRAN BAZAAR was a legend that did not disappoint, one of the fabled domed havens scattered throughout the Red Desert offering rations and goods to nomads and travelers. Sleek, robe-wrapped bodies sweated under the chinks of sunlight falling from glass domes over the brick-brown vendor booths; bulbous ghostlamps swung on strands and gathered in gentle clusters at the center of every smaller dome, sprinkling the floor with cups of light in filigree patterns.

Cistine would've loved this place.

Tatiana's head pounded under the weight of her fighting armor and the emerald robe that concealed it, but she had to blend in, marking the entrances and any Vassoran presence while Quill searched for this myth from Helga's stories. For no reason she could fathom, he'd actually begged to be the one on watch rather than charming some stall vendor for whispers about this so-called Secret Keeper; but this was her hunt, so she'd won that fight.

Still. She wished he'd stop acting so stars-forsaken *strange*.

"Can I help you, *Yani?*"

The vendor's quiet voice snapped Tatiana from her reverie. She lingered too long at his booth already, rubbing the ends of a silk shawl between her fingertips while her mind wandered. "No, thank you. Just lost in thought. Can you point me toward the food stalls?"

The brown-skinned nomad leaned from his booth and pointed to Tatiana's right. "Down there some ways. Follow the smell of spices, it should lead you straight to them."

Tatiana dipped her head and stepped back into the stream of booths hawking expensive clothing, jewelry, and even weapons. Normally, she would love to browse, but today it just made her think of Cistine...and how desperately she missed her.

True to the old man's word, once Tatiana caught the scent of meat, curry, and garlic, it was easy to find the small room full of cookfires where vendors of spices and exotic food made their living, chatting amicably with customers while they robbed them blind for a tin of saffron or a bushel of sage. Tatiana bought a pair of lamb skewers and retreated to a support column at the room's edge, studying the smoke trap in the center of the dome; judging by the slant of light, it was nearly sunset. Back in Hellidom, she would be preparing for patrol—slapping on her armor, sharpening her weapons, and eating a quick dinner of Baba Kallah's delicious scones.

Tatiana's appetite wilted, the lamb heavy as stone in her gut.

A familiar, sweet scent tickled her nose, drawing her head to one side. Her eyes found a mead vendor pawning his wares from a wheelbarrow, offering free samples to anyone brave enough to try. Tatiana stared at him until the smoke made her eyes itch; she could almost taste that rich, sweet drink gliding between her teeth, the burn flaring in her sinuses and rolling down her throat. But more importantly, she knew it would steady the flutter of her nervous hands, her jangling fingers and toes, and quiet the ache of fear for Cistine and the grief of missing Baba Kallah.

Her mouth watered at the notion.

Two nimble fingers tapped her shoulder from behind, and she jerked up from the column, spinning to face Quill. "There you are!" Though he couldn't know what she was thinking, her palms sweated with guilt. She punched his shoulder. "You should know better than to leave *me* unattended in a bazaar for two hours. I nearly spent all our mynts on a new scarf!"

"Was it at least a good color?" Quill plucked a skewer from her hand. "I hope this one's for me."

"It's not, but help yourself."

Quill didn't smile at her obvious joke as he reclined in the alcove beside her and bore down on the lamb like a ravenous wolf. His eyes flicked from vendor to vendor, searching out potential threats. "The Secret Keeper is here, and she'll meet with us for a price...a secret for a secret. If you want information from her, you'd better be willing to give it in return."

A wave of unease crested along the back of Tatiana's legs, spilling over her shoulders and turning her chest cold. Warning shivers shot down into her core; she twisted her head and found Quill watching her, brows pulled together, brows scrunched.

She finished her skewer, tossed it into the nearest fire, and started walking. He pushed up from the curved wall to follow her.

The feeling didn't go away when they pushed through the crowd; it intensified, setting the hairs up straight on Tatiana's neck and rolling prickles down her limbs. "Quill, someone's watching us."

He grimaced. "I know. I feel it, too." He grabbed her arm and spun her around. Backing her into an empty alcove, he planted his hands on either side of her head and bent over until their brows nearly touched. "Take a good look. What do you see?"

Tatiana rested her face against his shoulder so that only her eyes peeped over the sweat-stiffened fabric of his shirt, taking stock of the recesses on the walls, the stalls spreading like stains across the central thoroughfares where foot traffic meandered through—

But not all of them moved.

She ducked her head, hiding her eyes. "Across the bazaar, to your right. My left."

Quill pressed his lips to her temple. "How many?"

"I couldn't see."

He pushed back from her, freeing one hand from the wall to grab her chin and tilt her head up. His nose grazed the column of her neck as high as the hinge of her jaw, and her body responded before her mind caught up with what he was doing, craning her head to his advances. Eyes at half-mast, she watched the men casually browsing the booths, but clearly taking note of what was—or really *wasn't*—happening in the alcove.

"Six," she growled.

Quill dropped his hand and withdrew. "Vassora?"

"Maybe. They're not armored, but they have that look in their eye."

"I hate that look." Quill took her hand and moved more swiftly through the booths.

"A little warning next time?" she hissed. "I hate when you make a plan without me."

He shot her one of his lopsided, disarming smiles, so rare these days. "But there's this noise you make whenever I breathe on your ear." Tatiana slammed her elbow into his ribs, and he grimaced, humor fading and gaze darting away. "I'm sorry. You're right, I shouldn't have...I won't do it again."

Her tongue knotted up. How was she supposed to tell him she loved it without ruining *everything*? And since when did she have to *tell* him anything—since when did he ever feel ashamed or need to apologize for this dance they did around each other?

There was no time to pursue the subject; they reached the bazaar doors and stormed through into the heat, racing to the stables where they left their horses. Quill selected a pair of mounts at random, led them from their stalls, and let them slip. Tatiana rushed them, flagging her arms and snarling, and the frightened beasts charged from the stable. She and Quill followed them out and climbed the stable's short side, then ran along the roof and leaped to the bazaar's domes, wedging themselves above the doors. Below, the Vassoran guards burst out into the open, cursing when they scouted the horizon and spotted the horses galloping away. In moments they reached the stables, gathered their own mounts, and gave chase.

"And there they go," Tatiana grinned.

"For now." Quill slithered around the dome and walked the bazaar's sculpted edge toward one of its back corners. "The Secret Keeper is in one of the upper rooms. Let's drop in from the window...first impressions are important."

"Not with you. No matter how you present yourself in the beginning, everyone knows you're a hopeless fool sooner or later."

Quill paused, meeting her gaze in a way she couldn't name but didn't like. "That's true."

Without another word, he swung down from the roof and in through an open window below, leaving Tatiana with no choice but to drop after him, straight into the Secret Keeper's room.

No sooner had she rolled from her crouch and picked herself up than she heard the music of many bracelets tinkling together and the harmony of steel leaving its sheath. Her eyes adjusted to the incense-riddled darkness to find a knife against Quill's throat, held by an old woman with sun-browned skin, a stern mouth, and fire in her ancient blue eyes. "Move, and he dies."

Tatiana froze, palms out, heart in her throat. "*Don't* hurt him."

Maybe she was pleading already, showing all her cards at once. Maybe she didn't care.

"Why have you come here?" the old woman demanded.

"To purchase truth from the Secret Keeper," Quill said. "If you could just be reasonable about it..."

The knife tightened. "There is a *door*."

"Well, doors, you know, *everyone* uses the door these days. Where's the fun in that? Windows, on the other hand, if you look at the lattice on yours..." He gestured broadly, and Tatiana tensed. That was a signal, just for her.

His eyes locked on her sideways, with that crinkled crone and her knife between them. No fear in his face—of course. His glittering stare conveyed a silent message and he craned his head slightly as the knife nestled a bit deeper against his skin.

Tatiana dove forward, tangled her legs with the old woman's, slammed a shoulder up into her sternum, and kicked the knife from her hand. Quill caught it and sheathed it in his belt as Tatiana wormed free and backed up to his side.

Flawless. Quick. But her hands shook as she and Quill faced the Secret Keeper side-by-side.

The old woman wobbled upright, massaging her chest, and shame fizzed in Tatiana's middle. Quill's life had been in danger, but still, she might've struck a bit too hard.

"You must be Quill and Tatiana." The Secret Keeper turned back the glittering shawl on her head, revealing her silver plait and the stark lines of antimony power around her eyes. "Where the tinker travels, the raven flies close behind."

Tatiana opened her mouth, and Quill perched his elbow on her shoulder, silently interrupting her half-planned tirade. "That's us. We've come to trade a secret for a secret."

Ever since they met as children, Tatiana loved the sound of Quill's voice. Something musical about it, flirting with an accent, belonged on a performance stage or in a tavern singing drinking songs with friends. But here the quality was different. Practiced. Reciting words someone taught him to say. She wondered if they were from Helga's stories, or if whoever he flirted information from in the bazaar told him exactly how to treat with this old scorpion.

The Secret Keeper regarded them shrewdly, then turned to a small firepit at the room's end where fruit crisped on skewers. Sitting, she gestured Quill and Tatiana join her, and in silent accord, they did—wary, on their knees, mimicking each other with their hands resting on their thighs.

"What secret do you seek?" The old woman locked eyes with Tatiana just as warily as Tatiana watched her.

"We need information on a ritual that took place over two decades ago here in Valgard," she began."

"You seek the keying of the Doors to the Gods."

Tatiana finally broke her stare to glance at Quill. He frowned. "That's right. Do you know where it happened?"

"Yes." She took the skewer from over the flames and shuffled the fruit onto a small plate before her. "And I will tell you for a price. To gain something precious, you must give something precious."

"Name your price. I'll pay it," Quill said without hesitation. "Whatever it is, for Cistine, I'll pay it. I'm ready."

His voice slipped back into that haunting cadence, and Tatiana wanted to hit him this time. They hadn't discussed this, who would pay with which secret. This wasn't how they did things; before every card-counting sham, every drinking game, every fight, they always consulted, always laid out plans *together*. In games, in battle, in *life*—

The Secret Keeper stared into the empty fire for a long moment. Then she said, "You will tell me what became of the Hive Lord and the beast-slayer and rain-dancer when the Blood Hive went aflame."

Tatiana blinked, sparing another swift glance at Quill to find her shock reflected in his face. Of all the secrets they could've been asked to tell—where Thorne was, what the cabal's plans were, where they'd been hiding all this time or what they wanted with the secrets of the Key—something like this had never crossed her mind.

"You want to know about Aden and Ashe?" Quill demanded. "*Why?*"

"Is that the secret you wish to trade for?"

He cursed, dragging a hand through his hair. "All right. They're alive, they escaped. Aden is in Jovadalsa. Ashe went back to Talheim."

"But," Tatiana added quickly, remembering that late-night conversation she wasn't meant to overhear, "our friends think she may come back."

The Secret Keeper went on staring at the flames for a moment; then her eyes flicked up to them. "The keying you seek took place in an ancient temple called Kalt Hasa...one of the few that remains from times before. It lies far to the west of here, down the spine of the Isetfells."

"Kalt Hasa," Tatiana echoed. "Why do I know that name?"

Quill shifted. "That was worth it to you? You just wanted to know Ashe and Aden were alive?"

"Oh, yes, very much. I see farther than you could possibly dream...that is why I am Secret Keeper and you are not." She tucked her hands into her sleeves. "Now, take your fruit and go."

Tatiana stood, snatching up the plate; the meat hadn't quite sated her appetite, anyway. Quill was slower to rise, watching the old woman narrowly. "Why do I feel like I know you?"

"Because I know so much about you, and you do not like to be disadvantaged in a battle of wits."

His mouth twitched. "Fine, keep your secrets."

"That is what I do, Quill. Now be gone...and this time, use the door."

Tatiana led the way out into a steep, rectangular stairwell, her stomach rioting. "Stars, I hope Aden's ready for whatever that old scorpion throws his way." Hot shame licked the back of her neck. "What do you think she wants with him?"

"I don't know, but it's *Aden*. He'll manage." There was no uncertainty in Quill's tone, his gaze fixed down the steps. "We need to keep our focus on finding Cistine. It sounds like this Kalt Hasa is a long way away."

"You really think we can do this?" Quill muttered.

Tatiana squared her jaw and nodded. "When you and I put our heads together, there's nothing we can't pull off. That's why we're here, isn't it?"

He glanced at her, and she let him see the faith blazing in her heart. It didn't matter how far Kalt Hasa was or why it sparked an uneasy memory in her; she and Quill had spent most of their friendship scraping miracles together from the odd ends of crude swordplay, card-counting, gods-given favor, and an intuition toward one another that ran deeper than any other bond in Tatiana's life.

They could do this. And they *would*; they'd bring their princess home.

CHAPTER SIXTEEN

C ISTINE'S TANGLED HAIR bunched and haloed above her as she sank beneath the cloudy mineral water in Kalt Hasa's natural hot spring basin. She'd been allowed from her chamber to bathe as soon as she woke that morning—another kindness from Kristoff, she'd assumed at first, who hadn't spoken to her in the days since his whipping. But it seemed Salvotor meant for her to hear the rumors swirling through the Wound instead.

Devitrius was gone on some mission of such vital importance, no one could fathom what it was; anything from the truth of the Key's ritual to a weapon that would loosen her tongue. Though she tried to shut out the whispers, her ears were too keen on gossip still, and now Salvotor had her precisely where he wanted her: distracted and uneasy, powerless to plan even in the heart-throbbing stillness below the water.

Lungs aching, she surged upright, dragging her hands through her hair. Her nails snagged in the tangles and she grumbled, yanking them out again. The chamber was quiet aside from the sloshing water; the unfamiliar guard who brought her here left a fresh dress and allowed her privacy to bathe. But she couldn't enjoy the delicacy even while she scraped her scalp, dunked herself again into the spring, then hoisted herself from its safe cocoon. No matter how pleasant, it was all just an illusion; the cold waited to embrace her, planting gooseflesh kisses along her arms, flanks, and legs as she hurried toward the flat rock where the guard folded her clothes.

But the dress was gone. The pajamas were gone.

"Well, well. Look at you, Wildheart."

Dread iced Cistine's middle. She stumbled around to face Salvotor—propped between two stone columns, grinning at her nakedness—and wrapped her arms around her chest and hips in a vain effort to cover herself. "Leave me alone!"

Salvotor shook his head, still appraising her. "I can see why my son was ready to die the Second Death for you. Almost a shame to waste you on the ritual."

"*Get out!*" Cistine flattened herself around the nearest pillar, heart thudding against her sheltering arm.

"And speaking of that ritual," Salvotor circled the column and planted himself against the basin, facing her, "all this ends the moment you tell me how it's conducted."

"*I don't know!*"

He clicked his tongue and studied her for an infinite minute, then pushed up from the basin and approached her. "Perhaps a meal of cinnamon-orange scones will enlighten your mind. They were always my mother's favorite...she insisted our apartment smell of them always." He gripped Cistine's throat in the flash of a hand, thumb pressing her windpipe. With the hand, he smoothed her matted hair. "I'm certain she *adored* you. Pretty, impractical, and soft, just like her. Perhaps it was mercy she didn't survive to see you this way."

He shoved her back against the column so hard her back spasmed and her legs gave out, dumping her on the floor. After a long moment admiring her crumbled at his feet, Salvotor swaggered out.

Cistine hugged her knees to her chest, uncontrollable shudders wracking her body. Shame and disgust made her want to crawl back into the basin and wash the impression of his gaze from her skin; but it wasn't there, it was *under* it, a blight on her spirit that would never endanger his coveted ritual.

"Don't let him win," she whispered to herself. "*Don't let him win.*"

But she was so gods-forsaken *tired*.

It was the cold that finally made her move, the sound of her chattering teeth reminding her she could be found any time. But when she tore around the bathing chamber, she came up with empty hands and a racing heart.

He'd taken her clothes and not returned them—leaving her to cross the temple in nothing but her skin.

Cistine couldn't muster anger about the latest dress Salvotor insisted she wear to supper. It didn't matter; prisoners and Vassora alike had ogled her shamelessly on the humiliating run back from the Wound, and beneath the gossamer threads of this satiny shell, she was still stripped bare by their eyes.

She plucked at the scones on her plate, stomach turning at the smell of orange spice and cinnamon. Salvotor, on his third helping already, peered casually down the length of the table. "This show of defiance hurts no one but you, Wildheart. What would your suitor think, knowing you're wasting his last valiant efforts just to prove a point?"

She stared at him, a flush of anger thawing the cold humiliation in her core. How dare he insinuate she was *betraying* Julian, that she was *selfish*—

Salvotor slammed his hand on the table. "*EAT!*"

Cistine cringed at the voice to match the scales cladding his flesh—the voice of the creature lurking in Salvotor's spirit.

"Eat," he repeated softly, "or go back to your chamber and consider how you sent that Talheimic boy to the Sable Gates for *nothing*."

Cistine wanted to kill him. Then she wanted to curl up in her seat and sink through it into the temple floor, into darkness and nothing below that.

"Get out," Salvotor said when she held her silence, and Cistine almost gagged. How could he replicate Thorne's inflections so perfectly? "Your company disgusts me, you self-interested, cosseted *korvat*."

Empty stomach cramping, she shoved back her chair and all but sprinted into the hewn chamber, angling toward the corridor and the relief of her chamber.

Relief. When had it become that? What had he turned her into? "Cistine?"

Kristoff's voice. Some sliver of her was almost relieved to hear it, relieved to see he wasn't dead or bedridden, but playing cards with the Six at the usual table—the first time she'd seen him since Baldvin led her from his room. But she didn't slow, pushing blindly into the dark hall. Kristoff called out to Krusar to keep the game going; then his steps clomped after her.

"Don't," Cistine snapped without looking back. "Leave me alone."

Even limping, he managed to catch up with her. "I can't. You know you're my responsibility, Salvotor hasn't revoked that yet."

"Then I free you from your responsibilities today!"

"That's not your choice to make." Kristoff caught her arm and pulled her around to face him. "Look at me, Cistine! Tell me why you have no guard tonight!"

"Because I don't need one—all I want is to be *alone!*" She snatched her arm from his grasp. "No one told you the spectacle I made? That Salvotor took my clothes and made me parade myself through the temple? Don't you see how everyone is *looking* at me?"

Rage, pure and righteous, exploded through Kristoff's eyes. He took her hand this time and hauled her into her chamber, slamming the door behind them. Then he took her by both shoulders and met her eyes. "Did he lay hands on you?"

"He doesn't have to!" Cistine shouted. "He's determined to wear me down a piece at a time. And I'm afraid he's going to *win!*"

She hated hearing herself say it, hated that Salvotor had broken her composure so completely today. But ever since Kristoff's whipping, she hadn't caught her breath, couldn't truly plan or think. She was alone, she was tired, she was *terrified*—and tonight, giving up and letting this end seemed almost reasonable. Almost like mercy.

Kristoff sat her down on the bed and lowered himself beside her, his hands still on her shoulders. "I'm going to tell you something I taught my son: It's not over when you're beaten, it's over when you surrender. A war is not one battle, it's *many* battles. Salvotor can win some, and you can win others, and none of that matters. Not one single fight matters except for the one where you surrender or he does. Tell me, Cistine...is this that fight?"

She covered her face with both hands.

Surrender felt so easy. Merciful. Like sinking into that basin again, warm and floating and forgotten. She ached for the release so badly, her heart cracked in two.

But if she surrendered, it would be the end of all things—not only for her, but for everyone who leaned on her. Talheim would have no one left to fight for it in the north, no one to lead it into the future; and nothing would keep the Key away from the Doors, out of Salvotor's hands.

Who would avenge Julian and Baba Kallah? Who would stand beside Thorne against his father?

She had made him a promise. She'd made the cabal a vow: Valgard and Talheim, united, and the end of Salvotor's march into all five Courts.

Cistine's breaths slowed, the panic abating. Clarity began to pierce the terrible haze of Salvotor's actions today; she raised her head to find Kristoff watching her, a strange glow in his eyes.

Pride. That was *pride* as he watched her sunder up from the depths of panic. "Well done."

She mustered a smile just for him. If he wouldn't fight for her life, then at least he gave her the strength to do it herself.

She pressed her hand over his against her shoulder. "Your sons were fortunate to have you."

Kristoff's fingers flexed and his eyes darkened. "I tried with everything I had. One was always in pain. Like you, nights were the worst. After the nightmares, I always held him like this..." He took her face in one hand, pressing it over the beat of his heart, and wrapped his other arm around her middle, tucking her elbows to her sides against the brawny strength of his embrace. "He never knew a father's love before he came to us. I tried to show him that he would never be alone again."

Cistine couldn't begin to fathom how much pain that child suffered, but she understood why his father's arms brought such comfort. Kristoff's embrace was steady enough to hold the broken parts of a person together. It made her feel safe in this place without safety.

She did not feel herself fall asleep; but when she woke, she was alone again, tucked under the burgundy dress. The lavender ghostlamps were snuffed for the first time since she woke in Kalt Hasa.

And despite the previous day's ordeal, she had not had a single nightmare.

CHAPTER SEVENTEEN

WITH THEIR NEW armor and boots, Ashe and Pippet made good time. The girl's resilience was a surprise, though perhaps it shouldn't be, given she grew up among livestock and gardens without servants to tend them. Ashe's hopeful bid for silence after Cerne Mosiar was a lost cause, but as the days wore on, she minded Pippet's chatter less. It distracted her from the bone-searing ache of knowing her princess was in danger every day; and though she would never confess it aloud, it was good not to be alone with bad dreams and fear for Cistine.

They emerged at last from the Wildwood and quickened their pace through long stretches of thinning trees, Pippet never content that Ashe didn't know the names of every single one.

"How much schooling do you have?" Ashe asked one day while they forced their bodies through the brittle thickets.

Pippet shrugged, battering more branches from her path. "Some. Helga made me read books and things, but I've never been to a school. Have you?"

Ashe smirked. "I hated it. I wanted to be out in the yard, practicing with a sword."

Pippet brightened, and before Ashe could call a halt to that wicked gleam in her eye, she grabbed her knife and hacked at the brambles.

Ashe lunged, catching her wrist. "This little butter-knife is too dull.

You'll glance off and skin yourself."

Pippet let her take the knife. "You know everything about steel, don't you? You should teach me about knives and things."

Ashe snorted, sheathing the knife in Pippet's belt again. "That wasn't part of our arrangement."

"Arrangements can change if people really want them to."

Scoffing, Ashe pushed deeper into the thicket. "You'd make a dangerous Tribune."

Pippet grinned. "Do you really think so?"

"That wasn't a compliment."

The girl's laughter cut short as they stumbled out on the far side of the hedge and into the narrow median of trees and tall, ancient stones beyond.

They had reached the border forts.

Ashe's guts clenched at the imperious array of barracks and watchtowers concatenated by pikes twice as high as her head. On the other side was a thin stretch of open land before Talheim's own forts demarcated the beginning of their boundary. The beginning of home.

"They're so tall," Pippet whispered. "How will you cross them?"

"Very carefully." Ashe judged the stretch of wall. Crossing here would be as good as anywhere else, but the guards were almost guaranteed to have augments. While Disa's armor would defend against those attacks, Ashe wasn't eager to invite them.

Still. She had to cross.

She readied herself to bolt, and Pippet laid a hand on her arm. "*Wait.* Ashe, you're not being sensible."

She shrugged the girl off. "This is for Cistine. I have no choice."

"I *know* that. I mean you're not being sensible about *this.*" Pippet gestured to the border forts. "You need a distraction."

Before Ashe could tell her that was also a terrible idea, worse than the knife and brambles, Pippet broke cover and ran toward the border forts. Ashe barely kept from lunging after her this time; wide-eyed and frozen, she watched Pippet careen toward the nearest watchtower with the same affected sobs as when she talked Ashe into bringing her along and Disa into sheltering them.

She was a dangerous little actress. And today, she was Ashe's greatest hope, even if some visceral terror screamed at Ashe to drag her back to the trees where she could protect her.

When the barracks doors opened and a slew of Vassoran guards streamed toward Pippet, whose wailing reached an ear-splitting crescendo, Ashe slipped from the trees and made a break for the pike wall. She only had moments before she was discovered, and returning would be another matter entirely, but for now she could only think of the late-day shadows concealing her; and then of the wall as she grabbed hold and began to climb it. Desperately scrabbling for purchase on the slick wood, she caught the sharp tip of a post at the pinnacle of the fence, swung over, and looked back.

Pippet had collapsed in a sobbing heap, sputtering about her trained raven flying away, while the helpless guards crowded over her and implored her to tell them her name. Ashe allowed herself a small smile before she slid down into the between, crossed the sliver of open land, and pounded gently on the Talheimic watchtower. "Open up in the name of King Cyril!"

Nothing from the far side, not even a whisper of sound.

The hairs on Ashe's neck rose. Any moment, the Valgardans might look down the length of the wall and see her.

"Asheila Kovar, Warden of the Princess, *demands* entrance!" she hissed.

The wind sighed through the pikes. Pippet's distant sobs ebbed.

At last, the watchtower door sailed open, and Ashe's heart stuttered to a stop. For there, framed in the doorway with his intimidating bulk, fully armored and frowning, was Rion Bartos.

CHAPTER EIGHTEEN

C OMMANDER," ASHE CHOKED. Of all the people she'd expected to face in the forts, it had not been her mentor, the man who entrusted Echelon to her—Julian's father. He was supposed to be in southern Talheim, holding the forts against Mahasar. She thought she had weeks of travel yet before she'd find him.

Rion's gaze slid over her. "I see you've changed your armor."

Shame pricked Ashe's skin as she glanced down at her ill-fitting Valgardan threads. "It was all I had."

"Indeed."

There was something in his face Ashe was tired of seeing: disappointment, the same way her parents always looked at her after yet another prestigious dinner where she couldn't restrain herself from rattling off the properties of certain lays of steel to their family's blank-faced guests.

She jerked to attention as Rion stepped back, granting her entrance. The watchtower's interior was dim and musty, more like an old storage room than an outpost, except for at the table Rion led her to, its ghostlit surface draped in maps of Valgard. A cluster of Wardens gathered around it, snapping straight at the sight of Ashe. Viktor, Rozalie, Symon, Lydie, Andrej, and Petra; people she'd known and trained with—trained herself, in Rozalie and Andrej's case—all staring at her like she'd just crawled out from the Sable Gates. If they even knew what those were.

"Ashe." Tall and ruddy, his brown hair cascading across his brow, Viktor beheld her with shock first, then with the usual hunger, just like the last time she forced him from her chambers and told him they couldn't see each other anymore.

Ashe slammed the thought away. "Why are you here?"

"I should ask you the same," Rion grunted. "You should be at my estate on Talheim's eastern coast. That, it seems, was a lie."

"Like Cistine's entire birthday celebration was a lie? A front for a private war council?" Ashe shot back, and Rion's shoulders stiffened. "I know about Jad and the forts. What I don't understand is why you're here when you were supposed to travel *south* to reinforce the ranks."

Rion leaned his fist on the table. "I am here because Cyril can't be. He's in Middleton now, awaiting Jad's arrival for the peace talks. But someone needed to investigate when rumors spread that Princess Cistine was *not* at the coast where we sent her...and you, and my son."

Ashe frowned down at the maps. "Why did you assume she was in Valgard, of everywhere in the kingdoms?"

"Because the North is renowned for its treachery."

"No. Because you *knew* it called to her."

Rion loomed over her like the child he once trained, his stare glittering adamant. "Wardens here at the barracks reported hearing rumors from the other side of the Talheimic princess seeking an audience with the Chancellors. What I would very much like to know is why *you* are here— without her."

Ashe's heart plummeted. "She's...gone missing. I came for Talheim's help tracking her."

No one gasped. No one looked as shocked or sickened as Ashe felt when Thorne delivered the news.

"Did you know?" she demanded.

Petra scoffed. "Of course we *suspected*, Ashe. It's *Valgard*. Every one of them would take her as a prize if they could."

The cabal's faces flickered in Ashe's mind—their fear for Cistine, sleepless eyes scouring maps, desperate to find her. But this was not the time to argue. "What was your plan? Storm the border and start another war?"

"If that's what it takes to retrieve our princess, yes," Rion said. "But Queen Solene dispatched us with a Writ of Nobility so we may *treat* with the Chancellors as well. Now, tell me everything you know of her whereabouts...and Julian's. Is he with her?"

Ashe's temples throbbed. How could she possibly tell Rion Bartos his only son was dead? He'd take revenge from every Valgardan hide he touched from here to wherever Cistine was imprisoned, because that was what Talheim did when it was wronged. What Ashe did to Thorne.

She shook her head. "I don't know where they are." Not really a lie. No one had told her where Julian was buried, if he'd been buried at all. "We traveled north to entreat Valgard for aid against Mahasar—"

"Unsanctioned by the King."

"Sanctioned by the sole heir to the throne," Ashe snapped. "Cistine and I were separated, and she was...taken."

Rion dragged a hand down his face, cursing. "Julian will not be able to keep her safe alone. We infiltrate now."

The Wardens peeled off, faces grim, but Ashe caught sight of bumped knuckles flashing between bodies. They were mostly her age, too young to have fought in the war, and unlike Ashe they hadn't tracked Cyril's entourage north to fight anyway. This was their first brush with the Valgardans they spent their whole lives being taught to hate and fear.

Ashe settled her fingers against her hips, tapping out nervous energy. "Why didn't you tell me what she was? What the *King* is?"

Rion stiffened. "How do you know?"

"It doesn't matter. Tell me why."

His scowl deepened. "I was his Commander. I had my orders."

"And I'm her Warden. I deserved to know."

"I decided otherwise. Your task was to keep her in Talheim, to keep her safe. And you *failed*."

Anguish filled her hollow chest. "If I'd known the truth—"

"Your duty would have been the same. You failed once. Don't let it happen again."

Her heels clipped together. He was giving her a second chance. *Thank the gods.* "To cross the forts—"

"We won't need to. We tunneled beneath them a decade ago."

She stared at him, aghast. "*Why?*"

"Because this is *Valgard!* If conflict arose again, we didn't want our people impeded by piked walls and augurs on the watchtowers. This way, we can go beneath them."

It was tactically brilliant, and it would save them the risk of being caught. But she couldn't ignore how they dug under Valgard's noses before there was a hint of aggression—before anyone took Cistine.

Preemptive strikes and revenge tactics and dead grandmothers—

A touch to her cheek halted her thoughts. Rion's thumb followed a new scar ripped along the arch of the bone from one of her many arena matches. "I don't remember this one."

She lowered her gaze again. "The price of keeping our princess safe."

His hand fell. "Wear it with pride, then."

Viktor led the others back to the table just then, tossing Ashe a satchel. "Some real armor in there, Kovar."

She slung it across her body as Rion turned. "You all know the mission: retrieve the princess and Julian by any means. Find them, kill any Valgardan who touches them, and bring them home without asking anyone's consent."

"Including Cistine's?" The words jumped from Ashe's mouth.

Rion's head slowly revolved back toward her. "I suspect your concern for the princess's consent is the only reason she made it to Valgard without a *Warden* exposing her plans to the King." He let the acid-laced words hang between them until Ashe dropped her gaze. "The time for coddling Cistine is over. She will return to Astoria where she belongs, where Cyril and Solene can teach her proper conduct as it comes to Valgard."

Ashe stopped herself just short of telling him they'd have to; Cistine knew too much to ever go back to thinking of the North as a bedtime story...if she'd ever really thought of them that way at all.

Half a dozen narrow tunnels, hollowed out under the Valgardan forts by human hands, funneled the Warden patrol from inside their own borders to the median where Ashe and Pippet first caught sight of the barracks. Ashe despised the close space, the stone walls rubbing her shoulders with every step. Her mind raced with thoughts of the fetid tunnels below Siralek, naming the tempo of the breaths ahead and behind her as Andras, Kalman, Rez, Tobor, *Nimea*—

Gasping for breath, she crawled out behind one of the stone heaps among the trees. Leaning against a sapling, legs trembling, she reminded herself this was not the Blood Hive. She was free with Wardens at her back, clever men and women who won wars by grit and stamina rather than augmentation.

Pulse settling at last, she squinted toward the forts. She could just barely make out Pippet, cross-legged with her back to the pike wall. Someone had given her a drink and draped a blanket around her shoulders. She was alone for now, perhaps while the Vassora conferred inside about how to handle her.

Their contract was over. She'd brought Pippet to the border forts as promised. Yet something grim and heavy slithered into her guts at the thought of leaving her. Ashe had yet to meet a single Vassoran guard she'd trust with a newly-bought blade, much less her own life. Much less a *child's* life. If she left her with these people...

Bait.

For a single blink, she saw Cistine lying facedown in a trapper's cart, sobbing while she thought Ashe was asleep.

If Salvotor learned Quill's sister was here, he might have her thrown in the back of a prison wagon and carted off to Stornhaz, or some other gods-forsaken corner of Valgard, and used as leverage against the cabal to stop them searching for Cistine. Ashe couldn't take that chance, arrangements be damned.

She whistled a two-note birdsong, and when Pippet's head swung up, she struck her thigh. Grinning, the girl shed her blanket, set down her cup, and dashed away from the forts. She skidded through the leaf mold and slammed into Ashe, both arms wrapped around her waist, grinning. "Did you hear me before? Did you *see* me? I was so *real*, wasn't I?"

Ashe ruffled her hair, shocked that the chill that came so fast at Rion's disappointment thawed so rapidly in the glow of Pippet's enthusiasm. "I saw everything. More importantly, I *heard* everything...you almost had *me* convinced with all that sobbing."

Pippet stuck out her bottom lip. "I'm just s-s-so *sad*."

Ashe pinched her neck. "You're dangerous, is what you are."

A throat cleared behind them. Arm looped around Pippet's shoulders, Ashe turned them to face the Wardens, their expressions a range from shock to disbelief to scorn. Rion's eyes were fixed on Pippet with insidious calm. "What is that?"

"This is Pippet. She helped me cross the border forts." Pippet straightened proudly, and Ashe parried slashes of guilt from different blades. She shouldn't need a Valgardan child's help, nor should she be encouraging Pippet's pride in creeping off into a battle she had no part in.

"Get rid of her." Rion said. "This is no place for a child."

"That wasn't the line you used against Cyril when I followed *you*."

"You have my orders."

"Commander, with all due respect, endangering *children* is not the Talheimic way." Even as the words left Ashe's lips, she tasted their hypocrisy. Pippet was out in these wilds because Ashe deemed any risk worthwhile to reach Thorne...but she couldn't betray that truth aloud.

Some strange emotion flickered through Rion's face. "If you bring a stray, then it's your responsibility. If it interferes with our search even once, it will be gone the next moment you rest your eyes. Do I make myself clear?"

Ashe's nape prickled. "Understood."

Rion flashed an arm. "Lead on, then."

A test. An offering of trust, and a truce. Despite everything, he was letting her take the lead. A burst of gratitude and desperation to please him arced through Ashe's chest, setting her gaze forward.

They would start where Cistine went missing: Jovadalsa.

CHAPTER NINETEEN

THERE WAS NO longer an illusion of peace in Kalt Hasa—no sense of quiet, no hint of relief. It was not Kristoff, but Grimmaul who escorted Cistine to dinners and the hot spring now; she didn't bathe or dress or even relieve herself in peace. There were no more moments of solitude to write things down or braid her rope; Grimmaul sat against the door night after night and joked with the guard outside, slipping in lewd comments to jolt Cistine awake whenever she started to drift off. And each time, she had the same blinding moment of clarity.

That day in the bathing chamber, she'd let Salvotor slip past her defenses, wearing her down toward some inevitable end. That night's reprieve with Kristoff was not enough to keep her feet under her, no matter how many times she reminded herself not to surrender.

She had to push back, regain lost ground.

She tried to imagine what her mother would do in this situation, but her thoughts crawled through an exhausted fog. She'd hardly slept yet again thanks to Grimmaul's chatter, her hand shaking when she stirred her tomato soup and struggled to *think*—

"No appetite again?" Salvotor didn't throw his voice for once. Cistine lifted her gaze from the brimming soup bowl and noticed something that made her hand, and the spoon, go still.

He hadn't touched his portion, either.

"Have you given any more thought to my request?" he asked.

Cistine mustered a glare, though her eyelids were so heavy they ached. "You know, Ashe always told me you can spot a madman when he does the same thing over and over, expecting a different outcome."

"Ashe. Was that the guard who gave her life so you could slip from Stornhaz?" Salvotor tipped his head. "She's dead, you know. Killed in Siralek's Blood Hive during a brief uprising."

Cistine's spoon dropped into her bowl.

Ashe, in the Blood Hive, just like Maleck feared. He'd been on his way there the last time she saw him. What if he'd died trying to free her? What if they were both gone?

"It's a shame," Salvotor went on. "I hear she was integral to so many things these past few months...tragedies in Blaykrone. Assassins running free. My own mother's death."

Cistine pressed her back and shoulders against the seat, relief sliding through her. That was one lie too many, showing his hand; her Warden would never betray her that way. Just another of his cruel schemes to chip away her resolve. "Are you finished?" she deadpanned. "If neither of us is going to eat, I might as well return to my room."

"Stubborn to the last." Salvotor rose. "As a matter of fact, Devitrius just returned with a gift for us. I thought we should see it together."

Cistine's guts tangled at that careful, articulate tone, the same as when he brought her to the balcony to see the mountains. *This* was what he'd worn her down for days and weeks to witness, and his icy gaze warned there would be no escaping it.

Slowly, she shoved back her chair and followed him.

The Six stood watch at the cellar tonight, bolting to attention when the Chancellor passed, though to Cistine's unease Kristoff was not with them for once. She met Dain's wide eyes and shrugged helplessly; Krusar and Baldvin exchanged a cautious glance.

Inside the Wound, Devitrius's name was in every mouth, a swarm of spectral whispers about his conquest and the prize he brought, though none would say what it was. Cistine followed Salvotor down a long, winding tunnel bathed in reddish-yellow ghostlight into a room half-lined with narrow straw nests separated by iron slats. There was no room to pace or train or properly stretch—a fresh kind of prison.

Perhaps hers now.

Cistine stepped back, heart pounding so viciously she couldn't catch her breath, and Salvotor pivoted and snatched her by the chin. "I've grown bored with this game. Tell me about the ritual, or I will kill you and chance that I'm already prepared to open the Doors."

She glared up at his face, the skin shivering like sun-licked steel in the ghostlight. "If you were willing to risk it, you wouldn't waste any more time threatening me. I'd already be dead. You aren't going to do anything without proof about the ritual."

His eyes narrowed. "So, the princess thinks she's fit to play at being queen." He shoved her head aside and glanced past her, toward the scuff of footsteps in the doorway, first stumbling, then slapping the stone. Devitrius joined them at last, eyes darting uneasily to Cistine, then to Salvotor. The Chancellor beckoned, and only then did he approach, leading a prisoner behind him—neck leashed, hands bound at his back, feet hobbled and a dark burlap bag over his head.

Cistine's breath caught. Vomit rolled up the back of her throat.

She would have known that body anywhere; the articulate lines of his arms straining against the cords, the arch of his back when he checked the wall with his shoulder, keeping himself upright. His sleeve dragged up, baring dark, new bruises down his arm, and Cistine's fingers tingled with the memory of what that skin felt like under her hands.

This couldn't be happening. It *couldn't* be.

Salvotor strode forward when Devitrius yanked the prisoner to a halt. "If you won't reveal the truth to save your own life, perhaps you will to spare your *selvenar*."

With a flourish, he ripped the bag from Thorne's head and kicked him to his knees on the floor. And the moment his body impacted the stone and his eyes flashed to Cistine, pinning her in place the way his hands had fastened her against a stone shelf in her dreams when he kissed her, she won the war.

Her enemy had grown arrogant, bored of chiseling away her resolve and unraveling her sanity a piece at a time. So he'd gone and done this, tried to break her, and now it would cost him everything.

He'd hurt Thorne badly; one of his eyes swollen shut, his lips broken open, cuts freckling his brow and cheekbones and blood soaking his upper lip from his left nostril. He wavered, breathing heavily and staring at her like he'd never known pain.

If Salvotor and Devitrius had not been standing there, Thorne Starchaser might've smiled at her; and she would have smiled back. Because the sight of him, even injured, even bound and battered, did not break her. It put a sword in her hand.

Salvotor buried his fingers in Thorne's hair and yanked his head up. "Tell me every part of the ritual, and I may decide to spare my son."

For one glorious moment, Cistine held absolute power in the room.

Right now, Salvotor believed he'd broken her, that she teetered on the edge of telling him everything—which meant she could bargain for *anything* except her own life, because *that* was ultimate prize.

That was the game the Chancellor wanted to play. Could she play it, for Thorne's sake and her own?

She met his eyes, trailing down from the harsh angle of his upturned head to lock with hers again.

Yes. A thousand times, yes, for the thousand deaths he would've died for her. She would gladly face this one for him—for *them.* "If I tell you about the ritual, you'll let him live?"

Salvotor smiled. "You have my word as Chancellor."

"Your word isn't good enough. Release him and send him to me."

Devitrius loosened the noose from around Thorne's throat and slit the ropes that bound his hands, and he freed his own feet in a few rapid yanks. Then he staggered upright, clutching his ribs as he walked toward her. Cistine didn't know if the desperation boiling in her chest was to her aid or detriment in tricking Salvotor, and right now, she didn't care. Thorne was half the room away. Then a dozen steps. Then half that.

Cistine put out her hand, and he reached for her, too. When their fingers met, a rebellious tear snaked down her cheek.

She pulled him close enough that the smoky smell of his dark shirt filled her nostrils and spun her head. For an instant, she laid her face against his racing heart; then she pushed him behind her and faced Salvotor. "I'll tell you every piece of the ritual but one. Once you have those pieces, you'll let Thorne go. Then I'll give you the last thing you need."

Salvotor exchanged a glance with Devitrius, the silence weighing heavy between them. With a thrill of unease, Cistine realized she was *not* fully in control—the balance of power was an undulating wave passing through her hands and back to Salvotor's like an augment traded among warriors on a battlefield.

After several tense heartbeats, the Chancellor nodded.

Thorne let loose a low growl, but he didn't argue. She had never been more grateful for his faith in her.

Keeping one hand back on his chest, feeding from his strength while she played at weariness, Cistine rattled off a list of items she'd spied in the Citadel shrines and Astoria's Temple of the True God—empty offerings to send Salvotor hunting and give her time to plot their escape.

Drunk with hunger, Salvotor and Devitrius hung forward on every word, believing she was a foolish, untested ruler who would shatter when held to a flame. And maybe she had been all those things when she first faced him in Stornhaz, but the cabal had helped scrape away that weakness, exposing the tenacious princess and clever deceiver beneath. Someone who could lie to the face she couldn't break with her fists.

"Devitrius," Salvotor said when she finally felt silent, "you committed all of that?"

"I did."

"Then you know what to do."

Devitrius strode toward them, and Cistine jolted backward into Thorne's chest. He slung an arm around her waist, shielding her against him, but it was not enough to keep them together when Salvotor buried his fingers into a wound in the meat of Thorne's side and yanked them apart. The Chancellor's reinforced fist smashed Thorne's ribs next, and he sagged against the wall so sharply only Salvotor's hand around his throat kept his knees from buckling. Cistine lunged, twisting to escape from Devitrius, but his hold around her wrist was fetter-tight.

"You know, boy, I'm beginning to see the merit to your survival. If I had killed you on the wetlands, what would have become of this glorious opportunity?" Salvotor thrust Thorne harder against the wall, driving a groan from his chest. "In these coming weeks, you'll begin to wish your *selvenar* begged a different fate for you. And every day, you'll know she handed away the keys to her own demise because you were foolish enough to be caught in a temple raid."

He let Thorne away from the wall only to twist his arm behind his back and shove him toward a cage. Thorne reached out with his unrestrained arm, and Cistine mirrored him, hand for hand; their fingers locked, eyes branding one another.

Then Devitrius and Salvotor yanked them apart for the last time. Thorne disappeared into the cage, and Devitrius marched Cistine back out to her own hollow prison.

CHAPTER TWENTY

For DAYS AFTER Thorne's arrival, Cistine saw no one—not Kristoff, not Salvotor, not even Grimmaul. Her only companions were her own racing thoughts, conjuring up horrific notions of what Salvotor might be doing to his son while he kept her locked away. No one visited her except to slide a tray of food onto the steps while she slept, and she felt the cold press of insanity knowing Thorne was *here*, just out of reach. That he might be enduring lashes or worse every day, and she was powerless to intervene like she had with Kristoff.

Finally, to chase out those thoughts, she resumed her training. Physical exertion sharpened her focus like a blade on a whetstone. She needed to move forward with investigating possibilities of escape—the balcony. The vents. The cellar. They'd brought Thorne in *somewhere*...and maybe he knew. He'd been conscious, and even with a sack over his head, he was too perceptive to have missed how he came into the mountain.

The cellar still seemed the likeliest place, and she considered her options while she began her regiment of push-ups. She needed to divert Vassoran attention from that doorway, but nothing less than a calamity would peel the guards away from the mouth of that cellar. And calamity would not doubt be punished...not just in her, but in Thorne now, too.

She huffed through her last twenty push-ups, collapsed to her chest, then rolled onto her back. Pressing her fingers against her burning abdomen in a steady, gentle cadence, she gazed up at the shadowy pocket above the trellis.

That air hole.

The door creaked open for the first time in days. Cistine scrambled to her feet and whirled to face Kristoff. "What are you doing here? Where have you been?"

"On patrol at the watchtowers." He descended the shallow steps to the floor, brow knit with worry, searching her face. "Stars, I wondered if he killed you already and kept me away so I wouldn't defy him."

Heat choked Cistine's throat. "Would you?"

Kristoff looked away. "He placed Grimmaul as your guard because I came after you that night, didn't he?"

She sank back on the edge of the bed. "I think so. He wanted to wear down my defenses for the worst thing he could possibly do to break me." And everyone in Kalt Hasa must believe he succeeded—even Kristoff. It was the only way to keep them alive.

Kristoff's well-worn boots slid into her path of sight when she dropped her gaze. "What has he done?"

"He brought his own son here and put him in a cage. I gave Salvotor almost *everything* just to keep him alive."

Kristoff was silent. Too silent, for too long. Then a soft, vicious growl. "Thorne."

Cistine's bowels clenched. Her gaze whipped up to his face, full of raw, ravaging fury like none she'd ever seen before.

"Thorne. His son. The silver-haired boy. He's *here*."

Cistine lunged to her feet, catching his arm. "Kristoff, wait—"

He tore free from her grip and sprinted out of the room, and in his rage he didn't even shut the door. Forsaking the thought of her own punishment for now, Cistine dashed after him.

It was good she'd trained enough to stay light on her feet, clinging so close to Kristoff it would seem he was leading her somewhere. She didn't dare breathe a plea or protest in front of the other guards while they flew past them; she had to save her strength to get between him and Thorne when it mattered.

Through the Wound, down that dark tunnel, never slowing. Panic gave Cistine a last burst of strength when they reached the prison room, and she finally grabbed Kristoff's shoulder, towing him to a halt. "Wait—*please*, whatever he did to you, don't hurt him!"

He plucked her hand off like it was nothing, but he didn't step forward, didn't look at her. Cistine followed his gaze, her heart slamming in her throat.

Thorne sat propped against the back wall of his cage, head and shoulder slumped to the bars, hair hanging across his brow. His clothes were tattered, yanking away from his skin; fresh blood ran from the lacerations on his face—someone had taken their fists to him already—and his neck rubbed raw where an iron hoop banded his bruised throat.

Her *selvenar*. Her Starchaser. They'd put a *collar* on him.

Fury sparked in Cistine's fingertips and pounded against her temples. His name choked from her lips, and his eyes flickered open, the first flash of light in this dim room ghostlit like blood and cradled in shadows. "Cistine?"

Kristoff snapped forward. Cistine leaped to get between them, but there was no space anymore, Kristoff's hands already wrapping the cage bars. "Thorne."

He struggled to his feet, gripping the wall behind him for support. His eyes flicked to Cistine and back to Kristoff. "Why did you bring her here?"

Slowly, Kristoff shook his head. "You don't remember me."

Thorne rocked back on his heels. The line of his shoulders dropped, his eyes glinting with confusion. "I do." He tilted his head. "I do know you. Who—?"

"Wayfinding on the courtyard walls. Fortresses of blankets in the parlor with all five of us crammed inside." Kristoff choked as if he would weep. "Hot chocolate milk with nutmeg and cinnamon. You clung to my leg and begged me not to go fight in the war. You asked me once if I would be your father instead of him, and I told you—"

"That you didn't have to be my father to love me with everything you are." Thorne broke down to his seat on the floor, staring up at Kristoff like he was seeing a specter. "*Nahdar.*" The Old Valgardan word was a breath on his shaking lips.

Uncle.

Cistine's hand clapped to her mouth, muffling a shriek of disbelief as Kristoff jammed his knife in the lock, ripping the cage door open. Hands buried in the front of Thorne's shirt, he lifted him like he weighed nothing and steadied him against the wall, gripping the side of his head. "They told me you were dead years ago, Thorne."

Tears carved through the old blood on Thorne's cheeks. "They told us the same."

Then their arms were around each other, Kristoff holding Thorne's head tight in his hand and Thorne's face buried in his uncle's neck. Tears slid between Cistine's clutched hands and dripped from her jaw—not terror or heartbreak for once, but wonder and shock. Though she wanted to be the one in that cage, the one whose arms were around Thorne, it was not her moment. Not her joy to feel.

Kristoff drew back first, taking Thorne by the shoulders. "After all this time, how did you *survive*? Salvotor told me he put you all to the sword for defying him."

"He drove us out of Stornhaz a decade ago...Baba Kallah and I, Quill and Tatiana, Maleck and Aden, and Ariadne, you never knew her—"

Kristoff dropped back against the cage bars, gloved hand holding his mouth. "Aden and Maleck still *live*?"

Cistine stared at his back, her heart stumbling to a halt, then quickening into a wild tumble. Thorne's uncle, a man with two sons, one with night terrors—the one Salvotor claimed hardly counted for a son.

Maleck.

This was Aden's father, the man he'd betrayed the cabal for, the one Salvotor claimed was dead, then alive, then dead again, just to make Aden suffer and tear the cabal apart.

Alive, after all.

"They're all right, *Nahdar*," Thorne said, and Cistine's heart raced. If Aden was alive, if he was *well*, then it could only mean Maleck had reached them in time. He'd gotten them out of that desert prison after all.

Relief nearly buckled her knees as well. It *was* just a lie—Ashe was all right. Ashe must be looking for her, too.

"Have you been here all this time?" Thorne's voice jerked her from the dizzy spin of joy.

"Nearly twenty years now," Kristoff said. "I tried to help you and your mother escape him, but Salvotor learned of our scheme. He intercepted us that night. I would be dead now if my sister hadn't pleaded for my life. Salvotor decided using me as a weapon at her throat was better than my blood on the docks at Spruce Harbor."

Rage tightened Thorne's mouth. "He'll do it again with us."

"I'm sure."

Thorne's eyes shot to Cistine, and her stomach turned weightless at the look on his face. "Then why haven't you helped her escape yet?"

"Because it would only end in tragedy."

"That's no excuse. That's not the nobility you taught me."

"Nobility has no place here! This is what your father does...he brings people to Kalt Hasa to taunt me. People who never deserved to be here. As soon as I remember who I am, *what* I am, as soon as I lift a finger to help them, he butchers them before my eyes."

Cistine's breath caught. "That was why he was bringing Maleck here when Sillakove fell."

Kristoff paled. "Thank the stars he never came. I've learned my lesson...it's better for everyone if I don't get involved."

"But we don't deserve to be here!"

"You think you're the only one? Do you believe *Dain* deserves to be here? Or Selanus and Suandi? They killed a Vassoran guard who attacked their mother. Dain stole rations to feed his seven younger siblings. *Injustices.* The Courts' faults, not theirs. As a former Tribune, I know every single law broken by every man and woman in Kalt Hasa. They're *nothing*. And that's precisely why Salvotor brings them here."

Thorne lurched forward, shoulders tight with desperation. "You know what happens if we stay. You *know* where this road ends."

Kristoff rubbed his stubbled face with both hands.

"Help us," Cistine pleaded. "If not for my sake, for Thorne's. *Please.* You know what Salvotor will do to him."

Kristoff dropped his hands and stared at his nephew, soaking in the sight of his bloodied countenance, the collar around his neck, the fire in his eyes. Thorne stared right back. "Can you help us escape?"

"I don't know, but...oh, stars damn it. I can *try,*" Kristoff grunted. "It will take time, and that means letting your father's plans play out until I can guarantee he doesn't turn you loose on this mountain to die or punish Cistine in some other way. Do you understand what's at stake? If I help you, I can't stop every different way he hurts you."

Cistine's stomach lurched. It would be a dangerous game for all three of them and the men Kristoff brought into the shelter of his guard. But it was better to play it with him as their ally than alone. "We understand."

"Good. You both know how to take a punch?"

Thorne nodded, and Cistine said, "Quill and Thorne taught me."

A smile traced the dimple on the side of Kristoff's mouth. "Good boys. I'll try to find a way to get you out, but in the meantime you'll have to brace against whatever blows Salvotor brings. As of this moment, we are at war against him, and we are fighting to survive. You're ready to fight?"

"Yes," Thorne said.

"More than I've ever been," Cistine agreed.

"Then keep both eyes open. We'll get you two home."

"*All* of us," Cistine said. "Your sons are out there. They still need you."

Kristoff rattled in a wet, shaky breath and shut his eyes for a moment; when he opened them again, life blazed back into him, a dead body buried under the mountain for twenty years slowly awakening again, shaking the dust from his bones and taking up his sword. He stepped back and shut the cage door, yanking the lock from it. "We'll replace this. He can never know I was here."

"Wait," Cistine begged. "Let me—"

Kristoff flung out an arm. "Not now. Back to your room, before you're missed. I'll tell you more about that air vent you were eyeing when I came in today."

Cistine blinked, and Thorne chuckled lowly. "You never change."

"I wish that were true. But the man I was before would never have let things go this far." Kristoff shook his head. "I have plenty to atone for. It begins today."

He led Cistine to the tunnel, and she twisted to look back as they went. Thorne's arms hung through the cage bars, his eyes fixed on her; he offered a crooked smile, a silent promise they would see one another again.

They were not alone on this battlefield.

THE
PRISONER

OF

LOVE AND
LOYALTY

CHAPTER
TWENTY-ONE

TATIANA WAS ALWAYS afraid to travel north of the Isetfell Mountains after the stories she read of dragons and frostwolves, perilous clefts and icy lakes like sheets of glass that could shatter in an instant under a traveler's feet. But when they returned to the Den, she was determined to sell those books and buy snowshoes for her return; because this was the most beautiful land she'd ever seen.

It was already winter here: deep green pines and winterberry bushes bridled with snow, smoky patches of rock and dirt peeping between drifts. The distant Red Desert, then the brown foothills disappeared the higher she and Quill climbed. Everything turned to rime ice and rock, and it was there that she remembered where she heard of Kalt Hasa.

"It was Maleck." The words popped out of her, pitched with surprise, while they made camp after another long day of trekking.

Firewood tumbled from Quill's arms as he slid onto the ledge beside her, a defensible jut of stone hanging over deep furrows of pine far below. "What was?"

"Kalt Hasa." Tearing the last of the dry-bark kindling to tatters, she heaped it into the small stone ring and pulled the flintrock from her thick coat—the best purchase she made in the bazaar, meat skewers aside. "That's where they were sending him when I pulled him out of that cart. I *knew* I'd heard of that place before!"

Quill swiveled his gaze northwest. "What do you think they wanted to do with him there?"

"A former *visnprest* acolyte, in an abandoned temple? I was always afraid to ask."

"And we never had to, thanks to you." Settling in beside her, Quill snapped the kindling into forearm lengths and lined them up. "How did you do it, Tati? That night, when everything went to Nimmus…"

She shivered at the nip of cold air on her neck, just like that evening when she stood on the banks at Spruce Harbor, waiting for Quill, and he never came. "It's been ten years, Featherbrain. *Now* you're asking?"

Another branch snapped like breaking bone. "I was always worried what would happen if I did, you know…before."

Guilt and defensiveness surged in her chest. Just because there was no flask, no wine-pot, no tavern for a hundred miles, he suddenly deemed it safe to rub at that old scar?

She struck the flintstone harder this time, sparking the kindling to life. Over its fresh embers, she met his gaze. "You know how I did it. You were there in Detlyse Halet."

It was a soft blow, a warning aimed at his weakest parts to deter without deeply wounding. A deprecating smile yanked Quill's lips as he stooped forward and cupped a hand to blow on the fire, coaxing new life into it. His gaze never left hers; an equal heat fanned in her core. "I know how you got *me* out. I think about it so much, sometimes I forget I wasn't the only one you had to save."

The memory tumbled back on her like a wave returning to its shore: wasting one of their few stolen augments to break into Detlyse Halet, attacking the jailor, bringing down the guards. She'd killed more men and women that night than she could count, a feral child of eighteen possessed with rage, panic, and desperation, hacking her way through layers of Vassora to reach her best friend. And then he left to find his sister, and she found solace in a bottle of mead to keep the screaming specters at bay.

The warm, honeyed memory drizzled her tongue, wrenching her gaze away from his. "It was just like any other fight. I started hitting and I didn't stop until they let go of everyone I cared about."

And after, when I needed you, you weren't there.

She forced that thought away. It was nothing new or revelatory; she'd learned long ago that needing Quill was dangerous, because she would never come first in his life. That role belonged to Pippet, maybe even to Thorne. She was third at best, and he didn't need someone needing him who put herself in danger, who took expansive risks; no more than she needed someone so dangerous, who saw so much of her and kept so many of her secrets. Quill would be better with a pretty barmaid, a quiet girl, someone like Cistine used to be, as much as that infuriated Tatiana when they first met. And she needed peace, a chance to find out who she was with the false armor of alcohol and aversion peeled off.

She didn't realize how quiet Quill was until the pop of kindling tore her from her thoughts. He'd settled in a sprawl, one leg cocked, half on his side and half on his back; his typical repose, but his eyes were more troubled than usual. "Salvotor underestimated you. He always does. Look where we are." He flicked a pebble down into the pines below. "We're probably closer to finding Cistine than anyone else, and all we had to do was listen to you for a change. Remind me again why *you're* not our leader, Saddlebags?"

Snorting, she threw a handful of kindling at him. "Because I never *wanted* it, first off. And second, I'm not cut for leadership. I crumble under pressure."

"If you don't think Thorne's been crumbling ever since Baba Kallah..."

Grieved silence strangled the rest of his words. Tatiana stared into the flames, throat bathed in a different kind of heat.

Slowly, Quill raised himself, arms linked around his knees. "I keep thinking maybe we should've gone after him. Brought him with us."

Tatiana shook her head. "It's still safer to divide our forces. We *may* be closer, but that's only if I'm right. And we both know that only happens half the time."

"Right. But the look on his face when he left..." Quill scratched under his hair. "I don't know. Something feels off about all of this."

Worry darted down Tatiana's spine, stabbed into her core, and flourished rapidly into defensiveness. "Well, if *you* were so worried about him, why didn't you say something before we went to Nordbran?"

Quill opened his mouth, then shut it with a sharp wag of his head. "Better if I don't make the plans."

"Are you joking? Since when do you *ever* hesitate to throw your opinion around?"

He rose, brushing off his hands, and started for the trees. "Remember the Izten Torkat?"

"That wasn't—Quill! Where are you going?"

"For more firewood."

Tatiana's gaze fell to the snapped branches, perfectly lined beside the fire, and her stomach plummeted into her knees.

Deprecation and self-loathing were *her* specters to wrestle; Quill was the confident one, the brash one who plotted and acted all in the same breath, wildly sure that luck or the gods would catch him if he fell. This wasn't how they danced; she wasn't the believer, and he wasn't the doubter. If she didn't know who he was, and who *she* was, and how they moved through the patterns of this cruel, unpredictable world together...

Fear punched into her gut. She needed him to come back, to talk to her.

But that night, he never did.

CHAPTER TWENTY-TWO

IT TOOK CISTINE and Kristoff days to construct a crude map linking Kalt Hasa's walls together, blending everything they knew into a path sketched on paper. She'd been in the right vein with the air vents, a web of tunnels within the roofs of different chambers, and tonight she would begin exploring them.

Footsteps clapped the stone hall outside Cistine's chamber, interrupting the excited sizzle of her thoughts as she studied their map; the door slid open, and Kristoff cursed when he saw her holding the sketch. "Put that away! You never know who could walk through this door."

"Yes, I do," Cistine said absently. "You walk. Grimmaul struts."

"You can tell me apart by how I walk?"

Cistine glanced up at the surprise in his tone. "It's something the cabal taught me about patrol. You learn the way your friends walk so you don't attack them in the dark."

A flicker of a smile turned Kristoff's lips. "I taught Aden that trick." He shut the door, and at the snap of the latch, all humor fled his face. He tossed the familiar wooden latchbox onto the bed so hard its clasp unbuckled, and it tumbled open.

Cistine stared at its contents—another sheer affair, this time with curlicues dripping down from the shoulders to the hips in garlands that barely covered the tips of the breasts. The middle of the gown from clavicles to waist was nothing but a gossamer web of fine, invisible threads. "I am not going to wear this."

Kristoff grimaced. "At the Chancellor's command. Remember...take the blows."

Cistine stormed to the relief alcove and carefully stuffed her body into the dress. It did nothing to ward off the cold, and the coarse patterns clung to her ribs and chest like hands clenching her sides. In Talheim, this would be considered negligee fit only for the marriage bed.

She stalked back out into the open. "I'm *ready*."

Kristoff glanced at her, then averted his gaze just as quickly and strode from the room, beckoning her to follow.

The moment the toe of her dirty slipper grazed the hewn chamber's threshold, the whispers started. Vassora glanced up from playing cards and drinking potted wine, shamelessly admiring her; a few hooted and whistled. For the first time, Cistine was glad to enter the corridor to the dining hall, blocking her and this glittering nightmare of a dress from their eyes.

But the relief was short-lived.

Salvotor was at his usual place at the head of the table, but this time they did not dine alone. Grimmaul and his own six guards flocked the seats, a dark inversion of Kristoff's men, but it wasn't even their hot, filthy stares that dragged Cistine to a halt.

Thorne sat at his father's right, hands bound behind his back, a gag stuffed in his mouth. The rough cloth abraded his cheeks when he looked up from the plate before him and caught sight of her—in that dress, little more than negligee.

She almost turned around and walked back into the hall.

"Kristoff, I have a gift for you." Salvotor cut a hand toward Thorne. "Look who survived that unfortunate incident a decade ago!"

Kristoff stared at his nephew, his hands forming slow fists at his sides. Shock stormed across his eyes, so believable that for a moment even Cistine forgot it was an act. "*Thorne.*" Love and desperation and heartbreak formed the breathless word.

Salvotor reclined on one elbow toward his son. "Do you know this man? He is your uncle, the one my mother dragged you off to see every day. As if someone so pitiful could take my place in your life...so weak he couldn't even protect his own family."

Thorne twisted forward against his bonds, a harsh breath slipping past the gag in his mouth.

"What of Aden?" Kristoff demanded. "Maleck?"

Salvotor leaned back in his seat. "It seems they survived as well. But Devitrius is on the hunt. It just seems a shame to waste so many family reunions." His gaze slid to Cistine. "Sit."

The men on either side of her usual chair shifted subtly when she sank down. Thorne's eyes cast from one end of the table to the other, darkening with blind fury.

"Out, Kristoff," Salvotor added. "You're relieved from duty tonight."

Cistine glared down at the platter of pale meat, leeks, and potatoes before her. She wasn't hungry, but she knew by now that if she didn't eat, the meal would go on forever. So she forced her limp hands to cut, her stiff jaw to chew while they stared at her like *she* was the next course. Thorne's eyes branded her, but she couldn't bear to look at him.

She had to take control back. Small steps, like when she first trained with the cabal. She nibbled at her portion the same way she tentatively balanced knives in her hands, keeping her eyes on only one task at a time, like when Ariadne gave her a chore to fulfill. In her mind, she recited Old Valgardan words and imagined the map of the tunnels like the one she and Tatiana used to study in her room. She imagined herself anywhere but here, plucking at her supper while Salvotor leered down the table.

She took the blows, just like Quill taught her.

"Cistine, that dress is absolutely ravishing on you," the Chancellor remarked when he realized she was marching the dinner along, not content to wallow in it. "Wouldn't you men agree?"

Thorne shifted, not looking at Cistine, only at the Vassora—assessing which one to kill first.

Grimmaul snorted and hooked his thumbs into his belt. "Bit bony for my tastes."

"But she'd be shapely if she ate a bit more." The man on Cistine's right speared a portion of meat and thrust it toward her. "Do you like to be fed?"

Now they were getting into the spirit of it, ranking every inch of her from her eyes, to her shoulders, to her breasts and hips and haunches. Grimmaul ordered her to stand, and when she didn't, her face so hot it felt swollen, Salvotor rolled his arm. "Rise. Show them the dress."

"No," Cistine seethed.

"Then I'll give them permission to strip it and send you back to your chamber in nothing but your skin."

Thorne's body vibrated with a muffled snarl. Salvotor picked up his knife and twirled it over his fingers, inches from his son's face.

Ears pulsing, Cistine rose and slowly turned. The Vassora whistled and clapped, ranking her legs and navel and the things *under* the dress, parts of her no man had ever seen or touched, that they no right to even *think* about. She burned with silent, vicious hatred, glaring at Salvotor with every turn.

"I wonder what that boy would've ranked you," he mused, and the laughter slaked. Thorne tensed. Cistine froze. "He certainly thought there was something about you worth coming back for, didn't he? Was he aware he guarded the Key his kingdom stole from us?"

Cistine gripped her seatback. "Don't speak to me about Julian Bartos." Not here. Not with these people. Not with Thorne present, guilt and grief crashing through his bright blue eyes.

"*Bartos*? Not the son of *Rion* Bartos, the self-proclaimed Butcher whose slaughters in the war were legend on both sides?" A few Vassora whistled, this time with derision toward stories Cistine had never heard. "I wonder what the Butcher would think if he knew how his son charred up like a flank of meat. If he learned Julian died for *absolutely nothing*."

"Shut your gods-damned mouth!" Cistine screamed. "*You're* the butcher!" She pushed forward, ready to punch him even if it broke her hand again—because he had no right, *none*, to say Julian's name after what he did to him. After he stole Julian from the world—from *her*.

She barely felt the knife graze her skin from breastbone to belly; she hadn't even seen Grimmaul pull it. All she knew was the cold kiss of air on her chest and navel as the severed halves of the dress flopped apart, baring her to the room.

Choking in shock, Cistine stumbled and snatched the ruined fabric in the cross of her arms, trying to hide herself as the cold wedged under her bare skin. The Vassora roared with laughter, and Salvotor smirked, lounging in his chair. "I wonder how my son would rank you."

He reached over with the knife and casually slit the gag, scouring Thorne's cheek with the tip of the blade. He twisted, cursing under his breath, eyes flashing to Cistine. "Go."

Her eyes welled. Even bound and imprisoned, he was trying to protect her—taking the punishment, whatever would follow, so she could scrape together the last of her dignity and flee. "Not without you," she whispered.

Salvotor spun the knife. "Well, Thorne? Rank her."

"You'll have to kill me."

"You already know I won't do that. But this is the lesson, after all." He flicked the blade, and Grimmaul shot forward, catching Cistine by the arm and throat. His fingers pinched her airway shut, and panic poured through her veins. She couldn't breathe, couldn't wriggle loose as he twisted her arm between her shoulderblades. Thorne staggered upright, wrenching against his bonds, and Salvotor rose beside him and touched the knife to his neck. "If you defy me, I will allow Grimmaul to punish her however he sees fit. And if *she* defies me, I will take the lash to you. That is how we'll maintain order until Devitrius returns with the ingredients for the ritual. Is that clear?"

Grimmaul loosened his hand from her throat, and Cistine sagged as air rushed back into her lungs. Her body ached with rage.

"Now," Salvotor said, "rank her."

If Grimmaul hadn't still held her arm, she would've covered her ears. She didn't want to hear any of this. Even with her eyes closed, she knew it was Thorne ranking her, not his father throwing his voice anymore. Whatever he said would be stamped onto her heart for the rest of her life.

"Look at me, *Logandir*," Thorne murmured.

She forced apart her tacky lashes and met his wild gaze, guttering and hot as the heart of a flame.

"Cistine," he said, "you defy every standard they hold you to. There is more nobility, compassion, and wisdom in your *fingertips* than in every man's spirit in this stars-damned mountain. And *that* is just the beginning. I rank you above them—above all of us. I rank you among the stars, *Logandir*, and I would follow your light to find my way home...as long and as far as I wander, for the rest of my life."

Scoffing, Salvotor grabbed Thorne by the shoulder and slammed him back into his seat. "Wrong answer, boy."

Grimmaul dragged Cistine away to the hall, her slick heels scouring the stone, ears ringing with Thorne's curses behind them, his furious roars that he'd done as he was told and if Grimmaul hurt her, if *any* of them did, he would turn Kalt Hasa into a graveyard—

Then they reached the end of the corridor. And Selanus punched Grimmaul in the face.

It happened so swiftly, Cistine didn't even register his presence before the guard's hold loosened. She yanked away from him, still banding her ruined dress to her breasts with her arm, staring wild-eyed at the Six crowding in the mouth of the hall.

"*Nadrian* can't take another lash." Selanus shook out his fist, staring at the dazed Grimmaul heaped on the floor. "But we can."

"Hurry, Cistine," Dain urged. "Back to your room, before this turns into a bloodbath."

Cistine's eyes burned. "Thank you."

"Thank *Nadrian*," Baldvin sniffed. "It was his idea."

Kristoff waited in her chamber, sitting with his head in his hands. He didn't look up when she entered. "Get dressed."

Cistine scrambled into her pajamas and considered asking Kristoff to burn this dress. But when she held the beaded folds wrapped around her fists like sparring cloth, a notion occurred to her. She shoved the slit fabric into the corner instead and emerged, leaning against the walls with arms wrapped around her middle.

"I heard them ranking you," Kristoff said toward the floor. "Tonight crossed a line."

"Take the blows, remember?" Cistine said, though her heart still raced and her skin felt branded with their lust. The moment she was alone, she would cry; for now, she had to ensure Kristoff wouldn't give up their escape for a seed of doubt. "I can endure him. But if you want to make things better, let me see Thorne."

Kristoff's mouth twitched. "You like to play with fire, don't you?"

"I *am* the Wild Heart of Fire. The flames don't frighten me." She dropped onto the bed beside him. "I can't let the only time I see him be at that table, with a knife to his throat and Salvotor commanding the room. You had your chance with Thorne. Now give me mine."

Kristoff hesitated a moment longer, his gaze turning to the roof. Then he said, "I know how you can see him."

CHAPTER
TWENTY-THREE

A SHEILA. HAVE YOU made a plan?"

Rion's gruff question jolted her attention away from the smoldering fire. Sunset dimness poured over Eben's plains and the small Warden camp on the edge of the marshes under a hanging shelf of rock. The others were off checking the snares, taking patrol; it was just Ashe and Pippet, napping across the dead firepit, and now Rion dropping down from the rock to land beside her.

"You've searched the plains and this Valgardan slum for days." Rion knelt, dark eyes searching her face. "We're wasting time. What's your strategy?"

She prodded the fire, coaxing life into the embers. "It's being made."

Exhaustion suffocated her mind. The journey back from the border had been twice as swift as the descent, and the moment they reached Jovadalsa's crumbling edge, she set to work searching the plains for clues, then searching every inch of the city that opened its doors to her...and some she had to force herself into. She left Pippet with Rozalie during those days and always found herself distracted until she laid eyes on the girl again.

None of this was going to plan. After days of searching, she still had no trace of which way her Princess was taken, and every time she tugged at the leash of her own restraint, ready to threaten another barmaid or drunkard and reach into this city's dark heart, she thought of shadowed catacombs and silty water. Of her last disastrous infiltration.

A heavy hand on her shoulder broke her thoughts. "We need to *move*, Ashe."

"I'm trying!" She cast the stick into the firepit, scowling. "I don't know where to start. I wasn't there when they were taken!"

"I'm aware." She couldn't tell if that was consolation in Rion's tone or a gentle reminder of her failure. "But I've seen you do much more with far less. You will find a way. You always do."

A shard of warmth pierced her chest, and she rubbed her face with both hands. She needed to track Cistine, she needed a plan, she needed *help*—

If you ever need aid, go to the Tavern of Six Thieves *in Jovadalsa. You'll find it there.*

A strange shiver snaked through her guts, setting her back hard on her heels, her gaze turning toward the derelict city.

No. She *couldn't* go down that road, and she shouldn't be excited at the prospect of what—or who—might be in that tavern. Of seeing *him*.

She'd tried everything. Pushed the memory out. Even walked right past the way into Hellidom, keeping Pippet with her, because she didn't want to risk meeting one of the cabal or being driven out by the sword. But here she was, in the very place Cistine was taken, where Julian died, and she couldn't muster a strategy better than breaking a few doors down and roughing up drunks.

Going would be weakness. It would give in to her basest desires, her most foolish wants; not just for one pair of eyes that looked at her with something other than disappointment, reserve, or undeserved adoration, but for something she shouldn't even seek.

Forgiveness.

The word burned in her chest as Pippet roused and sat up, rubbing her eyes, shooting a bleary look at Rion across the fire. They regarded one another with the same wary animosity as ever since the border forts; it still set Ashe's hair on end.

And that was what made up her mind; because going meant at least one more person to watch over Pippet. Maybe it even meant she could leave her with a friend.

She shrugged off that thought and stood, beckoning to Pippet. "Let's go find Rozalie. Time for patrol."

Rion smirked. "You have a plan?"

"I have a plan." And he would despise it, so she didn't tell him. If nothing came of it, he never needed to know. And if something did...

She'd break up that brawl when it came to it.

Rich notes of spiced honey mead and strong herbs saturated the *Tavern of Six Thieves,* filling Ashe's senses with the tang of indulgence she'd come to associate with Jovadalsa by now. Dark shapes in every corner might've been broken furniture or inebriated people. The upper level reeked of strong drink, but it was the lower quarters Ashe was interested in.

She descended a long flight of steps to find little more than a broad wooden platform below, stilts speared into the lake, planks shifting just slightly under the water's duress. It was open on three sides, allowing a view of the slate-gray water and the murky fog that spilled from its surface. Ghostlamps swung from the low ceiling, guttering in time to the pounding footsteps on the level above.

Beneath their garish amber light, a circle of erect wooden planks boxed in a pair of fighters tussling for their lives.

The blood drained from Ashe's face. Her skin pulsed with the memory of hot desert wind, of sand shifting under her sandals, of blood—hers, Dorsta's, Aden's, Briet's—slapping the ground and the cries of the patrons and nomads and Tribunes freckling the air.

Ashe, Ashe, Ashe—

She pinched the scar on her thigh, shook her head wildly, and shoved through the crowd to the edge of the ring for a look at the fighters. The breath gusted from her all at once, leaving her chest void, disappointment and then strange relief crashing through her.

Maleck hadn't waited for her. He sent someone else in his stead.

Aden bobbed and slewed around his broken-nosed opponent, skinned of his shirt and barefoot, making the brawl look like a dance. He wove effortlessly through the man's wild punches, then dove in and smashed an uppercut into his ribs, spun back out of reach and followed up with a roundhouse kick that tossed the fighter to his knees. Aden twisted back and slammed his elbow into the man's chin, knocking him unconscious on the planks.

A smirk crawled across Ashe's face, and she raised her hands to clap with the other patrons—then froze when Aden's eyes found her.

Still as stone plunged into sand save the heavy lift and sink of his chest while someone dragged his fallen opponent away, Aden watched her. Then he curled his fingers twice, a challenge as familiar as arena laps and sparring matches.

He hadn't offered that since Nimea revealed her betrayal.

Ashe unlatched her cloak and let it fall. Then she vaulted into the pit to fight the Lord of the Hive.

The moment she skimmed over the planks, a strange calm enveloped her. Aden's head sank slightly, greeting the puff of her boots on the bloodstained floor.

They said nothing. No words would do.

As one, they rushed in.

Clarity clapped through Ashe with every blow she threw, every one he blocked. Their steps matched, each swing parried perfectly, as if they'd never missed a day. The wooden planks turned to sand under Ashe's steps, the ghostlights transformed to the sun's relentless glare bouncing off the desert's glittering face, and the cries of the onlookers as mynts traded hands became Sander's voice, Noaam's voice, Nimea's—

She slammed her fist into Aden's open hand, arm buckling. He seized her elbow, eyes boring into hers. "Don't stop."

Ashe cracked her knee into his gut, then hooked out his legs. They fell together, her knees slamming the planks so hard a gasp wrenched from her throat. Aden flipped them in one smooth motion, pinning her elbows away from her body with his knees and pressing her down with his fingers around her throat. The pressure was light, in no danger of strangling her, but his wild gaze dared her to fight back.

Panic ripped through her chest, hot and daggered, a memory of Viperwolf talons and hot sand under her body, of frigid stone and Nimea's blade at her throat.

"*Let go!*" she roared, voice half-muffled by the storming crowd, and he did. Ashe slid her knee between their bodies and forced him off, surging up and smashing her brow against his. He barked in pain, toppling back on his haunches and rolling upright. Ashe staggered up after him, mustered her strength, and swung a finishing blow into his face.

The crack of her knuckles on his cheekbone silenced the crowd for a moment, and in the breathless pause Ashe stepped around him and slammed the bar of her arm against the back of his hips. Aden went down again only because he'd chosen to; she hadn't hit him that hard. But the fight was over the moment his touch brought her mind flashing back to Siralek.

Still, she played the victor's part, catching the few mynts they tossed at her feet. Aden slowly heaved himself up again, retrieved his tunic from the other side of the circle, and hopped the fence. Ashe followed, peeling away from the cheering onlookers toward one of the support columns holding up the tavern's first floor. Aden folded his arms and leaned his shoulder into the post, looking out across the dark water. Ashe copied him, the sound of the current soothing the fear that drummed under her skin.

"I thought it was Maleck I'd find here," she admitted after a beat. "Not you."

"Disappointed?"

Ashe bit back a scowl. "One Valgardan is as good as another." She wasn't going to do it. She couldn't ask where he was.

"Stornhaz," Aden supplied to her silence. "He sent word...he and Ariadne are searching for a witness and an accuser who could testify to some of Salvotor's more heinous offenses."

She'd only heard that certain twist in his tone once before. "Is this about Ariadne?"

Gaze fixed on the fog, Aden nodded. "There is a law that could place Salvotor in chains, if they could prove he broke it by what he did to Ariadne. But her sister, the sole witness, refuses to testify."

"Damn," Ashe muttered.

"He buried that law long before he drove us from Stornhaz. There's every chance he's committed this crime before. If he did, Maleck and Ariadne will learn of it...or else they'll find another means of bringing that *bandayo* to his knees." Aden leaned his temple to the post, looking across at her. "Maleck knew you'd come. What took you so long?"

Ashe shook off thoughts of laws and crimes. "It's a long story. What matters is, I'm back, and I need your help. I'm looking for Cistine—"

"As am I."

Ashe's tongue faltered midword. "What?"

"Contrary to your assessment of me, I don't take pleasure in bloodying men's faces for sport. I do this from necessity."

"Necessity for *what?*"

Aden motioned her from the throng with a jerk of his head, and spoke while they ascended the steps. "What happened to Thorne and your princess on the plains couldn't have gone completely unnoticed. Someone in this city saw what happened. So I've been tracing whispers."

"Like in the Blood Hive."

Aden's gaze flicked to her, then away again. "Precisely."

Nervous energy rang in Ashe's fingertips. "And?"

"That man you saw me bring down tonight was our witness. His name is Thrain, and if his tales have any merit, he witnessed the convergence of Kanslar's Tribunes and the battle on the plains. He's watched his flanks closely until now, but seeing as he's been tossed out to gather his wits in the gutter, I believe he may be in a conversational mood tonight."

They broke out onto the street. "What are we waiting for, then?"

Aden arched a brow. "We?"

"Do you really think I'm going to walk away from this? He saw what happened to Cistine and Julian!"

Aden turned, studying her by nothing but moonlight. "You left without so much as a farewell. Now you want my aid finding your princess. Valgardans aren't weapons for you to sheathe and unleash at will."

Ashe drew in a deep breath, steadying her rage. "I *know* that. I came to this tavern because Maleck told me I'd find help here. I am *asking* for your help, Aden."

If only to herself, she could admit there was some part of this that made sense—that felt *right*. Aden knew the best and worst of her. He'd seen it all in the Hive. If he helped her, it would be because some part of her deserved it; and if he didn't, she deserved that, too.

He studied her a moment longer, expression inscrutable. Then he jerked his head. "Let's find Thrain before someone else does."

CHAPTER TWENTY-FOUR

ADEN'S ACCOMODATIONS WERE among the filthiest Ashe had ever seen. There was no bed, the door didn't latch properly, one corner of the roof was ripped off entirely to expose the stars, and the doorless washroom was too small to turn a full circle in. But at least he had a chair to tie their captive to.

Thrain raised his eyes to Aden, gap-toothed mouth bared in a snarl, and wrenched against the ropes threaded around his chest, through his arms, and into the three-legged stool. "What do you want from me? Mynts? You've got plenty of them from all those fights!"

Aden stroked a hand along the dagger lashed to his hip. "What we want is of value to no one but us."

Ashe folded her arms. "We want to know what you saw on Eben's plains the day of the skirmish with Kanslar's Chancellor."

Thrain recoiled against the seatback. "Nothing. I saw *nothing*."

"That is far from what your gambling and drinking associates heard from your own lying lips." Aden's voice was deadly soft. "They claim you know who was there, and who attacked whom. Perhaps even *why*."

"I don't! I didn't see anything—I'd had too much to drink—"

"So much it made you clear-headed for once?" Ashe said. "Because these accounts match what we've heard from others who were nearby that day." It alarmed her how easily the lie rolled off her tongue.

Thrain spat blood at their feet. "If I tell you, he'll have my head!"

"Who?" Aden asked. "Chancellor Salvotor?"

"He was there?" Ashe pressed in. "What did he do?"

"I don't know where he was then, any day! I *told* you I know nothing!"

Aden slid the dagger from his belt. "Pity. If you knew *something*, we might've spared your life."

Ashe gripped Thrain's hair and shoved him back in the seat. "What do you think first? Tongue? Ears?"

"Eyes. He still needs to hear our questions, and he may yet choose to speak."

"Stars, no, please!" Thrain bellowed. "*Please...*"

Aden rested the tip of the knife at the corner of the man's eye. "Whatever you *believe* Chancellor Salvotor will do to you, he is not here. We are." He flicked the dagger, drawing a thin trickle of blood from the soft flesh. "And you *know* what we will do."

Thrain gasped with terror, and Ashe flinched. Had Baba Kallah made that sound when she felt the Tumult's poison working through her blood? Had Helga when she'd received word of her friend's death? Had Thorne when his grandmother died in his arms?

"Aden," Ashe hissed. "Wait—"

"There was a battle!" Thrain burst out. "Between the Chancellor and a silver-haired man. I saw it from my room at the edge of the city."

Aden lowered the knife. "What came of that fight?"

"There was a whipping, and then some sort of battle broke out, the horses were freed...and the augments, so many it turned the air static through the whole city! Saw him burn someone alive—"

Heart clenching, Ashe grabbed Thrain's chin and forced up his head. "And then what?"

"Chancellor Salvotor used a wind augment. Left all the Tribunes to clean up the mess behind him."

"Which way did it take him?" Aden growled.

"*I don't know*—" Aden lurched forward, pressing the knife's tip to the arch of the man's eye. "No! It was north!"

Aden froze.

"He traveled north," Thrain panted, "I don't know where in the north, I swear by all the stars, please—don't take my eyes, don't..." Sobs rolled from him, turning the muscled fighter to a weeping heap, and hot shame sliced into Ashe's chest. This was what she and Aden were, what the Blood Hive made them. When she was with him, it was easy to do these things. To be this together.

Almost too easy.

"Give me the knife," she murmured. He relinquished it, and she sawed through the ropes, heaving Thrain up from the chair. "If you tell anyone we were here or what we asked, we will find you. And you know what will happen." She thrust him toward the broken door. "Get out."

Thrain didn't look back, his footsteps drumming down the inn's staircase.

Ashe sheathed Aden's knife in her belt. "Why does it feel like we never left the Hive?"

Aden shrugged. "Because it hasn't left us." He snatched a satchel from under the blankets in the corner, rolled one inside it, then jerked his head. "We'll make good time if we leave now."

"Aden." She stuck out a hand, stepping between him and the door. "You're not coming with."

He arched a brow. "I believe we've proven how little you know about this kingdom. If you wish to stumble around in a desperate search while Salvotor fulfills all his plans, by all means, I won't stop you. But I know someone who keeps close watch over what transpires within Spoek and Nordbran. Someone who may offer information for a price."

Ashe grimaced. She'd been prepared to bring Maleck along as a help, a guide—someone quiet, sturdy, and strong. But Aden, impulsive as he was, bitter and furious like her...

It would ruin that seedling trust Rion placed in her. It would mean opening her arms to the memories of the Blood Hive that swarmed in whenever she looked at him.

But this wasn't about her. What was best for Cistine?

She hated that it wasn't even a question.

"Fine," she muttered. "But we have to stop somewhere first."

They left the inn, Aden dropping a few mynts on the empty innkeeper's booth. Humid autumn fog murmured from the water and wrapped around them while they walked, and Ashe rubbed her hands together, warding off more than just the chill.

Aden nodded to her. "Your knuckles."

She flipped her hands over, examining the scabs. "Your cheek looks about the same. You know, back in Siralek, I don't think I ever asked you where you learned to fight."

"My father first. Then, after he was gone, anyone who was too afraid to deny a Tribune's son his lessons."

Ashe snorted. "He was a fighter *and* a Tribune?"

"Almost as good at both as he was a *valenar* and father. He taught me to defend myself, not to attack."

"That must be rare for Valgardans."

"My parents lived a life of utter contradiction. It's rare that Valgardan unions are steeped in anything but social gains, especially where Tribunes are concerned. You can ask Quill...his father and mother joined for nothing more than political stature and good breeding stock."

Not unlike what Aden himself had suffered in the Hive. Despite all the shifts between them since, Ashe still felt a stab of fury at the memory of his sponsor and the things she and her associates did with him because he was, by Valgardan standards, a *prime specimen*.

"But my father and mother were different." Aden's voice took on a note of quiet nostalgia. "He was already a Tribune, his sister—Thorne's mother—married into the Chancellor's bed. And *my* mother was a prominent medico who worked alongside Tatiana's in the houses of healing. They stood to gain nothing from one another, and that offered them everything."

"Marriage for love. Romantic."

"When you consider how Thorne and Quill were raised, or how indifferent Maleck's parents were, I couldn't have asked for more."

Ashe studied him sidelong in the moonlight. "Salvotor knew you were close. He knew you'd give anything to see your father again."

Aden nodded. "But that was a fool's dream. And a mercy neither of them lived to see what their son became."

There were so many layers to the self-deprecation in his tone, Ashe couldn't hope to peel them all apart: his actions in the Blood Hive. His mistakes with the cabal. What he'd given to protect the fighters in Siralek. So she said nothing, leading him out of the city toward that shelter of rock. Her muscles were tight by the time they arrived, braced for the inevitable fight.

"It's me," she called quietly when the flare of the low fire broke the fog ahead. "And...someone who came to help."

Aden halted when the cluster of shadows rose to greet them; one bounded ahead of the rest, running to fling thin arms around Ashe's waist. "You've been gone for *hours*! What were you doing? You smell like Tati when she hides that flask...were you drinking? Why is there blood on?"

"*Pippet.*" The harsh rasp of Aden's voice halted her tumble of questions. Wide-eyed, she peeled back from Ashe, looking up at the frozen warrior staring back at her like a specter.

"Oh," Pippet whispered. "He's...*beautiful*. How does he know my name?"

Aden wandered two steps nearer. "Do you remember me, Hatchling?"

Her nose scrunched, eyes narrowing. "I feel like I do. You have a sad face, like Maleck's." She bit her lips together. "I don't know your name."

"This is Aden," Ashe said—not just for her benefit, but for Rion's, stalking from the fog ahead of the retinue, his hand to his sword. "He's a friend." It should've felt more like a lie, after everything they did to each other.

"Aden!" Pippet shrieked. "Thorne's cousin! Quill talks about you...what are you *doing* here?"

"Helping." Aden hooked his thumb through his satchel strap, eyes fixed on the Wardens. "Though it doesn't appear I'm needed."

"You're not." Rion's tone was glacial. "Why is he here, Asheila?"

She gritted her teeth. Best to get this over with now. "He's my plan. He helped me find someone who saw which direction they took Cistine and Julian, and he can help us narrow our search."

"You trust a Valgardan to help us?" Rozalie appraised Aden cautiously.

"I've worked with him before."

Rion's brows slanted. "You were busier here than I thought."

Ashe looked away from that furious glare. "Reaching Cistine and Julian is all that matters. He can help us do that. Valgardan or not, that's worth the risk."

"Is it?" Viktor drawled. "Maybe he leads us in circles. Maybe he doesn't want them found."

Aden's presence closed in at her side, boxing Pippet between them. "If we *don't* find your princess, I lose my kingdom to the man who murdered my father. Believe me, I want her found far more than you do."

"Unlikely," Rion scoffed. "The child is one thing, but I won't have a trained Valgardan warrior in our ranks."

Ashe sucked in a deep breath, praying for strength. "Then you'll have to search by yourselves. I can't spoil the chance for a guide based on fear. I'm sorry, Lord Rion."

"Fear?" he echoed scathingly. "I'm not afraid of this man. I'm *aware* what his kind are capable of."

"Then you should know better than to insult me," Aden growled. "We can waste time stroking your delicate Talheimic pride, or we can save your princess. The choice is yours."

Rion's gaze shot between them. At his back, the Wardens braced, hands to weapons, ready to follow whatever order he gave.

For the first time, Ashe wasn't. Not if it put Pippet and Aden at the tips of their swords, squandering every chance of carving a clear, straight path to Cistine.

"We leave at dawn," Rion said at last. "But one hint we're being led astray, and he dies."

Not a threat—a vow. Aden took it without blinking, his chin sinking a bit, eyes pinning Rion with an equal promise that death would not come swiftly or easily.

And Ashe wouldn't be sleeping for the rest of this journey.

The Wardens gathered up, muttering and shooting glances at Aden. Little to Ashe's surprise, they gathered their bedrolls and left the shelter, arraying in a broad ring away from the overhang—giving Aden, Ashe, and Pippet a wide berth.

They'd see the wisdom of this choice in time, just as she did. They'd realize some Valgardans weren't bloodthirsty animals.

They settled around the fire, Pippet huddling close to it for warmth. Aden pulled a blanket from his satchel without a word and offered it; Pippet cocooned herself inside, wide eyes never leaving his face. Ashe almost laughed. She'd looked at Lord Rion the same way at that age, like he carried the rising sun on his shoulders. Aden was in deep danger with this one.

They were silent until Pippet sank off to sleep, her snores weaving into the crackling flames. Then Aden said, "So, that was Rion. The man who made you what you are." She dimly remembered telling him something about that when he learned of her betrayal in the Hive. She'd been so proud then; now she was just weary. "I don't see the resemblance."

Indignation pulsed in Ashe's throat. "You don't know him. You barely know me."

"I know you better than either of us likes." Aden lounged back against the rock. "Why did you lie to him about Julian?"

"Julian is his son. It won't serve the mission if he hears what happened."

"Is it Cistine's wellbeing you fear for, or this kingdom's if he learns his son died on our soil?"

Ashe scowled at him. "Does it matter? He doesn't need to know yet."

Aden folded his arms. "Speaking of what one *needs* to know. Tell me why Quill's sister is with you."

She supposed she owed him that much. In hushed tones, she told him of Helga's fate and her encounter with Pippet in the Wildwood; of the Zabekas, and Disa, and her journey to Talheim.

"I don't know what to do with her," Ashe admitted. "I'm more aware than anyone that battlefields are no place for a child, but anywhere I try to leave her, she follows me. She's my gods-forsaken shadow."

"She's like Quill. Telling her where to stay is the only certain way to make her go."

Ashe tossed up her hands. "So what do I *do* with her?"

"What did you want when you stood in her place?"

Ashe snorted. "For someone to teach me how to stand for myself, how to fight for what was precious to me. But—"

"Why should Pippet be offered anything different?"

"I'm not the person to teach her. I'm..." *Deceitful. Guilty. Unworthy.* "Talheimic. A Valgardan should teach her."

"I could teach her the blade. But to be a strong woman who defends what's hers...that isn't my place."

"It's not mine, either. I'm not her mother."

"She has no mother. She only had Helga, and Helga is gone." Aden's eyes bored into her. "But now she has you."

Pippet whimpered and stirred suddenly, towing the blanket tightly around herself. "*Ashe?*"

She shot Aden a withering look and shifted across the fire to rub Pippet's back. "I'm here."

"I had a bad dream."

Ashe sighed, gathering the girl across her lap. The familiar Talheimic lullaby rolled from her so easily now she didn't even have to think of the words, and the tension melted from Pippet's body. In minutes, she snored again.

"I didn't know you sang," Aden murmured.

"I haven't touched music in years. Not since tending Cistine became my full focus." And she'd failed even that in the end.

"We will find her," Aden said. "We know the way."

The warmth in Ashe's chest wanted to be many things: gratitude. Relief. Excitement that at last, they had taken a tangible step toward finding Cistine. But when she saw the look in Aden's eyes, head leaned back to look up at the rock overhang, that thing in her heart named itself dread.

CHAPTER
TWENTY-FIVE

T HE WAY STEEPENED along the spine of mountains high across Spoek territory. The wonder of its beauty faded, the joys of ice-kissed rock and glinting powder melding into a monotony of rock and snow. Every mile seemed to tug against Tatiana and Quill, slowing their journey toward their princess.

Each night, Tatiana consulted her map by firelight, adjusting their course. Valgard lay to their left, the land of Oadmark stretching to their right. Most days were the same, the span of the world open around them, long silences full of labored breathing broken up by banter. But that banter didn't come as simply as it used to; Quill was frequently stern, sober, eyes fixed ahead. Conversation skirted the subjects they didn't want to broach: what Thorne was doing now; how Aden was faring back in Jovadalsa and what the Secret Keeper wanted from him; whether Maleck and Ariadne could find another victim and witness; what was happening to Cistine.

Tatiana tried not to dwell on things that reminded her in any way of what the Chancellor could do to those unprepared for his cruelty...and even those who thought they were. It always led to feelings of being stalked, like a mountain cat or a frostwolf padded on their heels—a sensation that grew as they climbed, leaving man-laid trails far behind.

Scaling sheer slopes and pine ridges, Tatiana looked often over her shoulder into the valleys below, scalp prickling. It felt like something was truly out there, watching them.

"No fire tonight," she muttered when they made camp one evening in a thick knot of evergreen. She'd chosen this spot specifically to deter watchful predators.

Quill, bent over his pack and pulling out rations, hesitated and glanced back at her. "You're not cold?"

"Freezing, actually, but..." she peered down the dark slope they'd climbed that day. "I don't know. Something feels strange."

Quill hesitated, then shrugged. "It's your hunt."

Tatiana stared at his rounded shoulders, heart thrusting into her throat. For the first time, even with him right there, she felt alone in these mountains.

Her bond with Quill was something she couldn't explain and never had to. A motherless waif and a Tribune's son shouldn't have gotten on like fire and wood, but they always did, and the brilliant thing about Quill was that he'd never forced her to ask why. Not when they played together while Aden watched them; not when he gravitated toward her in their classes. Not when he made appearances outside her house in the middle of the night or showed her places she could get into trouble, earning extra mynts along the way.

She remembered the last day he ever came to school, catching her on the terrace down by the channel to tell her his mother was pregnant and he'd be making his own way and his own mischief from now on. When he asked her to run away and cause trouble with him, it wasn't even a question.

Something sharpened when they fled from the school together and never looked back, like a door opened in their spirits and they found a path between where they could always cross to each other. Sometimes Tatiana found herself standing in his spirit rather than her own; sometimes it was the other way around.

But now she didn't *feel* that. Looking at him was like walking down a familiar street with every ghostlamp snuffed. She was knocking at the door of Quill's heart and finding it shut in her face.

Fury pulsed in her fingertips. She rolled a sphere of snow and hurled it, slapping the back of his hair.

Cursing and hollering, he swatted ice from his collar and whirled on her. "What was that for?"

"For not picking fights with me."

"You argue back when I fight, you hit me when I *don't* argue...there's no pleasing you, is there?"

"If you'd start acting like yourself again, I *would* be pleased."

Tiredness stamped his face, and he lowered himself against the tree across from her. "This *is* me, Saddlebags."

"No, it's not! You're acting like..." she cast her mind about for where she'd seen it before—this unsmiling, somber, scowling Quill—and it struck her like a blow to the chest why it unsettled her so much. "You're acting like you did after Detlyse Halet."

His expression shifted, not with the defensiveness that usually came from this topic, but a searing pain that took her breath away. Teeth gritted, she bent forward. "Tell me why."

"It doesn't matter."

"It does to me, stars damn it!"

"Tati, you don't know." He scooped snow from his collar and flicked it on the ground. "*Nothing* is like Detlyse Halet."

She didn't answer that. He hadn't been there after she killed all those Vassora setting him free; but she'd known better than to ask him about the Lightless Pit, either. A whole decade, and they'd never had this conversation.

But they'd never been alone with just each other for this long.

"It was like the Sable Gates," Quill murmured at last. "All the stories our parents told us of the places we would go if we didn't shape up. I crossed the line, and there I was. Salvotor gave me a chance to renounce my loyalty to Thorne, did you know that? If I turned, he would've let me out."

"But you didn't."

Quill shook his head. "That's why Thorne's never doubted me. He knows I went to Detlyse Halet because I wouldn't turn my back on Sillakove. Stars, Salvotor's always known how to break us."

Tatiana's teeth clicked together. That was true—and right now, he had *Cistine*, and the miles never seemed to shrink from here to there.

"I tried to get out," Quill said softly. "Kicked and clawed at the door...where I thought the door was, anyway. You know you can go blind in darkness that deep? I tried to find a light for days."

"Well, you aren't blind."

"Because I found it. Not out there, but...here." He tapped his scarred temple. "I slowed my breathing. Laid down and slept as much as I could, so I'd dream. I could see things in my dreams. I went back to Stornhaz, all the taverns and dinners. Spruce Harbor. Tati, I came back to *you.*"

Her breath snagged. "Why me? You had Pippet to worry about, you had *Thorne*..."

"Not like I had you."

She couldn't find humorous words to make light of what he was saying, not with that look in his eyes, that angle to his mouth like he might cry.

"I did a lot of thinking in that place...and after," he went on when she didn't speak. "How I heard them whipping Thorne, but I couldn't get to him. And then they burned our rooms, killed my parents, took Pip...I wasn't there for any of it. I couldn't help Ari or Mal, and when you got me out, I was gone. While everyone was trying to pick up the pieces, I was gone, and you know what I saw when I came back?"

"A cabal who couldn't think straight?" She chafed her thumb over her wind-chapped knuckles. "A tinker's daughter drowning in a bottle?"

"No. You were already putting the pieces together. Two months, and Thorne had his roots down, found you a home. He was already in charge. Ariadne was starting to find her way out, and so were you. Maleck and Aden were training...and here I came walking in with Pippet, changing everything, yanking Helga out of there and making her go to Starhollow. I realized I wasn't any different from Saychelle. You could move on without me."

"That's not true, Featherbrain."

"Is it? You tell me you need me to make it through this."

Anger tightened her throat. She had spent months, *years*, even, trying to convince herself she didn't—that things would be easier and better without every selfish way she wanted Quill. But somehow it didn't sound as noble and strong coming from his mouth; it sounded like giving up the best part of her life.

"Anyway, it doesn't matter," he said gruffly. "Ever since then, I've known how it is...what we can and can't live without. I saw how much Thorne missed when he didn't have you this summer. How bad it was after Aden left, even. I see how he is now without Cistine. So keeping you alive, and finding her, that's my duty."

"What about you?" Tatiana demanded. "Did you come with me because you believed in this, or just because you thought I might walk off a cliff and you needed to be the one to stop me?"

"Does it matter? I'm here."

"Yes, stars, Quill, it *matters*! Why do you always treat your life like it's a weapon you can just break off in an enemy's back?"

"Because *what else do I have to give?*" Quill lurched forward from the tree, hands smacking the icy rock beside his legs. "A pair of swords and a few augments? That wasn't enough to keep the slavers from taking Pip. It wasn't enough to keep Thorne from being whipped, or Maleck from being taken away, or Ariadne's entire life from breaking. It didn't save Baba Kallah or Julian. *It didn't save Cistine.*" He dragged a hand down his face. "I tried so stars-damned *hard*, but it's just not enough. And I'm not the loss that breaks this cabal, so I'll take the hits. Take the dangerous fights. It's what I'm good for."

Tatiana quivered with rage. "You think I wouldn't break without you?"

"Not a chance. You're stronger than I've ever been."

No compliment had ever stung so much. "Maybe I don't want to be."

A divot creased his brows. "Then why haven't you—?"

A strange, bleak comprehension dawned in his eyes. His mouth hung open; then he nodded, like all the pieces of some strange mosaic fit together in his head.

"Right." He rose, dusting off his hands. "I'm going on patrol."

"What did you just—? Quill! Stop walking away from me!" Tatiana barked at his retreating back. "That's not how we do things!"

"Yes, it is." He gestured between them. "We've been running from this our whole lives. But I finally see it...why you've never asked. Why you never wanted to try. And it's all right, I don't blame you. There's not much for you here, like I said."

Her ears turned hot. "What in the *stars* are you talking about?"

"Nothing." He slung on his swords. "Get some sleep."

She jolted to her feet, angry and frantic. "Don't you dare, Featherbrain—we're going to have this conversation!"

"What's there to say?" He looked back, sorrow creasing his brow. "We don't deserve each other, Saddlebags. This doesn't end in any way that's good for either of us."

He was gone before she could summon a retort, the way he was most nights; and now, maybe, she knew something of what he was thinking about when he left. What he was doing to himself out there in the dark.

She stared at the shadows that swallowed him, heart racing, rage hammering the backs of her teeth. How long had he been falling down this slope, and she never noticed, too focused on her own dark slide into self-loathing? She hadn't trusted him with all her heart, terrified he wouldn't be there when she needed him most...but had she been there for him?

Maybe he was right. Maybe they didn't deserve one another. Maybe this bond between them was nothing but another clever trick, a mirage dreamed by two people desperate to belong to someone and something better than themselves.

But if that was true...could they ever reach Cistine?

CHAPTER
TWENTY-SIX

SALVOTOR RESURRECTED THE spiteful shade of lavender during one dinner he didn't force Thorne to attend. Cistine was relieved at first that he wouldn't see her in tonight's attire of gathered, ruffled skirts, plunging neckline and pinned cape like lightning crackling from her shoulders. But with only Grimmaul and his men to rank her, it was worse; she had no ally, no anchor, nowhere to focus but forward, reminding herself that she was none of the things they spat toward her. She was the Key, she was a princess—and for the last several nights, she had become an explorer.

Today, with any luck, she would also no longer be alone.

Kristoff escorted her back to her room after the horrific supper and kept watch at the door while she changed. "Are you going hunting?"

"Yes. If we're right about the tunnels I've scouted so far..." her stomach wriggled with excitement at what she might find tonight. Rolling the dress in her arms, she slipped from the alcove. "Would you burn this hideous thing for me?"

Kristoff clenched the dress in his fists. "I'll keep the guards away from the prison tonight as much as I can. But go quickly. And *quietly*."

"Ha, Nadrian."

He rolled his eyes and stepped out, snaking the chain back into place. The moment it latched, Cistine returned to the alcove and retrieved her wrappings from a chink in the wall. She'd made them exactly how Quill made his, creating extra purchase with the tatters of that beaded dress Grimmaul slit from her chest. Fists wrapped, she lashed the braided rappelling rope around her hips, threaded one of the ghostlamps into her makeshift belt, and went to the trellis. What was left of the roses turned to powder under her hands as she climbed the wobbling wooden arch to the air hole. She waited for her pounding heart to slow, then lunged, gripped the lip of the rock, and hoisted herself inside the vent. The roof scraped the ridge of her spine and pressed the ghostlamp against her thigh as she crawled down the narrow passage.

The shadows pressed in like hot, heavy water, soaking her clothes in nervous sweat as she crawled past a hole that looked down into the dining hall. She took the left branch in the tunnel just past it, angling her course roughly toward the Wound.

As she inched along, the panic of entrapment in the narrow shaft dulled into the predictable thud of her heart, only leaping occasionally when her shoulders or hips snagged against the rock, her spine scraped raw through her shirt. The ghostlamp flickered when she took a new course, angling down a mouth of uncharted stone on the right.

Several minutes later, a draft touched her face; a ring of red ghostlight wormed through the narrow slit in the roof, painting small spears of rock that filtered the air through a natural current. Cistine lashed her braided belt around one of the stone teeth and shimmied down into the prison room across from Thorne's cage. Heart thundering with anticipation and relief, she freed the harness and spun toward him—then froze.

He crouched on the balls of his feet against the back wall, arms resting out on his thighs, head bowed. A dark chain wrapped across the width of the iron cell, links cloaked in augmented fire.

Come.

Cistine hesitated at that familiar whisper.

COME AND SEE.

She took an involuntary step back, a hoarse whimper sliding from her throat, and Thorne's head jerked up. He squinted at her like a mirage dancing up from the flames on the chain. "*Cistine.* How did you—?"

"Air vents." She gestured vaguely behind her. "Kristoff helped me find my way between our rooms."

Joy kindled in his eyes, but when he shifted, pain crushed it out. His eyes fluttered shut and a groan slid from his throat. Cistine darted to the cage and crouched, gripping the iron slats. "What is he doing to you?"

"The steel is reinforced. Atrasat blood—its properties are similar to ink. It bonds to the metal. The augment has nowhere to go as long as I don't lean forward."

"Maybe the whole cabal should bathe in it, then," Cistine rambled, trying desperately to distract him. "The ink, I mean. So we're never without armor."

A tired smile settled on Thorne's mouth. "They would appreciate that. Quill and Tatiana especially. Bathing in the blood of their enemies to prepare for battle."

Their names sent her heart racing. "How are they?"

"All alive, all accounted for. All afraid for you."

"Me? I'm not the one in a cage!" She wrapped her fingers around the bars. "How did Salvotor find you?"

Thorne craned his head back, but there wasn't room to rest it against the wall. He slowly snaked a hand around to rub his spine. "I was searching Azkai for you. Devitrius trapped me."

"And *defeated* you?"

He fixed her with a wry half-smile. "You'll be proud to know I *did* fend him off for a good while. It was a spectacular battle."

"Thorne..." she broke off with a sigh. There was no use trying to lecture the cabal about their battle choices. "Do you remember how he brought into the mountain?"

"A wind augment. We came in through a balcony."

Cistine moaned and pressed her head to the cage door.

"Don't do that. Look at me, Cistine." Thorne's quiet voice dragged her gaze up to him. There was no fear in his face. "We are going to walk out of this place the same way we walked from the Izten Torkat. Do you trust me?"

She clenched her hand so tightly her nails bit into her palm around the narrow iron shaft. "*Yes.*"

"Good. Then tell me what you've discovered so far."

Cistine shoved her despair into the recesses of her mind. "Besides that balcony and the air vents, there's a cellar. It's always guarded by no less than six men. I thought there might be a door down there that would lead from this place. But if that's not how they brought you in—"

"Don't be quick to dismiss it. A prisoner is one matter, but the food Salvotor served those Vassoran *bandayos* the other night wasn't something that could be hunted in the mountains." Cistine's stomach clenched at the thought of that supper, her nakedness, the things Thorne said about her; but he didn't seem inclined to revisit it, so neither did she. "They import rations from somewhere. And for that, they may have a hidden entrance Devitrius didn't want me to see. Does my uncle know what's down there?"

"No. He's never had duty inside. Only Salvotor's private retinue are allowed further than the top of the steps."

"Interesting." Thorne frowned. "I'll see what I can learn. Will you keep searching those air tunnels?"

Cistine shuddered. "And I thought *Quill* was cruel to me!"

"I can't help it if I'm too broad to fit inside."

"Well, if you weren't so ridiculously muscular..."

"You noticed that, did you?"

"It's difficult not to. How many times have I walked into your room while you were changing?"

"I knew you forgot to knock on purpose."

Cistine jutted her tongue at him. "Just for you, I'll risk all the dark, spider-infested tunnels in the world."

"Stars, I've missed you."

She stared at him across the chain, heart throbbing at the tender shift in his tone, the longing to touch him growing into the most powerful ache she'd ever felt. "I've missed you, too. You don't know how many times I've gone to the balcony on the Den in my mind just to escape this place. And somehow you're always there."

"I will *always* be where you need me, *Logandir*."

"Don't make promises like that. That was what Julian did."

Thorne hung his head. "There are...no words for how sorry I am about what happened to him. He's dead because of my grudge—my mistakes."

"That's not true. *He* made the choice to come back for me."

"That doesn't excuse my part in it. I'll spend the rest of my life atoning for it."

"Good," Cistine said fiercely, and Thorne raised his eyes again. "Because that will mean you're *alive* to atone. And I will be, too."

Thorne's gaze flickered in the ghostlight. "Not if Salvotor has his way. You shouldn't have given up that ritual, not for my sake."

"I lied. I don't know about any keying ritual. I just needed to give us enough time to escape." She rested her head against the cage bars again. "Thorne, if...if I wasn't the Key, but some other person was, would you want to use them to open the Doors, now that you know it would mean taking a life?"

"No. Not even if that life was my father's. The moment you begin to justify murder for your own gain, you've set foot down a road so dark most men never come back from it."

Relief bore breath down into her lungs, deeper and clearer than it had in weeks. "That's what I thought. I just wanted to hear you say it." She fumbled the slip of paper from her waistband and laid it out flat on the floor. "I need your help. Look at this." Thorne tilted himself to peer over the fire at her crude drawing. "I mapped the places where Kristoff thinks the tunnels intertwine. I've scouted a few already trying to find my way here, and he's been right for the most part."

"Do you have a pen?"

She slipped it from her waistband as well and shoved pen and paper carefully through the slats, under the chain, to the tip of his boot. Thorne dragged it the rest of the way up onto his knees and started sketching.

"Ariadne has a theory," he said while he worked, "that you only need half a map to construct a whole plan. I'm specifically interested in whether any of these tunnels intersect over the cellar."

"Why would a cellar need to be ventilated?"

"Why does it need six guards?" He flashed her a crooked smile.

"Fair point." She tapped her fingers on the cage bars. "If you're right, we don't need to worry about sneaking past the guards. We just need to find where the lines intersect."

Thorne toed the map back to her. "Try going straight instead of left from the dining hall next time. If you find another branching tunnel beyond that, it should cross over the cellar, given the shape of the mountain. If not, have Kristoff do some scouting. Between you two, you'll find the way."

Cistine stared at the paper until it blurred. "I can't believe we managed this. How do we *always* find a way to move forward when it feels like the gods themselves are against us?"

"Because we have each other."

Cistine stuffed the scroll into her shirt so she could grip the cage bars. "I should go. I wish we had more time."

"We will," Thorne said, "once we're free from this Nimmus-pit. Be careful, but don't be afraid."

"I *am* afraid. But that's not enough to stop me. I swore I would find a way to save our lives, and I will. This is not over."

Laughter floated down the tunnel, and she stiffened, swiveling on her heels. Thorne cursed. "Go. They check at random intervals. Go, now!"

Rocking to her feet, she held his gaze. These few pitiful minutes had not been enough; she wanted hours, she wanted days, weeks, *years*. She wanted to ask him if he meant the things he said at that humiliating dinner, and if he was really all right, with Aden alive but Baba Kallah still gone, his uncle back from the dead, the whole world in turmoil.

Next time she would make time for their hearts, not just the plan.

"I'll see you soon," she murmured.

"Not soon enough."

Three simple words. But somehow they made everything just a little more bearable.

CHAPTER TWENTY-SEVEN

THE JOURNEY NORTH from Jovadalsa was not easy or pleasant. Ashe straddled two lives: one as a Warden, familiarizing herself and her companions with the landscape, and the other as Pippet's caretaker. It was simple to ensure she was fed, that she slept enough despite the grueling pace Rion set, and that her clothing didn't tear and her feet didn't blister; it was another entirely to defend her from the Wardens' cruel banter against Valgard. Their voices dry as the Kroaken sands where they made camp every night, they told the kind of bawdy tavern jokes Ashe used to join in on, if not lead. But now she hoped neither Pippet nor Aden could hear from their own fires where they trained.

The regimen began when Aden took Pippet's knife from her the morning they left Jovadalsa. He weighed it, then asked the wide-eyed girl if she knew how to handle a blade.

"Maleck taught me how to hold Starfall and Stormfury so I don't hurt myself with them," she admitted.

"Interesting. Does your brother know?"

"No. He thinks I'm still a drooling little *tajall*."

"Because I used to call him that. I'll show you how it's done."

"Calling Quill names?"

"No. The blade."

Now he walked Pippet through basic footwork routines every night, showing her how to balance and grip the blade, how to draw it from either side of her body. Ashe sat between the fires most nights, quietly simmering; Rion's pointed glares made it obvious she hadn't earned her way back into his favor after bringing Aden along. And Pippet didn't need mothering while she learned weaponry.

This mission was her plan, yet she felt more useless than ever.

She jolted from her thoughts when Rozalie crashed down beside her, stretching and yawning. "You always sit off by yourself these days. Why not join us? There's plenty of drink."

"I don't think my presence is appreciated." Ashe tugged up dry handfuls of the malnourished grass and peered at Aden and Pippet from the corners of her eyes. He was teaching her impact and thrust tonight, correcting her footwork when she grew overeager and unbalanced herself.

Rozalie nudged shoulders with Ashe. "Lord Rion's always been...a bit difficult when plans change. But that's never seemed to bother you before."

"I've never sided with a Valgardan over him."

"True." Rozalie cocked her head. "But you're doing what you believe is best for the Princess. He can't hold that against you when we find her."

"*If* we do." Every mile toward Aden's informant in the north seemed to stretch unnaturally long. Some part of Ashe regretted all the time wasted traveling to Talheim; if she and Aden had begun this search the night she left Hellidom, would they have reached Cistine already?

"We have to," Rozalie said firmly. "You and I made a pact, remember?"

"No more stolen girls sold to bidders." She leaned her shoulder back into Rozalie's. "Is that why you came along on this mission?"

"Actually, Lord Rion didn't give me much choice. He said bringing the Princess home from where she wasn't supposed to be was the perfect opportunity to face my own past. If I don't, I'll always be just the farm girl stolen from her parents and sold to the brothels."

Ashe's jaw tightened. "You're *much* more than that, regardless of the missions you take. And he damned well knows it."

Rozalie shrugged. "He's the one who led the raid on that brothel. He knows me better than anyone."

"He led the raid. *I* pulled you out. You don't have to go back to those places to conquer them."

"Maybe. Maybe not." Rozalie strung her arms a bit more tightly around her knees. "But you *did* pull me out, Ashe, which is why I know we're going to bring Cistine home, no matter what. I trust Lord Rion. And I know what we're capable of."

So did Ashe; all the many horrors and all the ways she was capable of failing.

She glanced at Aden and Pippet again just as the girl lunged forward, stabbing dramatically with her blade. Her feet slipped, and Aden swung his arms around both of hers, pinning her against his chest and digging his fingers into her sides until she thrashed and shrieked with laughter, begging for mercy.

Something cracked in Ashe's chest at the sound; desperation trickled through her, a yearning for that closeness, for hands on her arms propping her up instead of striking out in fury, for eyes that looked at her warmly rather than with disappointment or a challenge or rage or *heartbreak*—

"*Ashe.*" Rozalie elbowed her. "Are you listening? Do you want to come drink with us or not?"

"Not tonight." She peeled to her feet and went to Aden and Pippet's fire instead.

Pippet wrenched free at Ashe's arrival and plowed into her, grinning. "Did you see me? Did you see how I *parried?*"

"I saw how Aden nearly put you on your backside." Ashe ruffled her hair. "He has a habit of doing that."

"Anytime you begin to miss the feeling," Aden said, "I welcome the challenge."

Hot sand and desert air and blood and venom. "Someday, maybe."

Aden sheathed his dagger. "That's enough for tonight, Pippet." She let go of Ashe and returned her own knife to its scabbard with a cold somberness just like his.

"How much farther to your contact's home?" Ashe asked.

Aden squinted up at the darkening sky, then spanned his fingers at the first flickering stars just as he'd done every evening since Jovadalsa. "A week at most with the pace we've set."

"Are you doing that to look wise and mysterious? Showing off for Pippet?"

She giggled, and Aden scoffed. "I've been called many things, but never those. This is wayfinding—charting one's place in the world by the stars, the sun, and the moon."

Ashe let Pippet pull her down by the fire, warming their hands. "Who taught you that?"

"My father. And I taught it to Thorne. The first Valgardans found their way by following the stars...and if you believe the old epics, the Wayfinders illuminated their way south from those same stars to choose the traitor who saved the land."

A traitor who saved everyone. It was a fine story; Ashe almost wished she could believe in it.

Pippet leaned suddenly against her side, wrapping both arms around one of hers. "Stay with us tonight, Ashe? I miss hearing you sing. Did you know Aden likes music, too?"

"My mother played," he said when Ashe shot him a raised-brow look. "What instrument?"

"Piano, mostly. She taught Maleck. It helped him after the war."

"I played violin," Ashe said. "One of the few things my parents and I agreed I should pursue."

"Will you play me a song someday?" Pippet begged.

"I haven't touched an instrument in years." Ashe poked her side. "I was too busy keeping *another* mouthy girl alive."

Pippet laughed, burrowing into Ashe's side, and she looped an arm around her shoulders.

All at once, the hair on her nape stood at attention. She twisted to look over her shoulder.

Rion watched her through the tall flames of the Wardens' fire, his eyes hooded and mouth downturned. Displeasure radiated from him as clearly as if he shouted at her, demanding to know what she was doing.

Cistine was in danger by Valgardan hands. Why was Ashe laughing and teasing other Valgardans around a fire like they were on a training excursion to the Calaluns?

She tugged free and got to her feet, cold at once in the absence of the fire. "I should take watch. Maybe I'll sing to you some other time, Pippet." The girl pouted, but she didn't protest.

"Care for company?" Aden's question was innocent enough, but he stared past her at Rion.

Ashe set her jaw. She wouldn't be prey caught between them. "I think I can manage one patrol by myself."

Ignoring his pointed glance, she stalked away from both fires, losing herself in the shadows of the quickly-falling night.

The augmented tundra spread out around Ashe, fanning further and further with each step she took. Darkness collided with the silvery terrain at the lips of the horizon, shadows guzzling the light. She couldn't run fast enough to escape what was coming.

The wind shoved her like a hand to the shoulders, and she tumbled to the boggy ground, rolling over to stare at the shadowed figure that pursued her, sword upraised, silver light licking the razor edge.

Meszaros.

When Ashe screamed the word, he lunged to silence her. His weight pinned her to the sand, four clawed feet against her abdomen. Viperwolf teeth closed around her throat, venom pumping into her blood while she screamed, thrashed, cried out for help, yelled for Aden, Cistine, *Maleck*—

"*Ashe*! Ashe, wake up!"

She jolted to consciousness, gasping, grabbing the scar across her stomach. There was no bright desert light, no bog or ice, no sword-wielding shadows or Viperwolves; the weight on her chest was a pair of hands, not claws. Pippet's face separated from the shadows, eyes wide and shocked. "It's all right! It was just a bad dream!"

Ashe yanked herself up on the Kroaken sands, casting her gaze wildly across the horizon. Both fires had died, only the moonlight rimming the world. She'd fallen asleep on patrol like a new Cadre recruit.

Pippet rested a hand on her cheek, turning Ashe's focus back. Her smile was crooked, wobbly, but full of hope that Ashe had returned to her. "I'm here, see? You're not alone."

Ashe's tight jaw and gritted teeth weren't enough to tame the strangled breath of sound battling free from her chest. Pippet surged forward and wrapped her arms around Ashe's neck, and she clung to the girl's solid warmth—more tangible than memories of the Hive, more real than any nightmare. Pippet's chest vibrated with a quiet hum; a Talheimic lullaby on Valgardan lips, and somehow she made it belong. Weakness fractured through Ashe's bones, and she slumped, holding Pippet tightly against her.

Deliberate footsteps brushed the sand, and Aden emerged from the dark, tossing his blanket around Pippet. "We'll sit the watch with you."

"Rion won't approve."

"I don't give a damn what he approves." Aden sat with his back against hers. "He isn't here."

He was right. Though her shouting and thrashing must've woken the other Wardens, no one else came but them. Punishment for tonight; if she was going to laugh around the fire with Valgardans, she'd be left to their company—and only theirs.

Ashe's shoulders slumped into Aden's. She slammed her head against the hinge of his neck and shut her eyes; behind the flickering lids, *Meszaros* stalked the shadows, dragging a shiver from her.

Pippet curled in Ashe's lap, head against her shoulder. "Do you want me to tell you a story Cistine made up about Tazra?"

Ashe swallowed. Aden said, "I would."

And to the steady cadence of his breaths rising and falling against her back and the dips and peaks of Pippet's voice while she told the story, Ashe hovered on the threshold of sleep and waking, the edge of peace and terror— the verge of two lives, uncertain of which one she belonged to anymore.

CHAPTER TWENTY-EIGHT

SILENCE, COLDER THAN the barren rock around them, continued between Tatiana and Quill as the days dragged on. This chasm was uncharted land; even when they argued about her drinking or his risks, they never went quiet. It weighed on Tatiana's back, heavier than any weapon sling or satchel, making the perilous trek that much harder.

She wasn't even angry with him—not really. She just didn't know what to say with all the truths between them. She was a tinker's daughter, but what if nothing she did was ever good enough to help mend this—mend *him*? What if he didn't believe he could be mended, or didn't want to fix the way he saw himself—the way he thought *she* saw him?

These thoughts haunted her on patrol every night, before the blackest hours when she shook Quill awake to take over. She had gone up into these mountains believing it was Cistine who needed saving; but how could she save her, and also mend Quill *and* herself?

It was a burden too great to bear, setting every nerve singing with dread that only deepened one morning when they rounded a bend in the latest high-walled stone pass to find their way blocked by a tumble of rock. Fresh by the life of the trees wedged among its fissures, it filled the gap from wall to wall.

They halted, side-on to a slope where tall pines gave way to bare saplings hugging the shore of a broad, frozen lake below. The great horns of another whitecapped mountain range rose beyond it. A necklace of pine and spruce hung at the base of those heights across the lakeshore, twinkling emeralds pearled with newly-fallen snow.

But before them, there was nothing but dark rock and uprooted trees.

Tatiana's breath tumbled out. "Well, *damn*."

"No way through." Quill skimmed his hand over the fallen rocks. "This couldn't have happened more than a day ago. Why didn't we hear it come down?"

There was no point telling him she was so deep in her mind, she would've been caught unawares by a bear rampaging into their camp. "Let's just be glad it fell *before* we walked by. Knowing our luck lately..."

Quill's hand swung back to his side. "It almost looks like an earth augment did it."

Tatiana's nape prickled. "Here? Why?"

"I don't know." He backstepped to her side, never taking his gaze from the rocks. "Lake?"

She picked up a chunk of stone and hurled it onto the ice below. It struck and thrummed—deep. "Sounds stable."

Quill finally tore his eyes from the pass. "Should we cross it?"

She gritted her teeth, wishing he'd make an actual suggestion rather than asking her. "That lake probably stretches into Oadmark. We might go days out of our way."

"Right. But we don't want to waste an augment on this, do we? Unless you think—"

"Oadmark it is," she snapped, hefting her satchel higher and sliding down the slope to the shore. Quill landed beside her, dusting off his hands, and Tatiana led the way onto the ice.

They walked for some time in the shadow of the high walls framing the pass. She couldn't see an end to the snaking height of sheer, icy rock, or any place where they could curve back around inside Valgard's borders; they might follow this spine of rock for days before it tapered off.

Snow crunched. The wind whispered across the open lake.

"I hate this," Quill burst out suddenly. "Stars damn it!"

"It's just a few more days."

"Not that." Quill cursed under his breath. "This. Us. It's not you I'm mad at, Saddlebags, it's—"

"Yourself?"

He scratched under his hair. "Sometimes I say things I don't mean. We should just forget about it—forget what I said that night. It's not important."

"Nice try. You're not getting out of this one." She snagged his shoulder, towing him to a halt. "Quill, listen to me…no one in this cabal is more important than you. No one is less, either. We all carry the burden, we all save each other. Isn't that what Sillakove stands on?"

"Maybe. But I wasn't there when it mattered. I didn't protect Cistine, and—"

The snap of a bowstring. The whistle of an arrow on the wind.

Cursing, Quill drove into Tatiana with his shoulder, slamming them both down on the ice. It creaked under their weight as they spun apart, scrambling to their hands and knees, looking back the way they came.

A line of Vassora fanned across the snow-dusted ice, led by the man who'd watched them in that bazaar alcove.

Tatiana gained her feet, hands rattling. Quill was right; that wasn't a natural landslide. Nor had she imagined they were being followed all this time.

"There's nowhere to flee," the leader called. "If you run, we will fire on you. Spare your own hides…come quietly with us back to Stornhaz."

"Isn't this a bit out of the way to make an arrest?" Quill's tone was casual, but tension banded his limbs when he stood. "Must be hefty charges."

"Sedition against Kanslar Court. Chancellor Salvotor has declared your capture of utmost importance."

Tatiana shot a glance around the lake. They'd chosen their place of attack perfectly; there was no cover here, nowhere to go but straight across the lake or back to the Vassora's waiting hands. She had her knives and sabers, her armor, her flagons of fire, water, wind, and healing inside her satchel.

She flicked a glance at Quill, his fingers already grazing his own flagons. He couldn't use his fire augment; the moment he did, the ice would turn to freezing water.

Wind. Lightning. That was all he had.

Not the best odds. But for their own sakes and Cistine's, they couldn't afford to turn themselves over.

Quill shot her one glance and dipped his head.

The Vassoran leader brought the covering back up over his nose and mouth, freed an augment of his own and broke it against his chest. At his shout, a storm of arrows broke across the sky. Tatiana snatched out a wind flagon and shattered it, hurling a shield of roaring wind around them. The arrows crumbled against it, but the snow it kicked up became a blinding gale; in dim flickers of shadows beyond, the Vassora closed in around them.

"Quill!" Tatiana shouted.

He unleashed the lightning augment in a whip of raw purple-white power, blasting through the snow and knocking two Vassora off their feet; but a third dodged and rolled, augment cracking, his violent gale slamming into Tatiana's in a swirling maelstrom. Cursing, she bolted straight toward him, dropping at the last moment and sliding between his feet. Before he could turn on her, she was up, slicing his neck with her knife.

In the tight quarters, augments were far less useful, and Tatiana's knives were reliable, ruthless friends. The ice and snow ran scarlet; sweat and blood dripped into her eyes and mouth as she punched, kicked, stabbed, and shoved between the guards. Most crumbled before her, just like every caravan raid, the battle in Stornhaz, the day she sacked Detlyse Halet; but one broke past her, dodging her singing steel on the way to bring Quill down.

Without pausing to think, Tatiana hurled her knives into his back and flung herself on their leader, stealing his attention and twisting away when he hurled the last gust of wind toward her instead of Quill. But she wasn't quick enough; the gale slammed into her lower body, knocking her legs from beneath her, ripping her saber harness and supply satchel from her body and sending them soaring into the trees on the shoreline.

The guard grabbed Tatiana's throat in one hand, slammed her to her back on the ice, and drew a fire flagon from the pouch on his hip. His furious eyes promised he would do it; he'd send them both to the depths before he let her escape.

Panic coated her throat. Quill bellowed her name. The guard smashed his flagon against his wrist.

The fire was gone.

Gone, because Quill was there, catching the augment before it fully ignited, bringing it into himself with one hand and launching himself away from them in a deft handspring, all in the same heartbeat.

The fire coated his body. His eyes met hers, just for an instant.

The ice turned to vapor beneath him. He plunged into the water.

CHAPTER
TWENTY-NINE

T ATIANA'S HEART STOPPED beating while she stared at the water sloshing in the mouth of the jagged crescent where Quill had dropped, waiting for him to reappear.

He didn't.

A wild, mighty strength possessed her body. With a feral shout, she grabbed the guard's wrist, broke it in a sideways snap, and kicked him away, then drove her knee into his chin so hard his neck crunched. She freed the last augment from his belt and broke it in her hands, casting it out with a sweep of her arm.

Ravaging darkness slammed into the last of the Vassora. Tatiana yanked her knives from the dead guard's back and hurtled into the shadows.

It was over in seconds. They couldn't see her, but she'd marked their positions when she dispatched the augment. Three corpses dropped to the ice, one after the other, and Tatiana soaked the darkness back into her armor and sent it skittering out in tendrils over the hole where Quill now clung with folded arms, his chin on his wrist. He shook violently, his face gaunt from chaining augments back-to-back.

"Careful—careful!" he wheezed when she ran toward him, sliding a hand up to halt her. "The...ice is...is thinner here. From the heat." His breaths were too fast, indeliberate, his eyes glassy with panic.

Tatiana dropped to her knees and eased herself toward him, distributing her weight as carefully as possible. Her pulse lunged when the ice creaked and groaned underneath her.

"Tati, stop!" Quill choked.

A web of cracks spidered beneath her body. She halted, forcing her eyes back to his. "You have to pull yourself out."

"Tried," he rattled out. "Can't."

"You don't know the meaning of that word!"

He coughed, spasmed, and his grip on the ice buckled. He slid backward into the hole.

Shouting, Tatiana lunged forward, grabbing for him. She caught his hand, but it slid from hers, leaving just his glove limp in her fingers. Tatiana dropped it and clutched the edges of the hole instead, searching the murky water desperately for Quill, *her* Quill—

A flash of pale hair, the sleek slide of armor. He was trapped under the ice shelf.

Bellowing, Tatiana pushed herself away from the hole, braced her weight on her hands, and slammed her heel into the brittle ice with all her might. Four swift strikes in the same place seemed to take a lifetime to land; then the weakened shelf caved and the curve of Quill's back slid to the surface. She skittered forward, slung an arm under his chest and towed his deadweight from the water, sliding along the creases in the ice until it steadied beneath them again. Then she laid him out on his back, grabbed the collar of his armor, and laid her cheek over his face.

He wasn't breathing.

"Don't you *dare!*" She grabbed his knees and thrust them to his chest; his body slid listlessly under her ministrations, head lolling. No signs of life.

Cursing, she forced him onto his side, jammed his knees up to his chest, and slammed her hand against his back at the same time. "Breathe! *Breathe*, Quill, don't you leave me in this stars-damned wasteland alone!"

He couldn't do this, couldn't abandon her like this, after *everything*.

Another blow of legs-to-chest, shoving his body along the ice. "*Nightwing, breathe!*"

At the sound of his Name—at the next slam of rough motion to his chest, stomach, and lungs—he heaved in a breath, retched, and vomited onto the ice. Panting senseless prayers, Tatiana crawled to his head, stretching her body against his and pulling him to rest his soaked hair against her chest while he hacked, spewing lake water from his nostrils.

What had Maleck and Baba Kallah taught her about this? Her mother had been a medico—what did all her old books say?

Clothes off. He needed fresh, dry threads...but where in Nimmus was she going to find anything like that? A fire would help; there was shelter, trees on the other side of the lake. If they stayed here, other Vassora might come, divided like in the Izten Torkat. She couldn't take that chance.

"Get up." She wrapped an arm around Quill's shoulders and propped him on his seat. He shuddered and vomited again. "Quill, get on your feet!"

"Can't feel them," he groaned.

Fighting her own shakes, Tatiana took his one bare hand, pulled his arm across her shoulders, and heaved him up. He bore almost none of his own weight while she dragged him across the barren lake to the opposite shore, up a steep slope and down into a deer-bedding hollow beyond. She couldn't remember him ever being this heavy—or maybe he'd never been hurt enough to lean on her this much.

She slammed down another trill of panic. This was *Quill*. He'd be fine once she got him warmed up.

Pausing to catch her breath, she looked around the rutting hollow, searching for a next step, a place to build a fire—and hesitated, gaze drawn to the lick of sunlight along icicles over a stone overhang to their left.

"Cave," she muttered, hauling him toward it.

The squat, deep hollow was mercifully dry, faintly musty, and clearly lived-in at one time—not by animals. A tarred crate stretched along one wall, an old firepit took up the center, and a few hewn monoliths framed the mouth to deter predators from bedding down inside. Best of all, there was a small heather nest at the back. She dumped Quill into it, and he groaned, rolling onto his back, teeth chattering.

"Just...let me sleep this off," he begged while she yanked away his boots.

"I'm feeling warmer already."

She'd heard him lie through his gritted teeth about pain too many times to be fooled by his show of bravado. "Take off your armor." She went to the chest and kicked it open, plundering the contents with shaking hands. "Holy stars! The gods still love us, Featherbrain, look! Furs, knives, snowshoes, water..." Her fingers encountered a familiar, bloated vessel, and froze.

A wineskin.

She cleared her throat. "No food, but I don't know about you, I'm not really hungry." Tugging out a heavy deer hide, she turned back to the nest to find Quill blinking sluggishly at her. His chest rattled with every breath.

"I could...use some help."

Hands threatening to shake, she jerked the wet shirt over his head, peeled off his trousers, freed the scarf that guarded his nose and mouth from augments, and took off his remaining glove. Then she hurled the hide over his body, crouched between his knees, and rubbed her hands furiously up and down his limbs. "You aren't safe yet. You could still die if you're warmed inappropriately."

He mustered a white-lipped smirk. "Does all—all this rubbing count as *inappropriate warming?*"

"I'm going to break your fingers and toes off."

"I'm not sure I'd mind, given how they feel right now."

His pain stabbed into her chest like it was her own, his dull groan when she helped him lie down jabbing blade-sharp into her chest. "Why did you steal the fire augment from that guard? You knew what would happen."

"I did."

"Then what were you thinking, Quill? You almost died!"

"So did you."

His voice was shaky, quiet, his eyes fluttering shut.

Tatiana slowed her ministrations, taking care of every scar she knew was sensitive, every patch of skin that had healed wrong from fights against the Vassora and animal attacks in the wilds around Hellidom. After all these years, fighting and playing deftly around one another, she knew the terrain of his body almost as well as her own.

Finally, when his horrific shivers eased and his rattling breaths fell to unconsciousness, she stretched out beside him and draped her arm over his chest. As long he didn't wake anytime soon, there was nothing it could hurt. Hadn't she read somewhere that it was good to share bodily warmth if someone was too cold?

Maybe that was part of some old Valgardan romance tale. But even so.

She rested her head over his staggering heart and shut her eyes. Behind them, she saw him fall again, the water surging over his head—a blow taken for her.

Tears slipped down the bridge of her nose. In the distance, a frostwolf howled.

Tatiana felt very, very much alone.

CHAPTER THIRTY

THROUGH A CAST of embers floating high on the chilly wind, Ashe spread her fingertips toward the frigid, distant taunts of starlight, trying to measure the distance left to conquer. They'd reached Nordbran's border at last, tawny dunes slowly grading into red sands. Four days to go, by Aden's measurements. He and Pippet had gone to retrieve kindling from the foothills of the lower Isetfell Mountains, a dark finger of jagged rock at the horizon, leaving Ashe alone at her own small fire.

She'd chosen loneliness frequently as her nightmares worsened. Better that than waking in cold sweats with the other Wardens' concerned gazes on her; better than Rion's unrelenting anger, the pain of being unable to please him even as her choices brought them closer and closer to finding Cistine. No matter what, she just couldn't win.

Footsteps shifted the sand, and Viktor, Lydie, Andrej, and Petra joined her; Lydie carried a flask, sipping while she stood across the lonely fire. Ashe's gut clenched with unease. "Was there something you wanted?"

"Well, you see," Andrej drawled. "We've told all the good stories around our own campfires already."

"And you always have the best ones," Petra chirped.

Viktor snatched the flask from Lydie, downed a long swallow, and flopped next to Ashe, offering it. "So. Tell us about Valgard."

"What do you want to know that you haven't seen with your own eyes?"

"Something has to account for all *this*." Viktor brushed two fingers on a scar traveling up the side of her neck to her hairline.

Ashe looked northwest across the flat expanse of the horizon. Every day, she hunted for a trace of Siralek's shape in the distance; and every time a mirage of high ellipticals and white stone shimmered in the midday heat, her heart faltered. "I was a prisoner—a fighter in an arena called Siralek. We entertained the elite and the desert nomads."

Petra cursed. "You're joking!"

"I knew Valgard was brutal," Andrej said, "but *that*..."

"What did you fight?" Lydie's eyes rounded in morbid fascination.

"What *didn't* I fight? Dahadts, Viperwolves, desert scorpions...serpents as large as a house..." A memory slashed across her mind: Briet, a girl around Cistine's age, forced into the arena's melee with Ashe and Aden and the other sponsored fighters. Ashe had felt compelled to keep her alive as long as possible, fighting that great serpent to save her—only to watch her trampled to death a moment later.

She took a long drink.

"What about the Valgardans?" Viktor prodded. "Did you fight *them*?"

"Plenty." Ashe wiped her mouth on her wrist. "There was a melee between special fighters. I killed..."

So many. She'd never tried to count. The horror of that day was a blur, most of it eclipsed by the riots, their escape, and Maleck—

The next drink stopped an uneasy anguish churning in her core.

"I would've liked to be there," Viktor said. "A few months in chains would be worth it for the chance to kill as many of these rat-eaters as I wanted."

Ashe raised a brow. "Still using that same tired insult?"

"He never shuts up about it," Petra said. "This is his latest joke: Where do you find gourmet Valgardan cuisine?"

"In the gutter!" Lydie and Andrej chorused, and Viktor roared with laughter. But Ashe tasted blueberry and walnut bread and orange scones on the back of her tongue, hot tea and mountain meadow air, braised fish shared around a table with tentative allies, and her ears warmed.

"Here's another!" Viktor wiped his eyes. "A Valgardan, a Talheimic, and a Mahasari walk into a tavern. The Talheimic orders a mead because he's smart, the Mahasari orders water because he think it's desert gold, and the Valgardan says, *I'll just follow you to the privy to fill my cup.*"

Lydie sobbed with laughter and Petra hung off Andrej's shoulder, beating his thigh with her fist. Ashe smirked down at the flask, but shame rubbed the back of her neck.

"One more!" Andrej gasped. "One more. Do you know the real reason Valgardan men were so obsessed with the wells? Because those were the only holes they were being let into!"

Face hot, Ashe looked away while her companions fell into fits of intoxicated giggles. But she could only turn so far, and then Viktor's arm dropped across her shoulders, pulling her to lean against his side. "One drink for every well-licker you killed in that arena." He pried the flask from her hand and raised it high. "To Asheila Kovar: doing the King's work even in captivity."

"To Ashe!" the others cried, and she pretended she couldn't feel blood on her hands when she smiled at them.

"Tell us more about the prison," Viktor urged, wiping his mouth on his sleeve. "Is that what keeps waking you up every night?"

Ashe measured him with a long stare. His concern sounded sincere, but warning still rang in her chest. "There's nothing more to say. I was caught protecting the princess. They threw me in the Blood Hive. I escaped."

"*The Blood Hive.* Could these Valgardans be any more dramatic?" Lydie rolled her eyes. "What's the harm in something just having a simple name? It's not as if we have to give sixteen different titles to the Calalun Peaks. They're just *the Calaluns.*"

"Names are important in Valgard." Maleck's words rolled off her tongue, stories he told her when she grudgingly followed him on patrols in Starhollow to keep her leg fit. "They name their weapons, their people each have a secret Name given by their Chancellors—"

"They name their weapons...you mean not as a joke?" Viktor snorted. "What a bunch of pretentious rot. And *these* were the people the gods gave the wells to? Pathetic."

Ashe eyed him sideways. "I thought the point of the war was to temper a power *no* one should have...no matter which kingdom they come from."

"Obviously. I'm only saying, between the three kingdoms, at least we Talheimics have our armor on properly."

"So, this Blood Hive," Andrej said. "What was it like?"

Ashe swallowed around a lump in her throat. "Dry. Dark. *Hot.* Full of too many bodies stacked together. Never a moment's peace."

"Just like the rest of Valgard, then," Petra snickered.

Ashe stared into the flames until their shade blurred into red sand and mirages fishtailing in the sunlight. "It wasn't what was above the sand we hated. It was what was below it...the catacombs. One of the old Hive Lords decorated his walls with the skulls of every dead fighter."

"Sounds brutal. How did you keep from going mad in that place?" Andrej demanded.

"Cistine," Ashe said after a beat. "I knew I had to return to her, whatever it cost me."

But that was only half the truth; there were moments where the thought of Cistine wasn't enough through glimpses of death around catacomb corners and in the haze of steam on the bloodstained sand. What had pulled her out then?

A hand jamming her dislocated shoulder into place. Nights running through the arena. Meals untainted by poison. A mirage in the sand, a voice telling her to rise, to get up, to take two more steps. Just two more.

"I understand how you felt about getting back to Cistine," Andrej's voice drew her from her reverie. "The sooner we take her back home where she belongs, the better off the whole kingdom will be."

Ashe's discomfort cooled into irritation. "What do you mean?"

"Well, we all love the princess," Lydie said, "but she has *no* experience with negotiations. She belongs in the Citadel."

"And even if she was a renowned liaison," Viktor added, "Valgard can't be reasoned with. They're like untrained dogs. The best you can do is bring them to heel with a flash of your hand. But more likely, you need the cane. These rat-eaters will never listen to someone like her."

"Someone *like her*," Ashe growled. "You'll want to qualify that remark before you taste my knuckles, Pollack."

At her careful stress on his family name, Viktor's arm dropped. "You've said it yourself, Ashe."

"Said *what*?"

"A few drinks deep, and you start complaining about how the princess can be so lazy and absorbed with her comforts," Lydie said. "We all know how beautiful her heart is, how open she is to the people, but..."

"But that isn't the kind of person who can convince a kingdom of barbarians to follow her," Viktor concluded.

Ashe's skin crawled. She'd vented those things over mugs of ale after particularly frustrating days guarding Cistine; she hadn't expected the Wardens to fashion their image of her from those few complaints.

"Anyway," Andrej said when the silence scaled long and uneasy. "All I'm saying is, the sooner this is over, the better for everyone, not just her. This journey is making the Commander uneasy. If that Valgardan doesn't deliver, it's going to be a fight."

"I'm sick of fighting," Ashe snapped, drawing their wide eyes back to her. "The wrong people keep getting killed."

"What do you mean, the *wrong* people?" Petra demanded. "You were saving your own life in that arena...what could be wrong about that?"

Baba Kallah and Helga's faces flashed through her tipsy mind, and she sucked in her breath, swaying to her feet. The spirits were already moving quickly through her blood, setting the desert swirling. "I need to...patrol."

"Easy, Kovar!" Viktor grabbed her wrist. "Symon and Rozalie are handling that."

"Don't go, Ashe, please!" Petra begged. "We've missed you."

Viktor's hand moved down to wrap around hers. "*Very* much." She yanked free again, and he came to his feet to clasp her shoulder this time. "What's the matter with you tonight?"

Knuckles slammed skin, and Viktor fell on his haunches, spitting out a tooth as Aden loomed up beside Ashe. Pippet, arms laden with firewood, gaped in his shadow. "Lay a hand on her again without her consent, and I will snap it off and feed it to you."

The Wardens lunged to their feet, hands to their weapons, and Ashe spanned her arms. "Stop! *Do not* start a fight over this."

"You're asking us not to retaliate when a Valgardan hits one of our own?" Petra roared. "Savage, limp-shafted well-rat—"

"*Enough!*" Ashe glanced at Pippet's scarlet face. "Not in front of her."

Viktor staggered up, thumbing blood from the corner of his mouth. "You're going to wish you'd never done that."

"The gods themselves couldn't make me."

"*Aden.*" Ashe gripped his arm, wrenching him back. "Leave it alone."

With a long look into her face, Aden receded, turning to Pippet and lifting the firewood from her arms. Andrej muttered a parting insult about Aden's anatomy and parentage that made even Ashe's heart skip with disgust. Aden froze, reading Pippet's mortified stare; Ashe stepped into Andrej's face. "If you ever say anything like that again, I'll nail your tongue to a tree with my knife."

Before their looks of scathing disbelief could find a home under her skin, Ashe yanked half the bundle of firewood from Aden's grip and led him and Pippet away.

"You didn't have to threaten them on my account," Aden said when they passed out of hearing.

"And you didn't have to punch Viktor on mine." Ashe glanced at him, then fixed her gaze ahead. "It wasn't just for you. I'm sorry you had to hear that, Pippet."

She scowled over her shoulder. "Helga would've made them wash their mouths out with soap."

Ashe met Aden's eyes, and at the thought of sweet, sturdy Helga prying open the Wardens' mouths and cramming a soap bar inside, they burst into side-splitting laughter.

CHAPTER THIRTY-ONE

For the first time in weeks, Cistine walked to the dining hall with her head high. Kristoff's presence was a small comfort at her back, a shield from the lewd remarks her latest attire accrued. She hadn't paid attention to the dress and she fought to pay no heed to their remarks about it now; she kept her gaze forward and her mind ahead.

Just one more meal, and she could explore the roof tunnels again. She silently recited the location of every vent and the distance from her room to where Thorne suspected the cellar would be as she stepped into the dining hall's boisterous chatter. Salvotor, Grimmaul and his retinue, and a bound but ungagged Thorne awaited her, and she flashed a half-smirk at the High Tribune. The corner of his mouth curled in reply; the memory of their unescorted meeting at the cage hung in the space between their smiles.

"Why don't you sit here tonight?" Salvotor gestured to the seat on his left hand, directly across from Thorne—the closest he ever made her come. She strode past the flock of Vassoran guards, their eyes and whistles floating on her heels. The arch of Thorne's shoulders hardened, and Cistine shook her head.

Kristoff was right. They just had to take these blows.

The dinner passed unremarkably, which was in itself remarkable; even the provoking looks and comments from Grimmaul did little to rouse her anger. She had a mission tonight, a goal of subversion their taunts broke easily against. With her platter clean, Cistine started to rise, eager to end this meal and begin her plan.

"Do you really believe it's wise to leave Thorne and I unsupervised?" Salvotor asked calmly.

Thorne's hand tightened around his fork, metal bending in the ghostlight. Slowly, Cistine sank back down.

"That's a good girl. Good, but foolish. That's quite the tether you have on this boy." He flicked a hand at Thorne, who tossed his fork down. "He doesn't seem quick to leap to your defense...no more than he was for the last woman he professed himself devoted to."

Cistine hunted under the table with her foot and pressed down on Thorne's boot with all her might. She didn't need him to rise to her defense, to lash out and bring down punishment on them. He'd come farther and risked more than anyone ever had on her behalf. Salvotor couldn't call that loyalty into question.

When neither of them reacted to his taunts, Salvotor stood abruptly and came to Cistine's seat, pushed it out, and took her face in one hand, guiding her upright before him. "All these lengths you've gone to, even sacrificing your own life through the ritual to save my son's. If I were a decent man, I would warn you he's not worth it. You were better off with the Butcher's son."

"I'm not searching for someone to save my life," Cistine hissed. "I'm looking for someone to share it with."

"Sentimental, but I doubt the feeling is mutual. You were only bait to him, as I recall."

Cistine hung a smile on shaking lips. "If you knew how deeply mutual it was, you wouldn't sleep at night."

Salvotor's eyes flickered. He let go of her face, stepped around the table, and in one deft jerk of his arm, slammed Thorne against the seatback with an elbow to the throat. He doubled up, retching and gasping, the sound a blade piercing straight to Cistine's core. She grabbed the table's edge—then froze.

Take the blows. Take the blows.

Thorne's eyes fixed on her, glassy with pain, his hand circling the red welt already blooming on his neck.

Punishment. Her fault.

"So much for mutual loyalty," Salvotor sneered. "All for the best, I suppose...you wouldn't want to betray Julian's memory *too* soon. Take my son back to his cage."

They dragged Thorne from the room before Cistine could gather enough breath to apologize, to plead for him—to make things worse with her brazen need to defy. The only small mercy was that Kristoff returned the same moment Salvotor left, so Cistine was not alone for even one moment in Grimmaul's leering presence.

She didn't speak again until she sat on her bed, pajamas donned. Kristoff folded his arms and leaned against the door. "What happened?"

"He hit Thorne." She squeezed her eyes shut against the echoing snap of impact, the sound of Thorne's gasping. "Because I couldn't keep my mouth closed."

"Salvotor craves the excuse for violence. That he goads you so hard is a sign you've done well so far."

"But tonight, I didn't." Cistine stared at her hands. She might as well have thrown that blow herself. "Maybe I shouldn't go. If he learns what I'm doing in the vents..."

"Cistine." Kristoff lurched up from the door. "Do not let him win this fight."

She stared at him, his chest barely rising and falling, tense shoulders straining at his armor. Of course he didn't want her to back away now...whatever was in that cellar might be the path to returning to his sons.

It might be the only way to spare Thorne from worse suffering.

She steeled herself and sat taller. "Will you go to Thorne, make sure he's all right? And tell him..." her voice broke. "Tell him I'm sorry. That I won't take the challenge next time."

Kristoff's adamant eyes softened. "Of course I will."

The moment he shut and chained the door, she was up, grabbing her hand-wraps and clipping the ghostlamp to her hip.

Tonight, the fizzing in her core almost passed for excitement when she shimmied down the tight confines over the dining hall. She would call this retribution for Salvotor's blow; if he struck them, they would strike back twice as hard, in all his softest parts.

She counted the distance to a new tunnel branch, just as Thorne predicted—and took it, veering away from the vents she knew.

For some time she crawled in weak, wavering lavender light, eyes fixed forward so the blush-purple ripples along the walls wouldn't remind her of lightning, of Julian, of *betraying his memory*. The swish of blood in her ears was the only sound for the time, her pajamas hardly whispering on the smoother, wider shaft here—carrying air away from somewhere larger than a small chamber or prison room.

She reached her arms out to drag herself the next few feet, and plunged her fingers into nothingness instead.

Scuttling backward, she fumbled the ghostlamp free and held it aloft. There it was, right where they marked it on their guesswork map—a wide hole once again rimmed in jagged, filtering spires.

The opening to the cellar.

Cistine dragged herself forward to look down. A pool of undisturbed blackness yawned below, barely cut by the ghostlight painting against stalactite fangs. There was no telling what waited at the bottom—but no sense waiting any longer.

She lashed her rope belt over the vent spines and shimmied down into darkness, the weak array of lavender around her a lonely, sole source of light. Her slippers found the floor and she raised the ghostlamp high, but it shed little definition over the darkness. She wondered if this was what the dark places between stars felt like, ashy and empty and cold.

Despair settled deep beneath her navel. This place felt worse than any other part of the temple, like a true prison. A part of her wanted to escape up the rope and forget she ever found this hole; but her raging curiosity peaked like a wave, forcing her body away from the moorings of safety and into doubt.

She walked, one hand braced to her right, one before her, stalagmites brushing her fingertips as she wove deeper into the cellar-cave. Even in the dark, she felt how vast this place was; the thin echo of her breaths, the darkness swallowing the tap of her feet. Somewhere in this expanse, there *must* be a way out...and if she kept walking, she might find it *now*. There might be a means of escape just out of reach.

Her feet quickened, the closest she dared to a jog in the unbroken blackness, hands outstretched and ghostlight bouncing wildly around her. Stalagmites jutted in her path and fell behind, jutted and fell—

Her hands smacked into something so hard and smooth it was almost slippery, jamming her shoulders backward in their sockets and sending her sprawling on the floor.

Ahead, light ignited in the dark.

Not the flare of a ghostlamp; but fissures of fire separating into crackling red-gold diamonds all linked together, stretching in a lazy curve around one of the stalagmites, blooming downward along four branches tipped with a razor-sharp talon.

The fire rippled and changed direction before Cistine's wide eyes, blurring with the swivel of a rising neck, a lifting head. Something sighed and rustled in what remained of the darkness, the sound like book pages ruffling in the wind and drums throbbing in the deep. His above her in the shadows, scarlet-flecked amber eyes revolved in their sockets, second and third lids blinking back, slit pupils fixing on her.

Cistine stopped breathing when she came face-to-snout with a dragon.

CHAPTER THIRTY-TWO

CISTINE CHOKED FOR breath, covering her mouth as the creature of legend and fable loomed above her, lips peeling back from bone-breaking teeth, hot breath singeing her hair. Sweat soaked the back of her neck, staining her collar, and sobs built in her throat with no release.

She was about to die a dragon's meal. A scrap eaten in the dark.

She wouldn't even get to say goodbye to Thorne.

The dragon's great fangs bared in the light of its own body, fire rippling under iridescent golden scales, jaws slinging wide—

"Would you *please* stop that insufferable blubbering?"

The deep, male croak of its voice burned off Cistine's unfallen tears like morning dew. She gaped into her hands, staring at the scaled brow that somehow managed to wear a look of offense. "You...you can speak the common tongue?"

"And seven other languages. Did you suppose because I am a beast, I must also be uneducated? And they call *my* kind impolite."

His neck curved, head turning away from her, and Cistine's arms swung loose at her sides. "You're not going to kill me?"

Quick as an adder's strike, he snapped back, broad snout pinning her by her abdomen to the rock. She whimpered at the heat climbing through her skin.

"Mmm...not, I think. My appetites are for far gamier prey. Besides, you don't look as if you'd be worth the work to digest." He peeled his head back, and Cistine's legs gave out, sending her to her seat so hard her tailbone throbbed. "However, you have disturbed my relatively-peaceful slumber. So unless you've brought literature with which I can pass the hours, I'm afraid I'll have to ask you to leave."

A dull, heavy rattle marked his steps away from her. A dark slip of steel wavered along his neck, interrupting the brilliant gold of his scales.

A chain.

Come. The whisper raised the hair on her neck. *Come and see...*

"You're a prisoner, too?" she asked.

The dragon snorted smoke and flopped down with his broad back to her, wings shuffling against his sides. "I prefer indentured guest. Ill-accommodated patron. Forcible boarder, if you will."

"Restrained tenant. Or trapped sojourner." The dragon's hide twitched. "Call it what you want, but you're being held against your will. Just like me."

He sighed as if her words were babble, vague and annoying. But he still hadn't eaten her.

"You mentioned literature." Cistine pushed herself up. "I'm fond of books, too. I've been learning to read Old Valgardan epics."

The silence was as long and deep as the forbidden cavern around them. Then the dragon's ribs lifted in another long-suffering sigh. "Truncated, or complete?"

Cistine's lips tugged into a smile. "Truncated, for now. Have you read them?"

"Every one. Truncated *and* complete."

"Do you have them here?"

"Well, I must have *some* means of entertaining myself." He rolled partway onto his back and craned his neck to look at her. "And why are *you* here, sojourner?"

"Because I'm useful. And you?"

The dragon's tail scraped across the stone floor, coming to rest in a loose coil around her body. A bare, raw patch stretched from the tip to midshaft; no fire moved beneath it. "The same."

Cistine's gaze flashed back to his angular face. "It's *your* scales Salvotor used to reinforce his skin! How long have you been *down* here?"

"Long enough to have forgotten the scent of the wind. Long enough that I've given up hoping for a better life. They'll chip away at me to make their armor until I'm little more than a naked lizard clawing for a scrap of sunlight."

"You can't free yourself?"

He huffed with humorless laughter. "Do you notice anything about this chain that seems unusual?"

The chilling hum slithered through her body again.

Come. Come and see.

She sidled closer, and the dragon watched with a half-lidded eye. Carefully, she rested a hand on the dark metal.

It sizzled on contact, a flash of purple energy arcing from the steel to her fingers. Panic lit through Cistine's body, knocking her in a scramble to escape the lightning augment that coursed through the chain. Her back struck the stalagmite again, and the dragon blinked after her. His massive, barreled side no longer moved with breath. "Well, tie my tail. That should have killed you, yet here you are."

"You should have warned me!"

"What do I care if an augment kills you? But that it didn't..." he turned onto his stomach and folded his front limbs at the elbow. "Now, that *does* interest me."

Cistine snaked her arms around herself and shut her eyes, but even in the darkness she saw those whips of white-hot power shattering from Salvotor's hand and cutting Julian down, melting his eyes. "You're disgusting."

"We can't *all* care deeply for whomever stumbles into our cave. But tell me, little sojourner...why aren't you a crisped husk now?"

Her eyes snapped open under a fierce prod of rage. "Maybe your books can tell you."

She turned to walk away from him and his augmented chain, her fingertips still tingling with the horrific memory of the wetlands.

"You may take a book, if you wish," the dragon said after her. "Great Father knows I've read them plenty of times. Knowledge, after all, should never be hoarded to the value of only one."

Cistine stopped, looking back. At the tip of one claw, he nudged out a volume of truncated Valgardan epics. A peace offering, perhaps...but also a bartering for information.

Two could play that game. "I make it a point not to accept gifts from anyone who won't at least give me his name."

"In the language of my race, I am Bresvek'aiz-Latanoknair'Moranyar. But to spare your uncultured tongue...Bresnyar." When Cistine knelt to take the book, his nail dug into the cover, fastening it in place. "And yours?"

"I'm Cistine."

"What a deplorably human name."

Cistine scooped the small book to her chest. "At least mine is pronounceable."

His eyes narrowed and his nostrils flared. "Get on your way. I'm bored of your company."

But Cistine's didn't move. Hope spiked through her, shattering the melancholy at finding not a cellar with a door, but a cavern with a dragon at the base of the tunnels. "Wait. I have a proposition for you."

Bresnyar scoffed. "Didn't I just say I'm bored of you? Be gone."

She almost had to shout to be heard above the drag of his chain when he hobbled away from her. "But how do you feel about freedom?"

He halted, swiveling his head to peer at her. "Why do you ask?"

She flicked a glance at the chain, stomach churning at the thought of augmented lightning climbing the cracks of her skin, coursing along her muscles and surging through her fingertips, just as it had coiled around Julian before it killed him. But the dragon didn't need to see the notion terrified her. "I have a...a way to free you."

"Do you, now? And what do you expect from me in exchange for such a gift? Surely you don't intend to loosen my fetters from the goodness of your heart."

"Not entirely. I want you to carry us away from this mountain."

"Us?"

"Myself and my friends."

Bresnyar tapped his talons slowly on the floor. "You are offering *me* freedom? You, who stink of fear when you touch my chain?"

She swallowed the lump in her throat. "Let me worry about that. I'm leaving this mountain with or without your help. Do you want to keep losing more scales and rotting down here in the dark, or do you want to put in a little effort and help save your own life?"

The force of the words punching from her chest reminded her of Ashe in their ferocity and tenor, and unbidden tears sprang to her eyes.

Bresnyar regarded her more intently, talons clicking on stone. "There is more fire in you then first meets the eye, isn't there?"

"You can't even begin to imagine." She stepped nearer, craning her head back to meet his fiery stare. "I don't have days to waste begging you. It won't even be safe to come back here after tonight. Decide, right now...are we helping each other, or do I need to find a different way?"

She held her breath, praying he wouldn't call her bluff. As of tonight, dragonback was the best way to ensure a swift and safe escape from Kalt Hasa.

Keen interest guttered in Bresnyar's face. He watched her like he was looking for something hidden under her skin—something no human eye could fathom. "Find a way to release me from this chain, and I will carry you and your companions from this mountain. But after, you and I will have a plain and honest conversation."

"Anything you want," Cistine said. "Once we're safe."

He grumbled under his breath about the aggravation of obstinate women and lumbered off into the dark, the chain dragging between his feet with a deep, rattling taunt.

Just one last obstacle to conquer. But with the echo of lightning over steel ringing in her ears, it seemed almost an insurmountable one

CHAPTER THIRTY-THREE

Q UILL WASN'T GETTING better.

It was comforting at first when his shivers eased and he slept deeply. Tatiana built a fire and dried out his armor, then ventured from the cave and trapped a few snow hares to keep them fed until Quill bounced back to his feet, ready to leave. But when he finally woke, the shakes and chills returned. Even when Tatiana helped him back into his armor, bundled him in pelts and hides, and curled up next to him, he trembled so violently she couldn't fall asleep lying with her head on his shoulder. He barely plucked at his rations and started coughing after the smallest sips of water. And it *hurt*, he complained, like having a knife jabbed between his ribs. But he still insisted he just needed to sleep it off.

She was fed up with that argument; but at least when he slept, she could hunt without feeling guilty for leaving him alone.

The dazzling light of deep, newly-fallen snow striped her vision mint-green when she ducked back into the cave from another morning hunt. Her gaze adjusted to the guttering fire and the shadows rippling at the back of the cave where Quill struggled up, reaching for his boots. He coughed with every movement, deep, wet rattles in the pit of his chest.

Tatiana's heart somersaulted. "What do you think you're doing?"

"Leaving." His voice was rougher than she'd heard it in days—if ever.

"No, you're not. You're delusional."

"How long has it been, Tati? Two days? Three?" He didn't wait for her to admit it had been longer. "Cistine needs us."

Tatiana hurled the hares beside the fire and crossed to him, kneeling on either side of his ankles and grabbing his wrists. "She needs *you* alive, which is why you're not going *anywhere*."

"Yes, I am, Kalt Hasa can't be that far..."

"Quill." Tatiana pinned both his wrists in one hand and grabbed his chin with the other, forcing his dull, bloodcracked eyes to meet hers. "We can't just go stumbling into the mountains right now."

He stared at her for so long, his gaze so detached, she wondered with a pang of horror if he just slid silently back into that addled state where he hovered for days and nights after the lake. Then his metallic breath brushed her face. "You're right. I'm useless. Just like he said I'd be."

"Who said that? Who do I need to punch?"

"My father."

It was the first time he'd mentioned Corvus since his family's apartment went up in flames. Tatiana's guts trembled. "He was Salvotor's most outspoken supporter, Quill. He was wrong about a lot of things."

"But not about this." Quill sank back on the nest, tugging his hands from her grasp so they flopped palms-up in his lap. "You know the one thing I always thought I was good at? Protecting the cabal."

"You are good at that, it's why you took that augment. I still hate you for that, you know."

No humor touched his face. "The night Cistine and Julian left Hellidom, do you know where I was?"

Tatiana grimaced. This was one road she wasn't certain she wanted to walk with him.

"Tavern." The word fell harshly from Quill's mouth. "You and Ari had a good excuse. You were on patrol. But I was in the stars-damned tavern, drinking to drown out Baba Kallah's voice in my head, and she *needed* me. She needed me, I was right there, but I wasn't close enough. And I've been thinking ever since Thorne came back, maybe if I'd stayed put like I was supposed to and watched over the cabal instead of worrying about my own specters, Julian wouldn't be dead. Cistine wouldn't be gone. She's my responsibility, she's...like Pippet. I couldn't keep Pippet safe, either. And I couldn't help *you*."

The breath gushed from Tatiana's lungs. "What do you mean?"

"Should've been there for you," Quill mumbled, "after Detlyse Halet. I know you killed for the first time when he took us. That must've hurt, because it hurt *me* when I killed those slavers for Pip. But I just wasn't there, I was in Detlyse Halet and then I was hunting and then that stars-forsaken tavern and I just...I don't know, Tati. Maybe I deserve every second of this."

"Quill, that's not true." But she had nothing else to give, no wisdom like Ariadne would've offered, no comfort like Cistine always provided. The right words failed her as she stared at Quill's vacant face and truly saw what she'd been looking at for weeks in all the silences, the void without his laughter, his smile, the familiar light in his eyes.

He blamed himself. Loathed himself. Hung Julian's death and Cistine's fate on his own shoulders. And he was killing himself to atone for it.

Heat bloomed in Tatiana's throat so fiercely she almost choked. Ever since they were children, she'd been right beside him and never had a name for that look on his face, for the anger after the Izten Torkat, after she pulled him out of Detlyse Halet—for the pain that lurked behind every failure.

Quill had been drowning long before that lake.

He stared at his lap with that same glassy, unfocused look as when he fell through the ice, and Tatiana's heart skipped. "Quill?"

"I can't feel two of my fingers."

"What?"

"My right hand. The two smallest fingers...I can't feel them."

Tatiana buckled forward on her knees, straddling his, and held out her upturned palms. He slowly laid his hand in hers, and her stomach dropped. The fingers looked almost augment-scarred, pocked and textured with blisters. Stars only knew how she hadn't noticed it before. "You don't feel anything?"

"They did hurt, until today. Not the skin, but...deep. Like the bones were stiff. And now it's just..." he shrugged helplessly.

Tatiana let go of his hand and turned back to the low fire, hoping he didn't see how her own fingers rattled. "You need to eat. You remember Baba Kallah's philosophy? There's nothing wrong in this kingdom that can't be solved with a good meal..."

She had to stop shaking. So what if he lost the feeling in his fingers? Things like that just happened. People went through ordeals, and they were slow to recover. It was what people *did*.

People...but not Quill. She'd never seen him hurt so badly he didn't hop right back to his feet, swinging wisecracks as smoothly as his swords. And he'd never been so honest about his hurts, never let her see this far past his armor. Now he was just quiet, and when she turned back, she found him slumped down deeper into the nest.

"Quill! Look at me." His eyes flicked open, roving over her face. "Don't you think you've slept enough?"

He grimaced. "Sleeping is the only other thing that doesn't hurt. My chest...feels like there's an iron band around it."

Tatiana slid the plate of hare meat to the edge of the nest and crouched before him again, feeling his brow. Her stomach plummeted at the pulse of heat from his tacky skin. "Eat. Don't make me force-feed you."

"Like all of my wildest fantasies," he deadpanned, scooping the plate listlessly into his lap. After a few unhappy bites, he put it aside and shut his eyes.

"Eat more," Tatiana snapped.

"I'm not hungry."

She should've felt sympathy, but there was only rage. "You heard me, Nightwing."

His eyes snapped blearily open. "You're not Thorne. Stop trying to be."

"If Thorne *was* here and he told you to eat, would you?"

Quill was quiet, passing through several long, torturous shudders. "I don't think I could."

With a low groan, he rolled onto his elbow and coughed so violently, he retched and gagged against the side of his hand. Tatiana crawled over to help him sit up, half-sprawled in her lap, holding his hair from his brow while the hacking fit went on and on. When he was finally spent, he wiped his mouth on his hand...and cursed.

His skin was ghosted with blood.

"Nimmus' teeth." He sank more heavily into Tatiana's grip, resting his head in her hand with a groan.

She stared numbly as his blistered fingers and the blood smeared on them, horror slamming into her heart while he drifted back into unconsciousness in her arms.

What if he hadn't coughed out all the lake water? What if there was infection festering in his chest? No amount of limb-rubbing, pit fires, hare meat or even coughing could drive out infection. Whatever had happened to him in that lake, whatever was happening to his body *now*, she hadn't gotten him warm and dry fast enough.

Quill was dying.

She let go of him and scrambled to her feet, stumbling to the mouth of the cave—but where in the stars could she to go? If she got lost wandering this small slice of Oadmark, she might never find her way back before Quill...

She grabbed the rounded mouth of the dark stone and hung against it, holding back vomit with her hand. Her eyes cast frantically around their small shelter, searching for something, *anything*—a thought, a plan, a way to save him—and they fell on the untouched wineskin.

A deep, visceral need stabbed through her core. If she could just remove herself from this problem for the day, clear the fear that fogged her mind, then maybe she could plan. If she could forget for now that he *needed* her help...

She uncorked the wineskin. Deep, blushy grape notes filled her head, easing the tension in her fingers, and she relaxed against the cave mouth, bringing the skin to her lips, already tasting the sweet relief it promised.

Quill stirred with a weak cough, and Tatiana froze. She was still frozen more than a minute later after she was sure he was restless and not really awake.

If there was no harm in this, why was she so paranoid he might see her drinking? Quill, of all people, who sat with her on the roof of their prestigious lodgings in Veran and listened while she poured out her heart about everything she was running away from—Cistine's friendship, the memories of Stornhaz, her own specters. He trusted her word that she was done with the drinking, whatever came.

She was still learning who she was, what she could be without a flask in reach—but she knew she couldn't be *this*. Not when he needed her.

She swung the skin with all her might, bursting it against one of the trees outside of the cave. Shaking the emptiness from her fingers, she hopped up and started to pace, thoughts darting over possibilities and scenarios. She forced herself to face every one...even the worst of them, where Quill died in this cave and she had to find Cistine by herself.

She would do that if she had to. But her spirit would die on this mountain, waiting for her body to catch up so she could find Quill in Nimmus.

Stars, if she had just gotten away from that guard fast enough, before he stripped her of her swords, her satchel...

Her feet caught on the stone.

For a moment, everything was silent, filled with the resonate echo of dripping icicles.

She had the healing augment in her bag, hung up in that tree with her sabers.

She glanced over her shoulder at Quill's slumbering form. She could be there and back before he even noticed she was gone. And with that healing augment, everything would be right again.

Maybe that made her no different from the people she despised, relying so heavily on their flagons they feared they'd die without them. But Quill *would* die without this one, and if Tatiana had to be a hypocrite to save him...well, she'd repent later.

She stole one of the pelt coats from beside Quill's nest, strapped on the snowshoes from the chest, wrapped her armored scarf around her face, and ran from the cave. Slipping and scrambling up the rutting hollow's slope and down the far side, she slid to a halt on the lakeshore, surveying the massacre they left behind days ago.

Scavengers had come and gone for the Vassoran bodies; there was more blood, more gore scattered across the ice, the brittle hole wider and something bloated floating inside. Entrails carved a grisly path to the treeline where she lost her satchel.

Grimacing, Tatiana started across the lake.

The wind cut across the ice like a scythe from the east, slamming through the pelt and freezing her cheeks. Every exposed inch of flesh hurt when she reached the pines, peering up through the thick weave of branches to the faraway glints of black leather and beaded suede strung above.

"Just like climbing buildings in Stornhaz." She unlaced the snowshoes and cracked her knuckles. "Quick up and down. No mistakes."

Gripping the lowest boughs, she thrust herself up.

It was slow going, shoving head and shoulders through the dense needles, sap freckling her cheeks and chin. Everything that wasn't cold stung, and everything that was cold started to burn.

"You should've done this the day the Vassora attacked, *Tati*," she mumbled to herself. "Too dangerous, oh? *There might be more Vassora*! I don't *see* any, do you? No, just trees! Could have...been most of the way to Kalt Hasa by now, but *no*, you just *had* to be afraid of Salvotor's *friends*..."

With her next desperate reach, her fingers brushed suede, and she whooped a prayer of relief. Wrapping both legs around the tree's thick trunk, she stretched up, slung her arm over the branch, and leaned out to wiggle her satchel and harness loose.

The branch buckled, bowed violently—then snapped.

Cursing in a half-scream, Tatiana slipped sideways, dangling almost upside-down, holding onto the pouch by the tips of her fingers. But it slithered loose, tumbling into the snowbank below.

Jerking upright, Tatiana shielded her face with her arm—but no eruption of light or fire came. The powdery drift cushioned the satchel's fall.

Muttering under her breath, she shimmied down, lunged from the lowest branch, and snatched up the satchel, surveying its contents. To her relief, the flagons were unbroken, steadied by the leather band that held them together and the other contents of the bag—her favorite scarf, a drawing from Pippet, the photograph of the cabal. She pocketed the pictures, wrapped the scarf around her wind-bitten cheeks, and turned back to the ice.

Her way was blocked.

She'd never seen wolves so massive, each one the size of a small horse. Pelts snow-white, eyes red like precious gems, three prowled in a crescent near the Vassoran bodies and two more flanked, silently enclosing her. Either she was prey to them, or another predator stalking their food; regardless, those booming growls promised a fight to get back to the cave. Back to Quill.

Slowly, Tatiana let the bag slide lower in her grip. If she could scare them off, get back to her sabers, she could make a real fight out of this.

One wolf tossed its head, the hunting howl echoing thinly across the ice—and lunged. Tatiana swung the bag, and the beast recoiled at the last instant before it struck. Another pounced from her left, and she sidestepped and swung again, clipping this one in the muzzle and praying the flagons held.

The third wolf was smarter. When she swung, it caught the bag and ripped it straight from her hands, the cord skinning her palms. Paws pounded her ribs, knocking her to her shoulder on the ice, and she barely rolled clear of the jaws snapping for neck. Gasping, she lurched upright and drew her knife, backing away to take wild stock of the pack.

Four of them were closing in on her. A pair of adolescents fell on her bag, wrestling the strap between their teeth until the sturdy threads gave way, sending all the flagons rolling across the lake.

"No!" Fury twisted Tatiana's voice into a shriek as the healing augment looped lazily down the ice—and dropped through the hole.

Tatiana screamed as the last hope for Quill's life disappeared into the same void that sealed his fate. And she kept screaming as she charged the nearest wolf, sabers forgotten, and swung onto its back, stabbing wildly. She whirled away from its floundering body and pierced the next beast in the chest, and the next in the ribs, and the next in the hocks.

The pack scattered as Tatiana cleaved through them; she was augmented fire, an ocean tide, a windstorm, a cyclone—a disaster against these beasts that *destroyed* her best hope of saving Quill. Blood splattered the snow and pained, panicked yelps split the air; Tatiana sprang on one of the adolescents, plunged her knife into his shoulder, then bellowed when pain plunged into *her* shoulder and down along the top of her right breast. Though her armor protected her from being pierced, fangs bruised to the bone when the pack leader's jaws closed over her arm. It yanked her backward and dragged her across the ice in a galloping tumble, so disoriented all she could see was a blur of her dark armor clashing with the white snow. Her feet dragged for purchase, trying to kick her body free.

A second wolf landed on her chest, knocking the wind from her. Tatiana stroked dizzily with the knife, slashing its muzzle, but it caught her arm and bore down against her with all its might. The pack leader pried its jaws from around her shoulder and lunged toward her head.

A furious, broken yell pierced Tatiana's ears, and a flat birch snowshoe wielded like a club slammed into the wolf's broad skull, sending it reeling. Tatiana could barely comprehend what she was seeing when Quill tackled the second wolf off her chest, freeing her to breathe. She sprang up to help, then fell to her knees again when the pack leader caught her leg, dragging her backward.

She cursed, flinging the knife straight into the animal's forehead. It seized and crumbled, and she yanked the weapon free and ran toward Quill and the last wolf. It held him pinned, battering at his armored back while he shielded his head. Lunging at its flank, she buried the knife behind its elbow, bringing it down in a whining heap.

She came down with it, releasing the knife, tossing her hair from her eyes with a mad sway of her head and grabbing the collar of Quill's armor, pulling him up to face her. "What in the stars is *wrong* with you? What are you doing out here?"

"Woke up, heard the howling. You were gone." He squinted at her. "Why didn't you wait for me?"

"Wait for you to do what? There was no time! I needed that healing augment..." The one that was currently resting at the bottom of a frozen lake. She tightened her grip on his armor. "And I needed *you* to stay where you were *warm*."

He shuddered, his eyes falling shut. "You think I would just...lie back while you got eaten by wolves? You aren't—you aren't getting out of this that easily. I'm enjoying you being my medico too much."

He buckled forward, spasming when he coughed—barely more than a pained gurgle this time. Blood misted from his lips.

"Quill," Tatiana took his face in her hands, sitting him up straight again. "Quill, you can't keep doing this, do you understand me? You can't kill yourself over and over for me. For *any* of us."

His eyes trailed listlessly over her face. "Preferable to the alternative."

She thumbed blood from the crevice of his blue lips. "Let's get you back to the cave." She hauled him up, his arm around her shoulders, and dragged him to the shore; but the slope at the end was unnavigable in his condition. She couldn't manage her limbs and his too, with her shoulder and leg throbbing and blood dripping from his lips with every errant jerk of his body.

"Tati," he panted after the fourth time they made it halfway up the slope, then skidded down again. "Stop. Just stop, I can't...I can't."

He slid out of her grip into the snow, face contorted with pain. Tatiana crouched beside him, her hand on his chest, his heartbeat fluttering unevenly against her palm.

"Don't do this," she panted, her throat burning. "You can't give up."

He turned on his back to look up at her, an unconvincing smile teasing one corner of his bluish lips. "Do you remember Spruce Harbor? That night I brought you as my escort to the Tribune's party?"

Tatiana wiped her weeping nose on her arm and settled next to him, legs curled, stroking the hair from his brow like she did whenever he was hungover or ill. "How could I forget? You in your filthy clothes, and me in that hand-stitched dress. No one wanted us there."

"I did."

"I think your father nearly drowned himself in the wine fountain that night, he was so furious with—"

"Tati," Quill wheezed. "*I* did."

Snow dusted his face. She brushed it off with a trembling hand.

"I remember racing each other down to Spruce Harbor," he added. "Sitting on the shore and skipping rocks into the channel."

She remembered that, too; moonlight dancing on the opalescent beads she sewed onto one of her mother's old dresses to make it seem new. Quill with the collar of his rumpled school clothes undone, sleeves rolled up, carefree smile the best part of his attire.

"That was the first time you told me why you did it," Tatiana said. "The vandalism, the fights, the gambling."

"You mean how I didn't want Thorne and Aden's lives? Becoming a Tribune like my father?"

"Actually, you never told me what you *didn't* want, it was all about the things you *did*. Like seeing a sunrise in the Vaszaj Range or swimming in the Agerios. Sampling Veran's market. Making love on the Black Coasts. Seeing the auroras."

"I did almost all of it, didn't I?"

"I wouldn't know about the lovemaking part." Not that she hadn't daydreamed when she was feeling brave.

"What else do you remember about that night?"

When she closed her eyes, she could see the sky traced with clouds, feel the wind warm on her skin and the crunch of Spruce Harbor's grayish-blue gravel under her while she gathered her ankles and watched Quill flick stones out across the channel as far as they would go. That was the night she fell in love with his voice, the first time she ever had the *real* Quill, alone, all to herself.

She remembered when he came back to join her on the shore, hands stuffed in his pockets, unruly hair wind-tossed in a storm settling from the north. "Do you think this is all there is for us? Just this city? Just nights like these?"

"If it is, can you survive it?"

He dropped onto the gravel and draped an arm around her shoulders.

"As long as I have you, I can survive anything."

She blinked, looking down at him, because that wasn't a memory at all. He'd whispered it toward the darkening sky.

She stretched out next to him, resting her head on his outflung arm. Tears froze on her cheeks and she did nothing to stop them.

"I think I did all right," Quill rasped. "There were only two things I never did." He raised a weak arm and waved at the sunset sky, darkness spreading like a stain over the lake.

With the last gasp of sundering daylight, glassy green ribbons, pink banners, and soft blue streamers fanned out like silk through the sky. Cords of light chased one another from horizon to horizon the same way Tatiana and Quill chased each other from one dangerous place to another, ever since they were children—a pattern of peril, a portrait of beauty and brashness as perfect as any dress Tatiana ever held or any painting she ever saw.

"The auroras," she breathed.

"Better than I imagined." Quill dragged himself up on one elbow, sliding his arm from under her head and leaning above her. "There's one other thing I always wanted to try."

His undamaged fingers grazed her hip, pressing her deep into the snow. Then her mouth was frigid with the press of his bloody, ashen lips against hers.

She had kissed her share of men—some she remembered, others inebriated blurs, drunken back-alley fumblings or tavern teases. One or two slower, sweeter kisses had roused some slumbering chamber of her heart before those men tasted the hopelessness inside her and withdrew.

This was not like any of those; it was needing and desperate, careful and shy all at once, and unafraid of the darkness that made her want to pull back the moment her mind caught up to her mouth and realized who she was kissing, and *how* he was kissing her.

She grabbed Quill's face, ready to shove him away, but instead her fingers latched into his hair and brought him down against her, body-to-body, every familiar contour of his lean, muscular frame pressing hers into the slope. His chest hitched, and for a moment she was breathing for them both, tasting the blood on his breath.

She eased her vigor, and the kiss softened into a slow, gentle meeting that didn't just rouse Tatiana's heart this time; it threw her spirit wide open, and she drank Quill in—the roughness of his ice-glazed hair, the shape of his mouth melding to hers, the way his curves hugged her body so comfortably, belonging the same way he always gave her a place to belong even when the whole stars-forsaken world turned her away. She'd always fit to his side, into his plans, inside his heart.

She never wanted to let him go. She'd waited so damned *long* for this—

His jaw slackened suddenly. His body crumbled. He slid off her.

Shrieking his Name, Tatiana grabbed for his collar, his face as he tumbled to his shoulder in the snow beside her, eyes closed, utterly still.

"Quill!" Tatiana sobbed. His lips were blue, his eyelids blue. His fingers, on her waist still, were blue in the nailbeds. "*Nightwing,* show me your eyes! Don't you *do* this!"

Nothing. His face didn't so much as twitch.

"*No!*" Tatiana shook him. "Quill, *please*—"

An angry, unfamiliar shout cracked the air. Feet skimmed snow and crunched ice. Tatiana whirled, straddling Quill, spreading her limbs over him and facing up the slope toward a dark line of bodies gathered at the ridge. She couldn't make out their faces in the dark, and with wild grief pounding through her, she didn't care who they were.

"What are you waiting for?" she screamed.

One of them lunged, tackling her off Quill and slamming her onto the ice. Her head jounced, brain jolting against her skull, and darkness slid into the corners of her eyes.

The others were coming down the slope, circling around Quill, toeing him over onto his back. He rolled without resistance. His chest didn't rise.

"Quill," Tatiana panted.

The darkness took her voice, took everything.

Above the lake, the auroras paled into shadow.

CHAPTER
THIRTY-FOUR

Aden's bearing changed when he turned their retinue hard east toward the foothills of the Isetfell Range. For once, he and Pippet didn't train when the day's heat leached away into cold desert darkness; he set about quietly teaching her how to build a fire instead, then watched her do it twice—once for them and once for Ashe, who settled off on her own again, jittering with nervous energy.

A brief but violent sandstorm had slowed them down, but tomorrow they would reach their destination and find their heading to rescue Cistine.

"Ashe?" Pippet prodded her foot. "How does the fire look?"

She forced a smile. "Perfect, Pip."

It was true. The flames blazed high and strong, chasing out the desert chill from Ashe's fingers. She only wished it could thaw the frost in her chest from the Cadre's irritation with her; Rozalie was the only one who'd speak to her after Viktor and Aden's argument. Adrift between the two camps, she felt like the thinnest shred of sinew holding their mission together.

Pippet plopped down next to her. "Did you teach Cistine to do this? Build fires?"

Ashe's smile flickered away. "No, I didn't. Tatiana and Ariadne did."

"Aden says it's good to know these things. It keeps us safe, that's why he's teaching me how to use my knife. Why didn't you teach Cistine?"

Ashe hated the first answer that came to her, but Pippet felt the safest person to say it to. "Because I thought I'd always be there to protect her. I was afraid if she became too strong, or if I pushed her too hard to do things she didn't want to do, she'd dismiss me." Like Ashe's parents dismissed her when she professed her loathing of their profession. Like King Ivan tried to dismiss her when she came to the war. She was always fighting the same tired struggle: banished from her family. Banished by her king. Banished from the Hive Lord's chambers and the Den. And now, banished from the Cadre's camp. "Maybe I didn't want things to change."

But they'd changed anyway; and if not for the cabal, Cistine would be in these dire straits without a fighting chance.

"I think Quill is afraid of change, too," Pippet said. "He wants me to stay in Starhollow forever. But I'm like Cistine, I have to go places and see things. Stories aren't enough when there's a wide-open world out there."

It was wide, and vast—so much that even Ashe felt lost in it. She risked a glance at the Wardens' fire and found them all circled up, heads bent together. Rion gestured broadly, nowhere in particular, but somehow it felt like he was talking about her and the Valgardans whose company she seemed to prefer.

As if he wasn't the one pushing her away.

"Ashe, do you think *I'm* too strong?" The quiet fear in Pippet's question made her stomach drop.

"No. *Never.*" She laid a hand on Pippet's back. "I want you and Cistine *both* strong enough to fight the battles that matter to you. I just didn't realize it with her until it was too late."

But she had another chance now—a better choice to make.

Ashe stood and offered her hand to Pippet. "Here. Let me teach you something I should've taught Cistine."

She whistled for Aden to join them, and he swaggered over from his fire. "You summoned?"

"I want to show her something. Put your hand on my shoulder."

The moment his fingers wrapped her arm for the first time since their fight in Jovadalsa, the sensations of blinding sunlight, the chafe of sand, the taste of blood and sweat rolled over her. Sickness surged in her gut, and she fought down the Hive instinct that told her this touch, from this hand, meant harm. "Pippet, if someone grabs you here, take their arm in both hands and push them off."

She demonstrated, slashing her knee toward Aden's legs for good measure. Pippet laughed. "Tati always does that to Quill!"

Ashe smirked. "No wonder he's terrified of her. Now, if someone covers your mouth, you bare those teeth like a dog—perfect, like that—grab his wrist and sink your teeth in as hard as you can."

"Twist your head and wrench," Aden added. "You can tear out more flesh that way—even render a man's hand entirely useless."

"What if they grab my throat?"

Aden turned to Ashe. "May I?" When she nodded, he brought his hands around her neck, pressing his thumbs gently in the dip above her clavicles. "You may have only seconds to escape this hold. After that, you're unconscious and at their mercy."

"What do I do?"

Aden nodded to Ashe, and she pressed her palms together and yanked them up inside his arms, snapping his hold from her throat.

Pippet shrieked with delight. "Again!"

Ashe grinned, Aden chuckled, and they obliged. "It gives you a stronger hold and better leverage," Ashe said. "You'll be smaller than most of your attackers for a few years yet. Grabbing elbows and wrists won't always be enough."

"Break the hold quickly and firmly," Aden said, "and get out of reach."

"And if that break doesn't work?" Pippet asked.

"You can also go for the eyes—soft and vulnerable," Ashe said. "Press in with all your might. Either he'll let go—"

"Or he'll be blind," Aden finished, stepping back. "Your turn."

Pippet surged into his place, fists up. "I'm ready."

Ashe shook her head and laughed, brushing her arms down. "Not yet." She circled her fingers loosely around Pippet's neck. "Now."

Pippet's arms flashed up quicker than Ashe anticipated, breaking the hold easily. "Well done!" Aden called, and Pippet grinned.

"Again, Ashe!"

She was ready this time, resisting, letting Pippet feel the firmness and chinks in the hold. They repeated it twice more, and the third time, Pippet broke the hold and dove forward, kneeing Ashe in the stomach so hard it forced a laugh from her.

"Are you *sure* no one in the cabal ever trained you?" she gasped, rubbing her middle.

Pippet spun a strand of dark hair around her finger. "I watch them grapple sometimes. And Tati's shown me things, but never like this."

"Let's try something else." Ashe curled her fingers, beckoning her closer. "I don't want you to underestimate the power of your voice. An attacker may not care what you say, but you can frighten him by how you say it. So when you attack, I want you to roar. Not scream like you want someone to help—*roar* in his face."

Pippet planted her feet and pressed her palms together. "What do I say?"

"Whatever comes to mind," Aden said. "Tell him to take his hands off you. Tell him to get away. It matters less what you say as *how* you say it."

Pippet drew her lip between her teeth and nodded. Ashe necklaced her throat, and she breathed deeply, hurled her arms up and broke Ashe's hold, then planted both palms in her chest and knocked her backward, bellowing in her face, "*I'm not afraid of you!*"

Ice and darkness and tundra and blood and a boy's eyes, dead eyes, wide eyes with life trickling back into them...

Ashe's haunches impacted the sand and Pippet danced a triumphant circle around her. Aden's eyes fixed on Ashe, full of concern.

You augurs don't frighten me. You never have!

"Well done, Pippet." Ashe sounded breathless to her own ears.

"That was incredible! I could fight anyone!" Pippet whirled on Aden, jabbing a few mock blows into his torso, and he caught her head and pushed her gently away.

"There's a difference between hold breaks and combat. Everything in time, Pippet."

Grinning, she spun back to offer a hand to Ashe, who took it, dazed, and pulled herself up. "You're so good at this! Let's fight again!"

Ashe shook her head. "Not tonight. Settle in, I'll sing your song."

Though Pippet whined that she wasn't tired, she was asleep with her head on Aden's thigh before Ashe finished the Talheimic lullaby. Carefully, she stroked the hair from Pippet's temple. "She may be strong, but training takes its toll on her."

"Why do you think we do it in the evenings?" Aden smiled. "I learned quickly with Thorne that grappling sessions made all the difference at bedtime."

Imagining Thorne as a child full of boundless energy lurching around Aden's weary feet only twisted the knife in Ashe's chest. "You're good with her. Good *for* her."

"Despite everything I've done." Aden peered off to the horizon. "Everything I'm going to do."

He didn't elaborate, and Ashe let her gaze drift back to the Wardens. They'd stopped conversing and stole glances at her instead.

Her skin crawled. They'd seen her training a Valgardan child, wrestling with Aden. Was she a traitor in their eyes, spilling Talheimic combat secrets to the enemy?

She heaved herself up. "I should go on patrol."

"Ashe." Aden sounded more tired than she'd ever heard him, even in the Hive. He didn't look at her, his gaze still turned north. "Stay. Please."

Slowly, Ashe folded back down beside him. "Something on your mind?"

He tugged the blanket more securely around Pippet's chin. "I owe you an apology. I can't number the criminals whose paths crossed mine in Siralek...thieves and murderers, defilers, slavers and conspirators. I never met anyone who wrestled the same specters as me. And that made me feel like this monstrous thing. For all the horrors they committed, they never betrayed their friends, never destroyed their family legacy or broke the trust of their Court as I had.

"Then you came along, and your loyalty to your princess drove me to dream of redemption again. When I learned what you and Nimea did, my anger wasn't only at you. It was at myself for never noticing how your devotion drove you down the same path I took, straight into the jaws of Nimmus. I should have done better as someone who dared to call you a friend even in that place. For that, I'm sorry."

Ashe shifted uncomfortably, looking away from him. "What I chose to do with Nimea wasn't your fault."

"The secrets I kept certainly were." Aden rubbed Pippet's shoulder when she shivered, curling closer to his side. "I know the pain you're feeling now...why you never sit at the Cadre fire anymore. I shouldn't have let you leave the Den alone, knowing your pain is the same as mine."

"I would've pushed you away even if you tried to follow me. I wasn't interested in Valgardan help that night. I thought my kingdom was the only one I could trust anymore."

"Do you still?"

Ashe slid her finger along the dark scarf girdling her throat. When she tugged it just right, the smell of charcoal and cedar still floated from the creases. "I don't know anything anymore, Aden."

Boots scraped the sand, and Ashe twisted around as Rion led the Wardens to join them. Aden let Pippet down gently on the sand and stepped away from her; Ashe rose at his side.

"You say we reach our destination tomorrow," Rion said. "But I don't appreciate being led in the dark. I've allowed things to go this far, now you tell us who we're going to see."

Aden's jaw shifted, eyes gleaming. "We're going to speak with Deja, a powerful Valgardan elite who keeps an ear to all that happens in the northern territories. She will strike any bargain to sell information for the right price."

Ashe's breath hitched, her gaze spearing back to him. She only heard that particular rough note in his voice once before—the day he told her of his sponsor from the Hive who bought him against his will, then used him to service herself and her friends in exchange for keeping the rest of the fighters from spectators' beds. "Aden. *No.*"

"What makes you so certain this woman will share secrets?" Rion curled his lip. "I know how you Valgardans protect your own interests."

Aden shifted at that, blocking Rion's view of Pippet. "She'll help because I have the one thing she wants. If a Chancellor is hiding secrets in the north, she'll know of it."

Ashe put her back to the Wardens, facing him. "You can't do this."

"Would you prefer to discuss this opportunity while your people rot in Salvotor's grasp?" Aden snapped. "I am doing this. I'll find the information you need, and then you'll save your princess and her friend."

The Wardens traded battle-ready looks, knuckles cracking; but Ashe watched Aden, her stomach in a riot.

He hadn't included himself in the retinue saving Cistine. And he would not meet her gaze.

CHAPTER THIRTY-FIVE

Deja's home was an oasis amid red sand and foothill shadows, built around a moonlit pool and waving palms, its three-winged structure and well-groomed desert garden framed by a tall outer wall. The household steward received them without a flicker of surprise, led them to a parlor on the upper level, and left to fetch the lady of the house—all with as few words as possible.

Not that Ashe could blame him for his silence or his hasty retreat. Rion held the bearing of a predator on a leash as he reclined in one of the tall, recessed windowframes. Viktor and Lydie stood post at the doors, and Petra, Symon, Rozalie, and Andrej at the windows. Aden paced, hands tucked in the small of his back, looking at nothing. Every so often he glanced out the window over Rozalie's shoulder, toward the stone crags where they'd tucked Pippet away in case of combat.

Ashe wasn't sure what sort of fight Aden anticipated, but it had her guard up; as did the thought of Pippet huddled in those dark clefts, alone, with only her knife and a fortnight of training under her belt.

"You're tense," Aden remarked—the first words he'd spoken to her since he shouted in her face about coming here.

"Another astute observation from the Lord of the Hive," Ashe muttered. "You never told me how *Deja* acquired all this wealth." She refused to call her a sponsor in front of the Wardens; it would raise too many questions she didn't want to answer. Nor did she want to think about her own sponsor, or what he was doing these days.

"Her family roots lie deep in Valgard's crust, almost as deep as Noaam's. There are rumors of an understanding between their families, that Deja's *valenar* was a slaver supplying Hive fighters for generations. Not from the prisons, but pulled from the territories." Aden rubbed the back of his neck. "He was executed for that. She, on the other hand, pleaded ignorance and maintains position through blackmail. Her chain of spies stretches far across Spoek and Nordbran...most of them elite families whose reputation would be tarnished forever if it came to light they did business with her husband."

"She extorts the people he enriched," Ashe snorted. "Clever."

"How do you know all this?" Symon demanded.

Aden shot him a glare so chilling, he looked away. But Ashe already knew, her stomach plunging at the notion.

Forbidden whispers in the haze of the afterglow. How many times had she nearly bared her heart to men like Viktor when she found some imitation of affection, perhaps even love, in their strong arms with nothing else between them? Deja might extort secrets over her husband's hidden allies, but Aden had taken some in turn—an advantage of sharing her bed.

Rozalie cleared her throat, leaning in on their conversation. "This place was paid for with slave blood?"

Aden shrugged. "If you believe the rumors."

She lurched away from the wall, rubbing her arms.

"I hope your friend won't keep us waiting long," Rion growled.

As if she'd been listening for that, Deja opened the parlor door.

Sleekly intimidating as a Viperwolf, her dark dress shining like armored scales, she glided into the parlor with two attendants behind her. The heavy combs in her graying chestnut hair and the waterfall of jewels around her throat suggested she was indeed a widow of riches and power— and she didn't mind flaunting either. The Cadre instinctively came to attention at her arrival, and Aden...slumped. His gaze lowered, his shoulders curled in, and his head bowed slightly.

Deja's eyes, barren as the sand-scraped foothills beyond her home, traveled from each Warden to the next and finally settled on Aden. Her artfully-painted mouth curved up; not a smile, but a predator's snarl. "What a lovely surprise to see *you* alive. I was heartbroken when I took word of your passing in the riots...just heartbroken. Won't all of you sit?" She spanned an arm to the fine couches scattered throughout the parlor. "I'm sure whatever Aden's returned from Nimmus itself to discuss, it must be *very* interesting."

Rion folded his arms. "This conversation will be brief."

Deja pivoted to the Cadre Commander, her glittering stare a dead match for his. "And what *conversation* was so urgent you pounded on my door at the brink of night to have it?"

"We've come to inquire after recent movements in the north," Aden said. "Specifically, Chancellor Salvotor's."

"I see." Deja stepped toward him, smoothing her hand over a wingbacked sofa between them. "Well, you've learned that information about people above your station doesn't come for free. If I'm to divulge truths about the current season's Chancellor, I will need something ample in payment."

"We have mynts and weapons," Rion said. "We're prepared to use one or the other to loosen your tongue."

Deja scoffed. "Do I look as if I want for mynts? I'm not a poor woman. And I do not think you want to shed my blood...not if you hope to leave this oasis alive." Her orchid-striped smile clashed with Rion's scowl. "But don't fret, I'm not unreasonable. I can be bought into any agreement for the right price."

"Name it."

"Not from you. What I am, above all else, is bored. And my boredom, only one of you has any means of sating." Her eyes traveled back to Aden. "I'll tell you everything I know about Chancellor Salvotor's recent whereabouts if Aden stays with me when you go."

Rion's eyes narrowed. Rozalie and Viktor exchanged a weighted glance. And Aden, breathing harshly, looked at none of them.

He knew all along what price Deja would demand. His fireside penance to Ashe, all this training with Pippet, the way he held her against him and told her to be brave when they left the foothills; he'd been saying goodbye for gods-knew how long, walking back into Deja's hands to find *Cistine,* to stop Salvotor.

He was selling himself once again for someone else's safety.

A Valgardan, selling his body to save Talheim's princess. And he'd never even *met* her.

That nobility knocked Ashe breathless, sent her slamming forward, an arm fanned between Deja and Aden. "You can't have him. Choose something else."

"I'm afraid there's nothing else I want but this man, in subservience to me and my household, for as long and in as many ways as I say."

Aden shut his eyes, jaw creaking as his teeth mashed together.

"Aden is not currency," Ashe snarled. "We won't haggle with him."

"Then perhaps you'd like to carry on your search for Chancellor Salvotor without my help?" When no one spoke, Deja crooked a lazy finger at Aden. "Come, then. Let's see if you're still as talented a bedfellow as you are a fighter."

Bone shattered when Rozalie lunged and smashed her knuckles into the older woman's powdered cheek, knocking her to the floor.

Aden's head shot up. Ashe gripped Rozalie's shoulder and thrust her back as Deja struggled up, cradling her cheek, tears slicing through the cosmetics on her face. "You stars-damned *slynar*! How dare you come into my own house and strike me?"

"Believe me," Rozalie seethed, "that's the *least* of what I want to do."

Deja took a threatening step forward, and Aden blocked her path. "Enough of this. Ashe, it's the only way."

"No, it's not. You can't just *go* to her."

"This was the mission. We agreed to it in Jovadalsa."

She gripped his arm, wrenching him to face her. "I never would've agreed if I knew it meant *this*!"

Viktor's quiet scoff made her sharply aware how damning those words were to her reputation and rank—and still true. She wouldn't sell Aden back to his nightmares, not even to save Cistine. She wouldn't end one person's suffering at the cost of another's. Especially when both were her friends.

"Not like this," she insisted, holding Aden's gaze.

"Then this negotiation is finished," Deja snapped. "Get out."

Ashe dropped Aden's arm and caught his patroness by the throat instead, ramming her against the wall. "Let me introduce myself. My name is Asheila Kovar, and I was a Hive fighter, too." Sick pleasure roiled in her gut at the flash of fear in Deja's eyes. "If you aren't going to tell me where Chancellor Salvotor has been hiding, then you are of absolutely no use to me, and I have *plenty* of reasons to make you bleed. Enough that I really don't care what your guards *try* to do to me...you know how brutal Siralek's warriors are, so you know what I'll do to them. And what I'll do to *you*." She pressed in close, dropping her voice. "Don't worry, I'm sure someone will come scrape what's left of your corpse off this rug in a fortnight...but it's anyone's guess if they'll find every piece of you." She drew her dagger and placed it to Deja's neck, drawing a hint of blood. "Two seconds."

"*Very well!*" Deja barked, and Ashe relented the pressure. "He traveled to Kalt Hasa some time ago. I don't know why he's there, of all the stars-forsaken corners of Valgard, but that's all I know!"

"There. Was that so hard?" Ashe let Deja drop and turned away. "Aden, do you know about this Kalt Hasa?"

"You're wasting your time," Deja spat after her. "There won't be anything left of the girl to find."

Fury locked Ashe's boots to the scarlet rug. Rozalie hissed, "What did you say?"

"You think I don't know the look of a Cadre Warden when I see one?" Deja rasped. "He has the princess who came to bargain with him, the one he told us to watch the slave markets for."

"What do you know of her fate?" Rion demanded.

"Only what Chancellor Salvotor does to women who defy him." She hurled every word like a dagger into Ashe's back. "Scars them, breaks their legs, nails them to doors—"

The parlor erupted—a roar of fury from the Wardens, Rion shouting them back, Ashe catching Rozalie as she lunged at Deja, and Aden grabbing his patroness by the chin and slamming her back into the wall.

"*What did you say?*" Spittle flew, spattering her face. "What do you *know* of that?"

Deja paled before the Hive Lord's unbridled fury, her arrogance evaporating in the dry heat of his rage. "I don't...only rumors—"

Aden jerked her forward until their noses nearly brushed. "The only people who know what happened that night are scattered to the four corners of Valgard, and I know you didn't come close enough to any of them to have heard it from their mouths. Tell me what you know, or face the Hive justice people like *you* taught me."

When Deja didn't speak, Aden dropped her chin, took her arm, and snapped it at the elbow. The Wardens recoiled at the horrific crunch; Deja screamed, then vomited, then screamed again when he twisted the broken limb around her back.

"I saw it happen!" she wailed. "I saw what he did to her that night at your house—"

Aden's shoulders stiffened, his grip loosening. "You were there. *Why?*"

"Why do you think?" Agonized tears rolled through Deja's muffled voice. "I came f-for *you.*"

Disgust licked Ashe's belly. How long had this woman prowled the corners of Aden's life, waiting to strike, waiting to claim a young Tribune's son for herself?

"You saw him nail Ariadne's bleeding body to my door," Aden seethed, "and did *nothing*? I knew you were depraved, but that—"

"You think I didn't...didn't intervene? *I did*! And Salvotor threatened me—everything, my way of life, my legacy—"

"Stars damn your legacy! Ariadne was *hanging from my door* for *hours* before I found her!"

"And my l-*life* hung in the balance!" Deja gulped and retched. "He let me keep this place, gave me more power in Siralek, more spies to control, so I kept my peace. But I never forgot. Why do you think I agreed to your contract terms? My penance for what I didn't—didn't *stop* that night—"

Aden released Deja and rocked back so sharply he slammed into Ashe. She rested a hand on his back, facing Deja as she bent over her knees, weeping in agony.

"Bought into anything for the right price," Aden growled. "You're a baser creature than any Hive fighter I ever knew."

"Kovar." Rion's voice jerked her attention aside. "It's time to leave."

But Ashe stared at Deja as intently as Aden, a common thought binding them in silence. They had before them a witness to Salvotor's cruelty, an unexpected viper coiled in these desert sands.

And Maleck and Ariadne needed a witness.

"Ashe!" Rion barked. "We're leaving—we have what we need!"

They did. But Valgard didn't. Maleck didn't.

The choice almost made itself.

Ashe slammed her fist into Deja's temple, knocking her in a heap to the floor, and kicked her onto her back. "Aden, can you carry this? We'll take her and Pippet to Maleck and Ariadne, then travel to Kalt Hasa."

"That will delay us by *days* at least!" Petra protested. "Days Cistine and Julian might not have!"

Grief lashed Ashe's chest, but her words emerged firm. "They'll hold on. And Cistine will thank us for this."

She would want Ashe to set right some of her wrongs; if she couldn't give Thorne back his grandmother, Pippet back her nanny, or Julian back his life, she'd at least face the Cadre's fury and deliver the weapon Maleck and Ariadne needed to rip Salvotor from power.

"Ashe," Rion growled, "this is our princess and *my son* they're holding captive. You would forfeit their lives for Valgard?"

"I'm making the choice Cistine would make if she were here. And unless you want to stumble around in the north searching for this Kalt Hasa yourself, you're coming with us."

She had them, and she knew it. Rion never taught her more than the base details of the North because he never bothered to know them himself. Without her, he was as lost as she'd been when she followed Cistine here— before Maleck taught her the stars. Before Aden taught her the land.

Bending, Aden slung Deja's body over his shoulder. "The hunt is yours."

Ashe set her jaw. "Let's find Pippet and go."

Though the Wardens went without argument now, something broke in Rion's eyes when he turned away from her. Something Ashe knew could never be repaired.

CHAPTER THIRTY-SIX

T HE BRAIDED ROPE nearly slipped from Cistine's hands as she slid to her seat on the prison room floor, shaking with days of pent-up excitement. "Thorne!" she hissed, breaking for the cage. "Thorne, wake up!"

He was slow to rise from his straw nest, collared and shackled to the wall again, and Cistine slowed, her elation faltering. She'd forced herself to wait to visit him until she was certain her exploration of the cave had gone unnoticed. The news about Bresnyar was bursting inside her, but she wasn't sure how to say it when Thorne looked at her with such dull, detached eyes.

She sank down at the cage door. "What's wrong?"

"Nothing." But the harsh rasp of his voice betrayed him, and he averted his gaze. "Hurts to move."

Shame pulled her eyes away from him, too. "Is it your throat still?"

To her shock, he laughed. "You mean from that supper? I don't know what that was, but Salvotor may be losing his edge. He hit me harder than that *before* he reinforced his skin."

She blinked at his half-smiling face. "Were you *acting*?"

"It did hurt, but not as much as I wanted him to believe. I learned long ago that feigning pain ended the beatings sooner."

Cistine's stomach twisted. "No one should have to know those things."

"At least it helps us now." He shifted, then winced, falling from a crouch to his seat with a dull *thump* like his legs gave out.

Heart racing, Cistine gripped the cage bars. "Thorne, *that* wasn't a trick! What did they do to you?"

He grimaced, massaging the back of his calf. "It's the positions they make me sit in with that augmented chain in the way. Whenever I move, it feels like a dagger to the muscles."

Fury pulsed in her fingertips. "Tell me how I can help."

Thorne's eyes softened. "You can't. As long as Salvotor's focused on me and not hurting you, I'll endure it. Now tell me why you looked like you just read the greatest book in the kingdoms when you came down that rope."

She bit back the urge to argue; they both needed a distraction today, and another step toward escaping this place. Thank the gods she could offer both. "You were right about the tunnels, the cellar's vent was exactly where you said. And it's not really a cellar, it's a cave." She chewed her lip, but still the grin slipped through. "He's keeping a dragon down there."

Thorne surged back up to his knees, pain forgotten, eyes wild with excitement. "A *stars-forsaken* dragon? That's..." a chuckle burst from him, his hand sliding back through his hair. "He's lost his mind. Six guards are too few. What did it look like?"

"Golden. *Glorious.* He was as big as four or five horses lined up, and that's not counting the tail!" Cistine spread her hands for emphasis. "And he lit up with fire inside, like...like cracks in a mirror!"

"Secondary flammable veins," Thorne said. "I wonder if their venom sacs are real as well."

"His *mouth* was certainly full of venom." Cistine cocked her head. "You seem to know a bit about dragons."

He shrugged halfheartedly. "Baba Kallah smuggled a book about them into our apartment when I was a boy. It helped pass the time."

They sat for a moment in silence, heavy with the grief for his grandmother. Then Cistine added carefully, "There's more. He has a chain like the one they use for you, only his is wrapped in lightning."

Thorne frowned. "I'm not surprised. Every element in nature has its own weakness, even the ones we craft armor from. Lightning can cut through dragon scales in a direct blow. That's why I preferred not to use lightning augments with my old threads."

Cistine folded her arms and huddled against the bars. "Neither of us has any armor. So if we're going to escape..." The words trickled off into the panicked void stretching across her middle ever since she realized what breaking that chain would require of her.

"I have nightmares about the lightning, too." Steel rattled when Thorne shifted. "If I could help you carry that burden, I would."

"I know. But you can't, it has to be me." Terrified tears scalded her throat. "I just wish I knew *how*." The cabal had never trained her to wield augments. The nearest she'd come were long conversations on the Den's porch with Thorne about different flagons and properties and how warriors could share a single augment between them in battle.

"You'll find a way, *Logandir*. You always do." Thorne slumped back against the wall and bent his legs with both hands.

Cistine twisted to watch him. "How badly does it hurt?"

"Not badly enough to be a distraction." He flicked her a smile, smaller this time. "You should go. The guards could come at any time."

She knew that tone, that look on his face—a quiet attempt to shield her from his pain. Salvotor was chipping away at his resolve a piece at a time.

They had to end this.

She hopped up. "I'll find a way to get us both into that cellar and take the lightning off that chain. We're leaving soon. I promise."

Thorne struggled to his feet, pushed to the end of the chain, and reached toward the door. Cistine plunged her arm through, seeking until their fingers met. "I've seen you walk through storms and shadows to fight your enemies. You face Chancellors with your head high. You can do this, Cistine...you can conquer anything."

She flexed her fingers in the perfect fit of his, soaking as much strength and faith as she could from his gentle, callused grip. "As long as I have you."

"You always will."

Heart skipping, she dashed for the rope, hiding the heat in her cheeks from his too-keen gaze.

CHAPTER
THIRTY-SEVEN

F OR A TIME, there was nothing but the cold.

To escape it, she went back.

Back to Stornhaz and its rainbow of streets—the Rouge, the Quicksilver, and Onyx Way; back to Spruce Harbor, to skipping stones, to the feeling of a warm arm encircling her shoulders and a stubbled cheek resting on her curls. Back to firelit taverns and gambling houses, the slip of feathery old cards in her fingers and the reek of hard spirits and body odor all around her at the table where the card sharps played...not their cards really, but their minds against one another, hers as fluid as theirs.

Back to his eyes across the table, not watching the game, not fascinated by the card-counting or the gambling. Fascinated with *her*.

Back to the Tribune's Ball, her beaded dress, his hand clasping her waist while he taught her how to dance like an elite. His breath, a whisper against the shell of her ear. "*There was something I wanted to try...*"

His lips, cold, soft against hers, the taste of his blood in her mouth.

Tatiana jolted awake, swinging up in a nest of furs, pain arrowing through her shoulder and ankle where the frostwolves had gnawed her armor. But she wasn't wearing her armor anymore; she was layered in a heavy coat, a pair of pants, thick wool socks, and mittens, none of it hers.

She cradled her shoulder and surveyed her surroundings, dim and hazy—a braided hide tent with a fire burning low in its center, the smoke escaping through an open flap at the peak. A woman sat at the fireside, tending a pot of broth.

"Quill." Tatiana's throat ached around his name.

The woman glanced up, revealing a broad, flat nose and brow, narrow eyes, and a dark braid peeping from her collar. "Good, you're awake." She spoke the common tongue with an accent Tatiana had never heard before: thick, with heavy emphasis on the vowels. "I am Nunajik, but you may call me Nuna. This is—"

"Where's Quill?" Tatiana shoved back the furs, though her body cried for rest even while she was just sitting up. Those *bandayos* at the lake had hit her harder than she thought.

Nuna's face softened slightly. "You are in The Village of the Moon in Oadmark."

"I don't *care!* I don't care where *I* am. Where is *Quill?*"

The woman averted her gaze. "I am sorry."

The moment the truth dropped from Nuna's mouth, Tatiana was out of the tent and into the blinding glare of sunlight bounding on new snow. A small path wound between a dozen similar structures, lined with women and children—the entirety of this village, by the looks of it.

"Where's the medico tent?" Tatiana shouted at a pair of mothers hurrying by with infants strapped to their backs. "Medico? Where—where are your *sick?*"

Up and down the trail, heads turned, mothers and children blinking in mirrored confusion. But one woman shouted back, "Healer! *Innuin!*"

"Yes! Healer, medico, *Innuin,* whatever you call them!"

She pointed to the back of the encampment. Tatiana broke into a sprint before Nuna caught up to her, bursting into the largest tent of them all—more of a pavilion supported by a circle of struts and a broad central post. The interior was hot, lined with firepits and wooden pallets.

Quill was draped across one of them.

Tatiana caught herself against the support post, knees weak as her panic ebbed. He was here; Nuna hadn't lied, he was *alive*.

But not moving. Sweat streaked his face, his lips blue, his lungs gurgling with every labored breath. Two men hovered near his bed, halting their quiet conversation when Tatiana entered, blinking owlishly at her.

The pavilion door flapped open, and Nuna panted out an apology as she took Tatiana's shoulders. She shrugged her off and stalked toward the medicos. "What are you just standing there for? Treat him."

"Your friend is very ill," Nuna murmured. "An infection of the lungs, and other wounds."

"I don't care! *Treat him.*"

"Our supplies are limited. It already cost the boys much to revive him at the hollow. To use the god-power and reawaken someone not of the tribe is indeed unusual."

Tatiana craved a knife in her hand, an augment, *something*—anything she could use to force their cooperation—but she shoved that thought down. She would not use her fists, her weapons to force them to do her bidding. She wasn't like Salvotor.

She had so much more to lose.

Her legs wobbled as she knelt at Quill's side and pressed her knuckles to his cheek, clammy but feverish, tacky with sweat and slippery with tears. His stubble rasped against the back of her hand when she dragged her knuckles and the pad of her thumb along the curve of his jaw.

Nuna knelt beside her. "Our hunters say you took their cave in the reindeer rutting hollow. That you fought and killed frostwolves and men in dark garb." She laid a hand on Tatiana's shoulder. "I am sorry for how you were treated. They are boys, and they were frightened when they saw you fight the wolves. But they did what they could to bring him back."

Tatiana slid her palm up the curve of Quill's other cheek and stared at his pale, flitting eyelids. She'd never wanted to see his eyes so badly before, knowing they would never open again. "How long?"

Nuna conferred with the men beside the pallet in Oadmarkaic. "He has only hours."

Dampness plopped from Tatiana's cheek onto Quill's parted lips. His breaths rattled viciously, mortally through his ravaged chest.

She had told Cistine once that she didn't dream of the future, because running and hiding was all there was. And that was true, but she'd never told the princess how she was better than resigned to it. A hundred years of fighting and protecting, pillaging and thwarting...she welcomed every second of it, because she knew Quill would be at her side until the last moment. When the Undertaker came, he'd take them together.

Now the best and brightest part of that future was slipping away faster than she could hold on to him. She'd squandered so many days and nights desperately trying to define what lay between them, trying to decide if he was right for her and she for him. And none of it mattered now, because it was over.

The men said something to Nuna, beginning a rapid conversation full of rolling syllables with abrupt ends. Tatiana gave up trying to understand any of it and occupied her fingers with memorizing the angles of Quill's face for the last time—the shape of his nose and lips, the arch of his cheekbones and brows, every tiny scar along his jaw and forehead.

She'd wasted every other chance with him. She wouldn't lose this one.

Silence returned. Then Nuna cleared her throat. "There is...a way to heal him. But it will require something in return. In Oadmark, we do not give for nothing."

Tatiana's head snapped up, desperate hope pounding against her raw nerves. "Name your price. I'll pay it."

"The bodies in dark garb on Hrob Lake...those were Valgardan, yes? You are Valgardan warriors?"

"We are."

"Good. That is what we need." Nuna's gaze drifted, her jaw tightening slightly. "A great evil has descended on The Village of the Moon. Many hunters have gone to confront it and failed. But if you fight as the boys said, and if you killed those men on Hrob Lake, then perhaps you can succeed where they failed. If you will swear an oath to free my village, then we will save him."

Tatiana gritted her teeth. She and Quill could triumph over any enemy on any battleground they took together; but if she did this, she'd as good as agree that all his life amounted to was being a blade in someone else's arsenal, something to gamble with when it suited her.

But it wasn't really a gamble. He was halfway through the Sable Gates; this was a second chance to teach him his worth and tell him every truth she kept secret for years.

He was wrong, that night on the mountainside. She wasn't as strong as he thought; she was breaking. *This* was breaking, the thought of life without him. If that made her a coward, so be it. She wasn't ready to be broken without him to help her pick up the pieces.

"We'll do it," she said. "We'll fight anyone you want. Just heal him."

CHAPTER THIRTY-EIGHT

THE LONG HOURS while the *Innuin* labored to bring Quill back from the brink of death were the worst of Tatiana's life. They wouldn't let her into the pavilion; they allowed her to pace outside while a pair of boys half her age guarded the entrance with crossed spears and nervous glances. Nunajik disappeared, then returned with thin pine-needle tea in clay cups.

Tatiana sipped hers and kept pacing while Nuna sat cross-legged beside the path. When her rattling nerves turned to a cramping stomach, she finally broke the silence. "So. The Village of the Moon. Are you the only village here?"

Nuna shook her head. "There are many Villages here in the mountains. In the meadows and warm places to our north, order is maintained by the Wingmaidens and their dragons."

"Why don't *they* fight off this evil that's plaguing you?"

"They have tried. Many have fallen. Now they fear going into battle." Nuna stared into the distance, hands slipping into her opposite sleeves. "The *Aeoprast* is a young god who takes what he wills from whoever he wishes. I...fear him greatly."

Tatiana choked on her next sip of tea. "I'm sorry, a young *god*?"

Nunajik sketched a strange rune over her heart and pressed her knuckles to her brow. "Many gods have awoken these past ten years, but the

Aeoprast is the fiercest of them all."

That wasn't possible. Ariadne had taught her plenty about the True God and his vassals; they didn't walk among men. And they weren't *evil*.

Light footsteps pounded the village's well-worn path. A girl half Pippet's age ran to Nunajik and offered her a handful of dull river rocks. "Look, *Arnaq*! Moonstones!"

"They are lovely, Chena." Nuna cupped her palms, and the girl let all the rocks tumble into her hands. "I will treasure them always."

Chena scuffed her boot shyly on the path and bit her mitten, glancing up at Tatiana.

"Do I have something on my face?" she patted her cheeks, and Chena giggled, then squealed when Nunajik swatted her on the backside.

"Go. Play with the other children."

Tatiana arched a brow as the girl scampered away. "I didn't realize I was quite that breathtaking."

Nuna smiled heavily. "Chena is my daughter. Her father, Shesh, was the last warrior to face the *Aeoprast*. It has been...difficult for her."

The silence that followed was more strained than the one before it. Tatiana wondered if this was how Cistine felt when she first came to Valgard, constantly treading on a world she didn't understand, awakening hurts throbbing under the surface.

The sooner they finished this new mission and returned to their hunt, the better.

The pavilion flap lifted suddenly, and an *Innuin* poked his head out. He spoke to Nuna, but Tatiana didn't wait for the translation. She tossed her cup aside and barreled past the man, ducking into the warm shelter and bracing her heart for whatever she would find inside.

The other *Innuin* leaned against the tent post, stripping off his dark gloves—familiar. Armored. A tinge of power rode the firelit-air, setting her hair on end. Her eyes fell on Quill's bed, and her heart stopped beating.

He was sitting up. Bundled in a bear pelt, mismatched hair askew, folded arms cinching the covering tightly to his broad shoulders. There was color in his cheeks, his lips a healthy pink again. And his eyes...she hadn't realized how dull they were after the lake until they met hers, lighting up from their depths "Tati!"

He cast off the pelt and struggled up to meet her, drawing her focus to his right hand.

Her heart plummeted. Then her body moved of its own volition.

She grabbed the *Innuin* by his vest and shoved him back against the post so hard, the whole tent shuddered. "*His hand!* Where are his stars-damned *fingers?*"

The man shouted a jumble of indistinguishable syllables just as Nuna ducked into the tent. She translated rapidly, "He says the flesh on the last two fingers was dead...rotten! They couldn't breathe life back into it."

"Tatiana!" Quill's arm circled below her breasts from behind, and he heaved her away, letting the man drop on the pavilion floor. "Stop!"

She thrashed instead, spitting at Nuna and the *Innuin*, "You let me agree to this fight when he's missing two of the fingers on his sword hand!"

Quill's arm hitched around her middle, stopping her breath. Then he yanked her around to face him. "I said *stop*. Let it go, Tatiana."

"He took your fingers!"

Pain danced in Quill's eyes, as vivid and tangible as her own face in a mirror; but he brushed it aside when he brushed away her curls and took her face in his hands—*both* hands—and trapped her gaze with his. "It doesn't matter. It doesn't matter, Tati! Because I can still do this." He tucked her hair behind her ear when it swung loose again, this time with the three remaining fingers of his right hand. He grinned when she shivered at that touch, a crooked, desperate smile. "Right? *I can still do this.* No harm done."

This. Did he mean touching her? Living his life? Was he as afraid as she was that he would never be able to fight as strongly as he once did?

Tears threatened. Tatiana blinked them away. "Don't ever, *ever* try to leave me like that again."

His grin broadened, became more genuine. "No. I won't."

He looped his arm around her shoulders and Tatiana stopped caring which land they were in—because right then, she was home.

"So," Quill said. "What's this about a fight?"

Nunajik helped the *Innuin* up and murmured to him. He and his companion departed, and Nuna motioned Quill and Tatiana to sit. "I will tell you what you must do."

He obliged, snatching up his blanket again; but she didn't, body still humming with rage and relief. She leaned against the support post instead while Nuna settled in front of Quill.

"Long ago, before Shesh and I led the tribe, men came to us much like you...injured. Sickly. Weak. They brought no provisions, only gifts. In trade for these gifts, we agreed to heal them, and friendships formed." Melancholy touched her tone. "We cared for one another. They learned our language, and we learned theirs. They became familiar with our customs, the lay of our land. We were happy, peaceful together. And then, after the first thaw, it all began to change."

The *Innuin* returned just then, carrying platters of crisp fish and cups of tea. Quill sat up straight, his stomach growling audibly; some of Tatiana's tension melted, and a smile prodded through.

"I'm sorry," she said to the man she'd attacked. He blinked at her, then dipped his head—not understanding the words, maybe, but the tone that delivered them.

When they were alone again, and Quill tackling his portion with an intensity that made their argument in the hunter's cave feel like nothing more than a nightmare, Nuna resumed her tale.

"Our guests grew suspicious of us. They no longer wished to share their gifts, they spoke cruelly, they were selfish with our rations. They threatened our women and took too much interest in our children. So finally my father, who was patriarch at the time, mustered the men to drive them out." She touched trembling fingers to a carved necklace around her throat. "I have been matriarch ever since that day."

Tatiana leaned her head back against the tent pole. "But he did drive them out?"

"Oh, yes, they fled. Though the battle was brutal and countless of our elders lost, the visitors were not used to fighting in such climes. And we stole many of their gifts."

Tatiana glanced at Quill just in time to see his three-fingered hand flex.

"We have heard nothing all this time since," Nuna went on, "but in other Villages—the Village of the Sun, the Village of the Earth, the Village of the Winds—their people are taken at night with no trace. Sometimes, days before, they see the *Aeoprast*. The young god. And now we have begun to see him, too."

"Where and when?" Tatiana asked.

"Around the edge of the village this season. He never lingers, but his presence frightens away game. We must travel further every day to hunt. That is why the boys were in the rutting hollow where they found you."

Quill grimaced. "This young god, what does he look like?"

"Taller than any mortal man. He wears the face of a beast and moves between places like the wind. He fights for the ones we drove out. It was they who first invoked his name against us all those years ago, promising that when the hour of retribution came, a god called the *Aeoprast* would arise to avenge our betrayal against them. Now he comes for us."

"Do you know where he is?" Quill asked. "Where those people are?"

"Shesh believes they dwell in a cleft high up in the mountains, where the *Aeoprast* drags its victims. He planned to track it, but it used its gifts before he climbed the mountain. It did not leave enough of him to bury."

Quill's eyes jumped to Tatiana, his mouth jerking down at the corner. "All right. We'll need a few days to prepare."

"Take as much as you need. We are in your debt for this," Nuna said. "Come, I will show you to a tent."

They walked in silence from the pavilion to an empty shelter near the village edge. Tatiana wondered if it had belonged to someone the *Aeoprast* killed—an elder, a mother, a father like Shesh.

Nuna left them inside to discover their armor, a pair of sleeping pelts, and kindling for a fire already supplied. Tatiana built it while Quill paced, rubbing his thumb over the stumps of his missing fingers. The sight ached worse than she thought it would. "What are you thinking?"

"Augurs," Quill said. "Rogue ones, it sounds like."

"That explains how the *Innuin* healed you." Another pang of shame shot through Tatiana's middle; she really should've been more grateful from the start. "A healing augment. That's why they used the gloves."

Quill nodded. "They must've realized a long time ago that only people with the right armor can wield flagons. And if those really are augurs out there, we're the only ones who can really stop them."

"So we go up the mountain?"

"We go up the mountain. Take whatever flagons this Village still has, bring down a rogue band of augurs. Simple enough."

Tatiana sat back on her heels, away from the crackling fire. "This *Aeoprast*. What do you think *he* is?"

"Someone who likes dressing for a part. But there's nothing in this world you and I can't bring down together, Saddlebags."

She hoped that was true. Because something prodded at the back of her mind, like a story she heard long ago...something that made a journey up the mountain to face this *Aeoprast* seem like a dance with death.

Scooting back on the pelt, knees cradled to her chest, she watched Quill move around their small tent. He shook out his own bedroll and examined his clean armor, movements bunching with awkwardness only when he used his right hand.

As if he hadn't been as good as dead that morning; as if she hadn't gambled both their lives to save his.

"Can't use a bow the same way," he mused. "I'll have to retrain my hands to the sword, too. But that's all right...I can fight double-handed with one blade, if nothing else. Do you think they'll give us weapons when we go up the mountain?"

She cleared her throat. "They'll have to. The only thing I walked away from that lake with was my knife."

"Well, what more do we need?" Quill joked. "One knife should be plenty for hunting a god, saving a village, going to Kalt Hasa and rescuing Cistine." He flexed his three-fingered hand. "Training should be interesting from now on. I wonder what throwing a punch feels like without..." Voice snagging, he turned his hair shakily across the top of his head.

Tatiana's hands shook, trapped in the hinges of her elbows, and she dropped her chin to her knees. Quill shook himself and swaggered over to join her, balancing his left hand on her shoulder and his right on the pelts as he folded down cross-legged beside her. "What's wrong, Tati?"

What *wasn't* wrong? His hand, this hunt, the time they'd waste keeping their word before they could save Cistine...

"Tatiana." Quill nudged her shoulder with this. "This isn't your fault. I'd rather be alive with a hand like this than dead with all my fingers."

Dead. He really had come too close this time. "How much do you remember from the cave?"

"Bits and pieces. I think I dreamed a lot. You trying to feed me. Fighting wolves. Seeing the auroras."

"What about...after that?"

"Ah," Quill said. "Right. I guess that part wasn't a dream this time."

Tatiana's heart kicked up its rhythm. *This time?*

"Nimmus' teeth," Quill muttered. "You know, whenever I thought about this, all the kissing came *after*."

"After *what*?"

His eyes flashed over to her. "You know what."

She did. As much as she tried to run from it, as often as she reminded herself that wanting and needing him were dangerous, self-destructive things because she could never come first for him...he'd proved her wrong. Out there on that lake, he'd put her first. He laid down his life for her, even if it meant robbing Pippet, Thorne, Cistine, and the rest of the world of his safeguarding arms.

But that wasn't right, either. Was one truly better than the other?

"I don't want to be just another sword you fall on," Tatiana said. "That's not what this is supposed to be. Your life is worth more than being the thing this cabal hits when it's breaking."

"If I hadn't done what I did back at the lake, you'd be dead now."

"Wrong. I found a way to save you. You would've saved me, too."

Quill's shoulders bobbed in a scoff. "Is that what you think this is, then? Us saving each other, instead of dying for each other?"

Tatiana gripped his face with both hands, towing his head around until he had no choice but to meet her eyes. "All I know is you have a purpose and a place in this world, Quill. A place with *me*. You're gods-forged from the stars, and that's something *no one* can take away." He tried to shake his head, but she held him fast. "I need you to hear this, Featherbrain. I never wanted you to take my pain for me. I want you to help me carry it."

His mutinous gaze softened. His mouth curved into a half-smile. "I know you do. That's one of the things I love about you."

The words hung on the air, cold and clear and undeniable. Still, her mind struggled more to make sense of them than a riddle in a wine-washed frenzy. "When did you know?"

Quill blew out a long breath. "When those Vassoran *bandayos* shot you on the Vingete Vey. When Ariadne told me the state you were in, and I ran all the way back from patrol. I'd fantasized about kissing you plenty of times, but when I saw you in your bed, so pale, in so much pain, it was different. I wanted that hunt, even though I didn't trust myself with it. I wanted to hurt everyone who ever hurt you. I never wanted to spend another day of my life without you beside me."

And he hadn't. He'd never walked away again, even when she was drunk for days and lashing him with cruel words and snide remarks. Even when she screamed in his face in Geitlan, he stayed.

He *was* putting her first. He had been for months, and she never saw it until now.

When she didn't speak, Quill's gaze dropped. "I understand if you don't want that from me. I have less to give you right now than I've ever had. Just a pair of swords, my back against yours in battle, and a warm bed on the good nights."

"I told you, I'm not here for what you can give me," she rasped. "Not anymore. Just for you."

This time, when she pulled his head down and his mouth crashed against hers, warm and soft and sparking with life like she always imagined, it meant so much more than that brief, desperate kiss beside the lake. She poured every ounce of love and intent into the place where their bodies met, where their lips fit together as seamlessly as the rest of them.

When they broke apart, flushed and panting, Quill rested his three-fingered hand on her cheek. "You want to forge the bond, don't you?"

His voice was that strange, dark music from the Secret Keeper's room again, the one she loved ever since Spruce Harbor. It sent pure fire lacing through her body. "Is that even a question? I'll do it right now."

"Then it's a good thing you still have your knife, because I'm ready, too." He took her chin and breathed the next words against her lips. "I've always been yours, Dawnstar. Always will be."

With the last of the fear shattering inside her, she finally saw the truth. She'd always been his, too.

It was only after that she realized the sheer, awe-inspiring importance of what they'd done. Lying in the furs, her palm stinging from the *valenar* cut clumsily but gently wrapped in Quill's scarf by his own unsteady hands, she watched his face while he slumbered.

She'd seen him like this so many times: head pillowed on his folded arm, enviably-long lashes flickering while he dreamed. Sometimes they slept side by side on the Den's porch, watching the stars; sometimes on a blanket in Starhollow with Pippet nestled between them. Sometimes they curled up to read on his bed and she woke with his head in her lap, stealing precious minutes to watch him so perfectly at ease before the change in her breathing woke him and they pulled apart.

But this time his other hand was on her bare hip, and there was nothing between them but skin and bones. Their intrinsic bond fizzed with a brighter awareness than ever before. Her mark sealed his hand, the one twisted under his hair; the sacred words of the *valenar* vow still branded lips bruised from his passionate kisses.

She was his. He was hers. When he woke, neither of them would pull away again; they'd find healing together, better ways to love themselves and each other.

They would never be alone again.

CHAPTER THIRTY-NINE

Rion's rage was palpable when their retinue left Nordbran for Kroaken's gentler yellow dunes. Had they dared venture near any cities, Ashe would've expected him to buy a map, find Kalt Hasa, and leave her and Aden behind with Deja and Pippet.

Worse than the notion she might one day wake up abandoned by her Cadre was that it wasn't the worst fate she could imagine. Aden, at least, still spoke to her; he told her what little he knew of Kalt Hasa, an ancient temple far in the north, and over fires after Pippet nodded off, they watched Deja and speculated quietly why Salvotor chose that place to hold Cistine captive.

Though Aden shared what he knew, he never told her precisely where it was. Perhaps he feared she'd use that knowledge to smuggle away back into Rion's favor, leading the Cadre away and abandoning him to deal with Deja and Pippet alone. And she knew he wouldn't fully trust her even if she said it, but that course of action wasn't even a consideration for her anymore. They were too close to risk everything on foolish gestures and kingdom pride. They needed the Hive Lord's cunning and prowess, his blades, perhaps even his augments, if they could find any, to free Cistine.

When she broached the subject with Aden one night, camped on the verge where Kroaken's dunes gave way to hardy vegetation and rivers pooled down from the north, he nodded. "Very likely. Blades will not be enough."

Ashe grimaced. "Rion will never agree to it."

"I take it he agrees with very little." Aden prodded the fire with one hand, the other stroking Pippet's back where she curled up beside him. "What will *you* do?"

"Make trouble for myself, like I've been doing."

His eyes flicked to her over the flames. "You haven't told me why you did it...argued for my freedom over the knowledge of Kalt Hasa."

She shrugged, but it didn't lessen the discomfort weighing her gut. "I couldn't let you sell yourself back to her. There's nothing more despicable than a person who tries to own someone else."

"True." Aden's gaze flicked to the Cadre's campfire, outside of earshot, then back to her. "Whatever their methods."

The hair on her neck prickled. "Anyway, Cistine would kill me if she learned I sold your hide to find her. And I have to start thinking about what she wants, not just what I think is best for her."

"She would be proud, I suspect. You're making a great sacrifice."

It certainly felt like it, a war locked between her head and heart every day they traveled south when instinct screamed to go north.

"Thank you," Aden added when she didn't speak. "I was prepared to make that choice, to protect both our kingdoms and save your princess. But I'm grateful it wasn't needed." His gaze flicked to hers, warmer than she'd seen since he learned of her actions with the Tumult. "It seems my secret was always in good hands."

Ashe wished his gratitude was enough to ease the tension in her heart. But when she settled across the fire to sleep, her dreams were dark again—shadows and blood, ice and snow and flames. She woke in the dead of dark, panting and sweating from a nightmare of *Meszaros* chasing her through Deja's home. Vomit climbed her throat and the too-real sensation of blood poured between her fingers, the ice of *Meszaros's* presence crawling down her back.

She needed to move, needed to be alone before she emptied herself all over their dead fire.

Leaving Aden and Pippet curled up back-to-back and Deja slumped against a tree nearby, she staggered up and blindly followed the sounds of moving water through the small grove of stunted trees. Her thoughts popped and blazed too sharply, too loudly, her breaths tearing from her chest. She skidded down a short slope and fell to her knees beside a small waterfall breaking the river's flow; cupping handfuls of water into her mouth and splashing the clammy sweat from her cheeks, she struggled for calm.

She had to stop thinking about Deja and Aden, about Cistine. One mission at a time: first the witness, then the temple. They would go with augments, maybe even with Maleck and Ariadne at their backs, if they could ever trust theirs to her in battle again. This was the wiser, safer, *better* choice.

The undergrowth rustled, and Ashe groaned, knocking her wrist against her mouth. "Pippet?"

"No. But I am not surprised the raven's sister is with you."

Hand to Echelon, Ashe spun off her knees to face the lonely figure emerging from the undergrowth: an older woman, willowy and brown-skinned with deep, dark eyes. Tasseled bells whispered on her ankles with every stride, wrists singing when she raised her hands to lay back her shimmering hood.

"Peace," she said. "I didn't come here to fight."

"Then what?" The words emerged harsher than Ashe intended. "You enjoy sneaking up on people in the dark?"

"If you were not in need of the help I bring, I would not have been able to sneak up on you."

Ashe's fingers flexed on Echelon's hilt, then fell. There was no point in pretense; she wouldn't kill another old Valgardan woman. "Who are you, where did you come from, and how do you know Pippet and Quill?"

"My name is Sigrid," she said. "Though for many, many years, I have been called the Secret Keeper. And I know Quill and Pippet because I know the one who raised them."

Ashe swallowed sharply. "You knew Helga?"

"Yes, and I know how she died. Kallah as well."

Ashe's fingers flicked back to Echelon. "Why are you here?"

"Not to avenge my sisters. That is in the gods' hands. I come not as their divine agent, but as their messenger." She stepped nearer, the whisper of music around her ankles awakening a long-buried yearning in Ashe's hands—not for the sword. "I have a gift the gods bade me keep until the proper time. They told me I would know when the one it was meant for came to our borders. Some months ago, I felt the stirring, and when the Blood Hive fell and whispers began of the woman who helped topple it, then I knew." She slipped a hand into her pocket and withdrew an onyx chain; on its setting swung a stone, dark as night and smattered with mineral deposits like stars. In the very core, a flicker of amber-red burned like a lidless eye. "Take it. It was meant for you."

Ashe snorted. "Whatever you think the gods are telling you, I promise, you're wrong. That's not meant for me, I'm..."

Talheimic. A liar. Lost.

"The True God makes no mistakes." Sigrid said. "Are you not Asheila Kovar, Warden to Princess Cistine, beast-slayer and rain-dancer of the Blood Hive?"

Ashe frowned at those last titles, spoken by Nimea just to her the night Siralek fell. "How did you—?"

"The gods speak, and I listen. I've listened to many, many voices in this kingdom over the years." Sigrid took Ashe's wrist and tugged her hand from her sword. Half-numb with shock, she let the necklace coil in her palm. "This is a starstone. Some call them the Eyes of the Gods. In the ancient epics, they were used to summon aid from all corners of Valgard."

Ashe batted away the memory of Lydie's jab at Valgardans naming everything sixteen different ways. "What am I supposed to use it for?"

"You'll know when the time is right...when you're ready for it. Help will come, and your true journey will begin."

Sigrid's gaze shot past Ashe toward the waterfall. A look of urgency crossed her face, and her bony fingers seized Ashe's and curled them tight over the stone.

"War is coming," she hissed, and the rough shift in her tone sent chills cascading down Ashe's spine. "Not the kind you expect...not something you or your people can face alone. The gods chose you for a reason, Asheila Kovar. When you use this stone, you'll start to understand why."

A yell boomed above the rushing water, and a throwing knife whistled end-over-end past Ashe's shoulder and jammed into the old woman's chest.

A Warden's knife.

"No!" Rage and heartbreak cracked Ashe's voice, her fingers clutching Sigrid's arms as the old woman crumbled. Together, their knees struck the cool ground. "No, please, not *again*—"

"It's all right," Sigrid murmured. "I go to my sisters in Cenowyn. If you see Iri, tell her...tell her we will always be with her."

"Who is *Iri*?" Ashe shouted. "What does—please, no..." She slid a hand around Sigrid's neck, lifting her limp head. "What does all of this have to do with me? I'm just another Warden!"

"You are more," Sigrid whispered. "Even if you do not see it yet. When you are ready...use the stone. Find who you were made to be."

Her head dropped back, eyes flickering shut.

"All right there, Kovar?" Symon called down from the top of the falls. He and Viktor squinted at her in the moonlight, faces tense with concern.

Scarlet washed her vision. Howling profanities, Ashe spun to her feet. "What in God's name is wrong with you *bastards*? She was just an old woman!"

Just like Kallah and Helga. Another Valgardan dead because of Ashe.

Symon slid down the slope, frowning. "It looked like you were being attacked. Why didn't you fight back?"

"Because I wasn't *under attack*!" Ashe slammed both hands into his chest, knocking him to his seat on the shore. "She wasn't hurting anyone! None of them were!"

"Well, we didn't know that! All we saw was one of our own with a Valgardan grabbing her wrists, in the dark—"

"So you threw without looking twice? You didn't stop to think that *maybe* she was innocent? Maybe we were just *talking*?"

"Why would a Valgardan sneak up on anyone in the dark just to *talk*?" Viktor strolled up with thumbs hooked in his belt, his knife belt emptier by one. "You know better."

A shrill cry echoed from above the falls. "Ashe? Ashe, where are you?"

"Pippet," she cursed under her breath, moving to block sight of the dead body.

Pippet slid down the slope, boots digging into the damp sod, with Rozalie behind her trying to catch her arm. But Aden caught hers instead, towing her gently but firmly to a halt. "Leave her."

Pippet crashed into Ashe, hugging her waist. "We heard you scream— are you hurt?" Her gaze fell on Sigrid's body, and she let go of Ashe to hold her mouth. "Oh. Oh, *no*..."

Ashe pulled Pippet's face against her stomach. "Don't look."

"Who was she? Who hurt her?"

Symon looked away, jaw clenched, rubbing the back of his neck. But Viktor's half-lidded gaze dared Ashe to start a fight.

"She was an innocent who just came to talk," Ashe growled, holding his stare without flinching. "And she was struck down like prey for it."

Rozalie shook off Aden's hand and descended the slope, gripping Viktor by the shoulder. "She's right. You didn't need to do this. It wasn't part of the mission."

He shrugged her off. "Going soft for the North, Dohnal?"

She grimaced. "The next time, you might shoot someone important to this kingdom. What then?"

"Then maybe they think twice about creeping up on our camp in the dark."

Pippet wrenched out of Ashe's hold, pivoting and shoving her face as close to Viktor's as she could with their mismatched heights. "Why are you so *cruel*? Why do you hate *everything* you don't understand?"

Viktor bent on Pippet's level, his smile indulgent and cocksure—a look Ashe once found appealing from across smoky taverns over steins of ale. Now it made her stomach turn. "Let me teach you something my commander taught me." He seized Pippet's chin and drew her closer. "Little nasty things in this kingdom grow to be larger, *nastier* things. The sooner you stomp out Valgardan filth, the more pain you save yourself."

Aden shoved past Rozalie, his hand halfway to Viktor's back when Pippet broke his grip with a strike of a hand to his wrist and shoved him away with all her might. "If I was a princess, I wouldn't want to be saved by the likes of *you*."

"Pippet." Ashe lashed an arm around the girl's chest, drawing her back. "Enough. That's enough for tonight."

Viktor's gaze shot between them, brimming with disdain. Then he motioned Symon back up the slope, leaving Rozalie, Aden, Ashe, and Pippet beside the pool.

"I hate him," Pippet hissed.

"Don't give him that much power over you." Aden rested his hand on her head. "Don't let him make you *feel*. Remaining aloof is the greatest weapon you can wield against him."

Pippet dashed her arm across her eyes. "Why do they hate us so much?"

"Not all Talheimics are like him," Rozalie mumbled. "This...this wasn't right. Some of us know that." Throat tight, Ashe turned back to Sigrid and drew up the old woman's hood, arranging her limbs in an imitation of peaceful slumber. Rozalie crouched at her side. "Who was she?"

"Someone who believed in something that isn't real." Ashe's fists flexed, the starstone's linked chain biting into her palm. "*Someone* who isn't real. And she died for them."

Aden knelt on her other side, and the gravity of his presence heightened her shame. Perhaps he'd known her once, this friend of Kallah's. She couldn't bear to meet his eyes and ascertain if that were true. "It was an accident." Though she knew for her fellow Wardens, it was anything but.

"I know," Aden said. "Take Pippet back to camp. I'll build a pyre."

She didn't bother arguing; she'd done enough damage. She went to Pippet, wrapped an arm around her shoulders, and led her up the slope toward the camp, leaving Aden—and, to her surprise, Rozalie—gathering stones and branches.

It was an act both of penance and shame that rather than throwing away that necklace, the cause of yet another senseless death on her head, Ashe slid it into her pocket instead.

CHAPTER
FORTY

A WEEK SLID past like sand through Tatiana's fingers, every day stuffed with studying rudimentary Oadmarkaic maps and constructing battle plans with Quill. Much to her dismay, they had no battle flagons left—only healing. They were back to trusting their steel for this fight; thankfully that, at least, was not in short supply from the tribe.

At night they wandered the village, assessing the mountain path by full moonlight, tracking the weather patterns and discussing Hrob Lake, the cave, the attack from the Vassora, the impending hunt and their delayed journey to Kalt Hasa.

"I just hope we made Cistine strong enough to endure this," Quill admitted one night. They'd wandered to the edge of the village to study the snow blowing from the mountains in silver slants of moonlight—charting the wind patterns for approaching storms. Back propped against the last tent, hands stuffed in his pockets, Quill blew a shaking breath on the frigid air. "It's taking a lot longer than I hoped to get there."

Tatiana shrugged her shoulders deeper into her pelt coat. "She's always had that strength, we just helped her tap into it. She'll hold on. She has to."

Quill turned his hair across his head. "I just...feel responsible for her. Like I do for Pip, you know? *I* brought her into the cabal when I stepped into that mess in Veran with the slavers. Ever since, she's been like another sister to me."

Tatiana peered up at him, his strong jaw and sharp nose framed in harsh angles by the moonlight, the concern in his eyes brighter than the glint of snow all around the village. And she loved him for all of it. "We'll find her. Kalt Hasa is still out there. As soon as we kill this augur and his friends, we're back on our way."

"Right, that's—"

Quill cut off sharply, hands sliding from his pockets, straightening abruptly from the tent.

Where the mist from the nearby pond thickened into lazy curlicues at the base of the mountain and soaring stone walls framed the pass, a shape separated from the shadows. Nine feet tall at least and shrouded all in black, its face jutted like a gazelle's, the lower mandible crowded with jagged fangs that pushed the skull backward into a vicious, frozen grin. Horns climbed above the brows, sloughed with gory fibers, and it measured them through void eye sockets.

The hairs on Tatiana's nape bristled, and she sidestepped away from the tent to the open path; Quill moved with her like he'd been waiting for something to jolt him into motion. The creature extended a cloaked arm after them and bared a long, corpse-pale hand, beckoning with one gruesome finger.

Tatiana's knife was in her hand before her mind connected to the motion, and she hurled it with a shout straight down the path at the creature's masked face.

She didn't even see it move, but the blade struck *behind* it, bouncing and skidding on the cold stone.

Tatiana snagged Quill's sleeve and yanked him backward as the mist curled across the slope again. When it cleared, he swung around and pushed the small of Tatiana's back.

They ran, though there was no longer anything to run from. The mist swallowed the young god whole.

Even bundled in insulated furs, her armor stripped, Tatiana couldn't stop shaking. Whenever she shut her eyes, she saw that leering skull and ashen hand, the nails filed to riving points.

She shuddered, peeling her eyes open. Quill knelt on the pelts, stuffing provisions into a hide pack Nuna left for them, his jaw set and eyes glinting with the same madness as before every dangerous card game and act of vandalism since they were sixteen years old.

"What are you doing?" Tatiana demanded.

"It's time. If we don't do this now, that thing might be back to burn this village to the ground."

Tatiana lurched to her feet. "How are we going to face something like *that* with just swords and spears? You saw what it looked like—did you *feel* it? Steel won't be enough!"

"Well, we also have our fists." He wiggled his right hand. "Mostly."

Tatiana's heart somersaulted. Why wasn't he as terrified of that creature as she was—its unnatural presence, the danger fuming from beneath that hooded robe and the ruthless promise of its gaunt hand? "Quill. We need to reconsider this hunt."

His head snapped up, gaze jabbing into her. "The cabal is always good for its word. We swore that to Thorne when he Named us."

"We also promised we'd fight *clever*, not stupid!"

He yanked the rucksack shut and pushed to his feet. "Tati, what else can we do? This village isn't prepared to fight augurs. Only we can do that."

"And we could die! I could lose you again, and I'm not ready to take that chance." She gripped his collar, yanking him close. "I need you to choose *me* again."

"So do I, Saddlebags." His breath rippled across her face, warm and shaky. "I need you to put *me* first and help me do this."

They stared at one another, stalemated.

"I thought you said you were going to try to do this differently. Stop throwing your life away for other people." The words punched out of her, full of so much pain she felt embarrassed, weak from it.

Quill's tight jaw loosened. His three-fingered hand cradled her cheek. "Look at me...I don't want to go up that mountain and die. All right? I know things are different now for us. I don't intend to break that vow, either. But *you* deserve better than a man who runs at the first sight of trouble. That can't be the answer, either."

"I don't care if you run, as long as you *live*."

"Then run with me." His other hand joined the first, framing her face. "You want to know how I can always get into trouble like I do and never seem like I'm afraid? Because I know who's watching my back. We can *do this*, Saddlebags. Together."

His gaze was feverish, full of passion; he wanted to help these people. He *wanted* this hunt. There was no fear or doubt in his face this time.

Swallowing a surge of bile, she surged forward and pressed her mouth to his. "Fine," she muttered against his lips. "Let's go hunt a god."

Packs shouldered, they stepped from the tent—then halted.

The lonely figure waiting in the middle of the path was not the *Aeoprast*. But with her shoulders squared and a spear in each hand, Nunajik was no less intimidating.

"You go up the mountain." It was not a question.

Quill nodded, hefting his pack higher. "We saw that thing. You're right. It's time to end this before someone else gets hurt."

Something like fear glistened in Nuna's eyes, bright as the moonstones her daughter poured into her hands outside the pavilion. But her jaw remained firm. "I cannot thank you enough for what you do for us. You could have fled when you were healed, but you stayed. And now you go."

A trickle of guilt kissed every notch on Tatiana's spine. She stepped forward to meet the matriarch, gripping the spear beneath the head and meeting her sharp gaze. "We may not be from the same people, but our Court fights for everyone who needs us." She flicked a glance at Quill. "Sometimes we just have to remind each other of that."

Nuna surprised her by jerking her closer by the spear they both held, their brows brushing together. "May our ancestors go with you. May Shesh's spirit guide you up the mountain."

Tatiana wasn't sure she believed in anything like that; but with Quill beside her, she didn't fear the climb. And with the faith shining in Nunajik's eyes when they took their spears from her, she almost felt ready to hunt this skull-masked god.

"We'll see you on the other side," Tatiana said with the smirk she usually reserved for people in Blaykrone who needed their aid; the savior's smile, the look shared around the cabal. A promise that help was already here. "Keep an eye on the passes."

She and Quill lashed on the spears, then the knives Nuna offered. Then they started for that treacherous, dark mountain.

CHAPTER
FORTY-ONE

THE COMFORTING AROMA of herbs and root vegetables whisked Cistine away to the garden in Hellidom, anchoring her like fingers in the soil, the brush of twilight against her eyelids, the sounds of life in the Den behind her. With her eyes closed, she could almost imagine she was there, not in Kalt Hasa's dark stone kitchens; that it was summer sweat, not the heat of the large flues trickling down her skin.

Coming here was something of a risk, but it presented her first opportunity to be alone with Kristoff since her journey to the cellar. Salvotor kept him frequently from her and Thorne now, perhaps growing wise to the new fire in his brother-by-marriage; Grimmaul's men were usually her escorts, and Kristoff assigned to duty among the watchtowers.

She'd taken advantage in the aftermath of another humiliating venture to the bathing chamber the day before, with Grimmaul on duty; begging Dain to help her sneak to the kitchens had been surprisingly simple once he knew how desperate she was to be somewhere Salvotor's private guard couldn't find her.

None of it was a lie, either. The cold burn of his touch still lingered where he wrapped the towel around her bare shoulders after her bath.

The three great stone flues blazed, chasing out the memory of those wandering fingers. Prisoners tended the fires with permanent scowls while they chopped and filleted and cobbled together platters for what promised to be yet another torturous meal that night, but Cistine didn't mind their company. While she worked under the pretense of a needed escape, whisking and folding with the rest of them, Dain reappeared with the company she asked for, shot her an uneasy smile, and made his escape.

Kristoff strolled to the worktable, brows rising at the array of fruit and eggs scattered before her. "Lemon custard. A bold choice."

Cistine's cheeks warmed. "An old favorite." Her smile came easily when she met his eyes, and with a jolt she realized how much she'd missed him. "How are the watchtowers?"

"Cold as Nimmus." He folded his arms, leaning against the chopping block. "And the cellar?"

She bent to zest the lemon rind, pitching her voice to a whisper to tell him what she discovered below their feet—and what obstacles still lay between them and freedom.

Kristoff listened, brow sketched intently, and when she finished he murmured, "So, that's why he allows no reinforced armor in this place. Any one of us might discover that dragon and free it."

"But some of us don't need armor," Cistine pointed out.

"Some of us don't." His gaze leveled with hers. "But that augment."

She sipped in a short, sharp breath, the notion still bearing terror down to her core. "It shouldn't frighten me. It's just lightning."

"And lightning took something you cherish." He brushed an untamed swirl of hair off her brow with his smallest finger. "Fear is natural. It doesn't make you weak."

Gratitude burned off the last kernel of cold in her middle, returning a sliver of steely resolve. "But I still have to conquer it. I'm the only one who can carry that burden."

"Do you have a plan?" Kristoff followed her to one of the flues where she popped the custard tarts in to bake.

"I hoped you could tell me something about how to channel an augment," she admitted. "I'd ask Thorne, but..."

Her visits to the prison room had lessened. Whenever she came, he seemed weaker, more exhausted, straining at his collar and rubbing his abused legs. And the guards came to him more frequently, leaving marks of their boredom in bruises and slashes across his face. She wasn't certain if it was because they suspected her sneaking in and out, but the strain it put on Thorne to keep his strength together for her visits was too much. She couldn't keep asking that of him just to sate her own desperation for his company.

Kristoff's brow darkened, keen to things unsaid. "I'll tell you what I can, as soon as I can slip away from watch again."

"The sooner, the better. Once I channel that lightning—"

A throat cleared behind them, stilling her tongue. Heart pounding, she whirled away from the flue.

Salvotor didn't just stand in the doorway. He *emanated* from it, the prisoners giving him a wide berth as he strode to the flue. "I can't say I ever expected to find the Key toiling away over the cooking. Surely you're not teaching her, Kristoff. I seem to recall you and Natalya were terrible at this."

"She needs no teaching," Kristoff said. "But I had nothing to do with this. I just came for something to eat, and here she was."

He lied so effortlessly, she wished he'd teach her that, too.

"Oh? Finished with your watch already, *Allet?*" The casual word, spoken with so much affection among the cabal, dripped like poison from Salvotor's smirking lips. Cistine winced; Kristoff's jaw tightened. "And who brought her here against my orders?"

"How should I know? You've made it clear her whereabouts are no longer my duty."

"Indeed." Salvotor swiveled to Cistine, scouring her with an intensity that made her feel unraveled—beneath her clothes, beneath her skin, all the way to her core. "Well, if you're so eager to be out of your chamber, you have the honor of preparing supper for all of us tonight. I'm certain Thorne would be delighted to sample your fare."

Cistine's hand curled into a fist at her side, thumb out, ready to strike; but somehow she mustered a nod instead of a blow, keeping her eyes down and waiting for him to leave.

He trailed behind her instead, bending to peer over her shoulder at her recipe book and grazing his fingertip along the page. "Why don't you prepare us basted brisket? One of my mother's favorite recipes."

At last, he strutted out, stealing a meat pie from another prisoner's tray. Cistine stared after him, tension rattling her bones, a glassy film of rage coating her eyes.

Kristoff's hand covered hers, squeezing her fist gently until it loosened. "Keep to the plan, and this will all be behind us soon."

She forced a nod, shoulders tight. "You should go. It seems I have plenty of cooking to do."

Despite the lingering taint of Salvotor's presence shrouding the kitchens, Cistine didn't mind the work. The memory of Ariadne and Baba Kallah wrapped around her, their fingerprints in the dough and basting the brisket, their hands raw with hers from scrubbing root vegetables. She practically floated when Kristoff, not Grimmaul, arrived to escort her that night. Even the cruel clasp of the sheer dress mattered less.

Kristoff would teach her how to channel that augment. Soon, Kalt Hasa would be nothing but a nightmare behind her.

Salvotor waited with Grimmaul and his retinue at the table, her feast of brisket, vegetables, and lemon-custard tarts arrayed before them. Their greedy eyes and smirks met her the moment she entered the doorway—the same moment her gaze found Thorne.

She slammed to a halt, every flicker of relief plundering to shadow within her.

Her *selvenar* was strung up by shackles from the dining chamber wall, shirtless and bruised, the healing wound Devitrius had dealt across his side held together by the thready teeth of black sutures and dozens more cuts and bruises freckling around it. Food spattered the wall beside him.

"Ah, Cistine, here you are at last. I see Kristoff's concept of promptness has deteriorated since his service as a Tribune," Salvotor drawled. "We had to entertain ourselves in your absence. A pity to have wasted your hard-made meal on it, but perhaps you'll consider the fruits of your efforts next time."

Punishment. This was *punishment* for leaving her chamber.

Kristoff stared up at his nephew, buckling with exhaustion against his bonds. Tears stamped his stormy gray eyes.

Salvotor waved a hand. "That will be all, Kristoff." But Kristoff didn't move, and Salvotor's gaze narrowed. "I said, that will be all. You may go. Cistine, come."

Grimmaul pushed out Cistine's usual chair with his foot and left his boot propped on its edge, smirking at her; she ripped her gaze from him back to Thorne, the chamber fuming red and rage throbbing her temples.

"*Sit,*" Salvotor repeated icily.

"Cut. Him. *Down.*"

Cistine's voice did not sound like her—brutal, deep, *murderous.* It was the voice of Solene standing between Eboni's shivering frame and Prince Jad's vicious advances; the voice of newly-named King Cyril on the last battlefield of the northern war, bringing victory for Talheim. It was the voice of a queen; and when she turned her rage into a glare speared at Salvotor, he lurched taller in his seat. Grimmaul laid a hand on his sword.

"If you don't cut him down this instant," Cistine snarled, "I can assure you I will find a way to take my *own* life before you gather even a drop of my blood. You will never see the last piece of the ritual, and Valgard will *never* be yours."

After a beat, Salvotor relaxed, folding his hands on the table. "Petty bluffs do not sway me."

"Call it a bluff if you want, but I stand to gain more from my death than my survival thanks to you, and you gain *nothing* if I don't die the way you need. Now *cut him down.*"

After a long, painful minute, the Chancellor looked at Kristoff, giving all the release he needed to drag Cistine's seat to the wall and slit the leather bonds on Thorne's wrists, bringing him gently down the floor. He hung against his uncle's arm, legs shaking, eyes fixed on Cistine. She took just one step toward him, and Salvotor murmured, "Ah. We have a supper to finish."

Kristoff settled Thorne gently against the wall and dragged Cistine's seat back to the table, holding it out until she sank into it. Rage and pain throbbed in his gaze, in his touch when he brushed the back of her neck, then strode from the room under Salvotor's glinting stare.

The moment he was gone, the Chancellor's focus swiveled back to her. "Why don't you take a different seat tonight?" His eyes snaked to Grimmaul, chair pushed back, legs sprawled and arms open in lewd invitation. Her throat closed with dread, but Salvotor's pointed look and the echo of Thorne's hoarse, quick breaths behind her were a plain warning what would happen if she defied a third time today.

So they passed the meal with Cistine planted in Grimmaul's lap, his hand wandering wherever it pleased. Whenever she squirmed away, Salvotor cleared his throat and glanced at Thorne, head leaned back against the wall, clutching his side, eyes smoldering at her like the heart of a flame.

The torturous meal lasted twice as long as any other, and Cistine's head thudded with anger and humiliation when Grimmaul finally released her and pushed her off by a handful of her haunch. She gripped the table's edge and leaned away from him, and he grazed past her with a provocative thrust that jolted her forward, yelping, her hand knocking over of the cups on the table—

Thorne exploded.

One moment he was against the wall, and the next he had Grimmaul in a headlock, smashing his gut and jerking them both away from the table—and from Cistine. Grimmaul's five swearing men lunged to their feet, and Cistine snatched up one of the discarded dinner knives with a shout. Thorne spun himself and Grimmaul toward her, and she smashed her foot into the guard's chest so hard he retched and doubled over. Thorne dropped him in a gasping, cursing heap, caught the knife from Cistine, and spun with her, placing their backs together as the Vassora converged on them.

Cistine feinted out of the first guard's reach, then smashed her knee into the hinge of his elbow and punched him straight in the nose. Thorne moved with her, dodge and swing, his shoulders never leaving hers. Two of Grimmaul's men dropped under his knife; another vaulted across the table and snatched Cistine's wrist. She let him have it, boxing his ear and chopping his throat with her free hand, meeting his groin with her knee when he folded over. The memory of Quill's laughter burned in her ear when the guard dropped squealing to the ground.

Skin ripped and blood slapped the floor when Thorne jabbed the knife into the last guard's throat, hurling him against the wall—and then there was only Salvotor.

He watched without intervening, eyes murky with fascination. "Now I see where she learned to cross blades with me."

A scrape of movement stirred in the mouth of the hall, but Cistine refused to look away when Salvotor strode down the table toward them. Thorne's arm pressed against hers, and she slid her fingers between his and squeezed with all her might.

A hand dropped on her shoulder, another on Thorne's. Salvotor's brows tweaked. "Kristoff, what timing. Have your men see to my retinue's wounds. And join us, if you would, in the outer chamber." He halted before them, eyes trained on Cistine. "Grimmaul, pick yourself up and bring the Key with us. It's time for a new lesson."

Grimmaul stumbled up and snatched Cistine under the arm, hauling her out to the center of the hewn chamber after Salvotor, Kristoff, and Thorne. The Chancellor forced Thorne down on his knees with one swift kick; Cistine's whole body tightened at the impact, and Kristoff tensed, lurching forward a step.

"It seems I did not make myself clear enough what your actions mean for one another." The Chancellor's sharp voice carried along the rounded walls, halting even Kristoff in place. "Allow me to demonstrate. Grimmaul, your knife, please. And the Key."

Pulse lunging with dread, Cistine jerked against Grimmaul's hold. His fingers tightened in a quick, vicious jolt, half-deadening her arm, and he freed one of the many knives from his belt and pushed Cistine toward the Chancellor. Salvotor took the knife in one hand, wrapped his other arm around Cistine, and jammed the hilt into her sweating fingers.

"You seemed familiar with the use of this weapon tonight," he murmured against the shell of her ear. "Now you learn what will happen if you ever touch one of them again at my table." He hooked her legs out with his foot and brought her down to the floor, knee-to-knee with Thorne, banding her fingers into fists around the knife. "Six cuts for six guards."

Cistine's body snapped taut like a weighed anchor. Numbness and then tingling stole across her face, and her breaths guttered in short, shallow wisps. "No. *No.* Don't make me do this."

Kristoff's composure shattered, and with a desperate roar, he lunged at his sister's *valenar*. Grimmaul slid between them like a shadow, striking Kristoff's side so hard something audibly snapped, plunging him to the floor. Thorne lurched forward, fingertips touching the stone as he coiled to rise, and Salvotor shoved himself—and Cistine—into Thorne's path. "If you move, boy, I will let Grimmaul take your *Nahdar* apart one piece at a time *before* he has his way with the Key. Tonight's meal was only a taste."

Thorne ripped his eyes from Kristoff's half-curled, hacking form to Cistine and Salvotor, hands flattening back at his sides. He was unbound, and yet he would have to kneel there and *endure* this—the blade, and *Cistine* thrusting it into his skin, guided by his father's hands.

How could she do it? How could any princess harm someone under her protection, especially someone so precious to her, someone she—

"Cistine." Thorne's voice pierced the haze of panic, and her eyes moved to his face, so calm, almost resigned. "It's all right," he said, though it wasn't, and it never would be again. "It's all right."

Salvotor pressed his weight against Cistine's back and brought her arms forward. She writhed and twisted, jabbing against him, but his inflexible skin resisted and his reinforced bones and muscles locked her in place, bringing the tip of the knife to Thorne's left shoulder.

"One," Salvotor breathed.

They started to carve.

It was worse than any lash or assassin or Vassoran strike, worse than any other atrocity for which he wore a scar. Six cuts across his chest, not deep enough to kill, but every one was a betrayal, a hurt she could never take back from him. A hurt she was forced to deal by her own hands.

She wanted to vomit. She knew she would later, but right now she couldn't take a breath deep enough to even choke. The only sound was the give of flesh, the ache of her own sobs, and the wet panting from Kristoff as Grimmaul knelt on his back, holding him in place, punishing him like Salvotor was punishing Cistine. Punishing Thorne.

With the fourth cut, Thorne sagged. His forehead rested against hers, his breath stirring her hair in harsh, wheezing pants. He gripped her knees with white-knuckled hands, and she didn't care how hard his fingers dug in or how much that hurt. She would endure *anything* if it brought him some relief.

Her fingers were drenched in Thorne's blood. His lips, chapped and unsteady, pressed to her brow. "It's all right," he gasped against her skin. "It's all right, Wildheart, it's all right..."

It was not all right. But it was done.

Cistine's fingers separated from the knife, and Salvotor let her go. She caught Thorne's shoulders, but he slid through her grip and sprawled against her chest, his ear to her aching heart. Streams of blood swirled on her hideous, sequined dress, red against white.

Thorne's blood on her clothes. On her hands.

"Remember *you* did this to him," Salvotor said. "As he did this to *you.*"

Cistine wrapped her arms around Thorne's bare shoulders and buried her face in his scarred back, whispering a litany of useless apologies as Salvotor walked away and Grimmaul hopped up and strutted after him.

Kristoff crawled to them, a man carved of broken ribs and broken curses. When he gripped her arm, Cistine tore free, fell back on her seat, and scrambled away. Someone jerked her to her feet; she didn't care who. She could only see Thorne's blood on her hands and Thorne's unconscious face, his head lolling in Kristoff's lap. And because she had done this to him, to all of them with her defiance today, Cistine let them drag her away.

CHAPTER FORTY-TWO

I T WAS TIME. Ashe had to do this.

Her palms slickened with nervous sweat, worse than the time she confessed to her parents she broke their best display cloches practicing her homespun slingshot from the top of the steps; worse than when she caught her first black eye scrapping with a fellow recruit who taunted that the daughter of bakers and confectioners had no place among the Cadre.

At least those times, she knew exactly what punishment awaited. But today, pushing through the rushes lining the same branch of the river they followed ever since the night of Sigrid's death, she had no idea what danger she walked into. She just knew the blood on her hands was too much, the burden in her heart too heavy, and the weight on her conscience too great to ignore.

Rion had wandered nearly a half-mile from their riverside camp when she found him, sitting on a boulder and tracing in the dirt. He didn't seem to notice her at first; his sketch reminded her of vague battle plans. Perhaps a siege strategy for Kalt Hasa.

She cleared her throat. "Lord Rion."

He hesitated, the tip of his stick digging into the earth, and kept his gaze on his drawing. "Julian's taken naturally to this part of his training. Always able to scheme because he knows how to think like the enemy...how they'll react, what methods to exert and achieve his desired outcomes. When we hone that, he will be the best weapon this Cadre has wielded in decades, if not a century."

Guilt arrowed through Ashe's chest, followed by a hollow thud of despair. He'd told her when they returned from the war that *she* was his best weapon, the sickle forging a new path for the young and fierce to train as Wardens. King Cyril had dropped the age of enlistment two entire years on her account. Julian had only been able to train so long as Cadre because of the precedent *she* set. And the same man who spoke of her in such glowing terms back then looked at her now with distrust and dislike.

She shook off that thought. What was this mission doing to her, making her *jealous* of a dead boy? A dead *friend*? "Julian is a good man."

"I know. And I trust he's holding the line." Rion erased the sketches with the side of his foot. "I worry more for the Princess, young and untrained."

"I worry for her, too."

"Your actions would indicate otherwise."

Ashe worked her jaw and slid her hands down the backs of her thighs, wicking away sweat. This was the conversation she came to have, but with his steely glare fixed on her, the words grew heavy on her tongue. "I respect her as much as I fear for her. I don't want to ruin the things she came to do on my way to save her."

"What she came to do, illicitly and without royal consent, will mean absolutely nothing if she dies."

"Maybe I have more faith in her than you."

"Her, or the Valgardans who claim to help her?"

Ashe cast around for an answer to that and found none.

Smile chilly, Rion reclined against the boulder and folded his arms, one heel propped in the dirt. "Have you come to absolve your conscience?"

"I came to mend this rift between us." Ashe gestured from him to herself. "We want the same thing. We're on the same side, we always have been. I'm tired of fighting with you."

"You always did tire quicker on the training pitch." Rion's eyes raked over her, inscrutable for once. "As for whether we want the same thing...do we, Kovar? If that were true, we would have reached this *Kalt Hasa* by now."

Anger rubbed the backs of Ashe's teeth. "Cistine's life means everything to me. You don't know what I've done for her, the lengths I've gone to, the blood I shed—"

"And yet she's still a Valgardan prisoner, and you are still dragging us on a mission that has nothing to do with her safety, my *son's* safety. We are *not* like-minded, and suggesting otherwise is an insult to me."

Ashe's throat dried. This was *far* worse than she anticipated. "If we fight among ourselves, fight with Valgardans who just want to help, we create more problems."

"And when we adopt enemy causes, we blur the lines."

"Believe me, Commander, bringing down this man Deja can bear witness against is important for *all* the kingdoms."

Rion threw his hands up. "Then *kill him* and be done with it, Ashe! Why do they *need* a gods-damned witness? Solve this with the sword!"

She hesitated, hand falling to Echelon's pommel. "From what Aden's told me, killing him isn't as simple as a blade stroke anymore. He's found ways to protect himself, he—"

"Taking one Valgardan's word on how to kill another is like asking a dog how to trap a wolf."

Ashe clenched her teeth. "Bringing him down by their law helps keep Valgard stable. That keeps *everyone* safe."

"I don't give a damn about their law when it's keeping me from my son and my Princess." Rion shrugged up from the boulder. "And neither should you. You wish me to absolve you? I refuse. You chose this path against my wishes, against my better judgement. I am only here because circumstances demand it. The moment we have our heading to Kalt Hasa, I don't give a damn if you keep up or fall behind."

"This is my mission!" Her shout cracked out of control. "My responsibility!"

"Oh, yes, and we've learned very clearly what becomes of Asheila Kovar's responsibilities!" Rion stepped into her face, finger jabbing. "This mission would have taken place with or without you...and likely been more successful without!"

Grief slashed through Ashe's middle. She searched for words and found none. What would he have done if he came to this kingdom while she was still in Siralek? Would he have even freed her? She thought she knew back then. But looking into those cold eyes now, doubt blossomed.

"Fine," she hissed. "If you're so worried for the integrity of the mission, at least call the others off their insults against the North. Their loose rein is slacking worse ever since...that forest grove." Sigrid's kind, dying face flashed through her mind, and she shook it away. "That doesn't help our cause, either."

"I fail to see how insulting these people is in any way *detrimental* to the morale and purpose of this mission."

"We've beaten Valgard. We defeated them over two decades ago! When is it going to be enough?"

"It will *never* be enough!" Rion snapped. "You can't just defeat an enemy once, you must defeat him a thousand times. Cut his legs from beneath him at every turn. Anticipate that he'll rise again and thwart him before he does."

"Cistine's disappearance was not about an uprising. It's one madman, not the entire kingdom."

"Where one madman goes, the rest will follow. Look at Mahasar! That's why I warned Cyril not to offer a hand of friendship to the Northern Kingdom—the moment we show a hint of weakness, they'll exploit it. And now, gods help me, they have our *princess* and my only son. So you expect me to raise a brow when the Cadre make jokes? That's mere play compared to what Valgard would do to us if we gave them an inch. I don't frown on their language, I encourage it."

Ashe scowled as he brushed past her. "That's your personal prejudice interfering with how you conduct the Cadre."

"I didn't hear these kinds of complaints when I was training *you*."

The blood drained from Ashe's face so quickly her cheeks tingled. He was right. She'd made all these same remarks, basked in them, embodied them; and worse, she'd *acted* on them, bringing about Baba Kallah's death, Julian's, and Helga's—and now Sigrid's.

And ultimately, Cistine's capture.

Rion halted among the rushes, looking back at her. "We've had this discussion many times. Valgardans are warmongering animals, and I leave the penance for our treatment of them to Cyril. He's always been the more righteous man between us. My job is not to feel remorse, it's to butcher the dangerous ones in their beds. And when I look at that man you travel with and that little girl with her quick mouth, all I *see* is danger."

He disappeared into the rushes, leaving Ashe's skin puckered in gooseflesh. She didn't like where that thought could lead—how many dark roads it could travel down. Even the ones she explored herself.

She glanced back at the boulder, the ruffled dirt before it, but it was impossible to discern what Rion was plotting when she arrived.

The riverside camp was mostly deserted when Ashe finally returned. Aden knelt on the shore, watching the water for fish. Pippet knelt beside him, copying his posture perfectly down to the wrinkle of her nose. Only Viktor remained on watch, reclining on his elbows on the shore. He squinted up at Ashe when she sat beside him, grateful that for once, a Warden wasn't pulling away. Even if it was *him*.

"I haven't seen that look on your face since the time you tried drinking Andrej under the table." He nudged her thigh. "Valgardan fare upsetting your stomach, Kovar?"

"It's always Valgard with all of you, isn't it? Cistine can't be found— blame Valgard. Stomach woes must be from their food. Our own kingdom trying to pick a fight at both borders...I suppose that's on them, too."

Viktor's thick brow dropped. "We didn't start this, Ashe. We're all here because the princess ran away...and you and Julian went with her."

"So now all of this is *my* fault?"

"Why do you think the Commander's been so furious ever since you found us?"

Ashe struggled to make sense of that. Disappointed, yes, she'd known that; but the fury had only become clear after Jovadalsa. Before that, he gave her the lead, he let her bring them to that derelict city.

Unless that was just a test he expected her to fail. Unless he was plotting her fall from grace from the beginning, clear and present proof she no longer deserved her place at the Princess's guard.

Cold sweat broke in the small of her back.

Viktor picked up a handful of stones and skipped them into the water, filling up the silence. "Lydie thinks you're rutting with the Valgardan. That's a rumor you might want to put a stop to before we take the princess home."

"Why? Are you afraid word might spread among the Wardens that I found a better lover than you among the northern rats?"

Viktor's eyes flashed wide. "Kovar. You *didn't.*"

"Didn't *what?* Dilute our pure Talheimic blood by joining with a Valgardan? When did we start worshipping ourselves like the North worships its augments?"

"Do you think it's wrong to have some pride in our own kingdom?" Viktor planted one hand on the shore behind them and waved the other at the river, the rushes, the land beyond. "Look at where you've been, Ashe! We defeated Valgard with all their augments using nothing but swords and strategy. If that isn't something to boast about—"

"We fought and killed *children!*" Disa's face and the whisper of *Meszaros* leaked cold strands into her tingling fingertips. "*I* was a child, and I fought augurs who were barely older than me. What do you want me to be proud of, Viktor? The heads I cut off? The throats I slit? You weren't there, you haven't seen the gods-forsaken scars we left, the people we hurt." Maleck's face flashed across her mind. Ashe rubbed her brow, forcing the image out. "You all wanted to know how I survived Siralek? It was because it was like a war, and I'd already *fought* in a war. I knew how to survive. But no one escapes that unscathed. The only reason I am not dead right now is because of Aden and Sander and Maleck, because they pulled me out. And I don't deserve that!"

And there it was.

Ashe did not deserve to be alive. Not with the innocents she'd killed, the blood on her hands. People were dead because of her hate, the same hate she saw in her fellow Wardens every time they looked at Aden and Pippet. In Rion's face when he looked at *any* Valgardan.

"Innocent people are dead because of what our kingdom did," Ashe said. "And if that means nothing to you, you don't deserve to wear the Warden uniform. A life should be a life to us, whether it's Talheimic or Valgardan or Mahasari. If we stop caring about the blood we spill, how are we any better than our enemies?"

Viktor's eyes hardened as he stood. "Wolves don't concern themselves with the deaths of sheep. I'm not going to sit here and cry over dead Valgardans. As far as I'm concerned, they deserve whatever's given to them. Gods, I'd stick my blade in that augur myself for putting his hands on you."

Ashe launched to her feet and gripped his collar, shoving him back a step. "Don't you *ever* presume that who I allow to touch me is *your* concern."

Viktor knocked her hand from his uniform. "What in the gods' names happened to you up here? It's like you've become one of them."

"Maybe I have. And maybe you'd better take that under consideration the next time you feel the urge to stake some sort of claim over me."

He shook his head. "I wouldn't want to, knowing where you've rolled since then."

When he left her standing on the shore, heaving with rage, a gulf opened beneath her feet. She had failed Cistine and the Wardens, been cast out by Thorne. All she had left were two people crouched further down the shore, watching the fish pass through the water, learning their way back to life together; but she couldn't bury herself in them, couldn't make this her life the way the Cadre and Cistine were her life. She had to face this emptiness, this anguish brought on by her conversations with Rion and Viktor. And there was no one to step in front of her, to shield her from the grief and loneliness that slammed over her like a tide.

The Cadre no longer wanted her. For the first time in twenty years, she didn't have a home.

CHAPTER
FORTY-THREE

OADMARK'S MOUNTAINS PROVED treacherous in the ascent, and Tatiana and Quill hardly spoke while they scaled the steep path. The *Aeoprast* left no markers; all they had was the map to the cleft, a day-and-a-half journey away by foot, and that strange mist curling off the rime-ice rocks and drifting from courageous pine clusters on narrow shelves.

Tatiana didn't like feeling lured, as if they were moving toward someone else's battleground, but Quill was right; they had to finish this before the *Aeoprast* and his misguided worshippers decided to take their vengeance against the Village of the Moon.

"We're closing in on the cleft," Quill remarked as they broke camp after a few hours of restless sleep. "Should be there by midmorning. If we can corner it on the cliff, then we have every chance of winning."

Tatiana kicked out their small bush nest. "What do you think is up there? A new village for those Valgardan guests Nuna's people drove out?"

"Most likely. I'm more concerned about why they're taking people prisoner."

"Maybe they aren't. They might just be hauling them off for slaughter, sending a message."

"Maybe." Quill didn't sound convinced. "Let's move."

The inevitability of a forthcoming battle kept things quiet between them, charged like their journey before Hrob Lake. Tatiana tried to slow her racing heart, to remind herself this was not like that fight; it was really no different from the times they plotted wagon raids on the Vey. Just more cowardly Valgardans leaning too heavily on the prize of augments, nothing worse than she and Quill had faced before..

She almost believed herself.

The pass turned winding, and after another hour Tatiana spotted thick white light at the end. Hands to her knives, she took the lead, jogging up the slick rock path and peering out onto the *Aeoprast's* cleft.

It was nothing like she expected. No tribe of Valgardan runaways camped here; no small village greeted them full of their own people. It was a bare span of rock, the nearest mountain a spear's throw away, the others spanning out across gorges and deep valleys for miles. Less a hideaway and more a lookout point; and utterly empty.

Tatiana wandered away from the mouth of the pass, squinting into the peak-fanged distance. "I expected more. Maybe the map was—"

"Tati."

Heart thundering at Quill's soft, dangerous tone, she swiveled to see what drew his gaze.

The *Aeoprast* had materialized like a specter at the edge of the rock, just like that night outside the village. Once again, it regarded them through its skulled mask, head tilted.

Well. They were here. It was time to learn what this young god was truly made of.

Tatiana and Quill unlashed the spears gifted by the Village of the Moon. Thoughts stormed his scowling face; she was plotting, too, how they could entrap it: lead it down the pass, then scale the walls and circle around behind it, one in front, one behind.

She caught Quill's sideways glance. He dipped his head.

As one, they turned—and slammed into a solid wall of ice more than thirty feet high that rose in the breadth of a blink, blocking their escape down the pass.

Pulse quickening so fiercely her chest pinched, Tatiana yanked Quill back around to face the *Aeoprast*. Darkness steamed around its body, tendrils of violet and midnight that took Tatiana back to the Den's attic the day they found Cistine on her knees with a broken flagon beside her, body unharmed.

They were right. The *Aeoprast was* just an augur posturing as a god. And an augur they could kill.

She stepped forward, spear propped across her shoulders. "You picked the wrong village to intimidate, but trust me, you don't scare *us*. It's time for a reckoning."

The *Aeoprast* cast back its head and *cackled*.

Its arms flung out, and wind and fire skirled from its palms, joining in a cyclone that melted the snow and whipped it into a rainstorm. Frigid drops crashed back down in a deluge, blasting across their faces and robbing them of their sense of direction. Tatiana screamed for Quill in the cold void, her breath stolen, her mind blackening with terror.

There was no augur alive, armored or not, who could endure the use of two augments at once, nevermind three, without breaking down under the strain—the bones crumbling, the muscles tearing, the organs failing. No one was capable of withstanding so much power, not even Maleck, who'd once been the strongest augur she'd ever met, who almost became—

The wind banked. Tatiana found Quill at last, and from the horror in his eyes, she knew he'd realized it, too.

The cold wind forced them toward the wall of ice. The second they struck it, they'd be flattened with godlike power, and the *Aeoprast* would burn them alive, entomb them in rock, slit their throats—or use them to continue whatever despicable experiments he was stealing villagers for.

Tatiana reached out, grabbed for Quill's hand, and snagged the rope on his belt instead. A sliver of hope pierced through her panic at the chafe of its fibers, brilliant as a shooting star; she yanked the rope from his belt and tied it around her spear, then tossed the end to Quill and ran toward the edge of the precipice.

The wind dropped again and the ice fell all at once when the *Aeoprast* realized they were fleeing—revealing the edge of the cliff much closer than she'd thought. She planted her boots and skidded, and Quill grabbed her arm, swinging her around in a full circle. When she faced the sheer edge again, she hurled the spear with all her might, with a scream that pushed her body forward.

The weapon left her hand and whizzed through the open air to the next mountain. With a sharp *crack,* the spearhead lodged into the stone clefts, burrowing deep.

Quill had already tied the rope off to a spire of rock and shed his parka. He took a running leap and lashed it over the rope, sliding in a wild streak toward the far mountain. Tatiana followed, not daring to look back even when a scythe of fire slashed against her back and sank into her armor.

The rope caught aflame.

Tatiana screamed as the twine frayed and snapped, sending them into an uncontrolled forward swing. They toppled far below the cleft and struck the mountain face, the rope snapping on impact. Tatiana plunged, stomach soaring upward, and Quill caught her wrist and heaved her against the rock where her hands and feet found holds.

Panting with terror, she scrambled up beneath him, fingers cramping, legs chattering with nerves and cold now that she lost her parka. They passed the burning rope for a narrow shelf of rock, hauled themselves up, and ran, glancing back only once before they swung around a bend in the stone path.

The *Aeoprast* watched them go, skulled mask tilted, its laughter echoing distantly off the mountains.

This was not over. They had not seen the last of that nightmare.

They ran until the thin air tore their lungs and neither of them could breathe. Quill was the first to fall to his hands and knees, gripping the snow while he gasped and choked. Tatiana tumbled down beside him, staring at the thick hedge of pines while the *Aeoprast's* face, the memory of his power, battered the walls of her mind.

Quill gripped her knee, fingers flexing in a gentle request. She pushed a trickle of fire from her armor into his, and his shivers eased as it warmed him through. "Are you going to say it, or am I?"

Tatiana's numb lips responded before her mind caught up to the question. "That was a Bloodwight."

Quill's eyes tumbled shut. He dragged himself up to lean his face into the back of her shoulder. "We should have known. The Valgardans that fled north...it must've been twenty years ago, right after the war ended."

"I want to know what's drawing them out of hiding *now*." A trickle of rage found its way into Tatiana's voice. "This is too close to Valgard's border for comfort."

Quill's breath deepened, harshened. "You remember how Mal used to look at Cistine when we brought her to the Den? He knew there was something different about her, and he was never fully a Bloodwight. What if they can sense that the Key's come back?"

Tatiana flexed her cramped, aching fingers. "We need to get to her before they find out where she is."

Quill nodded. "But first, we warn the Village of the Moon."

Though urgency nipped her fingertips, Tatiana nodded. It would be nothing short of murder not to.

There was nothing any of them could do against the *Aeoprast* now.

CHAPTER FORTY-FOUR

THE JOURNEY BACK to the Village of the Moon was brief but tense, watching for the *Aeoprast*. They didn't sleep this time, eyes wide and bodies wrapped together even when they stopped to rest. In the morning they were up and running for miles on the slick paths, crossing a perilous stone bridge between the mountains and descending the walled path into The Village of the Moon at last.

Relief nearly knocked Tatiana's feet from under her. It still stood—for now.

"Nuna!" she shouted, barreling past the pavilion, ignoring wide-eyed mothers and curious children who turned her way. "Nunajik! Where are you?"

"*Suki*?" The matriarch ducked from her tent, Chena bundled in her arms. Blinking curiously, she hurried to meet them. "What is it? Did you face the *Aeoprast*? Is it dead?"

Tatiana and Quill skidded to a halt before her, and Quill turned his hair across his head. "We wish."

"Nuna, your village needs to leave," Tatiana urged. "Pack everything you can carry and get off this mountain *now*."

Nuna's arms tightened around her child. "What has happened?"

"The *Aeoprast* isn't dead," Quill said. "We might've just made him angry. I'm sorry, we should've guessed what he was, but..."

"You faced it?" Nuna demanded. Murmurs rose from the flock of villagers clustered around them. "Who is it? What is it?"

"He's *not* a god," Tatiana said. "He's a man like the rest of us...one of the Valgardans your Tribe sheltered."

"It was twenty years ago, wasn't it?" Quill asked. "When they came to you."

Nuna's eyes narrowed. "It was. You know...him?"

"We know *of* him," Tatiana said, "of his kind. Those gifts they brought with them *are* from the gods, but that *bandayo* corrupted them."

"He learned to do it by feeding the least-deadly of those gifts to children in our kingdom." Quill nodded to Chena. "Children no older than your daughter."

Nunajik clutched the girl to her chest, eyes wide. Several of the villagers glanced at one another.

"They're called Bloodwights," Tatiana explained. "We can't fight them, not even with our armor. I'm sorry, but we can't save you from this. The only way to keep your people alive is to run before he finds you. Start over somewhere else and help the other villages do the same."

"The *Aeoprast* isn't the only one with those gifts, that power," Quill said. "Every Valgardan with him can use them, too. And they won't stop attacking until they have whatever they want. This is a battle you have to run from before it's too late."

Nuna was quiet for a long moment, looking around at her family's village, their tribe's mainstay. "But this is the only home we have. The only one we've known for generations."

"Home isn't a place, Nuna. It's the people." Tatiana glanced up at Quill. "You can take home with you if you flee."

"Don't lose them like you lost Shesh." Quill gripped the matriarch's shoulder. "There's still time to outrun him if you go *now*."

Nunajik's gaze hardened. She turned to the people gathered around and spoke in rapid Oadmarkaic; one by one, comprehension broke through their faces—then sorrow, then resignation. Mothers tugged children into tents;

men and boys unstrung hide coverings for satchels. Nuna watched them, regret lining her eyes but breaking against the determined set of her mouth. "If he is not a god, then he can be outwitted. Perhaps in time, we will return. But if there are none of us left, then the village means nothing. *We* are the Village of the Moon." She turned back to Quill and Tatiana. "Thank you. Though you could not kill him, you have given us hope."

Quill scratched the back of his head. "That's not usually what we hear when someone mentions Bloodwights."

Nuna's smile was sharp as her stare. "Because my father and the elders drove these men out long ago. They can be beaten again."

"Nuna, don't try to fight him," Tatiana warned. "He may not be a god, but he has strength now that even Quill and I have never seen before."

"Tati's right." Quill draped his arm around her hips. "The best thing you can do is let him think he won and rally your strength behind his back. Stay one step ahead of him."

"We'll warn our people, too," Tatiana added. "We'll try to send help when we can."

Sadness softened Nuna's eyes. "You're going, then?"

Tatiana nodded. "We have a friend who needs us. We were searching for her when you found us by the lake, and now that we know the Bloodwights are stirring, it's more important than ever that we get to her as soon as possible."

"And yet you stayed to help our village? Why did you not tell us of this?"

Tatiana flicked a glance at Quill. He hooked his thumb in his belt and shrugged one shoulder. "Our cabal keeps its vows."

"And we keep ours." Nuna dipped her head. "Go, with our blessing. Though you could not kill this creature, you have given us time to run. That is more than enough."

Chena beckoned shyly to Quill, and when he bent his head, she reached up mitten-clad hands to clip something into his mismatched hair—a twist of raven feathers and hide strips. He smirked when he straightened, thumbing the small gift with the same look in his eye as the day Maleck gave him his first custom-crafted dagger.

Nuna smiled at them. "May you always be as strong as wolves together. And if ever you are in need, the Village of the Moon will send aid, just as we will help the other Villages now."

"Just keep yourselves alive," Quill said. "We're already even for the rest of it."

Not quite even, in Tatiana's eyes; not when they brought her Nightwing back. That was a debt she could never repay. But as she and Quill hurried down the path from the mountain, passing villagers who gathered their belongings in rucksacks and satchels, preparing to set out at their matriarch's word for a new home and, stars willing, a safer future, hope budded in her chest as well.

At the edge of the village grounds, Quill halted, squinting up at the climbing sun. "Think they'll be all right?"

"For now," Tatiana said. "Sooner or later, this is a problem Valgard has to help solve."

"First things first." Quill tipped his head. "Save the Key. Stop the Doors from opening." He angled away from her. "Southwest it is."

She gripped his shoulder. "You take the hunt."

A shiver rattled the hide-and-feather twist in his hair; but then his shoulders set and his jaw clenched. He clasped her hand tight to his armor, three fingers to five, still somehow the tightest he ever held on. "All right, Tati. Let's finish this before that *bandayo* catches up. It's time to bring our princess home."

CHAPTER FORTY-FIVE

"GET UP, CISTINE."

Kristoff's hand rubbed her back, and she rolled over to face him, exhausted eyes and foggy mind fighting to bring him into focus. The only thing clear through the haze of too many sleepless nights was the aching in her hands, cracked and blistering with cold. She washed them dozens of times a day in the frigid bucket beside her bed, yet she could still feel Thorne's blood sliding between each knuckle, soaking under the nailbeds. She'd bitten them to the quick, but the blood was still there—when she woke, moved around the room, went to the dinners with Salvotor, came back and fell asleep, and dreamed.

Nightmares. Plunging her blade into Thorne's chest, cutting too deeply this time. Straight to the heart she'd betrayed.

She didn't know how many days had passed since that horrific dinner. There was no training, no learning about the lightning. She didn't dare be caught in the vents, moving between rooms; she couldn't bear to ask for even a moment's reprieve from Grimmaul's lewd taunts or his retinue's escort everywhere she went.

It was over. Salvotor won.

Kristoff cradled her cheek, his face swimming into focus at last—too gentle and kind after what she did. "Get up. I need you to come with me."

Cistine slowly rolled to her feet. She ached all over, the prison cold entering her bones from her throbbing hands. She stuffed them into her armpits and wavered before him. "Dinner?"

His expression was the same inscrutable as every time he looked at her since she cracked his ribs and striped his nephew with the blade. He didn't speak, just led her from the room.

She was only dimly aware that Grimmaul and his men were not in the hewn chamber—and neither were the Six. The only guards were at the cellar door, and none of them looked toward her and Kristoff today; she didn't want to look at them, either. But when she glanced away, her eyes fell on that gods-forsaken circle where she committed her unspeakable act.

Kristoff grabbed her shoulder when she turned toward the dining hall; instead he led her toward the kitchens. Surprise cooled rapidly into panic, and she dug her feet against the rock at the hallway mouth. "No. Take me to the meal or take me back."

Kristoff's eyes flashed like steel and he pushed her halfway down the corridor to the kitchens, halting them both before a door set into the dark stone. "It took more finesse than you can imagine to empty these halls for you today. I need you not to squander it."

"Squander *what*?"

He gestured sharply at the door. "Stars above, Cistine, just get in this pantry!"

"Not until you tell me why!" She wrapped her arms tightly around her hollow middle. "Is this a trick? Are you doing Salvotor's bidding now?"

"*Never*." Kristoff secured her shoulders firmly. "This is my penance for allowing him to put that knife in your hands. I should've intervened sooner. Better I'd died than let that happen...but what's done is done. And now I'm doing this."

"*Why?*"

"Because I know what Salvotor is trying to do. And if all I have left in me to resist him is one small deception, then so be it. I'll *resist* until my dying breath." He opened the pantry door to a deep well of blackness beyond. "You have just a few minutes, but I hope that's enough to help you hold on just a bit longer."

He touched her cheek, then turned and strode from the hall. Cistine stared after him, feet itching to flee to the safe confines of her chamber—but curiosity pulled her in the other direction. Heart racing, she nudged the pantry door wider and stepped inside.

The spicy smell of herb sachets and wood stroked her nostrils. The interior was too dim to distinguish much more than a few twisted, hanging plants and a shelf against one wall—and a figure, hooded and robed, stepping forward to meet her. A fistful of bioluminescent ghostplants broke between his fingers, shedding brilliant ribbons of greenish-blue light across his chiseled, stubbled jaw and the threads of silver hair framing those breathtaking blue eyes.

Heart thundering with dread, Cistine whirled away, halfway to escape when Thorne's hand shot past her and jammed the door shut. "Wait. Cistine—*wait*."

"He'll kill you if he finds us here!" Cistine yanked against the handle. How could he still be so strong after all these days of imprisonment—after what she did to him? "Thorne, let go of the door!"

"I will." His voice was low, urgent. "Once you look at me."

All she could see was the ghostlight dripping between his fingers held against the door, staining his hand like blood.

She revolved slowly to face him, keeping her gaze on the faint outline of his bare feet. "What do you want me to see?"

He cupped her chin in one hand, bringing her eyes irresistibly to his shadowed face. He was so close heat radiated from his body, and when he slapped his hood back, it left streaks of dazzling green in his hair. "*Me*. Cistine, I'm all right. I know you've been sitting in whatever chamber Salvotor locked you in, destroying yourself because of this. But you need to see that I'm *all right*."

She grabbed the front of his stolen robe and shoved him back a step. "How in God's name could you be all right, Thorne? Look at this!" She tore open the halves of drab gray cloak and rolled up his tattered shirt, revealing the six rigid lines of black suture across his front. Tears punched her eyes.

"*I did this.*"

"Not you. *Him.* And I've suffered far worse at his hands before." He grabbed hers, prying them from his robe; and though she should take advantage while he wasn't pinning the door, break free and flee to her room where she could hurt no one but herself—

She didn't.

She didn't draw her hands away, either.

Thorne's thumbs stroked her knuckles, painting them with phosphorescent light. She followed his wide-eyed gaze to the fissured, chapped skin, red even in the ghostlight, covered in dried blood from that morning's furious washing. When his touch grazed the cracks, she hissed sharply, surprised by how much that gentle touch stung.

His eyes snapped to her face. "Who did this to you?"

"I did. I can't...I can't clean them enough. Every morning, I still feel the blood. *Your* blood. No matter how much I scrub, it never washes away."

Thorne let go of her hands. "Listen to me. My wounds don't matter to me. None of it matters. I was prepared for this and worse when Devitrius captured me. You can't let my father overwhelm you."

"Overwhelm me?" Cistine snapped. "Thorne! *I put a blade in your chest!*"

"No. *Salvotor* did that. You put a knife in my *hand* at that dinner table. You gave me the power to fight off the *bandayos* who shackled me to the wall. You give me more strength than he has *ever* taken away from me."

She struggled to capture a full breath. If that was how Salvotor repaid the small strength she gave Thorne, what would he do if he learned they were together now, with nothing between them? "Thorne, this isn't right, we have to—"

"Listen to me. Focus, *Logandir.*" He gripped the sides of her neck gently. "Don't let him win."

"We can't keep defying him like this!"

"Yes, we can. It's how Baba Kallah and I survived for almost twenty years under his guard."

A thin cord of panic in her chest loosened. "Was it really like this?"

Thorne's laughter rasped softly in the dark. "Now you know

everything...every scar, every bit I didn't want to show you when you first came to us. What do you think of me now?"

The ache in her chest burst into agony, and she wrapped her arms around his neck, burying her face in the side of his neck and her fingers in his hair. The old, tantalizing scents of rain and leather and sandalwood had faded from his skin; he smelled like the cold stone and straw he slept on every night, yet he was still Thorne. It was still his familiar grip wrapping around her, lifting her away from the door; still his breath against her cheek when he kissed her temple and held her to his battered chest.

"I thought you would hate me," she whispered. "I thought you wouldn't be able to look at me again, after he—after what I—"

"Never." He took her face in his hands, the tacky ghostplant sap setting her skin aglow. "We are going to survive this, Cistine. But you have to keep fighting. Find a way to defy him, no matter how hard he hits you."

"I'm so tired." The truth broke her voice. "You can't kill him, I'm not strong enough to fight him...even if we escape, do we just keep running?"

"Not anymore. Not after this." His mouth hardened. "The cabal is already working a strategy to bring Salvotor to his knees. But that victory, and every one after it, will be hollow if you're not there with us. With *me*. Do you understand?"

Cistine pressed her hands over his against her cheeks. "I hear you."

Thorne's eyes softened. "You *will* go home, Cistine, I swear it." His shoulders bobbed with a soft, resigned chuckle. "And that will do what no knife ever could. It's going to break me."

She blinked, squinting in the dark. "What do you mean?"

"That I'm through with running away and denying things. I knew it the second I saw you in that prison room, when you looked in my face and you won that fight against him." He brushed her hair from her chapped lips, leaving a streak of sweet, earthy sap on her mouth, and cupped her burning face in his hands again. "I would cross oceans for you, Cistine. I would cross borders and kingdoms for you. *Nothing* will keep me away from you when you need me...not even a stars-damned mountain prison or my father's fury. I've made my choice."

Their breaths mingled in shadows tempered only by the stripes of ghostlight on his hands, on her face.

"I will follow you always, Wildheart." He traced the curve of her cheek with his thumb, forging a glowing path in the darkness. "With my whole heart. For my whole life."

All the things Cistine pent up through miles of wilderness wandering, through nights of stargazing and plotting and training, through mourning and longing with time moving against them, shattered at those words. She slid his fingers into his hair, pulled down his head, and kissed him the way she wanted to since the Izten Torkat and the cliffs above Starhollow, since that last moment she saw him before Salvotor stole her away.

His mouth tasted like sap and cool streams and all the wild and wonderous places they had yet to explore together. And when his hand fastened against her hip and he pressed her to the door, his tongue grazing hers, she was not afraid, not shy of his advances. This place had made her feral, stripping away the decorum of station and giving her permission to want and need desperately—to need *Thorne*, his beating heart and the safety of his arms curving around her back, snugging her body against his.

His fingers stroked her spine. Hers threaded his hair and brought his mouth back to hers when he tried to pull away and breathe. She drank him like water down a parched throat; and when it was her who felt breathless, lungs begging for air, she fell back against the door with a gasp, and Thorne's hands skimmed down to settle against her hips again.

He'd never looked at her with so much passion, so much affection before. Her High Tribune. Her blended heart. Her Starchaser.

"Wildheart, you're shining."

She glanced down at herself; everywhere he'd touched, her body sang with color not even Kalt Hasa's shadows could dim. Silver-blue spirals on the column of her neck. Freckles of ultramarine snow on her cheeks and eyelashes, glistening along the sweep of her nose when he kissed each of those places and drew back again.

She brushed her thumb over his sap-stained mouth. "So are you, Starchaser."

His eyes unfocused slightly. "Say it again."

Cistine smiled and rose onto the tips of her toes so she could say it against his lips. "Thorne Starchaser."

His hand fisted in the hair at the back of her head and he brought her mouth hard against his in a kiss that exulted and enticed first, then slowed and explored, satisfying every question they'd wondered but feared to ask while she still courted Julian and thought of Thorne as little more than a reluctant ally.

And still, even then...she'd wondered.

Thorne broke away first this time, pulling her tight to him and pressing the next kiss on the top of her head. "We are leaving this place *together*. As long as we both draw breath, nothing in these kingdoms will ever separate us again."

Despite her aching hands and his wounded chest, her faith rose like a sunrise and her hope like a war-standard. That promise was sealed in the glistening strokes of his ghostlit touch all over, like starlight against her skin.

A path to guide them home.

THE
CHANCELLOR
OF
STARS AND
STORMS

CHAPTER FORTY-SIX

Grimmaul's hand was tight around Cistine's middle, hitching her against his groin while he fished around her elbow for the last scraps of food on his plate. Whenever she tried to shift away from him, he pressed his lips below her ear and murmured all the filthy things he would do to her once Thorne, sitting across the table from them, finally broke and betrayed her with an attack.

She looked down at her bandaged hands, away from Thorne's livid stare and Salvotor's smirk, and remembered the ghostlit pantry, the feeling of different hands and lips on her skin. Remembered the lessons Kristoff murmured through her door now about how lightning was like a bottled storm with texture and weight, and how to seize it and direct it to her will with a single touch.

Soon. Soon...

"I would say this has been a pleasant meal." Salvotor scraped his chair back. "Grimmaul, would you accept the burdensome task of escorting the Key to the bathing chamber tonight? Devitrius is set to return in two days. She should look her best to greet him."

Grimmaul's hand stroked lower, and Cistine jolted, twisting away from his touch. "It would be my *pleasure*, Chancellor."

Sudden, sharp footsteps pounded from the walls, and Kristoff burst into the room, his blade drawn at his side. Salvotor raised a brow. "Don't tell me you've finally grown enough spine to challenge me, *Allet.*"

For once, Kristoff didn't even glower at the word. "Chancellor, I've received a disturbing report from the watchtowers."

Grimmaul gripped Cistine's hips and plucked her off him, shoving her to the side as he stood. "What have your incompetent *bandayos* done now?"

"It isn't what they've done. It's what was done *to* them."

Cistine met Thorne's eyes across the table. His brow creased.

Salvotor cursed under his breath. "All of you, outside. Kristoff, escort the prisoners to their chambers."

Cistine pushed herself around the table, and Thorne stumbled upright. He almost fell again when she crashed into him, and she had to grip the back of the chair and wrap one arm around him to keep them both from falling. "What's wrong?"

"My legs," he grunted. "From sitting in the cage, I can't..."

She laid a hand on his chest to silence him, shooting a glare at Salvotor. The delighted gleam in his eyes said enough—he knew precisely what he was doing to his son.

Kristoff beckoned harshly. "Both of you. *Now.*"

Cistine pulled Thorne's arm around her shoulders and helped him into the hall, whispering under her breath, "The watchtowers?"

"I don't know." Thorne looked ahead. "*Nahdar?*"

"There's only one thing you two need to do right now," Kristoff growled, "and that is keep your heads down, keep quiet, and thank the True God for loving you almost as much as I do."

Thorne pushed his feet hard to the rock, sending himself and Cistine stumbling forward so he could catch Kristoff's shoulder. "What happened?"

He turned stony gray eyes on them. "There was an attack. Three of our guards were butchered on the mountain watchtowers."

Cistine's stomach turned. "The Six?"

That fierce gaze softened at the concern in her voice. "Not them."

"Was it wild animals?" Thorne demanded.

"The towers are built specifically to keep those out. No, this was deliberate...their heads severed and their augments stolen."

Now Cistine could hardly swallow. "Who—what—?"

"I told you not to worry. I am handling it." There was no anger in Kristoff's voice, no fear. That faint tremble was almost *excitement*. He snatched Cistine's hand and pressed something into it. "Get to your room, Cistine. Thorne, with me."

As Kristoff took Thorne's arm across his shoulders instead, Cistine twisted back, and Thorne ducked his head. This kiss was a wild meeting of mouths and tongue, and Cistine gasped when Thorne's teeth sank into her lower lip hard enough to draw blood. Then Kristoff tugged him back out of the corridor, and Cistine fled to her room. She didn't dare look at the gift he gave her until she was safe behind the closed door, bathed in lavender ghostlight. Then she cupped it in her palm, staring down at it, trying to make sense of what it was. What it *meant*.

Shock knocked her to her seat against the door, staring at this small taunt, this small *gift* until it blurred before her tearstained eyes.

There, kissing her palm with promise, was something that should not have been in these mountains at all: a single, glossy black raven's feather.

Quill.

CHAPTER FORTY-SEVEN

CISTINE FORCED HERSELF to wait an entire day before she entered the hole in her roof and dragged herself through the familiar path of tunnels, her heartbeat loud in the dark and the feather's stem tickling against her chest. Bursting with joy, she slid down the braided rope into the prison room.

Thorne raised his head when she entered, gaze intent like he'd been waiting for her. He pushed to the end of his collar at once, spreading his hands to grip the sides of the cage and keep himself upright. "Cistine, what is it? You're shaking."

"Look!" She pulled the feather from the front of her shirt and flashed it before him, and his fingers tightened so brutally in the slats that the veins and muscles on his forearms bulged. "Please tell me this means when I think it means!"

"It does. The cabal's timing isn't always perfect, but when it is..." Thorne blew out a short, amused breath. "I should've known Tatiana and Quill weren't fooled."

Cistine frowned. "Fooled by what?"

His gaze dropped, face pulling with a different sort of pain than usual. "My plan to raid the temples searching for you."

Cistine's knees almost buckled at his averted eyes, the sheepish tilt to his tone. "You...no. Thorne, you *didn't*."

"I spoke to a *visnpresta* in Keltei," he explained, "who made it clear that it was wasted time. We might glean useful knowledge about the Key and whatever ritual Salvotor thought he needed, but we would never find you before he completed it. She suggested I lure Devitrius to Azkai and let him capture me, bring me wherever you were."

Cistine clutched her throat, the dip bobbing and trembling with shaky breaths. "You *let* them capture you? Thorne, you almost died here! I—*he* carved open your chest..."

"I know, I know." His voice softened. "But I know how my father thinks. I knew he wouldn't be able to resist the temptation, and I told you, I was prepared for anything. I knew we *would* fight our way free together."

She wanted to reach through the bars and punch his chest—for bringing himself here and for keeping it secret for so long. "You're a fool, Thorne Starchaser."

His mouth twitched. "My only regret is that I underestimated just how much he would use me to cause *you* pain. For that, I beg your forgiveness."

"Not for the choice," Cistine said wryly, "but for the hurt it caused."

"You know me too well."

Urgency cleared her irritation, and she struggled to breathe deeply, to think past her excitement and nerves. "Does Kristoff know it's them?"

"Most likely. He told me he wouldn't see me for some time—I suspect he's finding a way to contact them without Salvotor knowing. But we still have to get to Bresnyar. Walking home is...not a choice for me anymore."

Cistine's gaze flicked down to his bowed legs, and she gritted her molars until her ears ached. "We'll have to find a way to get you out of this cage."

"Why don't you leave that to me?"

That was not Thorne's voice, or Quill's. It wasn't even Kristoff's.

Cistine spun on heel to find Grimmaul leaning in the arch of the tunnel mouth, eyes fixed on the braided cord dangling from the ceiling. "Clever little *korvat*. I wonder how long it would take for you to suffocate if we bricked over the air shaft in your room."

Thorne snarled deep in his chest.

"Heel, *bandayo*." Grimmaul smirked. "You know, when the Chancellor invited us to this place, I was so eager. The chance to be among the first who laid hands on those augment wells when one of the Doors opened. And to see *you* again, Princess, without you pining over that dark-haired boy anymore."

Cistine pressed her spine to the cage door. "What do you mean?"

"I'm not surprised you've forgotten. I almost didn't recognize you, either, without your two Wardens and that book clutched like a shield over that ravishing chest. You should have burned it like Rolf told you to."

Staring at him now, with the slashes of ghostlight like blood streaking his face, with that gritty smile and a hand on his sword, she knew him at last. "You were one of the guards with the caravan from Veran."

"Sent by the Guide to ensure you reached Stornhaz unscathed," Grimmaul grinned. "Imagine my surprise when we finally learned the identity of the bandits who were raiding our carts all that time."

The guard who escaped when Quill and Maleck sacked the caravan on the Vingete Vey; the man Quill lost in the woods, who warned Salvotor of the cabal's presence along the Vey and prepared them for the arrow put through Tatiana's shoulder.

"You *coward*," Cistine seethed. "You fled while your caravan died!"

"I've tried to feel a lick of remorse while I enjoy the benefits of being in the Chancellor's personal retinue. But I suspect I'll have an even greater reward for catching the vermin we heard scuttling in the shafts."

He crossed the room in three strides, grabbing for her arm, and Cistine punched him in the jaw. She danced past him when he doubled back, then lunged for the rope, Thorne shouting at her to go, to get out.

But as quickly as she moved, Grimmaul was quicker. His knife bit into the braided cord, slicing it off just above Cistine's knuckles; his hand knotted in her hair, and he slung her against the floor so hard her cheek broke open and her teeth sliced into her tongue. She struggled to catch her breath, spitting blood on the floor. Thorne shouted her name, threatened Nimmus and death and worse than death on Grimmaul; then his legs gave way and he slumped to his knees, staring at her.

"I think it's time the Chancellor knew about your little expeditions," Grimmaul said. "Let's bring along the High Tribune for good measure. I suspect this is something his *father* will want him to see."

Two of his men appeared down the hall when he whistled, dragging Thorne from his cage while Grimmaul hauled Cistine toward the Wound. Her feet fumbled dizzily as she tried to grasp her bearings, head pounding from striking the floor.

A third guard went ahead to summon Salvotor; he waited among the tables when they arrived in the hewn chamber. One look at his unamused face, and Cistine knew she hadn't waited long enough to visit Thorne. She'd been careless, assuming Salvotor was distracted by the watchtowers, and made the same mistake as the Chancellor when he brought Thorne into Kalt Hasa: she'd overestimated her position.

There was only one way to fix it.

"This was Thorne's idea!" she shouted.

Salvotor raised a brow.

"*Cistine*—" Thorne's growl cut short when the guards slammed him to his knees on the floor.

"He told me about the vents!" Cistine rushed on. "He told me how to braid the rope and where to go."

"She's telling lies! She devised all of this under your feet," Thorne spat at Salvotor. "I just came to watch her burn your plans to ash."

Cistine whipped her head toward him. Why did he have to be such a convincing liar? "No, *you* did this, you told me about the vents, about—"

"Enough," Salvotor interrupted coldly. Cistine's muscles knotted, sending sizzling aches through her calves and forearms. "I am *through* allowing the pair of you to undermine me. It was entertaining at first to see how far you would go and how much you'd harm one another. But I have spent my patience for your outbursts." His eyes flicked to Grimmaul. "Break them."

Cistine knew. Even before the knife grazed the back of her shirt, tearing the threads apart, she *knew*.

Thorne swore at the top of his voice, three guards pouncing on his back when he tried to rise. Grimmaul yanked the shirt from Cistine's shoulders, and she tore forward, spearing her elbow into his gut and hooking his legs. But he leaned into the maneuver and brought her down with him, gripping the back of her neck, forcing her facedown on the floor.

Her mind turned to a howling void. She couldn't drag herself back to the pantry, shut the door, taste sweet sap or see the lines of glittering phosphorescence in the dark. Salvotor's greatest weapon was at their throats, and now they would shatter.

She screamed at Thorne to look away, to close his eyes. The only escape either of them could find.

"*Hands up, Stranger!*"

There was no hesitation; Cistine was trained to obey that command from that voice, no matter what. She bucked her weight one last time, yanked an arm from under Grimmaul's knee and cast it out against the stone above her head.

Glorious, blinding power erupted in her hand, a flagon's glass shattering through her fingertips.

"Thorne, *eyes!*" she shouted, and brought the light into herself—then unleashed it.

Grimmaul blasted backward. The guards holding Thorne screamed as the light augment blinded them, a sickle riving from Cistine's body and smashing the stone walls. Something dark landed over Thorne, shielding him from falling debris, and Cistine arched as the augment unspooled from her, unraveling muscle and bone and organ.

Then it was gone.

She sagged against the floor, head thrown back as the ecstasy of power faded from her limbs. The world blurred when hands secured her shoulders and lifted her up; someone shook her, shouting her name. Through the muddied swirl of pain and terror and godlike might, a pair of bright amber eyes swam into focus; a hand connected with her face. "Look at me! Say my name, *Yani!*"

"Tati," she gasped.

A mighty crack echoed in her bones, and Kalt Hasa shook to its foundations. Cistine half-twisted toward Salvotor—or the place where he'd stood.

The ground had opened up below him. He was gone.

Quill straightened up from his one-kneed crouch near the Wound, wiping the shards of the earth flagon off on his armor. "That ought to keep him busy for a little while."

The Six clustered behind him. Tatiana was here—and Kristoff, peeling himself off Thorne and yanking him to his feet. Cistine wobbled as Tatiana cast something soft and feathery over her body. "Where did you get a parka?"

Tatiana rolled her eyes. "That's our princess, always asking the important questions."

A shaky shout echoed from the Wound—Grimmaul, recovering from wherever Cistine had sent him with that blast and rallying the Vassora for a fight. She was sorry the blow hadn't killed him.

"You need to go," Kristoff said as Tatiana pulled Cistine up, shaking so fiercely she could hardly stand. "This battle will be bloody. The Vassora lost confidence in me after Salvotor returned...they won't stand with me against him, knowing the cost."

Thorne gripped Kristoff's shoulder. "Then don't fight them. Come with us, *Nahdar.*"

"I can't. Someone has to give you time."

Cistine's ears filled with a frantic hum. "Kristoff, please...you don't have to do this. We can still escape, all of us, together."

Dain shot her a pained smile and silently shook his head.

Kristoff drew the black sword from the sheath at his hip. "I've spent too many years rotting in the dark while my family needed me. I will never make that mistake again." He offered the weapon's hilt to Thorne. "To break the dragon's chain. First the lightning, then the steel."

"What about Aden and Maleck?" Cistine's voice cracked. "They don't even know you're alive!"

Kristoff turned to her, sadness burning in his eyes. "It's too late to give them back their father. But I can give them back their friends." He gripped her shoulders, his fingers a familiar, beloved weight. "Remember what I told you about channeling the lightning. You can do this."

Cistine pressed her lips together and nodded.

"Good girl." Kristoff's smile freed a tear, scouring his bearded jaw in a silver flash. "You're going to break open more than Doors. You'll break borders and boundaries and the Sable Gates themselves. I wish I could be there to see it happen." He ripped the leather cord from around his neck, the Wayfinder's sigil gleaming dully in the ghostlight as he slipped it over Cistine's head. "You give this to Aden. Tell him and Maleck their father never stopped loving them. And...tell them my *only* wish is that they live free. That you *all* live free."

Tatiana let out a soft, dry sob. Quill's jaw flickered as he ground his teeth, his eyes as damp as Cistine's. Thorne said nothing, but yanked Kristoff into his arms, burying his face in his uncle's shoulder; whatever Kristoff whispered in his ear was not meant for any of them. But when they broke apart, tears slid down Thorne's cheeks as well.

Grimmaul's shouts grew closer, echoing on the walls.

"Run!" Kristoff unsheathed his other blade and whistled to the Six. "Around me!"

"*Ha, Nadrian!*" they cried as one, brandishing their steel.

Tatiana pushed Cistine, and she tore her gaze away from them—Selanus and Suandi, Markvard and Baldvin, Dain and Krusar—and led the cabal in a dash for the cellar steps. They clattered down, voices mingling with the slap of their boots.

"What happened?" Thorne bellowed. "How did you get here?"

"We used a wind augment to reach the balcony," Tatiana panted. "Had some trouble with the guards there."

"And then those six attacked them from the flanks," Quill said. "And *Kristoff* was leading them—*Kristoff Lionsbane*. I thought he was dead!"

"There's a lot of that going around lately, isn't there, Featherbrain?" Tatiana said, and added before Cistine could question that, "Why exactly are we traveling down, not up?"

"Because Thorne can't walk from this mountain." Cistine glanced at him, and his eyes flashed with guilt. "But we don't need to walk. We're going to fly."

They leaped down where the steps cornered abruptly to the right. Two guards waited at the end of the hall, already reaching for their augments. Thorne grabbed Cistine's arm, and Tatiana and Quill surged past them, lighting up the cavern with ribbons of fire.

Thorne's fingers clenched around Cistine's shoulder. "I'm sorry."

She squeezed his hand and pressed a kiss to his shoulder. They could discuss everything after they escaped; the sounds of battle were above them as well as ahead now, the Six and the Vassora clashing in the hewn chamber, and sooner than later, Salvotor would dig himself from the augmented crater Quill had thrust him into.

Urgency bit Cistine's limbs, and she rushed forward with Thorne limping behind her as soon as Quill and Tatiana dispatched their opponents.

The cave's chilly darkness closed around them for a breath, then dispelled when Tatiana broke open another stolen fire flagon. She ran beside Cistine, keeping perfect pace, and a portion of Cistine's spirit yearned to put out her hand and beg for that fire.

She gritted her teeth and ran faster.

Behind them, a pained shout. Thorne broke down, clutching his calf, face twisting in agony. Quill dropped beside him, and when Cistine and Tatiana whirled back, they caught sight of flames pursuing in the distance.

The Vassora had broken through. Which meant Kristoff and the Six—

Cistine forced the thought away before tears could blind her. She plucked the *Svarkyst* sword from Thorne's hand, and Tatiana dismissed the flames so she and Quill could take Thorne's arms and bear him up at a half-dragged run, following Cistine into blackness now.

But it grew brighter every second; first from the flames behind them, then from the fire igniting before them. Bresnyar, scenting Cistine, rolled onto his feet and shook like a dog, wincing as the chain jangled and lightning tines lapped his armored hide.

Quill and Tatiana slammed to a halt, Thorne buckling between them. "Holy—Nimmus, that is *not*—" Quill breathed.

"Is that a *dragon?*" Tatiana yelped.

"Yes, it is." A vein of gloating cracked Thorne's voice.

"Ah. There you are, little sojourner," Bresnyar rumbled. "I thought perhaps you decided to flee without me. Or not to flee at all."

"I made you a promise, didn't I?"

"So you did. Have you found a way to free me from this insufferable chain?"

"We're about to find out." Cistine glanced back. "Tati, Quill, can you hold the line?"

"Already on our way." Tatiana let Thorne down, gaze lingering on Cistine and the dragon for a beat; then she and Quill darted into the shadows and Cistine approached the chain.

This should feel right; she'd already used one augment today and craved another. But now that Bresnyar's chain sloped before her and she watched the lightning dance along it—the same augment that murdered Julian right before her, that melted those midnight eyes—her pulse stuttered and her throat closed.

She put out her hand, and before she even touched the chain, the lightning leaped toward her fingers like she was a conduit herself, another reinforcement running through battle armor. She jerked back, cursing in a half-sob.

She couldn't do it. Couldn't give her body over to that murderous power. Kristoff's instructions fled her mind, leaving nothing but the memory of Julian's face, warped and smoking, dead on Eben's plains.

"Cistine." Thorne's voice. Not urging her. Demanding nothing. He'd stopped making demands so long ago. "You can do this. You can *be* this. It's who you are."

She whipped her head toward him, leaning against a stalagmite for balance and gazing at her with eyes full of wonder—the way he always did.

Key or not, he saw her no differently. None of the cabal did. She was their student, their friend. And right now, she had the power to save them—just as they'd all come to this place, risking death, to save her. As Kristoff and the Six had laid down their lives to keep her from Salvotor's reach, and Julian had laid down his life to keep her safe.

She would not waste those sacrifices.

The clash of blades further back in the cavern rattled Cistine from her thoughts. "Keep watch, Thorne."

He nodded, lifted the black blade in shaking hands, and turned back into the cave. Cistine met Bresnyar's eyes, amber-red pools watching her with depthless intrigue.

There was no time now for conscience, for emotion, for modesty. She shed the parka, the frigid air nipping the bare skin around her breastband as she stepped forward and grabbed the chain.

The lightning shrieked into her body like it was desperate for her. She screamed when the white-hot blaze seared painlessly, just like when it struck her on the Black Coasts. She'd rationalized it then and run away from it ever since, but there was no fleeing anymore. The lightning slashed through her muscles, along her teeth, bursting silver stars across her vision. She struggled to take hold of it, to conduct it like Kristoff told her, melding and molding it to her will—

But it was impossible. She would've had better luck stopping the Sea's tide with her bare hands. The augment broke and crashed around her, burying her, stealing her breath away. It slammed over and through her, again and again, breaking her like a wave against stones. She couldn't cling to it, couldn't channel it; it crushed her, forced the air from her lungs...

Armored hands gripped her shoulders, slid down to her elbows, then covered her fingers over the chain. A strong chest pressed against her bare back, and the burden of the tremendous power lifted somewhat. She gasped in air. She could breathe again.

"Don't stop," Quill said. "Just let me help. Let me carry you."

She squeezed her eyes shut as the augment transferred, building and breaking through her body, releasing along his armor instead. She wanted to bury her face, to hide from the light skimming between them—but hiding and fleeing was what Salvotor wanted her to do.

So Cistine opened her eyes.

The cavern blazed and danced in the heat of the lightning fizzing from her and Quill, slowing time itself, brightening everything in Cistine's line of sight. She could count the raised hairs on her body and every dance of light with the shadows writhing in the seams of Quill's armor.

Then, like a ghostlamp snuffed out, it was over. She transferred it all to him.

"Tati!" Quill shouted, brushing hands with her when she darted past. The lightning shot from his body into her armor, and she marshaled it and blasted it toward the pocket of Vassora they'd pushed back.

But not far enough back.

The ceiling cracked under the strain of the augment, hailing chunks of stone to the floor. Quill whirled away, drew a spear and dagger, and charged the Vassora with Tatiana beside him. Cistine grabbed the parka, dragged it around her bare body, and screamed for Thorne.

He was there at once, brushing her back and hacking at the chain. Cistine staggered out of reach of those swings, unarmed and unsteady to her core, sapped by the battle against the augment's insatiable pull and the terror from Grimmaul's advances.

Her eyes found that wicked guard like an arrow to the target, a scowling, bloody-nosed specter ripping free from the knot of battle Tatiana and Quill created. Wielding the same knife he used to slit her shirt, he charged toward Thorne.

Cistine's scream overlapped the last slam of the sword into the chain. It broke, and as Bresnyar flourished his wings, craned back his head and bellowed in triumph and primordial rage, Grimmaul brought the knife sailing toward Thorne's kidney.

The world blurred when Cistine lunged, grabbing Grimmaul's wrist to break it at the hinge. Only dimly did she register the angle was wrong for that maneuver; then she was between the two men, wrestling Grimmaul for the blade. The struggle lasted seconds—less time than it took the echo of Bresnyar's battle cry to rattle Kalt Hasa to its foundations.

Then Cistine felt something tear.

Warmth. Against her abdomen. Against her hip.

Grimmaul's eyes shot open in horror, and that was when she realized he'd stabbed her.

A cry of hatred and rage. Quill brought Grimmaul down the floor in one shove and impaled him through the temple. Cistine was falling, too, the stone rushing toward her knees.

An arm caught around her waist from behind, and her head wobbled back, suddenly too heavy for her numb neck. The dip of Thorne's shoulder supported her as he sank down, gripping her against his chest. His hand splashed in the blood soaking the front of the parka. "Cistine! Cistine, no. Look at me!" His palm covered her brow, pressing the back of her head into his shoulder. His heart leaped between her shoulderblades, as frantic as his voice. "Wildheart, please, no—oh, stars, *no*, not this, not this, *not this*..."

Death dampened the air. Cistine couldn't see, couldn't feel anything but his touch. Her body was weightless, suspended in a dark current dragging her away from them.

"Cistine?"

"Oh, stars, her belly, *Quill*..."

More hands joined Thorne's, stuffed against her middle, and a sizzling shock of pain brought clarity like the streak of a lonely star across the sky.

It was a mortal blow.

A chaos of thoughts wailed in her head all at once, fighting for dominance. Who would tell her parents? What would they do to Valgard? Who would rule in her stead? She didn't know if there was a contingency. She didn't know whose hands would cradle Talheim when hers went cold.

A visceral need branded her body and bones. She wanted to claw through the ceiling itself, out to the light, to her throne, her kingdom. The ache raised her body in an arch from Throne's lap, her feet digging into the stone, a scream of need, of want, of rage and agony and grief tearing out her throat as it went.

She *wanted* to be Queen. She wanted the press of that throne against her hips and spine, the weight of that crown on her head, to guard and defend everything it stood for. She wanted it with every scrap of her spirit...far too late.

She collapsed back into Thorne's embrace, her scream going out.

"Cistine, keep breathing," Thorne pleaded. "Don't leave me, not now, not like this—*please*. Wildheart, open your eyes!"

But it was not her choice. She was a star, burning and fading, blazing across the horizon, doomed to vanish. And wherever she would go afterward...

Thorne could not chase her anymore.

CHAPTER
FORTY-EIGHT

T HIS WAS NOT happening, it couldn't be happening, nothing in this entire reckless, half-planned siege was possible.

First Kristoff Lionsbane, his sword at Tatiana's neck, then his arms around her, his stubble catching at her curls like she was eight years old again and he was taking her from her mother's arms for another day of play in his home. Then the charge, Quill and Kristoff and his men like specters at her sides; then that stone cavern, and the things Salvotor and his men were doing to Cistine and Thorne, and Quill sending the Chancellor they all despised straight to Nimmus where he belonged. Then the dragon and Quill and Cistine, burning like falling stars together, the purpose in their eyes mutual, blazing, enough to break this mountain at the seams.

And now this, the blood, the screaming, the *sobbing*, the knife in Cistine's abdomen the only reason she hadn't bled out yet, but her head lolling and her body slack.

A corner of Tatiana's spirit jolted awake, crawling out of a dark pit where she stuffed it away a decade ago when she went to Spruce Harbor and Quill wasn't there, when she ran to Aden's house instead, heart jammed in her throat just like now, panic clawing her throat *just like now,* and found Ariadne sobbing and bleeding on the sofa while Aden tended her wounds. The night he grabbed Tatiana and said *I did this, I did this, he's coming for them because of me. Get them out, Tati, save them before it's too late.*

Save her.

Before it's too late.

All this time, she thought that horrific night and the days to follow were about the others—about how Quill wasn't there when she needed him. But it wasn't. It was about her. Because the destitute card sharp from the poorer districts in Stornhaz was there when everything else broke.

She was there. She was here now.

She leaped to her feet and yanked Quill up, spinning him to face her. "We can fix this, Nightwing, we can save her, but I need you to help me! Bring the dragon over here!"

Quill's eyes snapped to focus at the sound of his Name, breaking his staggered breaths. He lunged toward the dragon and grabbed the severed chain around his neck, and Tatiana crouched again over Cistine's sprawled legs and caught Thorne's face in both hands.

"Thorne, look at me. *Focus.* We have to get her out of here, somewhere there's a healing augment!"

Tears streaked weeks of grime on Thorne's face and panic blazed in his eyes like nothing she'd ever seen before. "Tati, if she dies—"

"She *won't.* Not if we work together."

A sizzle of clarity shot through the blind terror in Thorne's face. He jerked from her grasp and scooped Cistine up, every movement gentle. The knife wobbled dangerously, and Tatiana steadied it as she and Thorne staggered awkwardly to the dragon. Quill swung up behind the wing joints and put both hands down to them. "I've got her, *Allet.*"

Thorne shifted Cistine up to him, and Quill cradled her to his chest as Thorne vaulted up, then dragged Tatiana on behind him.

"Hold on to me!" With a snarl, the dragon hurtled upward and spun, slamming all four feet against the ceiling and shredding the stone like parchment. Tatiana wrapped her knees around his sides and clung to him with all her might, trying not to think of the dizzying drop or the rumbling in the belly of this stone Nimmus, a feeling like the walls were caving in around them—

Salvotor's wrath fanned out toward them from the hole Quill buried him in, just like it had the night he broke her friends. Broke *her*.

She hurled the thought out, hurled away the panic that made her want to withdraw. *Not now, not now.*

This was not about her, it was about them, about *Cistine*. About saving her before it was too late.

With a roar as mighty as his fire, the dragon ripped through the mountainside and burst out into the icy night. With a snap of those golden wings, they hurtled south, faster than Tatiana had ever traveled in her life.

Quill cursed at the top of his lungs, a stream of profanity and Cistine's name as he lifted her head from the crook of his arm and grazed his thumb over her lips. "She's not breathing—Thorne! *She's not breathing!*"

Thorne's wordless shout pierced the wind as Quill shifted Cistine back to his arms and leaned low on the dragon's neck. They picked up speed, streaming over the foothills and Spoek's pale stretches, down toward Nordbran. Thorne twisted toward Tatiana and laid Cistine between them. Her head lolled, and blood leaked around the knife. She was so *stars-damned* still—

But Tatiana knew what to do. Maleck and Baba Kallah had taught her. Her mother was a medico, her father an inventor and tinker, a fixer of the unfixable. This was in Tatiana's blood—saving lives. Mending things. It was what she was *born* to do.

It was who Tatiana Dawnstar truly was. And Cistine had seen it long before Tatiana saw it in herself.

She couldn't let her go.

The orders flew from her lips, telling Thorne to breathe for Cistine while she swung a leg over the princess's hips, pinning her to the dragon's back, and with the heels of both hands she compressed her chest.

Don't you leave us, Cistine, don't you dare.

I want all of you. Your hurt, your temper, your smiles and wisdom.

Tatiana's hands melded seamlessly into the familiar motions, forcing the blood to flow, forcing their princess to stay with them while pain and bloodloss and the Undertaker's own hands dragged her away.

I want to talk about our problems while we root through your closet.

Thorne pressed his lips over Cistine's and breathed into her lungs. Every brush of his mouth to hers and every touch of his fingers under her jaw looked too much like a farewell kiss.

I want to read books of Valgardan lore and drink tea and discuss politics and augmentation together.

Tears soaked Tatiana's collar as she jammed the heels of her interlocked palms into Cistine's sternum.

I want my friend back.

"Breathe, Cistine." Thorne's voice shattered as he pressed his brow to hers. "Please, *please,* Wildheart, I'm *begging* you—"

Cistine's heart jumped under Tatiana's palms.

"Thorne!" Tatiana shouted. "Say it again! Say her Name!"

Her jerked back, gripping Cistine's face in both hands and pressing his lips to her hair. "Wildheart, listen to me. Hold on. Keep breathing, Wildheart, don't let go!"

The wind turned his words shallow and void and ripped them away as he wrapped his arms around his *selvenar* and brought his mouth to hers again. And the only hope Tatiana had left was another slow, unsteady thump against her palms as Thorne's lips brushed Cistine's, breathing life into them both.

CHAPTER FORTY-NINE

THE TEMPLE HALLS were quiet after dark, Tatiana's steps unnervingly loud in the deserted stretch leading to Cistine's room. In just one day, she'd crossed it countless times, following Thorne inside with Cistine's limp body, helping fetch Saychelle and the other *visnprests,* then explaining things to Iri, sending word to Maleck and Ariadne, and finally, after more than two sleepless nights from Kalt Hasa to Keltei Temple, pausing to wash Cistine's blood from her hands.

She was just coming back from that, nails pared short, scarlet freckles scrubbed from beneath. She rounded the corridor to spot Quill sitting exactly where he was ever since they arrived at Keltei in a flurry of dragon wings and shouts and pleas for help: outside Cistine's room. Knees cocked, arms strung around them, he stared at her door as if he could see through it—see *her.* Saychelle had only let Thorne inside, and that, Tatiana suspected, was because he was the thread holding Cistine tenuously to life.

"Here." She dangled one of the cups in her hands before Quill's blank face. "Refreshments."

He took it in his good hand, leaning back into the wall and inhaling deeply. "Coffee?"

"Freshly imported from Nordbran." She settled beside him. "Any change?"

"No one's come out to say."

Tatiana swallowed a trill of panic and the wish for something stronger than coffee to dull her nerves. She would *not* face Cistine inebriated when she woke.

When. Not if. They couldn't come this far to lose her to a Vassoran blade.

Quill thumped his head back against the wall, keeping his damp, raw eyes pinned to the door, and Tatiana took the cup from his hand and pushed herself under his arm, into his side. That revived him a bit; his hand closed around her upper arm and he kissed her brow.

They sat like that for a time, quiet apart from the chafe of his thumb on her sleeve and her occasional sips of coffee.

"I've been thinking about everything you said," Quill broke the silence at last, "about sharing the burden instead of carrying it. And what you called me, back in The Village of the Moon. Forged from the stars. That's from a Valgardan epic, isn't it? How the True God forms a man by pouring stardust into a vessel and letting the light shine out."

Tatiana nodded. "Everyone you love and everyone you hate is only stardust."

"Right." Quill settled them both more comfortably back against the wall. "I spent my whole life worrying about how my father and mother saw me. First I tried to live up to it. Then I tried to run from it. I just saw a failure, all the time. The worst brother, a bad advisor, and a terrible friend. That's why I always believed I was replaceable. Expendable, you know? Like Thorne wouldn't have chosen me if we crossed paths on the street the way he did Nimea and Tobor and the rest of them." His hand tightened around her arm. "But back there in that cave, when I helped Cistine channel that lightning...stars, Tati. I felt it. The way she leaned into me. What she needed from me. I could've taken that augment off the chain for her, but that's not what she needed. It was just me taking part of it so she could carry the rest."

Tatiana swallowed around the lump in her throat. "Sharing the burden."

"Exactly." He rested his cheek on her hair. "I finally get it. I have to be there for all of them…for you. So that's what I'm going to do from now on. No more taking swords for people. I'll learn to block them instead."

"I appreciate that." Tatiana laughed breathlessly, twisting her face to press a kiss to the hinge of his shoulder. "I'd like to go a long time without blood from this cabal on my hands."

The door across the hall swung open suddenly, flooding ghostlight over them. Tatiana set down her mug and leaped to her feet. Quill pushed himself up, slower and stiffer from hours of sitting, as Thorne emerged, gaunt and haggard and dragging both hands through his filthy hair.

"What's the word, *Allet?*" Quill demanded.

Thorne's eyes flicked across their faces. "Saychelle thinks she's going to be all right."

Tatiana dropped back against the wall, dizzy with relief. Quill burst forward and clapped Thorne in an embrace, muttering something in his ear that dragged a hoarse sound, half-laugh and half-sob, from his chest. Quill didn't let go of him until the *visnprests* and *prestas* poured out, led by Saychelle. Tatiana met her weary eyes and dipped her head; after a hesitant moment, Saychelle nodded back.

Quill withdrew, keeping a hand on Thorne's shoulder. "What now?"

"We let her sleep as long as she needs. You sent word to Maleck and Ariadne?"

Quill nodded. "As soon as we touched down."

"Temple pigeons are even faster than ravens," Tatiana added. "They know we have her by now."

"Good." Thorne towed a hand through his hair again. "Are you two all right?"

"We've been better. And worse. Tell us what you need," Quill said.

"Food. And a few moments to collect myself."

Tatiana squeezed his arm in passing. "I'll join you two in a minute."

Cistine was more deeply asleep than she'd ever seen, swallowed in the lush bed. Tatiana leaned her hand against the headboard and watched her friend's chest rise and fall. She was so stars-forsaken pale, Saychelle must've used a blood augment to save her life—one of the rarest and most valuable, a prime weapon in the former Order's arsenal to corrupt children like Maleck. She'd always hated them because of that, but now she sent a silent prayer of thanks to the gods for that gift, and took Cistine's hand.

"Don't keep us waiting too long, *Yani*." She brushed a kiss against Cistine's motionless brow. "We still need our Wild Heart of Fire to help burn down Salvotor's Judgement Seat."

∼∼∽∾

In the dimness of Keltei's eating parlor, Thorne tackled his plate of fish with abandon and tore into a basket of sweet rolls, punctuating the meal with the occasional grunt of pleasure. Tatiana and Quill sat across from him, both fighting and failing not to smirk. The effort only became more difficult when Tatiana trod on Quill's foot under the table, silently warning him not to laugh, and he banged his knee and folded up with a groan.

Thorne paused mid-bite, raising his eyes to them. They were clear, icy blue again, losing some of the dull grayness from his imprisonment. "I owe you two an apology."

"For what?" Quill rubbed his leg, tone mild but eyes sparking like summer lightning. "Making us walk all the way to Kalt Hasa to find you?"

"Or lying to us about the temples in the first place?" Tatiana added.

Regret darkened the tight line of Thorne's jaw. "Both. I knew it was brashness, madness, even, to draw their ire on purpose...but I didn't know what else to do to reach her in time. And I thought my father would be more reticent to come for me if I had the pair of you at my back."

"You're damned right, he would've been." Quill thumbed his nose, then shrugged. "Apology accepted."

"Besides," Tatiana shot him a smirk, "it wasn't *all* bad, how things went."

Thorne gazed between them, brows arching. "How long have you two been *valenar*?"

Tatiana's mouth leaped open. Quill banged some other body part on the table when he snapped forward. "How did you—?"

"I've known you for twenty-three years. What kind of friend would I be if I couldn't tell how things have changed?"

Tatiana and Quill exchanged a sheepish glance.

"Also, you both have new scars on your palms."

Tatiana picked up a roll and hurled it at his head. "Cheating."

A smile tugged the left side of Thorne's mouth. "Well?"

"Since Oadmark," Quill admitted. "A little more than a fortnight."

Thorne returned to his meal. "And what was in Oadmark?"

"The path to Cistine," Tatiana said. "But that's not all we found."

He froze at her tone and raised his eyes again, a small divot forming between them. "Tell me."

Quill folded his arms on the table and ran his three-fingered hand through his hair. "The Bloodwights are on the move."

Thorne dropped his cutlery with a clatter and pushed back from the table, eyes blazing. "*What?*"

"We would've found you sooner if we hadn't been dealing with...that," Tatiana said. "They've changed, Thorne. The one we saw, the *Aeoprast*, it was nine feet tall and wielding three augments at once, terrorizing the Oadmarkaic villages in a skull mask."

"Passing itself off as a god, apparently," Quill scoffed.

Thorne's fingers curled around the table's edge. "Did you bring this *Aeoprast* down?"

"We wish," Tatiana muttered. "We never even stood a chance, not against that many augments. We had no choice but to run."

"They've been capturing villagers up there for years," Quill added. "I don't think they ever stopped what they started with people like Mal."

Thorne's gaze was unfocused, fixed past them on the tall windows that looked out over the Agerios. "The experiments."

Silence descended, as black as the edges of the room where their small ghostlight didn't reach. Quill slouched, folding his arms over his middle. "What do we do now?"

"Once we've dealt with my father, I'll bring this before the Courts," Thorne said. "If you two couldn't kill it, I take that as a threat beyond what the cabal can face alone. But a fighting force brought inside Oadmark's borders is a delicate matter. It's not my decision alone to make."

Tatiana grinned. "Already thinking like a Chancellor."

Thorne shot her a grateful smile. "I've had plenty of practice with all of you." He rose and stretched, then bent to rub his calves. "I'm going to be with Cistine. Call me if there's trouble."

Quill plucked a cinnamon stick from his pocket—gods only knew where he found it—and stuck it between his teeth. "We'll keep watch."

Thorne's warm gaze swept between them. "I'm happy for you. If every *valenar* bond was like yours, Valgard would be a better kingdom."

Tatiana took Quill's hand, scar to scar, and squeezed. "We'll just have to show them how it's done."

CHAPTER FIFTY

THE CITY OF a Thousand Stars loomed against a horizon strung with pearlescent stormclouds ready to unleash their rain. Ashe's retinue made camp along one of the ponds north of the city wall, and once Pippet was settled with her blanket wrapped around her shoulders and her knife in hand, Aden wandered south. Ashe bound Deja to a willow beside the water and joined him.

It was the first time they'd been alone since the forest grove and Sigrid's death; Pippet was always by Aden's side, and Ashe frequently alone, playing with the starstone necklace and considering whether to speak into it and sate her curiosity.

Tonight, she felt no curiosity, only dread while she and Aden stood side-by-side, staring at the city's outer wall. A shiver chased down Ashe's spine, knotting her muscles. "The Wardens are restless."

"They should be." Aden folded his arms and tapped his elbows. "This city holds no love for any of us."

"Plan?"

"I'll go in alone, find Maleck, and bring him to us. He'll know the safest route to bring Pippet into the city."

If she hadn't learned the cadence of his voice so well in the Hive, Ashe might have missed the worry chafing his words. "Are we doing the right thing, leaving her here?"

"Maleck will keep her safe. He knows where to hide her—somewhere she can stay."

Nerves rattled Ashe's hands at the thought of Pippet left behind in The City of a Thousand Stars, but she struck it down. Her hands were not always the safest. There were other people in Valgard who could be trusted with Pippet's life—with any important life. If she'd learned that sooner, they wouldn't be standing here now, and Aden wouldn't be leaving them for the childhood home he'd fled with the cabal after making all his worst mistakes.

Mistakes like hers.

"I'm sorry my actions brought us here," Ashe muttered. "If I'd been honest with you back in the Hive instead of leaning into Nimea's hate, we could've prevented all of this. Cistine and Julian, Baba Kallah, Helga, that woman Sigrid...none of them would be in danger. Or dead."

"Apology accepted." Aden flashed her a sideways glance. "But what's done is done, your mistakes and mine. We can only hope for redemption."

Ashe's throat ached with dangerous optimism. She'd come to hope for too many impossible things lately: to be forgiven. To belong. To redeem herself. To find Cistine, protect Pippet, bring Maleck and Ariadne their witness and have everything she wanted, and nothing she deserved.

Hope was pain. But she couldn't seem to stop hurting herself.

"Are you ready?" she asked.

Aden's back lifted in a long, careful breath. "I haven't set foot on these streets since I betrayed my cabal. Betrayed Nimea and the others. It's a risk, but I can demand it of no one else."

"You know I'd go with you if you asked."

"And you know I won't. Someone has to watch over Pippet."

True. But that meant there was no one watching over *him*.

They shifted their feet, neither one speaking. This was all time borrowed against Cistine's fate; they couldn't waste a second more.

And yet she didn't want him to go. She didn't want to be alone with the Wardens. And she didn't want to see Maleck when she still hadn't decided what to say to him, how to apologize for the hurt she left in his eyes when they parted ways in the Den. Or how to thank him for convincing Aden to stay behind and wait for her—knowing, somehow, she would find her way back to them.

"Aden," she said when he stepped forward. "Be careful."

He dipped his head and jogged away toward the city of his birth. Salvotor's city.

The other Wardens watched Ashe's return with the same shrewd, suspicious gazes as ever since Viktor murdered Sigrid, but she paid them no heed, joining Pippet in the windbreak of the willow tree and wrapping her arm around the girl's shoulders. "Are you excited to see Maleck and Ariadne?"

"I suppose." Pippet poked her fingers through a hole in her blanket. "But I don't want to leave you and Aden. I want to help you find Cistine." She peered up, eyes wide and resigned. "I'd just be in the way, wouldn't I?"

"It won't always be like this." Ashe hugged her close. "Now that you've left Starhollow, things will be different. You can go to school, maybe. Train with us. Stay with the cabal."

"If Quill *lets* me."

"If it's what you want, then make him hear you. You can raise your voice and still give respect. Make him see why it matters. Talk to him." She traced gentle circles on Pippet's sleeve with her thumb, working her mind through the next words. "If I'd listened to Cistine half as much as I did what *I* decided was best for her, we'd be in a different place."

"How do you mean?"

Guilt fizzed in Ashe's gut. "Just an expression."

Pippet didn't ask, only leaned into Ashe. "I'm scared for Aden."

So am I. The words clung to Ashe's lips, refusing to be given voice. Instead she fished in her pocket and withdrew the starstone, pressing it into Pippet's hand. "You can hold onto this, if it helps."

Pippet turned the stone over with two fingers, marveling at its delicate curves and mineral speckles. "I can keep this?"

"Just until Aden comes back." Ashe mussed the girl's hair. "It was a gift for me, remember?"

"Do you know why?"

Ashe grimaced, rubbing the memory of Sigrid's blood from her fingers. "I wish I did, Pip." But as little as she understood it, she couldn't bear to throw it away.

Pippet clutched the stone tightly in her fist and snuggled against Ashe's side. Silent, they watched the clouds roll closer; flickers of lightning danced in their depths and the wind banked sharply colder, promising that after this storm, change would come.

Ashe prayed it would be for the better. That in just a few days, she would have Cistine safe in her arms again, and Salvotor would pay for every crime he'd committed, for Julian's death, and more. And after...after was unknown, with Cistine and Rion at opposing ideals and Ashe caught between them. She wanted her princess safe, but she saw what became of ignoring Cistine's choices and threatening her consent.

She couldn't do it again—not even for Rion Bartos.

These thoughts chased circles around Ashe's mind until Pippet's slump grew dead against her and she began to snore. Ashe slowly wiggled free and draped Pippet on the lakeshore, the starstone still tucked in her fist. Then she went to check on Deja.

The woman was resigned to her fate, at least; she'd given up spewing threats when they removed her gag for meals days ago and was likely plotting how to use her leverage within Stornhaz to free herself from having to testify against Salvotor.

"Glare at me all you like," Ashe muttered, testing Deja's bonds and tightening her gag. "I'll still rest easier once you've done your part to put that bastard in chains."

"Since when did Valgardan politics become so important to us?"

By the distant forks of lightning and last shimmers of daylight, Ashe caught Viktor leaning against the far side of Deja's tree, watching her for an answer to his question. At his feet, Rozalie trapped and hauled up fish from the pond with a hand-crafted net.

Satisfied with Deja's restraints, Ashe rose and dusted off her hands. "Any Warden worth their steel knows a concern of one kingdom could be a concern for us all. That's why King Cyril hoped Valgard would stand with us against Mahasar." Stranger than hearing Cistine's argument come from her own mouth was that she felt truth when she weighed the words out.

Viktor snorted quietly. "Is that concern for the Middle Kingdom I hear, or for your Valgardan allies?"

"Leave her alone, Viktor." Rozalie climbed to her feet, fish strung in one hand, and she didn't meet Ashe's eyes. "I heard you talking to Aden before he left. I—*we* didn't realize how many people you hurt. The weight you were carrying. No wonder you've been so standoffish and having nightmares."

Her sympathy yanked Ashe's heart two ways: desperation to feel seen, and suspicion that after all this time traveling together, they were only now acknowledging the torment she wrestled with. "I...appreciate your concern."

"Who were they?" Viktor asked. "Baba Kallah and Helga? You've never mentioned them before."

Ashe dragged a hand through her hair. "It's not worth discussing."

"Viktor, I think she's right," Rozalie urged. "If she doesn't want to tell us—"

"Oh, give it a rest!" Viktor's voice was so loud, Rozalie winced. "Who can she talk to if not us?"

Aden. Pippet. Maleck.

But a part of Ashe clung to the invitation in Viktor's words—faith and a glint of compassion from the Wardens she'd grown up training with. The ones who'd been friends and lovers. Her family.

Rubbing her face, she sagged against the tree. "When I was in Siralek, I did something I'm not proud of. I betrayed Aden's trust, and that betrayal killed two of the only people in this kingdom who were ever kind to me."

Rozalie chewed the corner of her lip and shook her head sharply, eyes locked with Ashe's. Viktor tilted his head. "Is that what you meant when you said the wrong people kept getting hurt?"

Ashe nodded. "Kallah and Helga were innocent of everything we've ever hated about this kingdom," her voice shook with the shame she held off most days, "and I killed them. I'm the reason Cistine is in danger and

Julian—"

"What about Julian?" Viktor's tone sharpened, piercing through the haze of guilt and grief and jolting Ashe up from the tree.

And then, from behind it, the softest whimper she'd ever heard.

The blood drained from Ashe's head, and she snapped around on heel. Lightning broke the clouds apart, gripping the frame of Pippet's face in icy hands, painting every freckle on her cheeks, the sunken hollows of her jaw, the agony in her eyes.

"Ashe," she whispered, "what do you mean you killed Baba Kallah and Helga?"

Ashe's stomach gave way, and she reached for the girl's shoulder. "Pippet."

"No!" Pippet jerked back. "No, tell me, what do you *mean* you killed them?"

"It wasn't on purpose. It was a—a mistake."

Not an accident. She'd known harm would come to the cabal, but she hadn't anticipated the ramifications until she stood in the Den's kitchen and saw the anguish in Thorne's face and heard that Julian was dead and Cistine taken; until she met Pippet in the Wildwood and listened to her cry for her nanny that first night.

Tears glistened on Pippet's lashes. "But...Ashe, *why?*"

"I don't know!" Frustration cracked her voice. "I was angry, *I* was hurt, but I know that's no excuse. I was wrong, and I'm sorry, Pippet. I'm *so sorry.*" But Pippet shook her head, backing away, lips flaring as she fought not to sob. Ashe stepped after her, hand still outstretched. "Pippet, please—"

"*Stop!* Don't come near me!" Pippet's scream froze Ashe in her tracks. "I hate you! You're just like all of them, like all the Wardens!"

"Pippet, that's not true. I don't hate Valgard." It wasn't merely placation. Somewhere between broken bones and arena battles, between swords protected and songs sung, between Jovadalsa and Deja's home and every dark, frightened night, nightmare, and comforting touch on the journey, her hatred had faded.

But Pippet shook her head, still stepping back. "You do hate us! You hurt Thorne, you hurt Baba Kallah, you killed *Helga*! I never want to see you ever again!" She hurled the starstone to the shore and fled into the gathering storm.

Cursing, Ashe coiled to chase after her, but Viktor caught her elbow. "Leave her. This is part of growing up. She doesn't need you to sweep in and save her from it."

"Are you out of your mind? She's just a child!"

"She's a *Valgardan*, Ashe! You heard what she said just now, look at her—she's already growing up to be just like them. You can't save her."

Ashe faltered, staring at him. All the caring was gone from his eyes, all the compassion for Ashe's plight. "Did you know she was listening? Is that why you asked me when happened in Siralek? You wanted to push her away from me?"

Viktor held her gaze with dispassionate eyes, but true pain carved Rozalie's crestfallen face.

Ashe wrenched from Viktor's hold. "You're all gods-damned cowards."

"Wait, Ashe, *please...*" Rozalie began.

But she was through listening to them. They'd proven their loyalties tonight; they'd crossed a line there was no turning back from.

She snatched up the starstone and sprinted into the deepening darkness.

CHAPTER FIFTY-ONE

"PIPPET!" ASHE'S VOICE tore from shouting. "*Pippet!*"

Thunder swallowed her words as she crashed through the foliage around the pond shore. Pippet had run straight toward the city, either fleeing blindly or going to find Aden; either way, she was running into danger.

Ashe burst from another pondside grove and winced when lightning seared her eyes. Blinking the dazzling impression away, she squinted at a distorted shadow rippling ahead: two figures wrestling between the glades, one small and slender, the other broad and powerful.

Rion Bartos had his hands around Pippet's neck, trying to restrain her.

Ashe barreled forward, shouting in rage, just as Pippet clapped her palms together, swept up her arms, and broke Rion's hold. She screamed in his face and scrambled backward, and Ashe slid between them, slamming her commander back with a hand to his chest and sweeping her other arm out toward Pippet. "Rion, what in God's name are you doing? Leave her alone!"

"No. Enough of these games, Kovar." Rion's voice was cold as the rain that dripped from his hair. "We're not tromping off into the gods-damned wilderness, searching for some place your augur *might* know about, *somewhere* in the north. This ends here. Tonight."

"What do you mean?" Ashe shifted her weight, keeping herself between Rion and Pippet. "What does any of this have to do with Pippet?"

"Leverage."

The word struck with a clash of thunder. Fury cracked Ashe's retort: "*What?*"

"I have the Writ of Nobility from Talheim's royal family, and we have one of their offspring." Rion gestured sharply at Pippet, cowering behind Ashe. "With that, we can march into their own capital and demand they bring Cistine to *us*."

"Or else, what? We slit Pippet's throat?"

Rion's gaze was terrifyingly inscrutable.

Calm. The thought forced through the rage-addled haze of her mind. *The one who keeps calm wins the battle.* Rion's own lesson; she'd never despised it more. "We can't do this. It's a waste of time and it would expose a Talheimic presence on Valgardan soil for no reason. The Chancellors don't care what happens to Pippet."

Rion scoffed, prowling before them like a caged animal. "You don't know their minds as I do. They're like wild dogs, they always turn feral over their young...no matter how dangerous they are!"

A deep chill clawed down Ashe's spine. "How do you know that?"

Rion halted, fixing her with the look of arched-brow disappointment she always hated. But tonight, she hated something else more: the dawning comprehension of who and *what* she was truly facing.

"Who do you think chased away that augur boy who attacked you in the camp during the war?" Rion said. "Did you really think *you* frightened him off? That he stayed away because *you* somehow pierced his heart? They are *incapable* of change!"

The augur boy—the tundra—

Dark trees and ice and blood and marshes and dull eyes with life trickling back into them...

"You chased him." Ashe's breath formed thick billows against the cold rain. "Into Cerne Mosiar."

Rion stared at her, waiting.

"You're *Meszaros*."

The creature of her nightmares ever since Disa's home. The one who slaughtered the children in the Wildwood—who killed the matriarch's young daughter.

The Butcher. Rion's namesake from the war. She didn't need Aden or Cistine to tell her what *Meszaros* meant in Old Valgardan now—the answer stood before her, heaving with rage to rival the storm.

"Whatever they call me, my conscience is clear," Rion said. "And it's clear in this as well: I'm taking that girl and the Writ into Stornhaz and these *Chancellors* will bring our princess here, or they'll watch one of their offspring perish."

He stepped forward, and Ashe slung an arm out, backing Pippet and herself away from him. "You stay away from her."

"As Commander of the King's Cadre—"

"I don't give a damn about your title!"

"As *your* commander as a Warden of the royal family," Rion shouted, "I order you to stand aside!"

"If this is what it is to be a Warden, then I don't want it!" Ashe yanked her scabbard over her head. "*Any* of it!"

She cast Echelon at his feet, mud spattering the sheath and his boots. Though it broke Ashe's heart to see it fall, with its weight gone she took a full breath for the first time in twenty years. She finally saw the world clearly—saw *Rion* clearly.

He cast his gaze from Echelon to her face. "You don't want to do this. I know your mind, I fashioned you into what you are. You're nothing without the Cadre."

"If being Cadre means hunting and killing children, I'd rather be nothing than that."

"They aren't like our children! Your duty is not to them, it's to Talheim."

"I have a duty to my conscience as well! I wasn't trained to sacrifice children, that's what the man we're hunting wants Cistine for. And I'm not like him." She straggled in a chilly breath. "I'm not like *you*."

Rion's face twisted with rage. "You forget your place, Kovar!"

"I forgot where that was a long time ago." Ashe spread her arms slightly. "But right now, I know I belong between you and her."

Lightning gleamed on steel when Rion drew against her, and she saw he'd come too far now; he would do anything to bring Cistine home, even cut down Ashe to reach his bait.

Cursing her name, *Meszaros* of Cerne Mosiar attacked.

She twisted on heel when his sword descended, and Pippet's hand clapped against hers, passing the knife. Ashe shoved her aside, but not quickly enough.

Cloth tore. Pippet screamed as Rion's blade raked her shoulder in passing, thrusting her into the mud.

Ashe stumbled to a halt, the pulse in her ears turning sluggish. Pippet lay on her side, sobbing and clutching her bleeding arm, and Rion stood over her like a wolf over his kill, facing a challenging predator.

Ashe flipped the knife backhand and sank her boots into the mud. Let her muscles feel sand, not mire, beneath her feet.

Red desert sand and golden sunlight and blood and gray eyes, full of danger.

White tundra and shadows and blood and dead eyes with life trickling back into them.

A girl with blood on her hands and fury in her scream. *I'm not afraid of you!*

Roaring in Rion's face, Ashe attacked.

They spun through rain and mud and lightning, sword and knife singing together. They'd fought a thousand training sessions like this, fixed in lockstep, but Ashe had never stared into his face and seen hatred aimed at her like a second sword before.

He pounded blows against her, harsh shouts punctuated by thunder, setting her arms ringing. Ashe's hair sopped into her eyes, half-blinding her while she dodged, blocked, and parried, forcing Rion away from Pippet, who curled up with her head tucked under her arm.

The clash became monotonous. The Cadre Commander wasn't swinging to kill, just to release tension—to break Ashe down just like he did so often in training. Breaking her and reshaping her into his own shadow, stalking the princess's heels, ensuring she was safe.

No. Ensuring she *conformed*.

How had she never seen it? The man whose son was destined for kingship, who despised Valgard more than he loved anything else in his life. She'd all but handed Valgard's heart to him when she brought him here.

Her mentor, the man she'd sworn to follow to the ends of the world, was a butcher, a breaker of families, and a killer of children.

Hurt and betrayal guided Ashe's strike when she lurched forward, swept Rion's legs, kicked his sword from his hand and slammed her fist into his mouth. He cracked hers in return, the strike of his elbow jarring her so hard she let go of her knife and staggered back, clutching her jaw.

He'd never been afraid to hit her, even as a girl, but this time he didn't pull. He was fighting for the chance to spill blood for his princess, to repay Valgard for yet another slight and wave his victory flag above the Chancellors' heads.

She'd unleashed *Meszaros* onto the Northern Kingdom again, trusting the power and rage of a Talheim she didn't fully comprehend—had never truly known.

They grappled in earnest now, blades gone, hitting and kicking instead. Blows glanced, some landed; Ashe's ribs throbbed and her head spun from a clipped temple, and Rion's nose churned blood and he bore less weight on his left side. Yet still they came back together again and again, knuckles biting flesh like angry molars, boots jabbing at soft spots, bodies plowing in with ceaseless rage.

Ashe caught Rion's fist just shy of striking her mouth again, but this time he followed with his knee rather than his other hand, catching Ashe's gut and folding her in half. Broad fingers encircled her throat, and he lifted her up, squeezing. "Look at you! Wearing Valgardan battle armor, fighting for a Valgardan rat...I don't even know you. You've become one of *them*."

"If you think *I'm* like them," Ashe gasped, "you should see Cistine."

Rion dropped her, cocked back his fist, and struck.

Flesh slammed flesh with a resonate *crack*—but the pain never came.

A gloved hand caught Rion's punch, staying it with the same might that held Ashe up whenever her injured leg faltered during those long days of strength-training in the Den. A braided head faced against her, a broad body shoved between her and Rion.

With one blow, Maleck thrust the Cadre Commander backward, sliding awkwardly through the mud. Footsteps splashed in puddles to their left, and Aden scooped Pippet up and pressed his hand against her bleeding shoulder, backstepping from the battle.

But Rion did not attack. Maleck did not attack. They simply stared at one another. Ashe didn't like that look, the predatory stillness in Rion or the frozen quiet in Maleck.

"You," Rion breathed at last. "I thought the tundra took you."

"I'm certain you wish it had."

Rion cursed and kicked his blade up into his hand. "I'll finish what I began with your eye."

Ashe pushed between them, sweeping an arm across Maleck's front. "You'll have to kill me first."

Rion's gaze flicked over her, remote and cold. "I have no qualms about killing a thing that wears Valgardan skin."

It would have hurt less if he'd rammed a blade into her gut. Snarling, Ashe gathered herself to attack again—to finish him bare-handed if she had to, to deal back an ounce of the agony he birthed with his well-aimed blows—but Maleck grabbed her hand before it slid from his chest, halting her assault. "Ashe! We have Cistine!"

She froze, the wind knocked from her. Rion's sword wavered, but he didn't strike when she swung her back on him to meet Maleck's gaze. "*What?*"

"Thorne is with her, in Keltei Temple. Quill and Tatiana as well." Maleck's eyes shone with excitement, searching hers for the joy he knew that report would bring. "They sent word yesterday."

Rion's steps splashed nearer. "*I want to see her with my own eyes!*"

Ashe whirled back on him, spitting with fury. "If you think for even a *moment* I'll let you near her after what you did tonight—"

"You don't command me! If you try to keep me from her, I'll report to the King you've defected and return with an army at my back. We'll storm this temple by *force!*"

"Asheila," Maleck said. "Cistine can manage him."

Bitterness, petty hurt, and rage all cooled when she met his gaze again. She trusted those eyes; she'd never stopped trusting them after he helped her learn to walk again. And perhaps it would never flow two ways again after what she did in Siralek, but it didn't stop her believing his word.

"Your fate is in Cistine's hands," she told Rion without turning. "If I were you, I wouldn't rest easy."

"I'll take Pippet and the witness into Stornhaz," Maleck said. "You and Aden go to her."

"No. The girl comes with us," Rion argued. "There's no telling whether they'll surrender our princess without some incentive."

Ashe turned back to him, speechless for a moment. She hardly recognized the man before her; yet in the same heartbeat, it was like seeing her own hate-filled face in a pool, her likeness in Siralek through someone else's eyes. "Pippet stays with Maleck, and if you disagree, I welcome you to cross me. I don't think I've had enough after learning what you are."

Maleck stepped up to her side. "You will not fight alone."

Aden settled Pippet on the pond shore again and joined them, facing Rion from Ashe's left hand. "You've already lost this fight. *Back away.*"

At their unified face, even Rion Bartos faltered. Cursing, he sheathed his blade, fixing his eyes on Ashe. "Go to her, or don't. This retinue has no more use for you. I'll find this *Keltei* myself."

He snapped up Echelon, stowed it across his back, then disappeared into the shadowy undergrowth back toward his Wardens. Ashe, Aden, and Maleck held formation until the veil of night and storm swallowed him whole; then Aden dropped to his knee next to Pippet in the mud. Maleck crouched beside them and peeled back the torn halves of Pippet's sleeve, examining the gash across her biceps. "We'll have to amputate."

Pippet squealed in shock, and Aden slapped Maleck on the head. "He's *joking,* unbelievable as it seems."

Maleck snorted, blowing rainwater from the tip of his nose. "I am."

Ashe dragged her hair from her eyes, knotting it back. "Maleck, tell me that was the truth. About Cistine."

He nodded. "She was injured escaping Kalt Hasa. The *visnprests* are doing what they can."

The breath tumbled from Ashe so sharply, she nearly fell to her knees. "Rion was bluffing. He'll just follow us to her. But we have to go anyway."

"Then go." Maleck didn't look up from Pippet's injury. "Ariadne is already clearing the path into the city. We'll hold the line until you return."

His voice was calm, but tension banded his hunched shoulders as he worked over the shallow cut on Pippet's arm. She stared up at him, lower lip quivering when he dabbed blood from her wound. "Am I going to die?"

Maleck's face softened, and he pressed his lips to her hair. "Not while there's still breath in me."

Ashe stepped forward and offered Pippet the hilt of her knife. "You did well tonight, breaking Rion's hold."

A wobbly smile turned her mouth. "But I would've been captured like Cistine if you hadn't followed us."

"I don't know," Aden said, "I think you could've defeated him with an arm tied behind your back."

"No, I *couldn't.*"

"*Both* arms," Maleck added.

Pippet giggled unsteadily. "No, I couldn't—stop it!"

"Never underestimate the strength of a woman fighting for something." Maleck's eyes lingered on Ashe. "She falls for nothing."

Throat aching, she rested a hand on his back. "You and I need to talk when I come back." She tugged the scarf from around her throat and offered it to him. "For her wound. There's something about this cloth, I don't know what it is...maybe it helps bring lost things home."

Slowly, their fingers met over the cloth and he nodded.

Ashe turned to Aden, who rose with a swift kiss to Pippet's hair and dipped his head. "Come. It's time to see your princess."

CHAPTER FIFTY-TWO

CISTINE SMELLED SALT, soap, and fresh linen, herbs and moving water. She smelled her beloved sea.

The white blur of her vision annealed into the soft ivory outline of drapes moving in the breeze. The walls around her were sky-blue, the doorposts and windowframes tastefully gilded. Mother-of-pearl doors opened onto the balcony, and the Agerios Sea breathed deep and sighed out against the shoals.

She was not cold. This wasn't the mountain. She was dressed in cream silk pajamas and stretched out on her back, buried under a bedspread the same color as her clothes. Not a trace of lavender ghostlamps or dark stone walls flickered in view when she pushed the blanket back and sat up, laying a hand to her stomach.

Under the thin silk, the raised ridge of a scar met her fingers.

She sucked in a sharp, shaky breath and dropped her hand to grip the bedspread, shaking away the memory of Grimmaul's knife. She couldn't think of him now, of Kalt Hasa, of Salvotor or Kristoff and the Six. Her gaze traced the whole room this time, taking in everything, searching for a hint of where she was.

Instead, she found Thorne.

He slept against the wall at the foot of her bed, hands clasped in his lap, chin tucked to his chest and face obscured by the threads of his hair. She hadn't seen him so relaxed since before Baba Kallah died, every line of tension erased, the weight lifted from his shoulders.

She whispered his name, and his head rolled up, red-rimmed eyes shooting straight to her face. "Wildheart." His voice cracked and he scrambled to his feet. "Thank the stars you're awake. When Grimmaul—"

"I know." The words broke at the memory of what that knife felt like inside her.

Thorne stepped toward the bed, eyes wary. "May I hold you?"

Twin blades of unease and defiance slashed through her body She hated that he looked so unsure—and hated that she hesitated before she answered, "Of course you can."

Thorne fell onto the bed and wrapped his arms around her. She hugged his neck and pulled the ends of his freshly-washed hair through her fingertips. He smelled clean again, like himself, like sandalwood and leather armor—

Like a Vassoran guard. Like *Grimmaul*.

She stiffened, and Thorne withdrew, planting his hands on either side of her curled legs, studying her face. "We're in Keltei Temple," he said, answering the unspoken question there. "We're safe, though...it was close. Too close, *Logandir*. Under any other circumstances, the journey would have been impossible before we lost you, but that dragon..." he chuckled under his breath. "It's true. They're faster than any creature on land or sea."

Cistine breathed deeply through her nostrils, forcing down the panic of being in another temple. This was nothing at all like Kalt Hasa; the people here were not Salvotor. "Where are Quill and Tatiana?"

"Walking the grounds, patrolling for trouble."

"And Bresnyar?"

"He's kept to himself, but I think he's enjoying freedom as much as any of us."

A smile tugged up Cistine's mouth. "I want to see."

"You should rest."

"Thorne. I'm not going to shatter between here and the balcony. I want to see him."

Thorne sighed and took her hand, guiding her up from the bed. Though the movement left her woozy, she walked hand-in-hand with her *selvenar* to the balcony looking out over the sea. He pointed to the distant coast, where the gold glimmer of Bresnyar swooped and wheeled, chasing gulls across the surface of the water.

"I'm surprised he hasn't left Valgard by now." Thorne crossed his arms on the railing and leaned into it. "Given what he's suffered here."

Cistine mirrored his posture. "He's waiting for me, I think. I promised him an honest conversation once we all escaped."

"He's been patient, then. I don't think he held much hope for your survival." Though Thorne's tone was light, heavy shadows crowded his eyes.

"Well, I'm told I'm worth waiting for."

He brushed her hair behind her ear with his fingertips. "That you are."

The door to the inner chamber creaked open, and Tatiana's voice knifed the steady breath of the sea. "*Thorne!*"

"Out here." He took his hand back as they both appeared in the doorway. Tatiana raked her curls from her forehead, breathing out Cistine's name in relief. Quill dropped his shoulder against the golden doorframe, rubbing his brow. When his eyes met Cistine's, a sizzle of understanding ripped through her body, a memory of lightning linking between them, their power uniting.

She sobbed his name, and when he turned his hair shakily across his head and opened his arms to her, she ran and crashed into him, knocking him backward into the room. He swept her off her feet and swung her in a half-circle while she cried into his collar. "How—*how* did you find us?"

"It's a long story," he laughed breathlessly against her hair. "And it starts and ends with Tati being brilliant, as usual."

He set her back on her feet, and she grabbed his hands, his new scars chafing against hers. "*Both* of you were brilliant! That signal with the feather—" Her stomach plunged, her gaze drawn down. "What happened to your *fingers?*"

"Lost them. If you see them anywhere, let me know."

Before she could demand an explanation, Tatiana took her elbows, spun her around, and buried her in an embrace. "I can't believe you, leaping in front of a Vassoran blade like that! Maybe we trained you *too* well, if you think *that's* how we fight in this cabal."

"Well, look at you and Quill..."

"I don't want to hear another word from you," Tatiana snapped, pushing Cistine out and grabbing her chin. "Unless it's *I'm sorry, Tatiana, I will never do something so risky again, and I will never get my sorry hide captured, either, and I will in fact never do* anything *dangerous without at least two of my friends with me from now on.*"

Cistine smiled sheepishly. "I try not to promise *too* many impossible things at once."

Tatiana mock-groaned and pressed a kiss to her forehead. "Fine. At least tell me you're feeling all right."

"Mostly. A little tired and dizzy." And overwhelmed, but she didn't want to say it; they'd crossed a kingdom for her. The least she could do was make time for them, even if the attention was an unexpected weight reminding her too much of dark suppers with every eye in the room on her gaudy dresses.

In the balcony doorway, Thorne cleared his throat. "Someone should see to her wound, just to be cautious. Quill, will you bring a *visnpresta*? And Tati, see what you can scrounge up from the kitchens."

They swapped smiles, and Quill drawled, "Just like we never left the Den. But don't expect us to wait on you forever, Stranger."

They slipped out, brushing arms in the doorway, and Quill's fingers grazed the small of Tatiana's back—not unusual for them, but there was a new, arresting intimacy in the touch that left Cistine puzzled and hopeful.

Then it was only her and Thorne, and she glanced shyly at him. "Thank you."

"It surprised me, too." His voice was low, edged in regret. "I thought I'd be relieved to surround myself again with people I trust. But I've needed my distance more since we arrived here than I ever did before."

"Do you think it gets better?"

"Stars willing." He stepped to her side, the smell of leather wafting from his body again, and she fought not to move back from him—then lost the battle.

He retreated at her subtle flinch. "Would you like me to go?"

"No." She gripped her elbows across her chest and averted her gaze. "Oh, I don't know *what* I want." She'd waited so long for this, had dreamed of a day when she could touch him without cage bars between them or the threat of being discovered hanging above their heads. Yet now her skin blazed with the spectral memory of Grimmaul's hands wandering where they weren't invited, and fear churned in her core.

Thorne's hands were at his sides, in full view and safely distant. "Will you look at me, Cistine?" A quiet request, not the sort of command he'd give the cabal. Slowly, she dragged her gaze up and found him smiling, cooked and soft. "Don't feel ashamed. You owe me absolutely nothing, not one touch, not one word. I don't expect you to be all right after everything you endured there. Stars know I'm not."

His unsteady voice tugged her from that dark pit in the middle of herself, freeing her focus to take in his bruise-circled eyes and wan pallor. How much had he slept on that hard stone floor? *When* did he sleep, if he was worrying about her? "Go lie down."

He arched a brow. "What?"

"You heard me." This felt right—helping him, not focusing on herself. "You're going to sleep in a proper bed."

He mock-groaned and dug in his heels when she planted her hands in the small of his back and shoved with all her might. It was like pressing against the walls of Kalt Hasa. "I don't remember how to sleep in a bed. They're too soft."

"*You* are too soft, Thorne Starchaser!" Cistine wedged her shoulder into his spine. "Now *move*, will you?"

Laughing, he gave up, letting her shove him chest-first among the silk sheets and pillows. He dragged one under his arm and pressed his face into it, watching her with a thoughtful eye while she settled against the footboard. But in less than a minute, that eye drifted shut, too. The pillow tassels drifted under his quiet snores.

Cistine leaned against the woven-iron latticework, legs stretched out and hands folded in her lap. She had to worry her lower lip with her teeth to keep from falling asleep under the lullaby of the sea, the wind, and Thorne's quiet breathing beside her.

She wanted to believe it was over, Kalt Hasa at last a mere memory at her back. But if she couldn't quiet the panic zipping over her skin when Thorne stood near her, if she couldn't stop thinking of Grimmaul and Salvotor, then was she truly free of them at all?

Her eyes snapped open just as the door did. A *visnpresta* entered, robes glinting in the sunlight, silver hair bound braids around her skull. She eyed Cistine and Thorne, then beckoned. Cistine slid from the bed and followed her to the balcony, where they could shut the doors and leave Thorne undisturbed.

"I am Saychelle." A passing spark of recognition shot through Cistine at the name. "I'm the *visnpresta* who healed you. I've come to examine your wound."

"Of course." Cistine towed up her shirt, trembling slightly as Saychelle probed the knot of scar tissue—not only from the kiss of cool sea wind on her bare navel but from the memory of that knife sliding into her body.

"The risk of infection has passed," Saychelle straightened after a moment, and Cistine yanked down the lace hem and resisted the urge to wrap her arms around herself. "But you lost quite a bit of blood. I suggest at least a week of rest."

"Of course. Whatever you think is best."

Saychelle's upswept eyes narrowed slightly, setting off another clamor of recognition deep in Cistine's spirit. "A word of caution, Princess. Women who involve themselves intimately with Kanslar's High Tribune do not escape unscathed. Tread carefully."

Before she could muster a retort for that unsolicited advice, Saychelle floated back inside, passing Tatiana in the doorway. The warrior joined Cistine on the balcony, took one look at her face, and burst into laughter. "Oh, I know that look. Which side of Saychelle did you just meet?"

Cistine tore her gaze from the closed door. "She—she warned me away from Thorne."

Tatiana rolled her eyes. "Well, she comes by *that* caution honestly."

Saychelle. The angled eyes, the piercing look, that haunting familiarity— "Was that Ariadne's sister? The one Thorne was going to forge the *valenar* bond with?"

"The same. I've been fonder of some scorpions Quill has left in my sleeping pelts, but...you know. Everyone loves differently."

"Why did you bring me to *her*? Isn't that...painful for Thorne?"

"Keltei is the healing temple. Nowhere else stood a better chance of saving your life. Painful or not, Thorne would live out the rest of his days here if it meant keeping you alive."

Cistine rubbed her hot cheeks and looked out across the waves.

Tatiana pulled something from her pocket—slightly flattened, but still arguably a pastry of sorts—and offered it to Cistine, filling her nostrils with the rich smells of sour yeast and butter. Her mouth turned to a spring, and she snatched the roll, broke it in half, and offered a portion to Tatiana.

"Please, if you love me—don't," Tatiana groaned, patting her stomach. "Quill and I had a contest. I've eaten a dozen of those today."

Secretly relieved, she tore into the roll, savoring the melting threads on her tongue. Tatiana whistled under her breath, elbows propped on the railing, her gaze darting to Cistine every now and again, full of thought.

Cistine finished the roll with a whine of regret. "What is it?"

"Nothing, really. Just wondering about Thorne sleeping in your bed."

Her ears heated. "I don't...that was just..." Tatiana's brows arched. Flushing, Cistine dusted her hands on her pajama legs. "I don't know *what* it is. But back in Kalt Hasa, he...he kissed me."

"It was about time! Did you kiss him back?"

Her skin was so hot, she feared a fever was coming—worse, it might be a welcome escape from this interrogation. "What do *you* think?"

"I think you did, passionately, and with abandon—"

"Tati!" She shoved her friend's shoulder, and Tatiana bent against the railing, shaking with laughter. "Well, what about you and Quill? I noticed he has a new scar on his hand."

They both dropped their gazes to the twin mark on Tatiana's palm, her fingers flexing too late to hide it.

"*Valenar!*" Cistine shrieked so loudly Thorne snorted and groaned from the bed. "You and Quill swore the *valenar* oaths without *me?*"

"It's not like your Talheimic ceremonies, Cistine!" Tatiana's nose and cheekbones darkened. "The things that went on in that tent...trust me, they were *not* for your eyes."

Neck hot, Cistine sputtered, "But that's not the *point*! There wasn't a dress, there weren't even any *witnesses*..." Though Thorne had told her long ago that was the way of things in Valgard, it was still strange to imagine that one moment Tatiana and Quill were dancing around intentions, playing with each other's hearts; and then, swifter than Cistine and Julian had even had their first real argument, they became this new thing—eternally oath-bound, blended in blood and spirit.

A part of her was almost envious they'd known so quickly, free of the expectations of courtship, betrothal, and a magnificent wedding. What would *she* do if those things weren't expected of her?

You wouldn't want to betray Julian's memory too soon.

Cistine shuddered, and Tatiana frowned. "Cistine, don't tell me you're *actually* trying to imagine what went on in that tent—"

"I'm not!"

"—because, believe me, I am not above slapping an invalid princess."

Scowling, Cistine shoved her. "No. I'm happy for you. It's...different from what I'm used to. But it's you and Quill, so, really, what else should any of us have expected?"

Tatiana turned a fond half-smirk back toward the room as if she expected her *valenar* to swagger inside at any moment. "You know how the old epics go. All it takes is surviving the impossible for two people to realize they can't lose each other."

Following her stare all the way to the sleeping High Tribune sprawled in her bed, Cistine wondered if that was as true for Talheimics as it was for Valgardans.

CHAPTER
FIFTY-THREE

F IVE DAYS AFTER she woke, Cistine finally picked her way down the salt-slicked coast, wrapping her thick cardigan more tightly around herself to shield against the chilly late-autumn breeze from the sea.

Saychelle was right—the bloodloss had left her lightheaded for days, too tired to do much other than eat, shuffle to the relief chamber, and climb into bed again. But Quill and Tatiana came and went during those long hours, easing her back into the joy of their company with tales of Oadmark—a vast and vivid landscape of snowy peaks and passes, merciless climes full of wolves and auroras and wild, hardy people. Thorne was there for every story, every meal, his focus riveted on her, ready to send out the others or disappear himself whenever she grew tired and craved solitude in the warm chamber. And he didn't argue when Cistine finally woke feeling stronger and said she had to go down to the sea alone; he simply nodded and told her he'd wait for her, and to be careful.

She took that warning to heart on the slick paths down to Bresnyar's perch, a stone crag riddled with fish bones and the carcass of something larger—a shark or a porpoise. Bresnyar cleaned bones from between his teeth with one claw, glancing up when Cistine halted on his shelf.

"You look well," she said. There was a new gleam to his scales, a wild sparkle in his gemstone eyes. Freedom suited him; she couldn't wait for it to hang as well on her, to shed the shackles of her memories the way the dragon shed his steel collar.

"I appreciate the compliment." Bresnyar flicked a bone into the sea. "You, however, do not."

Panic clawed at her throat, an insidious notion that she might always be this pale, thin, unhappy creature her imprisonment forged. She forced it down. "I appreciate your honesty. Have you been waiting all this time for our honest conversation?"

"That I have." He studied her, scaled brows tweaking. "It took quite a bit of courage and cunning to leave that mountain. And strength indeed for you to survive what you did."

She tightened her arms in their cross, pinning the cardigan over her scarred abdomen. "I think I owe my survival more to my cabal than myself."

"Perhaps." He eyed her shrewdly. "Tell me, what do you know of Wingmaidens?"

Cistine shrugged at the foreign term. Bresnyar sighed, blowing steam into the air.

"Oadmark's Wingmaidens help keep the peace. We are hatchlings together. We carry the girls on our backs before they walk on their own legs, and our first flight together comes before their first bleeding. At their ascension, they're given armor with special talismans allowing them to call their dragons from across the kingdoms." His nails clicked thoughtfully on the stone. "A dragon without a Wingmaiden will go mad, in time. It's simply our nature to forget ourselves, our words, our higher ways when we're stripped of that bond."

Cistine studied him, a glint of understanding piercing through the exhausted fog of thought. "Did you lose your Wingmaiden? Is that how Salvotor managed to capture you?"

"Indeed." Bresnyar looked out across the waves. "It is...rare for a dragon to find another Wingmaiden if he fails his first. Rare, but not impossible. I had thought perhaps, if the Great Father allowed me to fall into that barbarian's hands, it might've been for a reason. That perhaps I was meant to find something after all those years in the dark. Or *someone*."

His fiery eyes flicked back to her. Cistine squeaked, *"Me?"*

Another snort, more amused than annoyed this time. "I haven't quite felt it with you as I've felt it before. But perhaps there is a chance, given time...if you should be so inclined to travel and learn the ways of dragon-riding..."

The hope in his voice shredded her heart. There was so little she knew about dragons, about any of the world despite all she'd learned yet; but she did know enough to answer him honestly. "I can't go flying with you, Bres. I'm sorry...I really am. But I have duties, responsibilities I have to fulfill." The night before, while she struggled to sleep, Thorne had finally told her everything—the law, the plan Maleck and Ariadne were trying to set in motion, hunting a witness in Stornhaz. It was a tenuous hope they'd find one to take Saychelle's place. But that hope was enough to take the next step forward, away from Kalt Hasa, away from Bresnyar and into the uncertain future.

The dragon heaved a sigh. "I suppose that answers the question, then. Wingmaidens feel a pull toward their intended mounts, or so I'm told. It's been some time since a dragon without its wing found another, and never outside Oadmark's legions." He rose, shaking all over. "If I had all my wits about me as I once did, I would've made you agree to fly away with me before I agreed to carry you from that mountain. Alas, the prospect of freedom blinds us all. And the sky does not call to you."

Cistine shook her head. "But I want you to go. Be free. And be happy."

Bresnyar studied her closely. "You are unusual for your kind."

"So are you, I think." She craned her head back to smile up at him. "Maybe we both need someone to see us for who we are beneath our scales."

"Philosophers and poets?"

"Sojourners trying to find our way home."

Bresnyar's nostrils fumed with a smoky chuckle. "We have a saying in Oadmark: *no dragon can fly with one wing.* When a warrior ascends to Wingmaiden, she becomes her dragon's second wing, and he is hers." He jerked his head toward the glittering temple high above the crag. "I think perhaps you have found your home and your second wing already. Whereas

I have far to go."

"Well, wherever you're going, be careful. Salvotor still has use for you."

"For both of us, I gather. I won't be the only one hunted after this."
Bresnyar spread his wings and dipped his head. "May the Great Father have
mercy on you all. You'll certainly need it."

The draft of his ascent knocked Cistine staggering back against the
cliffside. Before she could blink the stone grit from her eyes, Bresnyar was
gone—only a rumor of gold among thick late-days clouds to mark his
departure from her life as swiftly as he came into it.

Cistine gave a prayer into the song of the sea that somewhere out there,
he would find the second wing he was searching for.

A throat cleared above her, startling her up from the rock wall. "I can't
believe Thorne let you come out here."

She glanced up at the unfamiliar voice, relaxing only when she caught
sight of Saychelle's familiar face peering down from the trailhead, silver hair
tugged by the breeze. Hugging the cardigan around herself, she ascended to
the *visnpresta's* side. "Thorne doesn't *let* me do anything."

"That sounds just like him."

It took her a moment to catch the joke in that flat tone. When she
smiled, Saychelle returned it, beckoning her back toward the temple.

"You really should be more careful," she said while they walked. "You've
been through an ordeal. Behaving like you haven't won't help you heal any
quicker."

"I suppose not." Though she was already growing weary of the cycle of
sleeping and eating and occasionally bathing. "How did you know I was
down there?"

"Tatiana spotted you on patrol. She asked if that was allowed or if they
should go after you." Saychelle shook her head and scoffed under her breath.
"*Patrolling*. At *Keltei*. The years can't kill some habits, it seems."

"You don't think they have any reason to be cautious here?"

"The Order prides itself on helping anyone, man or woman, rich or
poor, good or wicked, who comes to our doors. That demands
confidentiality. *All* people in Valgard must feel safe to bring their ailments

to us, or none will."

Cistine considered that, craning her head to peer at the temple's high white walls. "But you won't help those same people by using your testimony to remove Salvotor from the Judgement Seat?"

Saychelle frowned. "I told Thorne to leave that subject alone."

"He has. I haven't."

"It's a moot point. The two kinds of help are not the same."

"I disagree. As long as Salvotor is in power, you'll never want for people who need healing. You've seen that."

"Yes, I have, which is why I refuse to be involved. This is life. You must wake up and see it for what it is."

"I *do* see it," Cistine snapped. "I see how being frightened of Salvotor gives him control over you. He'll control this whole kingdom if we don't stop him. And to do that, we need you."

"I didn't spare your life so you could feed me Thorne's ideals." Saychelle lengthened her stride toward the temple's glittering front doors. "If this is how you repay our hospitality, perhaps we can find another use for your room."

Cistine halted, watching the slope of her back and the tightness of her shoulders as she walked away. "You're afraid to die."

The *visnpresta* stopped as well, fingertips skimming the ornate door handles.

Cistine padded up behind her, keeping her voice as soft as her steps. "I know if you do this, if you come with us, you might die. We *all* might die. I was dancing with death the moment I chose to come to this kingdom to save mine, and I didn't even know it yet." Her fingers met the puckered scar along her hip. "But I faced death in Kalt Hasa between a Vassoran blade and Thorne's back. That might haunt me for the rest of my life, but if you put me in those circumstances again, I would make the same choice as many times as it took to save him."

Saychelle's head dropped, her body half-angling back toward Cistine. "What is your point?"

The answer rose in her like searing fire, raw with power—a strength she learned when Julian rushed Salvotor with sword in hand, when Kristoff and the Six stayed behind to confront Grimmaul's men, when she stepped forward to wrestle the guard himself for his knife. "That there are things in this life that *are* worth dying for. My kingdom is one of them. *Thorne* is one of them. And I think if you look deeply enough, you'll realize that freeing the Courts from Salvotor is worth the risk, too."

Saychelle's back shuddered in a deep breath.

"Sillakove will protect you," Cistine insisted, "and you'll save Valgard. Please, just consider testifying. Your kingdom needs you."

Saychelle glanced back at her at last, and for the first time without cool impartiality or disdain. Her stern brow softened, her expression much more like her sister's. "So, that's why Thorne begged us to save your life. You're as full of hopeless idealism as him."

"Maybe so. But he didn't build Sillakove Court alone, either." She laid a hand on Saychelle's shoulder. "I'm asking the girl who dreamed with him back then to dare with us *now.*"

A gleam of tears glazed Saychelle's eyes, her focus turning past Cistine—then sharpening all at once. She gripped her by the collar, yanked the temple door open, and shoved her over the threshold. "*Get inside.*"

Cistine spun to look over the flat expanse of Lataus territory, her heart stuttering in her chest.

Dark figures lined the southern horizon, more than half a dozen streaming in their direction. This close to the coast, with so little else around them, they could only be bound for one place.

Saychelle slammed the temple door in her face; somewhere high above, glistering bells pealed out a three-chime song. It sounded sweet, soothing, but all around the foyer, *visnprests* and *prestas* leaped up from their studies, leisure, and work, faces bleak with dread.

The temple's matriarch, Iri, appeared from an adjacent room and made straight for Cistine. "Back to your room."

They did not make the long journey alone; Quill and Tatiana flanked them on the temple's second level, Thorne on the third, all with hands to their weapons.

Cistine nearly choked on fear. "Who is it?"

"Not Salvotor." Thorne gave the only answer she truly needed. "I couldn't see any more than that, but it's not him.

They reached her room on the fourth level, and Iri ushered them inside "I will do my best to turn them away. Stay hidden." She cast Cistine a warm but unconvincing smile, then shut the door.

Pounding silence descended. Cistine collapsed on the bed, holding her head in her hands, tremors rattling through her limbs. "What if it's Devitrius? What if he and the Vassora kill everyone in the temple to reach us?" She'd left Saychelle outside, let her face them *alone*—

"They won't." Tatiana's hand descended on her back, and she flinched.

"I can't do this," she panted, fingers threading into her hair. "I can't let them hurt all of you, but I can't go back to him, I can't—"

"Cistine." Thorne's voice was on level with her. "Look at me."

She forced her gaze up, finding him crouched before her, a dagger drawn but laid on the floor beside him. His palms were up, open—asking. She rested her hands shakily in his, giving up the power to hide behind them.

"No one takes you," he murmured, thumbs brushing her knuckles. "And no one falls."

There was a mighty crash from the hall, and the sound of running footsteps. Tatiana barked something at Quill, a request Cistine couldn't understand, because at the echo of a voice from the hall her head hummed with disbelief. She realized she'd rocked to her feet only when Thorne released her hands, freeing her to inch toward the door.

She knew that voice, knew those steps.

"*Ashe?*" she screamed.

For a moment, nothing. Then furniture cracked and toppled, more voices shouted, and boots slammed down the hall so quickly the sounds all blurred together. Cistine lurched toward the door as it ripped open, banging against the wall.

But it was not Ashe who stepped inside. It was Rion Bartos.

CHAPTER
FIFTY-FOUR

For the first time in too many months, Ashe was face-to-face with her princess again.

She never imagined reuniting like this: with Rion Bartos leading the charge while Aden held Viktor and the other Wardens at bay in the parlor of a Valgardan temple; with Ashe on one side, blocked from the splendid room by Rion's body, and Cistine on the other, framed by three tense, glowering Valgardan warriors.

Nor had she ever expected to feel like she was on the wrong side.

"Princess." Rion slapped an arm across his chest in salute, but didn't take the knee. His attention swooped from Thorne to Quill to Tatiana and back again, assessing the threat. Thorne's gaze branded Ashe with unspoken accusation. Cistine stared at her, too, eyes large in a gaunt, haggard face—older and more haunted than the girl with features eclipsed in sewer darkness whose pleading cries wove into Maleck's when Ashe shut that grate.

"What have these rats done to you?" Rion demanded. "Where's Julian?"

The focus in the room snapped like a bowstring, arrowing back to Cistine. She wet her lips and grazed a thumb against the empty base of her marriage finger.

Thorne cleared his throat. "Julian is—"

"I wasn't speaking to you."

Thorne dropped back on his heels and Cistine stood taller, peeled back her shoulders and raised her head in striking likeness to her mother. "Julian was killed trying to save me. I'm...I'm so sorry, Rion."

Worse than the words dashing any lingering scrap of hope for Julian's miraculous survival was the look on Cistine's face when she uttered them—the crumble of her features, the crack in her voice over Julian's name, and again over Rion's. The way her eyes glossed with tears.

Rion's hand settled against the doorframe, knuckles leaping corpse-white against his skin. "That—that isn't possible. I would know."

"I saw it happen." Tears slid down Cistine's cheeks. "I tried to tell him to run, but...you know Julian." Humorless laughter rolled through the words. "He never listened to sense when someone needed help."

Rion's spine locked, pushing out the grief, the weakness, until he could mourn his only son in peace. A Warden's calm overtook his posture—and underneath that, simmering fury. "Who? *How?*"

"It doesn't matter. Neither of those things will bring him back."

"It was an augment, wasn't it?"

Cistine's eyes narrowed, the tears evaporating. "Would that be any different than if it was a sword? I told Julian to stay away. He didn't. That was his choice. However he died and by whatever hand, augmentation isn't to blame, the man wielding the weapon was. And we're already working to bring him to his knees."

"*We?*" Palpable rage radiated from Rion, and Ashe's body tightened with the need to be away from him before that fury found a target.

But Cistine didn't falter. "We. Myself and my cabal."

There was no mistaking the pride or the affection in Thorne's face when his eyes flicked to her; something had perceptibly shifted between them.

Disbelief and jealousy gave way swiftly to resignation; Ashe lacked the strength and focus to hold onto them anymore. It wasn't her choice, and not really a surprise to her, either. But to the Commander of the Cadre...

Rion studied Cistine for too long, too closely. Then he jerked his head.

"We're leaving."

Tatiana's brows arched. Quill scoffed. Fury writhed in Ashe's chest, bringing her forward on the balls of her feet, but Cistine only said, "I'm not."

"You are, by order of the King and Queen. There's a retinue of Wardens here, waiting to escort you home."

Cistine shifted her weight and dragged her lip between her teeth. "My parents know I'm here?"

"They suspected. They sent me to retrieve you."

Slowly, Cistine shook her head. "I can't go. My work isn't finished."

"Royal decree says it is." Rion released the doorframe and stepped into the room, and Ashe seized her only chance to slip around his side and take up post next to the door.

Her princess beheld her with a flickering gaze. Then her cheek ticked and her eyes slid back to Rion. "*This* royal says it isn't."

He pinched the bridge of his nose the way he always did when someone tried his patience. "*Cistine.* This is not a teahouse debate over which book your group of gossips will read next—"

"I am *perfectly* aware of what this is and is not." Cistine's frigid voice matched the cabal's vicious glares. Rion was flirting with a dangerous line. "And it's *Princess* to you, Commander."

"This is a matter of Talheim's security and future," he went on as if Cistine hadn't spoken. "You have been behind enemy borders for too long."

"Enemy borders, he says," Quill muttered. "Who saved her? Who brought her here?"

"Quill," Cistine said, and he clammed up at once.

"We aren't debating this," Rion said. "Your parents sent me with a Writ of Nobility and orders to bring you home at any cost. I *will not* fail them."

Cistine cinched her arms over her waist. "A Writ of Nobility."

"A document that establishes the bearer as an official liaison, endued with the full permission to treat with Valgard as the mouthpiece of Talheim—"

"I know what it is!" Cistine snapped. "Let me see."

Rion reached into the breastpocket of his Warden uniform, stepping forward. Quill and Tatiana laid hands to their weapons, and Ashe couldn't blame them; Thorne, by contrast, went utterly still, watching Cistine take the Writ from Rion.

"I'm willing to flaunt this parchment if need be," Rion added, "but make no mistake, Princess—my blade is also sharp."

"As ever." Cistine's gaze leaped along the Writ; then she rolled it and tucked it into her waistband. "Take the Cadre back to Astoria and tell my mother and father I'm sorry for all the lies, but I'm not coming home yet. My work isn't finished here. In fact, thanks to you, it's about to truly begin."

Rion's eyes narrowed. "Pardon me?"

"This Writ of Nobility is precisely what I need to treat for Valgard's aid against Mahasar. I appreciate you bringing it to me. And now you're dismissed."

Ashe almost laughed at how rapidly she'd flipped the situation, disarming Rion and putting his own knife to his neck.

But Rion wasn't smiling. No one was laughing at all.

"If you think I'm going to leave you here," Rion growled, "in this den of rat-eaters—"

"That's precisely what you're going to do, by order of your princess."

"I answer to King Cyril and Queen—"

"You answer to the royal family!" Cistine shouted. "Which I am part of, whether you respect me or not! And as future Queen of Talheim, I order you to keep your blades sheathed, walk out of this temple, and deliver my message to my parents. I am *not* leaving Valgard until my mission is complete."

Rion's lips peeled back from his teeth. "You aren't equipped to bargain with these people. You're still a child playing royalty's game."

Cistine stepped nearer to him, her fearlessness the loudest testament of all to the things she'd endured—all the ways she'd changed. "I am Talheim's Princess. And I am not playing a game."

Rion seized her wrist. "You're coming home where it's safe, if I have to throw you over my shoulder and drag you to the border forts kicking and screaming."

Ashe and Thorne snapped forward at the same moment, but neither of them moved as quickly as Cistine. Her hold break was effortless—a swivel of the hand to lock Rion's wrist, bending him over with a twist to the arm, driving her knee into his chest and snapping loose from his grip. He staggered back toward the doorway, grimacing as his glare swept over them: Ashe and Thorne at Cistine's sides, Quill and Tatiana at her back. "The King and Queen will never stand for this."

"Actually, this was my father's idea, if you recall. I think you'll find he's exceptionally agreeable, especially when you tell him I'm alive and well, and making this choice of my own volition." She stepped a half-pace closer to Rion, but kept herself out of arm's reach this time. "And you will tell him *precisely* that, Rion, or gods help me, I'll have your title stripped, your rank removed, and your pension cut off."

He gaped at her, a look of shock heartbreakingly reminiscent of Julian. Ashe wondered which side he would've stood on in this argument, whether he would've defended Cistine or fallen under his father's hand again.

It was a painful mercy he'd never had to choose.

"Cistine," Rion began.

"You have my message," she cut him off. "Deliver it. After today, I don't want to hear of a Cadre presence on Valgardan soil again."

Rion cursed, swiped a hand down his face, then stalked from the room. The moment the door banged shut behind him, Cistine turned to Thorne. "You need to send word to the border forts. I don't know that he'll heed me, but if he doesn't—"

"Talheim may invade." Thorne squeezed her shoulder. "I'll find pen and paper. You should write something, too...a cipher for your parents to prove you're staying of your own volition."

Cistine nodded, sinking down on the bed. "Good idea."

Thorne slipped out, and Ashe hurried behind him and took a different branch in the corridor—sprinting after Rion back the way they came, past the furniture the Commander kicked aside on his way to Cistine.

If he heard her pursuit, he didn't care, didn't slow when she fell into stride with him. Breaths labored with rage, he marched like a man going to war. But there was more than anger in that face; there was pain in his eyes. He was returning home empty-handed, stripped of the Writ, turned out by a threat from the princess. Bereft of his only son.

"I'm sorry you had to hear about Julian this way." And she was, even if she despised Rion right now.

He halted in the middle of the empty hall. "You knew. You let me go on believing I'd see my son again at the end of this."

"It wasn't my story to tell." The words were hollow, inadequate, but they were all she had. If she told him she'd kept it from him to prevent a rampage against Valgard, she'd ruin any chance of ever mending what was broken between them.

Rion scoffed, but he didn't hit her, so perhaps he'd spent all the anger he had to spare for one day; instead he stared down the corridor like he could see memories dancing among the late-day shadows. "He was going to become the next king. Cyril and I had it all planned from the moment we realized Solene was having a girl. They'd begin courtship on her twentieth birthday and be married by her twenty-first. That was why I brought him to her birthday celebration this summer. Gods, I never should have brought him."

"He protected Cistine, he saved her life more than once. I was glad to have him at my side here, as a Warden and a friend. He served his princess well."

"And that's meant to console me? Children born in times of peace shouldn't die in war. Where were *you*?"

Guilt hammered her chest. If she hadn't unleashed the Tumult, if she'd never been taken to Siralek, Julian would be here today. Cistine wouldn't be hurt. "I know I should've protected them both, but by the time Aden and I escaped Siralek, it was too late."

Rion studied her for several breathless moments, his eyes tracing over her face, over the bruises he'd dealt her in the fight beside the pond near Stornhaz. "You're a disgrace." She'd expected those words, but it still surprised her how much they stung, stealing her breath away. "You've become Warden to a Valgardan child, you've rutted with their warriors, you're clad in their gods-damned armor." Rion gestured sharply to her body. "I no longer recognize you as King's Cadre. I strip you of your title and your rank. You have no place among us."

Ashe stared at him—his twisted face, his heaving chest, his trembling hands fisted violently at his sides—and saw him clearly as she'd never seen him before. Gone was the strutting King's Cadre Commander who could not be touched by death, disarmed by the brutality that made him shine in her eyes as a child; a hunched, bitter, grieving father replaced him. And as she stared at him, a strange thing happened.

She *heard* his grief rising up like the shrill mourning notes of a violin, felt the pitches and falls of its music tuned to his harsh breathing—a ballad for a man who had evaded the Undertaker so long, its grim scythe chased his son instead. Ashe knew exactly how she would weave the mournful notes of the Commander and his kingdom and his only child; the twitching of her fingers was not constrained violence, but the memory of where they would be placed, how she would coax that heartbroken melody from the violin's neck...how she would immortalize and explain Rion's anguish and Julian's loss in song.

For the first time in over a decade, Ashe's mind made music of what lay before her, made sense of it through notes too achingly bittersweet to fathom. Their years together had not been enough. Like Helga and Pippet. Like Baba Kallah and Thorne. Even like Sigrid.

Eyes burning, Ashe stepped back from him. "Go home, Rion. Deliver the message and let Cistine do her work. Cyril still needs you—Talheim needs you."

"That makes one of us," he snapped.

Ashe winced, but didn't argue. "I know apologies make for poor grave dirt, but I truly am sorry about Julian. If it's any consolation...before I was captured, I'd rarely seen him so happy."

Rion shook his head, pivoted, and strode away, leaving her alone in the empty corridor. But not for long.

Thorne's feet made little sound when he arrived beside her, staring after

Rion's retreating figure. "Julian was my fault."

Ashe waited to feel anger at that, or at how he'd listened in, but she found only an aching emptiness in her middle. "You don't want Rion to know that. Believe me, the only thing keeping you alive and your kingdom standing is that he accepts Julian made his own choice."

Thorne's gaze landed on her from the side with the same intensity his cousin usually looked at her. "You found something you were searching for out there."

"More than I ever imagined I would." Nightmares of *Meszaros* darkened Ashe's mind. "He's not who I thought he was. Neither are the Wardens. And...*I'm* not someone I want to be. But I'm trying to become better."

"Aren't we all," Thorne sighed.

Ashe's stomach clenched. She'd known he might seek her out, that this conversation would happy eventually. The least she owed him was not to walk away from it. "I don't think there are words for how sorry I am about what I did to you and your cabal from Siralek, so I'm not going to try. You were right. It wasn't my mistakes I ran from. It was the reasons why I made them. I was selfish and desperate, and that wasn't Aden's fault or Nimea's. Even if they hadn't helped put a blade in my hand, I would have found some other way to lash out at you. I accept responsibility for my actions against your cabal...and I ask your forgiveness."

Thorne studied her differently from Rion. There was no disappointment, no seeking out of shame or guilt, but still she fought down the urge to cross her arms or smirk or build up some wall he couldn't scale over.

"It's forgiven," he said after a moment. "Not forgotten. But forgiven."

Ashe blew out her breath. "Just like that?"

"Just like that...like Cistine forgave me for the recklessness that led to Julian's death and her capture. I didn't deserve it. You don't deserve it. But here we are...forgiven."

Ashe crossed her arms and swallowed the lump in her throat. "Common ground."

Thorne nodded. "We all played a part in this. If I'd been a better man, you would've never had a reason to doubt my intentions toward Cistine. I accept my share of the blame for how we arrived here...you with your scars, and me without my grandmother."

Ashe laughed at the sheer absurdity of it. "We make quite a pair, don't we, High Tribune?"

"A dangerous one. If we'd spent as much of our energy helping Cistine succeed as we did loathing each other, my father would already be in chains."

As one, they looked down the corridor toward the princess's room.

"She was braver today than I've ever seen her," Ashe murmured.

"She's endured much, and it isn't over yet," Thorne's tone held the same reverence and affection as that look he gave Cistine when she claimed his cabal as hers. "But she has the strength to end this. She just needs us to help share the burden."

"Finally, something we can agree on."

Thorne clapped a hand on her shoulder and left, but she waited, shadowy arms of grief wrapping around her in the empty corridor.

Her title stripped. Her name disgraced. She couldn't stop thinking of that parting look in Rion's eyes—her Commander seeing her like an enemy.

She'd been furious with him after Stornhaz, ready to bloody his face for everything. But having the full brunt of his grief and anger turned back on her stung worse than her own rage against him. He'd taken back power when she let down her guard to offer consolation—and used it to cut her off at the knees.

Footsteps jogged down the hall toward her, but it wasn't Aden, who she was waiting for; instead, golden hair swinging over her shoulders, Rozalie slid to a halt beside Ashe. "Listen, I don't have much time. Rion is leaving and he's *furious*—"

"I'm not surprised. How did you get past Aden?"

She forced a smile. "You know I have my ways of getting around handsy men. Ashe, I have to warn you, Lord Rion isn't letting this go. He's going to rally the Cadre." Rozalie glanced back as if she expected to find him lurking at the corridor mouth. "You need the Queen's ear if you and Cistine are going to stay without starting a war."

Fear raked up Ashe's throat, but she choked it down. She wouldn't let *Meszaros* walk through this kingdom with blade hunting blood again. Once she was certain Cistine was safe, she would act. "Thank you. I know what defying him means to you."

Rozalie dragged a hand through her hair from temple to ends, eyes wide with distress. "I never let myself see him as anything but the man who led the brothel raid and saved my life. But I think sometimes he's more like the clients—he's trying too hard to feel powerful. That's why he grinds you into the dirt."

Ashe blinked away her discomfort. "He grinds us all down."

"Maybe. But only one of us fought with him in the war. And only one of us protected Cyril while Lord Rion was taking a piss." Rozalie raised her eyes, burning with a strength Ashe had never seen before. "*No one breaks you without your permission.* That's what you told me when you pulled me out of the brothel. *You* did that, not him. Protecting Talheim is what you do, so you wouldn't stay here if you didn't think it was in our kingdom's best interest."

"I *know* it is, Roz. Cistine can do this."

Rozalie nodded slowly. "I'll buy you as much time as I can on the journey home. Consider it an apology for everything that happened, especially to Pippet. I'll never forget the things that happened to me at her age. No one deserves that abuse. I should've stopped Viktor and the others, but...you're right. I was a coward." A wicked smile tipped her mouth. "But not anymore." She offered her fist. "I'll see you at home, Kovar. Or on the front lines."

They bumped knuckles, then Rozalie hurtled back down the hall, dodging Aden in the archway. He stared after her, eyes narrowing slightly. "She's slippery, that one."

Ashe smirked. "She learned from the best."

"I believe she did." Aden limped past her, massaging his gut like he'd taken a kick. "The Wardens are gone...for now. I think it's time I met this princess you and Thorne would tear down kingdoms for."

Heaviness hung in the room when Ashe and Aden entered. The furious warrior who faced Rion was gone; in her place was a princess bent with weariness, sitting on the bed with her head in her hands. Tatiana sat next to her, close but not touching, and Quill hovered near the balcony doorway, eyes brimming with concern. Thorne perched on the edge of a writing desk in the corner, scratching out his letter to the border forts.

Ashe shut the door as quietly as she could, but Cistine still jolted up straight, gaze shooting straight to her. They stared at one another for a motionless moment, Ashe's body humming with elation, grief, anger, and *relief.* Then Cistine staggered up and ran to her like she was six years old again, and Ashe caught her up in a hug so tight she worried it might break them both. Sobs pumped through her chest at the protrusion of Cistine's bones against her, the dullness of her rough hair, the hollows around her eyes when she pushed her back and cupped her face in both hands.

"God's bones, I missed you," she croaked.

"I missed you, too." Cistine's eyes sparkled with unshed tears. "We looked for you, I tried, I'm sorry I didn't do enough..."

"*No.* Your responsibility was to keep *yourself* alive. And I did the same. No...no harm was done."

The words caught in her throat. Mere seconds reunited, and already her lies came between them.

Cistine let out her breath in a long tumble and held Ashe's gaze with new wisdom that made her feel exposed, like Cistine could see her wavering on the brutal edge of her own mistakes and fears. Then her gaze flicked past Ashe. "Aden?"

Armor creaked when he shifted. "I don't believe we've had the pleasure."

"We haven't. But I know your face from Tati's photograph." Cistine pulled from Ashe's grip and offered Aden her hand. "And I carried your old knife. I somehow feel like I already know you."

Aden slowly clasped her hand. "The feeling is mutual."

Cistine flashed a fleeting smile, then returned to the bed. Ashe took a vacant chair from the wall and sank down in it, and Quill cleared his throat. "What do we do now?"

"I spoke briefly to Maleck and Ariadne," Aden said. "Salvotor's returned to Stornhaz."

Cistine paled, her lips trembling. "Already?"

Thorne looked up from his seat on the desk, eyes narrow. "I wish I could say that surprises me. But while he may have lost his hold over you, Cistine, that isn't the end of his ambitions. Even if he assumes you're dead, he's come too far to release his grip on the Courts."

"Then we have to go to Stornhaz, too."

Ashe clutched the sides of her neck, holding nausea at bay. "If we go back to the city, he'll tear it apart searching for you. We can't risk that."

"That's not your decision to make."

She grimaced. This was going to take some getting used to. "Consider it my assessment of the stakes, then."

"Fine. But my position is to protect the people who can't protect themselves, and right now, that's Valgard."

"What are you thinking?" Tatiana asked.

Cistine slid off the bed and paced, rubbing her silk sleeves with quick, jerky hands. "We have to put Thorne's plan into motion. Have Salvotor accused and arrested."

"Except we still don't have an agreeable witness, remember?" Quill pointed out.

"Actually, we do," Aden said. "A…contact within Siralek who was privy to Salvotor's actions that night. It isn't as strong a case as Saychelle's, but it's better than nothing. Maleck and Ariadne have her now."

"Then arguing about the risks is pointless," Cistine said. "We have to go to Stornhaz and end this."

When no one raised another protest—not even Ashe, though every nerve screamed at the thought of being in that city again—Thorne said, "We leave at dusk. Tatiana, see if Iri has a wind augment or two they can spare."

Ashe swung up from the chair, catching Tatiana in the doorway. "Wait. Iri? There's a woman named Iri here?"

"You probably met her." Tatiana's lips curled wickedly. "Tall, somewhat ethereal, she tried to keep your Cadre from entering the temple?"

Ashe released her arm and swallowed. "Could you take me to her?"

Tatiana's gaze swept her up and down. "Could you tell me *why?*"

"I...have a message to deliver. From a friend."

Tatiana's jaw worked, and after a tense pause, she shrugged. "Just keep your blades sheathed."

It might've been a joke, an attempt to soften the frigid atmosphere; but when Tatiana paused to cast an arm around Aden before they hurried out, and Thorne drew his cousin aside to bump brows and speak with him lowly, a chasm widened within her.

She could never belong with these people, no matter how many apologies she made; and she no longer belonged with her Cadre, either.

Utterly adrift, she followed Tatiana into the hall.

CHAPTER FIFTY-FIVE

T HE SUN SET in fiery ribbons of gold and pink, the cool tilt of its late-year angle spilling long garlands of light across the Agerios and in through the bathing chamber windows when someone finally knocked on the door, rousing Cistine from her stupor.

She sat against the wall with her face resting on her bent knees, hands locked around her ankles, working to calm her breathing. But the panting resumed every time she imagined confronting Salvotor, being captured again, seeing his cruel face or hearing his voice thrown in imitation of Thorne's—

She startled violently when the door swung open, her hand jolting down to her gut. In the doorway, Ashe held up both hands for peace. "I didn't bring any weapons. Don't attack."

"We both know your hands and feet *are* weapons." Cistine said hoarsely. "Are we leaving now?"

"No, not for a few more hours." Ashe shut the door and traded her weight between her feet. "I came to apologize."

Thick, seething dread pooled in Cistine's core. "For what?"

Ashe raked a hand through her hair and cursed under her breath. Then she folded her arms behind her back—a Warden's posture—and held Cistine's gaze. "After you left Stornhaz, I was...furious with Thorne. I looked back on him and all I saw was the war. So I created war with him from inside Siralek's walls. I know that was foolish, and it betrayed your heart and trust. I'm sorry, Princess."

Cistine's mind didn't want to make sense of the confession, awakening the harsh echo of Salvotor's words in Kalt Hasa. *I hear she was integral to so many things these past few months...tragedies in Blaykrone. Assassins running free. My own mother's death.*

Not just a lie, another trick. So much worse than that.

"Ashe, *no*," she whispered. "Please, tell me you *didn't...*"

Ashe spread her hands, a humble gesture—honest. Damning. "I thought you and Julian went back to Talheim, but that was no excuse for what I did. Baba Kallah died because I used other people's grief and anger to lash out at Thorne. I'm sorry for every one of those blows, against him and against you. I hope you'll forgive me."

Cistine's mind flooded with broken villages and assassins and Thorne's blood, Baba Kallah's dying breaths, Eben's plains, *Julian.* She planted her hands on the wall and pushed herself up, glaring at her Warden. "If you regret it, why did you bring Rion here? You know how he feels about the North!"

"I do." Ashe dragged a hand down her face. "Believe me, I know that now better than I ever did before. But I was terrified for you. I thought I could trust Talheim and only them."

"And now?"

Ashe snorted quietly. "After Rion's behavior today, I wouldn't trust him with my back, much less with your best interests or your heart."

Cistine studied Ashe's face, exhausted but full of conviction. She looked like she'd just marched off one battleground to face another; was that because of Rion, or something else?

"I never liked how he treated you," she admitted. "I think you would've hated Valgard less if not for him."

"That's true. The way he and the Wardens speak of this kingdom, of its people...gods, even in front of children—"

"What children?"

Ashe flashed a sheepish half-smile. "Don't tell Quill, but I've been dragging his sister all over this kingdom."

Shock dropped Cistine's haunches hard against the wall. "*What?* Why?"

"When Helga heard the news about Kallah..." Ashe trailed off, and a pang of agony shot through Cistine's middle. Another friend gone, another star fallen dark because of what Salvotor did. What *Ashe* did.

She almost wished the pain would last longer, but Kalt Hasa had taught her mind to adapt to emotional blows like Quill taught her to absorb physical ones. In moments, the anguish of Helga's death dulled and a yawning sense of unsafety opened through Cistine's middle while she beheld Ashe's downcast face. "I don't know what to say to you. Thorne wasn't the only one who betrayed me."

"I know. And I'm sorry I ever let it get that far. But hating Valgard was easier than accepting that Thorne made a mistake, like all men do, and you'd forgive him for it."

A mistake. Thorne *had* made mistakes; one led to Ashe's capture, another to Julian's death and Cistine's imprisonment. It was unfair to forgive one and not the other, but Ashe's betrayal stung worse because she knew Cistine better. Or so Cistine had thought.

"Whatever you want from me, I'll do it," Ashe said when she stayed quiet. "However I can help, anything you need...I swear to you, Cistine, you'll never know a better supporter or advisor from this moment on."

And she meant it. Ashe would tear herself apart to make up for what she did, just like after every argument where they screamed at one another over suitors and swords and poor choices, and Cistine woke in the morning to find her Warden waiting outside the room, a new book and tea and scones in hand, an apology on her lips before Cistine even tore open the door. But they had never fought with stakes so high, where lives rather than wounded pride were the cost to pay when they hurt each other.

She stared at her Warden's earnest face while a reckless, crucial plan began to emerge.

"I do need your help." Cistine slid back to her seat, the strength in her legs spent. "I was bluffing with Rion. I have the Writ, but I don't know how to do this, how to be diplomatic and fierce. The way I told him about Julian was all wrong...did you see how angry he was?" She buried her face in her hands. "Now I can't stop thinking my parents may come north and storm this kingdom, and then we'll be at war again, only—" Only this time, it would be her blood against her heart. Her Talheim against her Valgard. Maybe even her *selvenar* against her father.

Ashe slowly sank down beside her, Valgardan battle armor creaking when she folded her arms loosely out in her lap. "Thorne's suggestion was good, about sending a cipher."

"I'd rather send you." Cistine raised her head to meet Ashe's baffled stare. "My parents trust your word almost as much as Rion's...Mama especially. I don't think a note will be enough, and I don't trust Rion not to destroy anything I send."

"True." Ashe's head thumped on the wall. "Holy gods, how did we *not* see the kind of man he was?"

"I think my father knew. Maybe that's why he sent Rion to Practica when he retired. Maybe he was afraid of how Rion would feel about a Key who wasn't his closest friend taking the throne."

"But Rion still had a hand on the crown through Julian."

Cistine wondered if it was more for Julian's sake than her own that she'd never allowed herself to look too closely at Rion's behavior with the Wardens, with Ashe, even with her; because above all other things, above duty and title, even, Julian Bartos had loved his father.

Tears began a silent, steady march down Cistine's cheeks. She hadn't let herself cry for Julian since those first miserable weeks in Kalt Hasa, fearing how Salvotor would turn her grief against her if he knew it was still so fresh. But now that she was here, in the presence of the only other person who loved Julian as Cistine still did, and always would—not as a suitor, but as a fellow Talheimic and a friend—the sobs rolled through her in silent, heaving sweeps.

Ashe pulled Cistine over to lean against her, holding her close, stroking her hair and whispering a soothing "Shh, shh," while she stroked her hair.

"I never wanted Rion to find out like this," Cistine choked. "Oh gods, what about *Eboni?*"

"You had to tell him," Ashe murmured. "He would've torn this kingdom apart searching for Julian otherwise. You did the right thing."

"Doing what's right has been nothing but pain lately." Even as the words left her lips, her eyes dried; she couldn't seem to cry for more than a moment anymore, tears still frozen by Kalt Hasa's cold. A feeling of purpose seeped into the empty caverns scooped out by the agony of Julian's death and Rion's visit, and she tugged herself from Ashe's arms. "Will you go?"

"To Astoria? Absolutely."

"Beyond that?"

Her eyes narrowed. "What are you thinking, Princess?"

Cistine wiped her damp cheeks on her sleeve. "That the ruse about the coast is over. If we're going to make this negotiation with Valgard official, maybe we can put a weapon in my father's hand with it."

"I'm listening."

The same brashness that gripped her in Kalt Hasa when she lied to Salvotor about the ritual staked through her chest again. "I want you to go to Middleton and make Jad believe the alliance is already official and we have everything Thorne promised us—by any means you have to."

Ashe frowned. "That's a dangerous gamble. If Jad realizes we're lying, he may use that to muster all of Mahasar and march against Talheim."

"He's not going to find out. By the time you finish stalling him, Thorne and I *will* have that alliance. Consider it a...a note of assurance before the coins are in the coffers. But they *will* be there by the time the note comes due, Ashe."

Ashe studied her, head shaking slowly. "Something changed you in that mountain, Cistine."

Swallowing was like gulping icy wind and stale cavern air. "For the better, I hope?"

"I hope so, too."

"But you'll go." She was no longer asking.

Ashe nodded. "As soon as we're finished with Salvotor. I just hope these skinflint Chancellors can spare a wind augment. I'm no augur, but there's only one way to reach the capital before Rion does."

So many threads, delicately primed, ready to be strummed—or severed if they weren't careful. So much more to do. One last thing *she* had to do before they left the temple; and she'd put it off long enough.

It was time to speak with Aden.

She found him on her balcony, leaning out over the sea, arms folded on the railing and gaze fixed across the waves. She stole a moment to study him when she slipped silently outside, to piece together all the different ways he was familiar to her; Tatiana and Thorne's stories about him, his knife, his hovel in Villmark, perhaps even his old bedroom, all hers. The ways Tatiana said they were alike. All these things that bound them to one another long before they met.

"So," he broke the silence without turning, "you're the princess the cabal can't stop talking about."

She joined him at the railing, and when he swiveled his head to look at her, the strength left her legs. Her stomach dropped. She didn't have to search far on his face to find familiarity: the gray eyes, the shape of his brow and nose, the one-sided dimple when he smiled at her. She knew them all. And when she found Kristoff on Aden's face, suddenly he didn't intimidate her at all.

"I met your father in Kalt Hasa," she blurted out.

Aden's arms slid off the railing and he turned fully to face her. "*What?*" Gods, they even *spoke* the same.

"He was my guard," she explained. "Salvotor sent him there as punishment...and as a weapon against Thorne's mother."

"That's not possible." Aden gripped the railing with one hand, knuckles white against skin just a few shades paler than his father's. "He was dead, it was all just a *ruse*. Salvotor burned his body on a pyre almost twenty years ago."

"He told you whatever served his interests. But I...I think I know enough about you to say you would never have betrayed your cabal if the proof your father was alive wasn't as clear as the proof he was dead."

Aden locked onto her face with a warrior's focus. "Where is he?"

The quiet anguish in the question took Cistine's breath away. He already knew Kristoff was gone; he just needed to hear her say it.

She slid the Wayfinder's compass from around her neck and held it out to him. "He told me to give this to you, and to tell you and Maleck he never stopped loving you. That the only thing he wanted was for you to live free."

Aden snagged the cord gently from her. The tarnished surface of the raised star, rubbed raw a thousand times by Kristoff's thumb over two decades, struggled to wink when he held it up to the light. "This was my mother's. She was sworn to Traisende when she became a medico. She fell in love with a Kanslar Tribune-to-be who spilled his guts to her, quite literally, when they first met."

Cistine's stomach writhed at the thought that the beginning of all good things in Kristoff's life had been as violent as his end.

"I should've known," Aden said after a beat. "All this time, he kept him caged like an *animal...*"

Thorne's voice came from the balcony doorway: "Salvotor was always jealous of the influence Kristoff held in the Courts with compassion rather than cruelty. This punishment was as much to break that goodness as it was to use him against us."

There were tears in his eyes as he beheld the pendant. Not for the first time, Cistine wondered what parting words Kristoff had spoken in his nephew's ear.

"Did he break?" Aden asked through gritted teeth.

"We're alive because of him," Thorne said. "He was a good man who lost his way in that prison. But he found it again, just like his son."

Aden pressed his fist to his brow, the leather cord wrapped tightly around his knuckles. Thorne closed the distance to him, swinging an arm across his shoulders and pressing his forehead to Aden's temple. Shyly, Cistine wrapped her hand around Aden's waist from the other side, laying to rest Kristoff's final wish with a farewell to him across the waves.

Thank you for everything. For bringing us home.

The memory of his voice whispered back from the first blinking stars: *Never stop fighting.*

Cistine smiled through her tears.

Ha, Nadrian.

CHAPTER FIFTY-SIX

BENEATH THE GLARING moon on Keltei's outer grounds, the cabal gathered for their departure. They all wore armor, Thorne and Cistine's ill-fitting but suitable for the journey by wind augment to The City of a Thousand Stars—a return Tatiana absolutely dreaded.

She wasn't ready to set foot inside Stornhaz again. Once in a decade had been horrible enough; a second time in a few months was asking for trouble. But they *had* to go, just as they'd had to go when Cistine, Ashe, and Julian trekked to the city to meet with Salvotor.

Maleck had always taught her it was dangerous to *have* to go anywhere; the moment you had no choice, the enemy held the advantage. But here they were.

"All right there, Saddlebags?"

She straightened from her repose against the temple's glittering side when Quill swaggered up to join her, hands in his pockets, cinnamon stick jutting from his teeth. "Oh, you know me, always leaping at the chance to venture into Stornhaz. What danger could there possibly be?"

Quill laid his hand on the wall beside her head and bent nearer, filling her head with the harsh, powdery scent of cinnamon. "None that you and I can't conquer together, Dawnstar."

She blew her hair from her brow with a huff, her unease soothed by her Name, and glanced past him at the others—all checking their armor and weapons, stalling even though the course was set. The sight would've warmed Tatiana's spirit if they'd been going *anywhere* but Stornhaz, this entire mission more like a death plunge. "I can't believe we're taking Cistine back there. Putting everyone we care about in Salvotor's reach while he's desperate to take the Courts...this isn't a good plan."

Quill let his hand slide from the wall. "I know. But it's the only one we have."

The temple door creaked open, and Saychelle slipped out to join them. Her face and hair were alabaster in the moonlight, and the somber set of her mouth set Tatiana's shoulders back. "More bad news?"

"How much more do you think we can take?"

Saychelle meandered over to Thorne. "Rushing off on yet another daring mission?"

"There never seems to be an end to them," he said.

"Well, try not to get captured this time."

"I'll remind you that was *your* strategy." Thorne folded his arms. "But I'll do my best."

"See to it you do." Saychelle cleared her throat. "It would be a shame for me to risk my life if there wasn't a proper Chancellor to replace Salvotor when he steps down to stand trial."

Tatiana glanced swiftly at Quill. Thorne's arms swung limply back to his sides.

"Still thumbing out riddles?" Aden asked mildly.

"Still not clever enough to solve them?" Saychelle cocked a brow. "I'll say it plainly, then: I think you're all fools. I think a trial is as dangerous as all-out war against Salvotor. But I'm tired of being held prisoner here by his threats, afraid of death every second. I'm tired of letting him win. So if you think we can build a case that will be strong enough to convict him—"

"We can," Thorne said quickly.

Saychelle searched his face, quiet for a moment; then she thrust the satchel and a scroll into his hands. "Here. Your wind augments...and my written account, signed and marked by Iri. If the Courts choose to try

Salvotor, they can call on me to testify in person."

Thorne's eyes flashed from the scroll to her face. "You don't have to do this. Ashe and Aden found another witness."

Saychelle's back rose and fell in a deep, shaky breath. "So I heard. But she saw the aftermath. *I* saw the act. And as a certain High Tribune taught me long ago, if a trove of evidence from one witness is enough to convict, two can put a man in his grave."

For an instant, in that sharp half-smile, Tatiana saw the ambitious acolyte with dreams of a better Valgard, a better future, who helped Thorne build Sillakove Court from stardust to a power that made even Chancellor Salvotor afraid.

"This is not just about saving Valgard," Saychelle added. "It's about giving my sister the justice *she* deserves...the justice we built our Court on, Thorne." Her gaze flicked to Cistine, then back to the High Tribune. New confidence threaded her voice and raised her head high. "It's finally time. Let's bury this *bandayo* like we promised we would."

CHAPTER FIFTY-SEVEN

CISTINE, ASHE, QUILL and Thorne huddled in a small alleyway masked in shadows inside Stornhaz's fortified outer wall. The wind augments had carried them to it, but not over it; while they stowed aboard a barge traveling into the city, Thorne had explained why. "There are reinforcements inside the wall, woven in like our armor. Between that and the height, wind augments won't carry you in or out of the city."

Cistine supposed that made sense; what was the point of an impenetrable wall any augur could travel over? That left them riding the barge between inspection points, where they disembarked, swam to the docks, and ran the multicolored streets to a derelict, less-guarded quarter of the city. Tatiana had told them to wait in the alley, turned up her hood, and vanished with Aden down the gloomy avenue.

It felt like they'd been gone too long. If something happened to them, if Devitrius or Salvotor caught them prowling the city—

Thorne rested a hand on her back, abrupting the tense shudders that rolled down her spine. "It's going to be all right."

She wanted to believe him, but being in Salvotor's city was as good as asking to be sent back to Kalt Hasa—as if she didn't return enough in her nightmares.

Quill grabbed her shoulders, spun her toward him, and rubbed her arms so vigorously she yelped. "Sometimes I forget how thin-blooded you Middle Kingdom invaders are! No wonder we were almost able to freeze you out with a few ice augments."

"Don't forget," Ashe said from Thorne's other side, "we *won* that war."

"By a hair. Maybe we should have pitched your sorry hides into a cold river and won that way."

Cistine jutted out her tongue at him, and he grinned, mussing her hair this time.

Thorne straightened from the alley wall, and Cistine's blood ran even colder. She turned out from under Quill's hands, pulse pattering with relief when Tatiana and Aden slipped into the alley.

"Streets are clear," Tatiana announced. "No one is watching his house."

"Whose house?" Cistine asked.

"You'll see. If the door doesn't shut in our faces." Flippant words belied by her uneasy gaze, Tatiana led them from the alley.

There was so much of Stornhaz Cistine hadn't seen during her last visit through its finest streets, escorted by Yager spies to expensive shops. She only had Baba Kallah's stories over late-night cups of tea to prepare her for these dilapidated homes, as different from the whitewashed facades of the richer districts as Kalt Hasa was from Keltei. Various squares housed communal wells and booths, and one boarded-over mausoleum of a building that reminded her of the Temple of the True God in Astoria. The stone homes and shops were hand-mortared with brown bricks, their steep slopes and thatched rooftops glinting in the moonlight.

It began to sleet when they halted across yet another modest square, and Cistine tugged her hood lower to shield her face from the icy droplets and hide her features as Tatiana knocked out a tuned pattern on the door of a two-level home clapped between shops. After a moment, it creaked open, the narrow slit of doorway filling up with the face of a man who looked so much like Tatiana, he could only be her father.

"*Tatiyani?*" he breathed, flinging the door wide.

She ducked her head. "I'm back, Papa."

The man sobbed a prayer of relief, yanking her against his chest and clutching her face to his collar. "I've prayed for this moment every night for *ten years!* I'm not dreaming, am I? Tell me I'm not dreaming!"

"You're not dreaming, Papa." Tatiana's voice cracked. "If you were, I probably wouldn't smell like the barges."

Chuckling through the tears, he loosened his hold, but she kept her arm tight around his waist while he reached out a hand to Quill. "It's good to see you again, *Aftyam.*"

Quill's smile lacked its usual arrogant charm when he shook the man's hand. He almost looked *shy.* "You too, Morten."

Eyes twinkling, Morten crushed Tatiana under his arm and kissed her hair. "I believe I have a houseguest or two who will be *very* eager to see you."

Footsteps thundered inside the house, and a shrill voice shrieked, Quill's name. He fell back on his heels, cursing in shock as Pippet dove past Morten and Tatiana and flung herself into his arms. She tried to wrap herself around him, but he set her back, gripping her arms—then letting go when she hissed at his touch. "Who hurt you? Who do I have to kill? What are you even *doing* here, where's Helga?"

"Helga's...gone." Pippet's eyes flicked to Ashe. "I found Ashe, we were on a mission, then we met Aden and there were *Wardens* and we went all the way to Nordbran and found this woman, do you know her? Her name is Deja. She smells like a muskrat. Anyway, and then we came here, to the City, and this man, *Rion,* attacked us—"

Quill flexed his fingers lightly on her shoulder. "Slow down. How bad is your arm?"

"It hardly stings anymore! Maleck's taken care of it. I'm just so glad to see you, I missed you so much!"

"So did I." Quill folded her against his chest and let out a gruff cough of laughter, hoarse with unshed tears. "Have you seen Faer?"

"No, I think he's still in Hellidom or Starhollow or somewhere. But I don't care about him, I just care about *you.*" She leaped up, wrapping her legs around her brother's waist and her arms around his neck. Holding her on his hip as easily as a toddler, he led the others indoors.

The home's cramped lower level was a single broad room full of trinket-cluttered workbenches, a half-buried table, and a stove stuffed into one corner. Morten hurried toward it, muttering to himself about tea and sweeping up various-sized cups from the mess.

"Tati and Mort made half of what you see in here," Quill explained to Cistine, then bounced Pippet around, adjusting his grip under her legs. "Either I'm weaker than I used to be, which, *look at me*, that's not likely...or you're heavier than the last time I saw you. Have you gotten more muscle?"

"*Maybe*," Pippet sang, glancing at Aden, who became suddenly fascinated with a device on the table.

Feet brushed the staircase behind the front door, and Ariadne descended from the upper level, unbound hair swinging in a satin sheet to the small of her back. Her gaze lit on Cistine first, mouth parting in a silent breath of relief. "You're here."

"I'm so glad to see you!" Cistine pushed aside a workbench to meet her, wrapped in the smell of florals and weapon polish from her armor seams.

"I prayed for you so much, I lost words. How badly are you hurt?"

Cistine shook her head against Ariadne's shoulder. "I can't think about that now. Not if I want to finish this."

Ariadne separated gently from her, taking Cistine's shoulders in her hands. "I'm here. Whenever you need to talk, you have me."

She breathed deeply through her burning nostrils and nodded, turning back to the others. Ashe frowned, and Thorne marshaled his features too late to hide the sorrow in his eyes.

Quill set Pippet down, clapped hold of Ariadne's shoulders, and drew her backward, wrapping his arms around her collar from behind. "It's good to see you!"

"And you." She elbowed him in the ribs. "Have you lost weight?"

"He's at least two fingers lighter," Tatiana said wryly.

"I'm sorry to compromise you this way, Morten." Thorne planted himself on the edge of the table at the center of the room. "We wouldn't have come if we had anywhere else to go."

"As if I don't know this was my daughter's idea." Morten snatched the boiling kettle from the stove. "You know your Court is always welcome here,

Thorne. Both old and new."

"We're new," Pippet whispered, sidling up to Cistine and taking her hand. "Are you all right? You look sick. You look *tired*. Ariadne says I should be tired, but I'm not...I'm just excited to see you! Did Ashe find you, or did you find her? We went *everywhere* looking for you...did Ashe and Aden tell you where we went?"

Cistine laid her free hand over the girl's mouth. "I actually *am* very tired, Pippet. I'll tell you the story in the morning?"

Pippet nodded and wrapped both arms around one of Cistine's. "I'm just glad you're home."

Eyes hot, she kissed the girl's hair. "So am I."

"I see you're keeping up with repairing elite toys, Papa." Tatiana palmed a small globe on the table, tossing it gently from hand to hand.

"Well, it's something to pay for food and ghostlamps while I wait for my inventions to gain the notoriety they deserve. Oh, Tati, you ought to see what I'm crafting now, a needle that allows dyes to be cast *under* the skin...you remember how you and Quill used to ink one another's arms as children?"

"In my *sleep*," Quill muttered.

Tatiana tossed him a smile. "*You* were asleep. *I* was bored."

"You wrote Old Valgardan insults on my forehead!"

Pippet burst into giggles, and Morten joined in. "Well, this device would make those markings *permanent*."

"Mort, please, *don't* give her *or* my sister any ideas."

Smile waspish, Tatiana hauled Pippet away from Cistine and up onto the table where they sat side-by-side and back-to-back with Thorne, legs swinging. "Have you tried the dye-caster on yourself, Papa?"

Morten planted his foot on the table and drew up his trouser leg, baring the intricate beauty of a delicate floral design on his ankle. Cistine stepped forward to inspect it, smiling despite her exhaustion and nerves. "A clover."

Morten's eyes brightened. "You know flowers?"

"Gardening is one of her many specialties," Thorne smirked, and heat climbed the back of Cistine's neck.

Morten grazed his thumb along the inking. "This is for my *valenar*, Dataelina. It was the meaning of her name in Old Valgardan."

Tatiana blinked, bending forward to study the straight stem and cluster of clover bristles more closely. "I didn't know that."

Quill looked between them, face soft with sympathy. "Any other inventions you've been working over lately, Mort?"

He stomped his foot on the floor. "Plenty! The shop and shed are teeming. And now, on the side, it seems I keep a house of rest for refugees."

"If it's truly rest they seek," a deep voice rumbled from the doorway, "they've come to the right place."

Heart thudding with relief, Cistine whirled to face him, this gentle-eyed and stern-mouthed specter with face still clad in the last shadows of the waning night, shutting the front door behind him. His braids grazed against his stubbled cheeks when he dipped his head to her, a gesture of respect so subtle and unbelievably healing, Cistine almost sobbed. "Hello, Darkwind."

"Hello, *Logandir*." The familiar rasp of that greeting was a balm to her spirit. She lurched forward, and so did Maleck, gently clasping the sides of her neck and pressing his brow against hers. His breath shuddered against her face. "You're *safe*. You're safe, *Malatanda*. Welcome home."

And with all her friends around her at last, she finally was.

CHAPTER
FIFTY-EIGHT

THE CABAL HUDDLED together in the upper room of Morten's home around a low wooden table between th only two beds. The one where Pippet slept, cordoned off by glittery fabric, must've been Tatiana's once. The other was plain and tousled and warm-looking, like its usual occupant, but he wasn't sleeping there tonight. He'd laid out blankets near the door downstairs so any movement outside would disturb him. Cistine was so grateful for that kindness, she hadn't protested against him giving up his bed.

She clutched a cup of tea now, feet tucked up on her chair, falling into the comforting shadow of Maleck's tall musculature. Quill sat on her other side, tossing that same globular invention Tatiana had played with before from hand to hand.

"It's good Aden and Ashe brought us that elite woman," Ariadne said, so quietly Pippet wouldn't wake. "Though she's been an absolute nightmare to keep quiet."

"Where is she?" Ashe asked.

"The shop," Maleck said. "Morten invented a sturdy cage that allows her some movement."

"That token of kindness finally convinced her to testify," Ariadne added. "All we need now is to convince Bravis to try Salvotor himself rather than waiting for Yager's season."

"Could we write to him?" Cistine offered. "Convince him to come meet us here?"

Quill caught the globe in one hand behind his back and slung his other arm around her chair. "Not likely, not with Salvotor in the city."

Aden nodded. "The risk of intercepted communication is too great. We need to deliver the message face-to-face."

"Reaching the courthouse itself will be a problem," Ashe mused. "If we don't create a good diversion, we'll never make the doors before the Vassora capture us."

"That cannot be allowed to happen," Maleck said curtly.

"And we've only got one augment left," Quill reminded them. "Fighting our way into the courthouse, there's no way we could distribute it between all of us. It's just not enough."

"And our blades won't stand against so many Vassora, either," Thorne mused. "The guard will have doubled with Salvotor's return."

Cistine rubbed her face with both hands. "I don't know what's worse, not having any strategy to end this or having one and being thwarted right outside the courthouse gates."

"We could always turn ourselves in," Quill offered. "A few of us, anyway. It would be a good distraction."

Tatiana whacked the back of his head. "Excuse me, Featherbrain, what did we talk about after Oadmark? What did Maleck *just say*?"

Quill flopped back in his seat, dragging the discolored sheaf of white hair across the top of his head and shrugging mutinously.

"We'll find a way through somehow." Maleck laid a conciliatory hand on his friend's shoulder around Cistine's back. "Even with just one augment. We have to."

Hands rattling, Cistine set down her teacup. "Maybe...if *I* offered myself to him—"

"No," Quill, Tatiana, and Thorne chorused.

"Absolutely not," Ariadne growled.

"Is *anyone* at this table actually listening to Maleck?" Ashe snapped.

"Yes, I am! But if it's a distraction we need, I can try to hold him at bay long enough for you to make our case to Traisende. If Bravis agrees to try Salvotor, you can stop him before he takes me anywhere. It's the only thing I can think of short of plowing through the courthouse gates! We need to catch him off guard."

Tatiana sat up sharply, staring at Cistine. "Wait. What did you say about the gates?"

Cistine frowned. "That we would have to plow through them?"

"*Yani.* You are brilliant." Tatiana shoved back her chair and stood, eyes blazing with excitement. "I know *exactly* how to distract Salvotor."

"I really don't see anything here that's going to help us into the courthouse." Cistine peered around Morten's dim shed, pulse racing at the uneasy pinnacles of half-finished, broken, or unsuccessful inventions Tatiana wove through—the graveyard of a tinker's hopes and dreams.

Thorne bashed his knee into a heap of metal castings and groaned. "Tati, what in the stars are we doing here?"

"Just be quiet, will you?" She slowed as they neared the back of the shed, brandishing her arm toward a cloth-wrapped creature huddled in the shadows before them. "Here it is! Our diversion."

Cistine and Ashe glanced at one another, mirroring helpless confusion, but Maleck breathed, "He kept it all this time. Stars..."

Tatiana grinned. "I knew he would."

Thorne grabbed the cloth and yanked it from the beast, puffing dust into the air and unveiling the strangest wagon Cistine had ever seen. Sleek but faintly rusted, oddly streamlined like a wildcat coiled to pounce, it hunkered with its belly to the ground on four wheels made of a strange substance, not the usual wood. It reminded her vaguely of the harvesters left to rot near the augment wells in Lataus. "What *is* that?"

"An augwain," Tatiana explained. "These machines carried elites along those high bridges over the Channel."

"Aden and I used to race them." Maleck swept his hand over the augwain's top "How old were we? Twelve?"

"Barely that," Aden smirked. "Those were the days."

"It was powered by an augment?" Cistine asked.

"Lightning, to be specific," Tatiana said, and Cistine's chest tightened. "Which is the last one Quill stole from the guards we killed in Kalt Hasa. He's right, one augment isn't enough to get us all through the gates, but it's enough to power this augwain."

"We drive straight across the bridge," Quill said, "and onto the lawn."

Thorne folded his arms and assessed their eager faces. "What then?"

"Then we abandon it and infiltrate the courthouse," Tatiana said. "You and Ariadne and Cistine make your way to Traisende's wing. The rest of us find Salvotor."

"It would certainly be a distraction," Aden mused. "No one's driven an augwain in two decades. Salvotor won't expect it."

Quill grinned. "And he can't stop what he doesn't expect."

Thorne's eyes cut to Ariadne. "Are you ready to see this done?"

Her chest dropped, releasing a long, silent breath. "I've been ready to see it done for ten years."

Thorne nodded. "Mal?"

"Yes. It's time he paid for every crime."

"Ashe?"

She blinked, hesitated a moment, then nodded. "Of course I'm ready. I'd break down the Sable Gates to stick my blade in that man's throat."

Thorne looked at Cistine, his questing glance breaking through the suffocation of fear. She forced herself to nod. "Let's put him in chains."

Thorne broke into a broad grin, clapping Aden on the back. "How's your driving?"

Aden assessed the augwain with folded arms and a look that almost passed for excitement. "We'll find out soon enough."

CHAPTER FIFTY-NINE

THE CABAL TOOK the day to rest, prepare, and strategize, orienting themselves to the courthouse grounds by map and chiseling out a plan for the parts they couldn't foresee. It was nearly dawn again when they broke apart from conference at the table and trailed off to sleep, scattered across Morten's attic—all except Maleck and Aden, who disappeared to the roof, and Ashe, who sat on the foot of Pippet's bed with her head in her hands.

Sleep failed her. Every time she closed her eyes, she saw *Meszaros* and desert sands and Rion's hate-filled gaze turning into Cistine's, full of betrayal. Watching her princess now, asleep with her head pillowed on her arm and her back just shy of Thorne's chest, Ashe realized just how much hate had blinded her. Even when he came back to this city for Cistine and faced Salvotor for the first time in a decade, he was in love with her; and her tears on the long journey from Starhollow had not belonged to just a friend's betrayal—or many friends.

Ashe had been so gods-damned blind.

Small toes wiggled against her leg through the covers, and she picked up her head to find Pippet watching her with sleep-drunk eyes, hair sticking to the sides of her mouth from drooling. "Did you have another nightmare?"

Ashe shook her head. "Just thinking. Go back to sleep."

"I can't. I want to stretch out and you're in the way."

Ashe shifted to give her room. "I'm sorry I kept secrets from you about Baba Kallah and Helga. I didn't want you to hate me for what I did. But I realize it's not up to me whether you're allowed to hate me or not. You deserved the truth regardless of what that meant for me. I hope you can forgive me for that, at least."

"Maleck says you don't hate Valgard." Pippet tugged a loose thread on the bedspread. "You got hurt a long time ago, and being hurt made you put on armor. But he said he's seen you without armor and...you're good. And you didn't mean to hurt us, you were just trying to keep Cistine safe, like how Quill tries to keep *me* safe even when it makes me *furious*."

Heat pricked the backs of Ashe's eyes. "He's right, but that's no excuse. I promise I'll try to do better in the future."

Pippet rolled onto her back, peering up at Ashe through her lashes. "If you train me, I'll forgive you right now."

Ashe bit back laughter that would've woken the entire cabal. "All right, I'll see what I can do."

But even that was a lie. No one but Cistine knew Ashe was leaving for Talheim once this was over; she didn't have the heart to tell Pippet now.

Humor fading, she shifted to rise, and Pippet grabbed her wrist. "Sing me our lullaby?"

Heart aching, Ashe settled back beside her and finally freed the music pent up in her spirit ever since Keltei. The lullaby blended with the peaceful, slumbering breaths of the cabal and soothed Pippet's restless fidgeting. In minutes, she dozed again, fingers linked through Ashe's. When her voice was hoarse from singing, Ashe eased free, tucked Pippet in again, and grabbed one of the swords Ariadne and Maleck had scavenged to arm the cabal. Retrieving her pocket whetstone, she padded downstairs.

The room was mercifully deserted. She sat in a secluded corner between workbenches and sharpened the sword—steady work, but bereft of comfort. Her mind had plenty of opportunity to wander over the countless ways this mad scheme with the horseless wagon, the diversion, and the dash for Traisende's Chancellor could go wrong.

It was a mark of her distraction that she didn't hear Maleck arrive until he scraped a chair around from the wall and sank down before her. His knees nearly knocked against hers as he bent forward, clasping his hands loosely and watching her work over the sword. "That is not Echelon."

"Rion kept her after that fight beside the pond." The words pressed a fresh bruise into Ashe's heart.

Maleck gestured to the sword. "May I?"

She shrugged and handed it over, fingers brushing his gloves as he lifted the weapon gently from her hands. He grazed his palm over the blade, then held it erect, turning it toward the daylight peeping around the dark curtains. The way the thin glow caught the steel's honed, radiant edge sent chills scampering up Ashe's arms. "I name this weapon *Odvaya*, for courage and unbreaking hearts."

"Odvaya," Ashe tested the word on her tongue and found she liked the sound of it. "It's better than *Second Echelon*."

Maleck laughed quietly and relinquished the weapon to her. "You are the second of nothing. You are the beginning of yourself."

The shadow of *Meszaros* lurked in her mind, butchering its way through innocent people, bent on vengeance. "I'm not so sure of that."

"Asheila, you are not like them. They are controlled by hate and fear. And you? Tell me what you are."

The words were already on Ashe's tongue, blending over his: "I'm not afraid of you."

Silence fell. All around them, the house creaked, chuckling at their unspoken secrets.

She raised her eyes to him. "I think it's time we had that talk."

Maleck sighed and sat forward again, palms rasping together. "You want to know about *Meszaros*. About Cerne Mosiar."

Ashe nodded.

Specters flitted through the depths of his eyes. "During the war, I was a weapon of the temples. I had no thought, no personal aim...I simply did as I was asked, enslaved to augmentation. I was tasked with clearing a path to kill Prince Cyril, and I might have succeeded if not for a girl Warden, even younger than me, who stood in my path. She was poorly-trained and half-frozen to the tundra, yet she stood between my augments and her prince and screamed in my face that she did not fear me."

Ashe knew this story. She'd *lived* it, the tundra and shadows and blood and snow.

"That day our paths first crossed," Maleck went on, "I was not the man I am now. But when you roared your bravery at me, it was like coming awake from a long slumber. *You* woke me, Asheila, and the first thing I saw after years of nightmares was your face."

Ashe's mouth hung open. All she could see when she looked into his face were dead eyes with life trickling back into them.

"I have visited you many times in my memories since that day," Maleck said, "because there are people who are brave for themselves, and then there are those whose courage inspires others to be courageous. You gave me back my bravery that day. Because of you, I fled the war and never looked back. I believe *that* is who you are...a roaring lioness and a maker of courage. You must not let anyone manipulate your fears, or it will become brashness, and people will be hurt."

Ashe touched her pocket where the starstone was hidden away. "I know that now."

"I can see in your face how your experiences have humbled you. Just as mine humbled me." He rubbed his bearded jaws, gaze distant. "I will never stop regretting what my presence brought to the Wildwood, the horrors its people endured not from the war, but from *Meszaros*, because of me."

Ashe winced. "I'm sorry you had to face him again for us. And I don't blame you if you see him when you look at me."

Maleck dropped his hands. "I only see you. I've only ever seen you."

Looking into his eyes, Ashe saw that was true. And it terrified her.

She stowed the whetstone in her pocket. "Rion...*Meszaros* is gone. Cistine sent him back to Valgard." And then she told him what she'd told no one else. "She wants me to go after him, to bring a report to the Queen and then go to Middleton and convince Jad we already have an alliance with Valgard while she fights for it here."

Maleck frowned. "That will be a difficult lie to tell, if the Mad King is everything Cistine claims him to be."

Ashe shrugged, though it felt like lifting the weight of a kingdom on her shoulders. "If this is how I prove my loyalty to Cistine again, what choice do I have?"

Maleck studied her, dark eyes full of thought. "It would be more convincing if a Valgardan accompanied you."

Something flighty battered the walls of Ashe's stomach. "Is a Valgardan offering?"

"I'm told I'm quite the convincing liar, when needs must."

"Doubtful."

"If I'm not, wouldn't you know it now?"

Ashe held his gaze until he cracked a grin, one corner of his mouth sliding up in a way that bared his teeth and made her stomach flip again. She'd never seen him smile like that before. "Oh, God's bones, all right! You Valgardan stowaways!"

"Yes, Pippet told me all about that adventure."

Ashe slid Odvaya back into its scabbard, avoiding his gaze. "And she said you two had a talk about me."

"I hope that did not cross a line."

She snorted with half the strength she intended. "Aside from Cistine, I don't think anyone's ever advocated for me like that before. I'm grateful."

"It was my pleasure."

She set the scabbard aside and shot him a rueful look. If he was going to be this sincere, even leave his cabal to help her sell Cistine's ruse to Mahasar, then she owed him more than a grudging agreement and passing gratitude. "I'm sorry for hurting you with my actions in the Tumult. *You* didn't deserve that, no matter what I thought Thorne was guilty of. I always knew that, I just didn't let myself dwell on it."

"Did you ever hesitate?" Maleck murmured. "Even once?"

Red sand and fetid water and dark roots and a mirage, bright eyes and a hand reaching to pull her from the sand. "Yes. When I thought of you."

Maleck's smile spread, flickered, then fell abruptly. He studied his gloved hands, upturned and trembling, then flipped them to grip his knees.

Concern pushed through Ashe's guilt. She set aside the newly-named Odvaya and gripped his wrist. "What is it?"

A deep breath rattled through him and came out as a sigh. "Aden took me up to the roof to tell me his father, the man who helped me return to Stornhaz after the war, is...gone. Salvotor finally ended his life the way he claimed to, years ago. It seems he was vital to Cistine and Thorne's escape, but he fell in the fight to free them." A humorless chuckle slid from his throat. "I didn't imagine it would hurt, knowing he was there all along and now he's gone again. But somehow, it does."

Ashe rocked back on her heels, sympathy tightening her throat. "I'm sorry. I know how much it hurts to lose someone you respect like a father." She glanced down at Odvaya, searching for words. None seemed adequate. "I'm not much of a comforter, but I'll listen if you ever want to talk about him. We'll have plenty of time in the coming weeks."

Gods only knew how she'd fill up a single second of it with Maleck of all people, the least-conversational of the whole cabal. But she'd listen, if that was all she could do. And maybe, somehow, it would be enough.

Maleck's wrist twisted, quick as lightning, his hand turning to squeeze hers. "I would like that."

Footsteps brushed the steps in the room's opposite corner, and they pulled swiftly apart. Cistine descended on dragging feet and leaned against banister, eyes glassy and cheeks red. "Tatiana says it's time."

Maleck stood and offered his hand to Ashe. "Let's finish this."

And because it felt like forgiveness, like an understanding between warriors who had done terrible things and were struggling still to come back from them—and never walking alone—Ashe took his hand.

Under the cover of night, the cabal pushed the augwain into the narrow street. Morten joined them, opening the beast's upper jaw to examine an array of parts within; then he shut it and turned to them with a nod. "She should be all right. I've tinkered with her many times over the years—kept her in good shape."

"Thank you, Papa." Tatiana wrapped an arm around his side, and he hugged her against him.

"We appreciate this, Mort." Quill hooked his thumbs into his belt. "We'll try to return her in...relatively the same condition."

"See that you do." Morten kissed the top of his daughter's head. "But more importantly, be sure you return *yourselves* in good condition."

"We'll try," Ariadne smiled.

Morten hugged his daughter one last time, cast a lingering glance around the cabal, and slipped back inside the shop, shutting the door softly behind him.

Thorne rolled his shoulders back and slid his hand over the augwain's top. "Everyone inside."

It was a tight fit. Quill took one side of the back bench with Tatiana in his lap, Ashe beside them, and Maleck wedged in next to her. In the front, Ariadne piled in, then Thorne with Cistine tucked carefully on his knees. Aden slid in behind the jutting wheel Tatiana claimed would guide them like reins turned a horse, and pried open a cavity next to his leg, slamming their final augment inside and sealing it shut.

With a growl like thunder, the augwain came alive, lurching into a stride as smooth as sailing on glass-clear waters. Aden cranked the wheel when they reached the alley mouth and slid onto the colored street beyond.

Ashe had never traveled so fast in her life. Her stomach dropped through her navel and made a new home in her ankles, and she grabbed onto the top of the front bench to keep herself steady as they barreled into the night. She hoped Aden remembered the streets of his childhood, because all she could see was a dash of black against the windows and dim hints of light like shooting stars beyond.

Her stomach churned when they ascended into a subtle climb like gliding up a mountain, and Maleck nudged her, nodding outside.

They sailed across one of those towering bridges over the Ismalete Channel, its waters a glittering ribbon far below. Perhaps the height should've terrified her; even Cistine buried her face in her hands. But the soaring sensation awakened something fearless in Ashe, a wild, desperate daring. She gripped the seatback next to Maleck's head, held onto the bench before them, and leaned across him to press her forehead to the window. "You drove these before the war?"

"Yes." Maleck's tone was strained, breathless, like he was trying not to draw in too much air.

"This is..." A laugh jerked from her chest as the road tilted beneath them. "It feels like falling."

Maleck's eyes lit on her, sharing a glint of her enthusiasm. "So it does."

The augwain dove, abandoning the exhilaration of the bridge for a series of sharp corners that forced Ashe back into her seat. Abruptly, they cantered down to a trot, then to a halt.

The courthouse gates loomed ahead across a shorter bridge, just as sharp and impressive as the first time she saw them—and flanked with guards, inside and out. Though they must have seen the augwain simmering with lightning, crouched on the far side of the bridge, they didn't leap to intercept it. Maybe they were as shocked by the sight of it as Ashe had first been.

But that pause wouldn't last.

Aden shifted his hips, sinking deeper into the seat and resting his hand on a knob that poked up between Ariadne's knees. "All of you, *brace yourselves.*"

Quill wrapped an arm around Tatiana and grabbed hold of the door. Maleck bent forward, and Ashe dug her boots into the footwell. Thorne snapped an arm around Cistine, and Ariadne twisted to anchor herself on the seatback as Aden pumped the lever and the augwain lunged forward again. Bellowing like a true beast, it gobbled the distance to the gates, the finial-tipped pikes filling Ashe's whole line of sight.

And then Aden cranked the lever again and whirled the wheel, sending the augwain into a vicious spin.

Shouts and screams ripped above the crackle of lightning, Vassora diving out of the augwain's path as its haunches careened into the gates with all the force of the augment in its veins, the momentum of its headlong charge, and the added weight of its spin. It smashed the bars clean off their hinges, slamming the cabal in their seats and blowing glass inward from the windows. Shards sliced Ashe's face, jerking a curse from her clenched teeth.

A moment later, Aden had control of the lever and wheel again. He straightened the augwain and sent it barreling straight ahead, plowing through any Vassora too slow to leap clear. The beast skidded under broad arches, through a short, dark stretch of hall, and into the peristyle, drifting in a smooth arc around the circular pond by the lightest touch of Aden's palms; then it bucked, jerked forward with a last surge of power, and rammed to a halt with its snout cratering the doors to the inner courtyard.

A narrow path. But it would do.

"Out!" Thorne shouted, and they surged from the augwain. Panicked cries rose from the glass dome in the peristyle and the courtyard ahead, but no one had reached them yet.

So they started running.

CHAPTER SIXTY

THERE WAS NO place for farewells or good luck; time moved against them now. Cistine reached out a hand to Tatiana as the cabal broke apart, their fingers catching and squeezing in a silent promise they would see one another again. Then Aden led the others in a sprint for the courthouse, and Thorne, Cistine, and Ariadne veered left, racking through the crowd of startled onlookers and making straight for the statue of the Four Wayfinders on their pedestal before Traisende's private wing. They broke through the crowd and shut the door at their backs, locking a few bellowing elites out behind them.

High, roofless walls enclosed them, funneling down a short stone path lined with doors and low shrubs and ending in an archway at the base of a broad tower. Its face, skirted with steps and balconies, gleamed in the moonlight.

"Hoods up." Thorne tugged the back of Cistine's in passing, and she obliged. They ducked into the cobblestone hoop around the tower base, framed with low-walled terraces and fine seating, and made straight for the steps of the tower itself. At the top, a jutting balcony sprouted out, lined with doors into the tower—each one manned by a guard.

Thorne motioned Ariadne and Cistine down with their backs to the edge of the staircase and crouched one step above them, balancing his wrist on his knee. "From now on, we spare as many Vassoran lives as possible. Cistine, your face is the least-recognizable of any of ours. If you can distract the guards, we'll knock them unconscious."

She swallowed harshly and slowly rose from her knees. "I think I can manage something."

He squeezed her wrist as she slipped past him. "We'll be right behind you."

Cistine forced her spine straight and glided up the steps. Her heart stumbled when the nearest guards rose from beside the doors, armor glinting in the moonlight, beholding her with the same blend of interest and arrogance Grimmaul always did.

Shaking the thought of him away, she brushed her hair across the top of her head, adopting Quill's lazy mannerisms and purposeful swagger. "Chancellor Bravis sent for me. I hear he's in need of company tonight."

The guards exchanged a glance. "We weren't informed."

Cistine spun to the side, drawing their attention—and the tips of their halberds—toward her, away from the staircase. "If I had a mynt for every guard who's said that." She prayed her shaky laughter passed for sensuous rather than rattled. "How many times must we tell you? Your Chancellor's business with us is not *your* business. Now, where can I find him?"

The guards exchanged a glance, brows slanting down, spears rising. They didn't believe her.

Thorne and Ariadne caught them from behind all at once, smothering their noses and mouths and dragging them back to the lower steps. Cistine caught the halberds before they clattered on the stone and glanced down the curve of the balcony where other guards were visible only by the occasional flash of their armor.

They hadn't noticed anything. Yet.

Thorne and Ariadne stashed the bodies on the staircase and returned faster than Cistine hoped. Thorne tossed a keyring to her. "You take the door. We'll take the guards."

Sweat soaked her fingers as she fumbled with the keys. Her back felt utterly exposed to watchful eyes from the ring of apartments all around. Any moment, someone could see her, recognize her, descend and capture her—return her to Kalt Hasa—

A key finally snagged, the door clicked open, and Cistine gasped in relief—then gasped again when a hand curled over her shoulder. She spun and slammed a punch into Thorne's ribs, and he groaned, doubling up.

"Thorne! I'm so—" she caught sight of his face and bit off the words. "You're hurt."

His brow bled, his eyes glowing with pain, but he shook his head and tugged her aside so Ariadne could enter the tower. "The watch changes again in fifteen minutes, and distraction or not, Salvotor will hear of a disturbance in Traisende's wing and know where we are. It's time...are you ready to face Bravis again?"

She forced a nod.

They slipped inside the tower and sprinted up its winding inner staircases, every few levels clustered with gardens or eating rooms on private balconies. Curious eyes followed their charge, but there was no time to explain themselves—no time to slow at all. They ascended through a solarium and a viewing parlor and finally emerged on the uppermost level, a stone crescent and a short bridge joining it to a gold-capped dome.

Sixteen Vassoran guards watched over the dome's ornate door.

Thorne halted, cursing under his breath. "Bravis."

Ariadne cracked her knuckles. "It seems we're going to have a fight on our hands after all."

Cistine's ears throbbed with the sounds of sixteen dual-wielders drawing the sabers from their backs; despite Thorne's orders, if they did not kill at least a few of these guards, they would be killed themselves.

But they were all faces and hearts, all breath and body and blood. They were all Kristoff and the Six.

Cistine darted forward, ignoring Thorne's shout and Ariadne's warning cry, blocking her friends and facing the Vassora. "I am Cistine Novacek, Princess of Talheim, and I've come to bargain with your Chancellor. Tell Bravis we've brought what he needs to save Traisende!"

Swords dipped; the men and women exchanged wide-eyed glances.

Sweat soaked the back of Cistine's neck with the ticking away of precious time.

"Tell him *now!*" she bellowed.

One guard nudged his companions and slipped through the door while the rest surged forward, training their weapons toward Cistine. She refused to fall back even when the tip of a saber hovered over her chest; if they were testing her mettle tonight, they'd find it honed by Kalt Hasa's cold and the nearness of their victory. She would give ground to no one.

It felt like they spent all that remained of their time between Vassoran shifts standing opposed on that bridge; finally, the door swung open again and the ashen-faced guard shouted, "She's telling the truth! Make way!"

The dome's interior was not as large as she expected, nor as brightly-lit, its walls unadorned apart from several pieces of uninspiring artwork. A table filled the center of the rotunda's recessed floor, Bravis occupying the seat of honor there, and beside him—

"Maltadova," Thorne greeted as the guards dragged the door shut behind them. "I'm glad you're here. This may involve you both."

Bravis regarded them with weary malaise, face stamped in sleepless lines. "Breaking into my own wing, making demands of my time...you've gained some nerve since Veran, Thorne. But whatever *this* is, I'm not really in the mood for it." He rubbed his brow. "Do you know what day it is?"

Cistine glanced at Thorne's mystified face; their long imprisonment in Kalt Hasa had left them both bereft of passing time. Ariadne answered for them: "Kanslar sets tonight."

Bravis nodded. "We hoped Salvotor might prolong his so-called absence of affairs until long after his season ended. But he returned some days ago, making outlandish claims that if we didn't surrender to him by dawn, something worse than death would follow."

"Did he say what?" Thorne demanded.

"Not directly," Maltadova said. "But he implied a force we couldn't withstand...something that would sweep any resistance from his path."

Cistine shivered. Was he referring to the might of augmentation unleashed, or was he plotting something else?

"We were just discussing if we ought to call his bluff," Maltadova added.

"It seems our return was timely, then," Thorne said. "You wanted something worth challenging him for? We have it." He told them in succinct detail about the law buried for far too long which Salvotor blithely broke for his cruel ambitions, his body and his victims all weapons wielded to unite the Courts under a single King. Cistine's spirit wailed with indignation now just as the first time he told her inside the rush of Keltei's sea breezes and peaceful healing halls.

Nowhere was safe from Salvotor's cruelty.

"I know this law," Maltadova said when Thorne finished. "It has not been brought before the Courts in nearly twenty years. You're certain Salvotor's broken it?"

Thorne's gaze skimmed to Ariadne. "I am. And if I'd known about it a decade ago..."

Ariadne clasped his shoulder. "What's past is past. We have it now...the law, and the crime to condemn him with."

Maltadova's eyes settled on her, wide and full of pain. "You?"

"Me." Shoulders set, Ariadne stepped to the table's edge. "I said nothing before because I had no witness to stand with me, but now I do. In fact, I have two." She flashed the scroll from her sister, and when Bravis extended a hand, she surrendered it.

Cistine fidgeted while he read. Though they'd been granted audience, the Vassora didn't know that; they would still raise the alarm when they found their unconscious friends, and Salvotor might interrupt if Bravis delayed any longer.

"Well," he said at last, "I see this was signed by the *visnpresta* Iri of Keltei Temple. She's a good woman, an honest one."

"It is all honest." Ariadne leaned her hands on the table. "We are also holding a woman who witnessed the aftermath of Salvotor's crime. She has agreed to testify. I'm prepared to press charges this very night if Traisende is bold enough to try a Chancellor."

Bravis glanced at Maltadova. "Yager already agreed, in their season—"

"We can't afford to wait another cycle!" Cistine snapped. "This is happening *tonight!* We just handed you a case that would force Salvotor to step down for immediate arrest...why in God's name would you *hesitate?*"

"She is right," Maltadova said. "This cannot wait for Yager's season. *You* must try him *now.*"

"How convenient for you," Bravis grunted, "not to have to lay your own neck in the noose trying the most dangerous Chancellor of our lifetime."

Thorne stepped to Ariadne's side, fingertips balanced lightly on the table. "I know what we brought you in Veran was tenuous at best. I didn't blame you for protecting your Court then. But if you refuse now, your fear of facing Salvotor would go before what's best for Traisende."

"I'll thank you not to tell the business of Chancellorship to me, Thorne. You aren't one yourself."

"But he will be," Cistine said, "if you remove his father from the Judgement Seat."

Bravis scowled, looking away.

"Trust us," Thorne urged. "And save your Court. All the Courts."

Bravis dragged his hand down his face and stared at the signed testimony before him; then his eyes returned to Thorne, burning like fire. "I hope you're right about this law." He stood, shaking out the edges of his fine robe. "Maltadova, would you gather the Vassora at the courthouse steps? Apparently, I have charges to write and deliver. And Thorne, send word to your other witness. I want her here immediately."

Cistine gripped her face with both hands and rocked on the balls of her feet. "*Thank you,* Bravis!"

The Chancellor snorted. "Step carefully, Princess. You—"

A concussive blast thundered through the tower, quaking it to the roots. Cistine staggered forward and Thorne caught her shoulders, steadying her beside him. Maltadova leaped up, holding his swaying seatback. "What in the stars was that?"

Ariadne glanced at Thorne, and Cistine's heart dropped. "Salvotor."

CHAPTER SIXTY-ONE

THE CABAL PUNCHED straight into the courthouse parlor on Aden's command, knocking between shocked loiterers and suspicious onlookers and tipping the vending carts where people spent their time waiting to meet with Tribunes and Chancellors; anything to draw the Vassora after them, away from Cistine, Thorne, and Ariadne. They only slowed once for Maleck to swipe a pair of ghostlamps off a table before he kicked it from his path.

A pair of guards held a door tucked away at the back of the lofty room, and Quill and Tatiana shot straight toward them, swords drawn. The resounding slam of blade on blade sent the people in the market screaming and fleeing, and Ashe grimaced at the shrill echo; they wouldn't find any diversion better than pure panic.

The guards were down in seconds. Quill and Tatiana stole their augments and Aden their keys, opening the door and motioning them into the dark stairwell beyond.

"What is this?" Ashe demanded.

"A place we are all forbidden to go." Maleck offered one ghostlamp to her. "A diversion guaranteed to bring Salvotor straight to us."

She forced herself to take that first step and accept the ghostlamp from him. Then momentum, with the steepness of the stone stairs, did the rest.

They went deep, down into the foundations of the courthouse—then deeper still. There was no light but what they carried, revealing where the fine bricking ended and became a long, dark gut of rock funneling into the heart of the world.

After several minutes, Maleck caught Ashe's elbow and raised her arm higher with his, shedding light over Tatiana, Aden, and Quill's dim outlines. The darkness deepened ahead; even the ghostlight didn't carve through it.

"We're here," Aden said. "Quill."

Fire ignited as Quill shattered one of the guard's augments, setting Ashe's hair on end. He swept out his arm, unleashing fire through a room at the base of the steps and highlighting the slabbed floor deeply engraved with spiraling twists and Old Valgardan runes. The flames blazed across them and struck the curved walls in a spray of sod and rock, booming through the chamber like thunder. Even when the sound faded, it still echoed in Ashe's head, resonate percussions spearing into her temples and vibrating in her chest.

"Again," Aden barked.

Quill rallied what remained of the fire, and Ashe looked at Maleck. "What *is* this place?"

His face was pained, his eyes trained on the ceiling, away from the runemarked floor. "One of the Doors."

Quill's fire cracked against the ceiling in a dazzling scythe at the same moment a violent burst of power slammed into Ashe and Maleck from behind. Pain erupted along her body as her feet left the steps, knocking her reeling into Tatiana and Aden, and Maleck into Quill, sending them all sprawling across the Door. Ghostlamps burst, spattering streaks of scarlet-and-lilac phosphorescence like blood among the runes.

Cursing, they all rolled apart, springing to their feet and spinning back to face the staircase where Chancellor Salvotor descended—blocking their only way out. Without missing a stride, Aden stepped ahead of the others to face his uncle, hands to his sabers, every muscle bristling with tension.

"Aden," Salvotor purred. "What a relief to see my only nephew alive. Though I hardly expected to find you here, desecrating the Doors with these outlaws. Finally reconciled into their fold, have you?"

"You're one to speak of desecrating the sacred." Aden prowled before the others, keeping Salvotor's attention on him.

"Do you refer to my presence here? Or are you thinking of *Ariadne?*"

"I'm referring to everything you are and everything you do. What you've done to my cabal." He spoke of them differently from Thorne, something almost primal in his tone—as if they were all a part of him as much as his beating heart and the blood in his veins.

Salvotor laughed, descending onto the Door. "That was far more your fault than mine. You sold them for the lie of your father's life." He paused, stroking his chin. "Or did I fail to mention that lie was really truth?"

Maleck drew Starfall and Stormfury, stepping forward to Aden's side, and glass shattered with a soft *ping.* Fire climbed Salvotor's arms, burning away his fine robe and revealing the armored skin of his bare chest. "Really, boys, I don't think you want to do this. How many augments do you have? And how many do you suppose *I* have?"

"Not enough to stop us after all you've done," Maleck growled.

"Let me take a gander," Salvotor said. "Kallah and Julian? Cistine and Thorne? Or your *father?*"

Maleck's grip whitened around his sabers. Aden stilled, his chest barely rising and falling.

"You ought to know he suffered. Not just at the end...for nearly twenty years before that. But those last few moments were exquisite, well worth the two decades of food and drink wasted on keeping him alive." Salvotor's lips drew up at the corners. "He died on his knees, begging me to spare you both. And I told him every heinous way I would make you suffer before I cut his throat like a squealing hog, left him drowning in his own blood, and buried his corpse in the rubble of that mountain."

Aden and Maleck exploded forward, their crossed sabers slamming into his face. Even the *Svarkyst* steel barely nicked his enhanced skin, and Salvotor thrashed Maleck's arm aside with a cut of his hand and kicked Aden away. Quill rushed in with a battle cry shaking the walls, Ashe and Tatiana on his heels.

Salvotor's fists and feet snapped out left and right, blocking blows and dealing them back, forcing the cabal to dodge and roll beneath gouts of flame. Maleck and Aden struck Salvotor and slithered around each other like entwining rivers, playing flawlessly with one another's patterns and movements, yet they couldn't break his guard. Ashe, Quill, and Tatiana hammered in unpredictably, but Salvotor batted those strikes aside, too.

Frustration keened along the back of Ashe's teeth like she'd bitten ice; she overstepped her next strike, and Salvotor's retaliatory punch snapped her head back so hard her world went white. She barely felt the second blow tossing her up against the wall, but the taste of blood on her cut tongue revived her. Spitting and shaking, she crawled upright, blinking through the pale dapples in her vision just in time to see Salvotor's reinforced fist smash straight into Maleck's shoulder, dislocating it with an audible tear.

Bellowing, Maleck staggered backward, dropping Starfall. Salvotor pounded his elbow into Quill's throat and tossed him against the wall, too, then stabbed a kick into Aden's ribs so hard something cracked, and plucked Tatiana from her next charge with a knee to the face, shattering her nose. Roaring with rage, Quill bounded back up and caught the Chancellor in a chokehold, dragging him away from Tatiana; he drove his elbow into Quill's gut so hard he retched, then flipped him onto his back and brought his boot down at his throat.

Aden slammed into him before the blow could connect, spinning him away across the Door, but Salvotor followed through on that momentum in a deft pirouette, driving his foot into Aden's broken ribs and dropping him in a winded, groaning sprawl on the floor.

Salvotor strutted slowly between the mess of bleeding, dazed warriors, lifting Stormfury as he went, hungry eyes hunting for his next victim; but before he could strike any one of them, Tatiana was on her feet, weapons lifted, charging in.

The clash that followed bought Ashe enough time to pull the men to their feet—and without that diamond-hard skin, Salvotor would've been dead already. Tatiana was graceful as a dancer, lithe as a serpent, twisting, lunging, parrying and skipping in and out of his reach. Salvotor's retaliations, though primed and practiced, were useless; she was never there when he struck back.

So he cheated.

Glass burst again, and this time lightning arced through the room, cracking into Tatiana's chest and blowing her backward against the stone wall. It cratered with the impact of her body, and she crumbled to the floor, hair twisted and smoking across her face. She did not move again.

Quill's agonized shout broke like he'd been the one thrown across the chamber. He attacked blindly, ignoring Ashe's warning shout, and the next burst of lightning sent him down like a fist to the face. Aden made it farther, almost within striking range, but the Chancellor sidestepped neatly and slashed Stormfury across his ribs, shredding his armor and butting him away with a shoulder to the jaw.

Ashe and Maleck attacked as one, but his stride was a hair shorter than hers, hindered by his useless shoulder. Salvotor struck him first, two clashes of blade to blade and a thrum of lightning that knocked him to his haunches; then his blade circled Ashe's, diverted her attack, and sent her staggering back with one more lash of energy. The room dimmed, lightning crackling low on the Chancellor's form, just enough to light his leer when he planted his boot on Maleck's back. One deft twist, and he'd snap his spine.

Ashe froze, mind racing, body coiled and straining.

"Not even half the leader Thorne is," Salvotor's gaze slid to the target of his latest attack. "And that is saying something indeed, Aden."

Spitting blood, Aden dragged himself up on his elbows. "I'll kill you."

Salvotor bent, pressing down on Maleck's back and laying Stormfury to his neck. Maleck groaned in anguish. "Not if you're half the weak-willed coward your father was."

Ashe lunged across the carven floor and spun a kick into Salvotor's ankles, knocking him away from Maleck. Stormfury wheeled in his hand, and pain ruptured down the length of Ashe's sword arm, deadening her hand. Odvaya clattered from her numb fingers, and her back struck the wall.

Salvotor was on his feet again in a heartbeat, lightning stringing between his fingers, its glow crackling fuchsia-and-lilac against his eyes. "You Wardens all make the same mistakes. And you'll all meet the same end, just like the Butcher's son on the plains."

On the corner of Ashe's vision, a figure struck the base of the steps and shot forward—just as the lightning arced out.

Godlike power slammed into the palm of Thorne's armored hand and streaked across his entire body as he stepped into its path, shielding Ashe with his own body. A High Tribune blooded with lightning, he crackled and fumed, balling the augment between his fists and hurling it back against his father's chest. The blow threw him gasping and choking at Ariadne's feet, a shadow descending the stairs with fury in her face and a kick to the Chancellor's throat for good measure.

Another set of steps, light and familiar, clattered through Ashe's ears. Panic raised her voice to a shout. "Cistine, go back up the stairs!"

The Princess halted on the last step, wide eyes taking in Salvotor, the cabal, and the floor—then sliding out of focus, fixed on the runes.

Salvotor chuckled wheezily, sitting himself slowly back up. "Well. Wildheart. Don't you look—?"

It was Thorne who kicked his throat this time, flinging him prostrate on his back. "We are not playing that game."

Dozens of steps reverberated on the curved walls now, a swarm of Vassoran guards pouring down the stairwell and forcing Cistine onto the Door. She stiffened when she struck it, peeling back to press against the curved wall while two men in fine clothes passed her: one so pale he nearly glowed, the other dark enough that his features blended with the shadows dancing outside the ghostlights in their hands.

"Salvotor," the pale man said, "you are under arrest."

The Chancellor laughed, stumbling to his feet. Thorne slid into his path, holding firm between him and Cistine. "On what charges?"

"The rape of a *visnpresta* acolyte," the other man growled. "If you come quietly, you may retain an apartment under house arrest for the duration of your trial. If you resist, you will be caged with the common men in the city jail. Or killed, if needs must."

"I am begging you," his companion added, "*resist.*"

"Bravis," Thorne murmured.

Salvotor's eyes snaked from Thorne, to Bravis, to the other man. His mouth twitched, but it was not a smile. "So, this is the game you wish to play, Thorne?"

"With every bone in my body."

"Very well. You found a law, a so-called witness, and a self-proclaimed *victim.*" Salvotor spat the last word toward Ariadne. "But at what cost?"

Thorne's eyes skimmed to Quill, face-down and motionless; Maleck, twisted on his side, holding his shoulder; Tatiana, limp in Aden's hold, and Ashe, her injured arm useless at her side. When his gaze met hers, despair crossed his face, and remorse so deep it knocked her breathless.

Salvotor didn't resist the pair of Vassora who clapped him in fetters. His eyes lingered on his son, full of spiteful glee. "Things have been set in motion in this kingdom that you could never possibly dream of. Do you think I've been idle since Kalt Hasa fell? The lessons I'm going to teach you, Thorne...they'll make you *wish* for the whip."

He laughed while the Vassora marched him away, and Ashe's blood chilled. Somehow, he was still the one in control of the room.

The moment Salvotor's voice faded, Cistine dashed across the Door and fell to her knees beside Quill, pulling him onto his back and taking his head onto her knees. "Lie still." Tears choked her voice. "Does anyone have a healing augment? *Anyone!*"

Bravis motioned a pair of guards forward, flagons in hand, then turned to Thorne. "We'll begin the proceedings to name you Chancellor. Kanslar will need a leader when this chaos comes to light."

Thorne nodded, but there was no trace of triumph in his face, only worry. While the Chancellors trailed up the steps behind Salvotor, Thorne fell to his knees beside Maleck, snapping his shoulder back into place with one deft stroke. His guttural groan prodded at something in Ashe's core, and she avoided his gaze when it cast to her, then skipped on to Aden and Tatiana and the Vassoran guard dividing a healing augment between them.

Ashe let out a long breath when Tatiana stirred at last, eyes fluttering open, head lifting from Aden's grip. "Did we win? Where's Salvotor?"

"In irons," Cistine said. "*Under arrest.*"

"Stars, we did it?" Quill grunted, propping himself up out of her grip. When she nodded, he laughed in bewildered wonder. "We actually *did* it."

He dragged himself over next to Tatiana, and when she crawled into his lap, he slung his arm around her and buried his face in the side of her neck. Aden struggled up from beside them and limped toward Ashe, outstretched hand glinting silver with a portion of the augment given for his wounds, a question hanging heavy in his face.

She nodded. It was no time for pride.

At his careful touch, the warmth of healing spilled through her arm; their gazes linked with the memory of another healing augment, in another dark stone pit like this, and his hands helping hold her together then. Twice, the power of the gods mended her brokenness. It was a shame it couldn't do anything for her shame, her regret, or the damning nerves that stormed her middle when she looked at Maleck again, rising beside Thorne and pulling Cistine up with him.

He caught her staring and cast her a smile, far too fleeting for the strength it spilled through her. That was dangerous, more than anything she'd ever feared about him when they reunited on the Vey after all those years since the war...but she wasn't complaining about it, not tonight. She could use a bit more strength, no matter the source.

Especially when she saw how Cistine's eyes lingered on the Door, full of reservation and a strange, desperate hunger, before she let Thorne take her hand and tug her up the steps to the courthouse above.

CHAPTER SIXTY-TWO

IT WAS NEARLY dawn before the adrenaline faded and Cistine tasted the first dregs of exhaustion from the long night and the restless day before it; but even then, she didn't want to leave her cabal.

They'd found a deserted parlor in Kanslar's wing of the courthouse, escaping the whispers of new rumors and gossip about the courthouse-shaking calamity of the night. Gathered around the circle of couches and chairs with a hearth roaring at their backs, the cabal shared a jug of mead and watched an early-season snowfall hurl its violent white flurries against the windowpanes.

Tipsy and content, Cistine curled against the arm of the couch with Tatiana beside her. She felt like calm waters...almost too calm. After seeing Salvotor led away in chains, and the state of her friends from that battle, and the *Door*—the sensation when she stepped on it, the gong that rang through her body at the contact of boot on stone—she expected to curl up in her apartment and weep. Instead, she was oddly numb; not as if there wasn't a storm to stir the waters, but like she sheltered in a cave and hadn't emerged into the raging tempest yet.

Perhaps she owed that to the four glasses of mead. Her head was floating and everything felt funnier than it should, but at least she was laughing instead of batting down brushes of panic.

Quill reclined on the lounge he shared with Ariadne, dragging a hand through his hair. "Well, Nimmus' teeth. Here we are, drinking in Kanslar's wing and *not* getting arrested. It's really over."

"Sillakove claims Kanslar," Maleck murmured. "It will be an interesting season when the Conqueror rises again."

"How do you feel, Thorne?" Ariadne asked.

He rubbed the back of his neck, something Cistine's inebriated mind found disarmingly attractive. "Unprepared. It was one thing to envision this as a boy. It's another to put all those dreams into practice."

"You'll do fine," Aden assured him, fingers absently tweaking the compass pendant at his throat.

A knock at the door came almost concurrent to the knocker letting himself in. Clarity burst through Cistine's tipsiness at the sight of his face, and she sat up sharply. "*You.*"

"Me," Tribune Sander grinned. "You broke my nose that day on the plains, you know, thank you for that...half my lovers couldn't stand the sight of me, the other half smothered me with concern. Oh, is that mead? Good, I'm parched."

"I'm sorry, who invited you?" Ashe asked.

Sander snatched the jug from Maleck's hand and tossed himself down on the sofa next to Aden, who shifted pointedly away. "Seeing as you wouldn't have this victory if not for me..."

"Don't expect any of us to fall over ourselves to thank you for that," Aden grunted.

"We should *all* be grateful," Thorne said. "Better than half of us wouldn't be sitting here today if not for him."

Cistine blinked at the Tribune, struggling to bring his features into focus. He stared back at her, wiping his mouth when he finished drinking. "I have something for you, Princess. It belonged to that boy, the one on the plains. I found it when I burned his body and, well...I have so many lovers, I know how sentimental some women can be. I'm sure he would've wanted you to have this." He fished in his pocket and withdrew a warped, half-melted circlet that once fit Cistine's finger so well: a betrothal ring, its gemstones opened in the shape of a rose.

Thorne's eyes were on her, full of grief and regret as she put out her hand and Sander dropped the ring into it. She didn't remember it weighing so much. "Thank you for giving him the goodbye he deserved."

"It was the least I could do."

Somber silence descended for several moments while Cistine rolled the ring around in her palm. Julian was not avenged yet—not while Salvotor stood accused but uncondemned. She would have to change that; she would bring aid to Talheim and justice for Julian. She wouldn't rest until both were accomplished and she could return home with an army at her back.

Slipping the ring into her pocket, she reached for her cup again. Tatiana sat forward as well, circling the rim of her water glass with one finger. "All right, I have to know. Who in Nimmus *Named* you, Sander?"

He chuckled, reclining into the couch and flinging a lazy arm behind Aden. "Ah, sorted that out, did you?"

"Well, it clearly wasn't my father," Thorne said. "Otherwise you would've told him you voted to keep my title long ago."

Sander swirled the mead jug, his smile no longer filling his face. "My mother did it. She taught me how the Courts ought to be—not existing to provide us with position, but position existing to provide for the people. She warned me over and over how a single Court with a single Chancellor would endanger our way of life." Sander shrugged. "Schooling alongside Salvotor gave her plenty of time to learn the heinous *bandayo* he was, and when my ambition set me on the path to becoming a Kanslar Tribune, she took matters into her own hands to keep me safe from him."

"And Salvotor never suspected it was you?" Aden raised a brow.

"What do you take me for, an imbecile? I had another Tribune take the blame, naturally. *Someone* had to be lying about the vote."

Thorne blinked. "Who?"

"Rathgan of Eben. He was a boring fellow and a bit too interested in one or two of my lovers. I learned his Name and a few others delicious secrets, convinced him to confess when Salvotor questioned us, and stood back while the rest handled itself." Sander shrugged. "Salvotor was eager to move ahead with his glorious conquest, so he dealt with the matter swiftly, replaced him with Njal, and all was done." To Thorne, he added, "I like him, you know, Njal. He has a good head on his shoulders."

"I'll keep that in mind."

Cistine draped her head over the seatback. "All of that, just because of one Name."

"They're powerful things." Quill's voice was the sort of soft it only reached when he was looking at Tatiana. "They can bring you back from places you never thought you'd crawl out of."

"That's true," Thorne said. "A tether and an anchor in the right hands."

Cistine picked up her head and held his gaze, a spark of daring flickering down her spine. Bouncing to her feet, she held out her hand to him. "Walk with me?"

He blinked, coming back to himself, and carefully took her hand. With a parting flutter of fingers to the rest of the cabal, Cistine towed him out of the parlor, into the hall—then halted, looking left and right. Both ways were exactly the same.

Thorne chuckled, propping his arm on the doorpost above her head. "What are you doing?"

"Trying to remember the way out." She gnawed on her lip. "There's something I want to do tonight. Right now."

His hand slid lower on the frame, eyes widening. "What is it?"

She tipped her head back and flashed him her most dangerous smile. "I want you to take me to the House of Visions and make my Name *real*."

CHAPTER
SIXTY-THREE

THE HOUSE OF Visions was a monolith near the very heart of Stornhaz, so tall it took them nearly half an hour to mount its interior staircase guarded by *visnprests* and *prestas*. The walk from the courthouse in the snow flurries and the climb up the steps sobered Cistine completely, but her resolve remained unchanged; the sobriety mattered more to Thorne, who reminded her over and over she didn't have to do this. She owed him no fealty. No ruler from one kingdom ever Named another.

She didn't care about any of that. She and Thorne were already the first of so many things; she wanted her Name to be one of them. She trusted him never to abuse it, to force her into decisions or joinings she didn't want. And she needed the anchor. The tether. Something to cling to when her panic started to churn.

The pinnacle of the House of Visions was an unwalled parlor, wide and railed and looking out over the City. At its center was a plain pedestal, the gemstone-studded chalice atop it breathtaking in its fine make, the liquid inside shivering in the light of Kanslar's setting constellation.

Cistine circled the pedestal, facing Thorne and taking up the chalice. "What should I expect?"

"It's difficult to say...everyone dreams differently when they drink. But whatever you see, follow it like a wayfinder follows the stars. The gods will show you exactly what you need to empty yourself so you can be filled again."

"And what will *you* do?"

His mouth crooked up at one corner. "I'll just say your Name."

She smiled nervously over the rim of the cup and raised it in a toast. "To a Valgard free of your father."

Then she drank.

The taste was like a crisp, flowing stream, the tingling sweetness of melted snow with the afterbite of herbs burning down her throat and rioting in her stomach. She set down the chalice with a clap on the stone pedestal and gripped its edges, closing her eyes against the bubbling nausea.

The smell of ash, dust, and brine filled her next breath; when she opened her eyes, the House of Visions dissolved around her, turning to black sand and pouring away in gentle curlicues. Only Thorne remained, his eyes fixed on her, but he turned to dust at the corners too. "Stay in the vision."

Pushing away from the pedestal, she lunged and grabbed for him—and stepped *through* him, bare toes grazing marble.

She twisted left and right, staring down the ornate, empty hall. High windows shed glittering moonbeams over her midnight dress, dusted in diamonds like starlight. She knew this hall, had crossed it so many times to listen in on meetings at the throne room doors as a child—had been dragged down it against her will while she grew, and finally slid down it by night's cruel shadows the evening of her father's private war council.

Astoria. The Citadel.

She was *home*.

Come, the wind whispered through chinks in the mortared walls. *Come and see.*

Feet limped on the marble behind her. "Look at you. An absolute vision of Cenowyn. What a queen you will make, Wildheart."

Wildheart.

Cistine swung around, heart jamming into her throat. "*Baba Kallah?*"

The old woman smiled, mischief dancing in her glittering eyes and lined, cheerful mouth. "Didn't I tell you that when your moment came, I would be here?"

Stunned laughter burst from Cistine, and she threw her arms around Thorne's grandmother, breathing in the cinnamon-and-orange scent of her clothes. Baba Kallah stroked her hair, then set her out at arm's length and took her chin, studying her face. "Oh, Wildheart. How much you've endured."

Wildheart.

Cistine looked away from the piercing gaze that saw through her flesh to the tatters Kalt Hasa made of her heart. Memories of the lash, the knife, the rankings and insults and mockery struck her like the sea struck the shore. "What do I do now?"

Baba Kallah released her and offered an arm. "Now we go to your crowning."

Come. Come and see.

Whispers sighed through of her home, wedging under the glass domes of parlors where she gossiped and sunned herself; twisting down the hallways where she walked, nose buried in books, trying absentmindedly not to bump into servants; guiding them through empty spaces where her family's legacy paved their path. They walked through splashes of moonlight and starlight to the throne room doors, and halted. Cistine's arms fell to her sides, tingling with dread. "I don't think I'm ready."

"For what? For this?" Baba Kallah gestured with her cane to the door. "For your responsibility, or to make the treaty?"

"Any of it. For being the Key our kingdoms need."

"How can they know what they need yet? There's only ever been two Keys, and few know they're human." Baba Kallah raised a brow. "You have the power to decide what a Key can be, just as you're deciding every day what it means to be a princess or a queen."

Setting her cane aside, she braced her hands on the throne room doors and pushed through every inch of resistance to the other side.

King Cyril's ebony chair and Queen Solene's ivory seat were gone. Only one remained: the princess's porcelain throne. And there, resting on its plush cushion, was a silver circlet studded with rubies and diamonds.

Cistine hesitated, chewing her lip. That throne seemed so impossibly far away.

Baba Kallah rested a hand on her back. "A princess could not have survived what you have, Wildheart. But a warrior queen would indeed."

Wildheart.

"You have earned the right to wear that crown," she added. "Daughter of kings and queens. Warrior of blood and mercy. Key to the Doors to the Gods. These titles are not your burden, they are your *birthright.* Take hold of them and save our people."

The words prodded at the yearning she felt in Kalt Hasa, those last bitter moments while her life slipped through her fingers; the ache, the need a power in itself beyond reckoning.

Baba Kallah's hand fell away. "I am here. I will always be here, *Yani.* Even when you cannot see me."

Cistine didn't turn at the fading of her voice; she didn't look away from her destiny anymore. Instead she set her jaw, gathered her skirts, and strode forward, every punctuated step declaring her purpose, her right, her *choice* to be here.

She was the Wild Heart of Fire. She would burn as long and as brightly as they needed her.

She was *Wildheart.* And they could not stop her. *Nothing* could.

She stepped up to the throne and lifted the circlet, the weight she feared so much as a child—but no longer. She was worthy. She was born for this. And with the call singing louder than ever in her veins, Cistine Novacek rested the crown on her brow.

A glorious wind cracked through the room, breaking the walls apart, blowing the throne to rubble and unraveling her gown at the seams. Threads of night and starlight blew from her body, baring the battle armor beneath, the stars on the satin fabric scattering across the stone floor and springing up in the illumined outlines of bodies kneeling at the foot of the dais.

Six people. Six names whispered in the dark.

Quill and Tatiana, Maleck and Ashe, Ariadne and now Aden, arms across their chests, genuflected before her. Tears budded in her eyes as she looked through the dancing light of these diamond-studded figures, her gaze coming to rest on Thorne in the throne room doorway, arms folded, eyes reflecting her joy.

This was the moment he told her about on the banks of the Muunvat River all those months ago. She was a cup spilled over, emptied of everything except—

"Wildheart."

The Name sliced from Thorne's mouth, branding Cistine's chest, lifting her lungs in a reckless whoop of breath.

"*Wildheart.*"

That was who she was, the Name gathering her very essence into a single word as powerful and fierce and free as the woman who carried it— and the man who gave it to her. She was bound to him, to his Court, to his very heart by that word.

She leaped down from the dais and ran, hands skimming the kneeling bodies of her warriors, each one shattering into starlight under her touch. The throne room walls shivered and rippled and collapsed, and she laughed, reaching for Thorne's hand—

Iron-tight fingers seized her wrist from behind, spinning her away to face the shattered room and a desperate face annealing from the darkness of its falling, another figure built of stars. Her heart knew him before her mind did...that tight grip, his wing of dark hair, those midnight eyes.

"Julian!" She wrenched against his hold, but he held her fast, panic bright in his stare. "What are you—what *is*—?"

"Come with me, Princess!" His voice cracked with urgency. "There's something else you have to see!"

He dragged her through the crumbling room, the sky turning from starlit black to scarlet-tinged above the buckling walls. She could barely keep up with his dead sprint leading her toward something that felt wrong, foul, *dangerous.*

"*Wildheart.*"

She glanced over her shoulder at that faraway whisper.

"*Wildheart, come back...*"

The floor tilted into a slope, a hill, the world around them stained in black skies and silver horizons. Panting, she stumbled to a halt with Julian at the top. "Julian, *stop*, I don't—"

She broke off, hand flying to her mouth.

A battlefield spread out below them—a massacre. The ground was so sated on blood, it no longer absorbed it, cradling it in puddles and streaks instead. The dead were *everywhere*, heaps of bodies evaporating into the dark, furious sky. And beyond that...

War.

Augments flashed in dazzling sickles of light, banners of lightning, and great spews of fire. Blades smashed together and dying screams flew on the wind. The world perished around them, turning to cinders and ash floating up to the black-bellied clouds.

"What is this?" Cistine whimpered, sidestepping nearer to Julian and tightening her grip on his hand.

"The end. The beginning." The voice wasn't just his; it was layered, high and low, solemn and furious all at once. Flickers of power rode the current of every word. "So many possible paths lay ahead, but they all lead to this place."

Cistine gripped Julian's shoulder for balance as augments tipped and swayed the ground beneath them. "What happens here?"

"Everything. The creating and the undoing. The opening and closing." His eyes turned to her, freckled with glints of lavender lightning from the clouds above. "War. Peace. Death."

At the tug of his hand, they sailed over the grass together, halting in the middle of the battlefield where draconic roaring sundered the black clouds. Bresnyar banked and glided through the smoke-choked sky, golden scales flashing, his fire painting the world. Through the haze of heat and darkness, the cabal came into view.

Ashe on her knees, gripping Maleck's hand, facing a line of shrouded figures writhing with augmented power. Beyond them, Ariadne and Tatiana dueled against a drove of augurs. To her left, Quill and Aden fought back-to-back in a tide of their own blood against a winged army whose screaming shook the sky itself.

Another voice, a bellow added to theirs—a battle cry.

Thorne.

Cistine's gaze whipped to him, a specter charging through the ranks, his silver hair glowing in the firelight, streaked with blood. His twin *Svarkyst* sabers flashed in his hands.

"Cistine!" he shouted. "You have to stop this! *Let it go!*"

The stroke fell.

Ashe and Maleck's heads separated from their bodies. A tide of augments rushed over Ariadne and Tatiana. The creatures crashed into Aden and Quill, tearing their limbs from their bodies. All at once, it was only her and Thorne still alive. She tore free from Julian's grip and tried to run to him, but her legs were still moored in the bloody dirt. It ate at her legs, climbing toward her hips, dragging her into a smothering tomb. Thorne changed course, sprinting toward her as the blood soaked her ribs, covered her breasts, and lapped at her throat.

"This only ends one way," Julian said quietly, watching her sink. "Either you stand alone..."

Cistine's head plunged under the tide of blood. Thorne's hand slammed into hers, their fingers entwining, and light burst through her whole world. He tumbled into the crimson tide, dragged down by her weight, sinking into the ocean of blood and death with her. Hands joined. Never letting go.

"Or you fall together."

Breathe.

Air shuddered into her lungs.

Beat.

Her heart leaped in her chest.

Either you stand alone...

"Come back, Wildheart..."

Or you fall together.

"*Cistine! Open your eyes!*"

She gasped back to reason, yanking against the grip of Thorne's hand around hers. Sobs ripped from her chest, her focus casting wildly over the railing, the parlor, the city far below. No broken world, no battlefield, yet she still felt the burn of Julian's hold. "What was that? What happened?"

Thorne released her hand to take her face in his callused grip, desperate eyes hunting hers. "I don't know! You were coming out of it, and then you were gone again. What in the stars did you see?"

"I saw—I saw—" *The opening and the closing. War. Peace. Death.* "I saw a battlefield, and Baba Kallah…" Another sob broke free. "I saw *Julian*…"

Thorne's brow softened, and he pulled her against his chest, pressing a kiss to her hair. "I'm sorry. None of that was supposed to happen. I don't know what went wrong, I'm so sorry…stars, look at you, Wildheart…"

The words struck her like a slap.

Look at you, Wildheart.

Thorne drew back when she stiffened, peering down at her. "Cistine?"

The dam burst without warning at the sight of his face and the sound of those words, his *father's* words, in his mouth. The storm she'd held at bay all this time to save her own life bashed apart her defenses, and the tempest and tidewaters bore down on her.

Every muscle in her body locked tight, and she lunged backward out of Thorne's hands, the pedestal's angled edge biting into her back so hard she cried out. Her fingers were numb, her nose and upper lip tingling, her heart racing, and she couldn't breathe, she couldn't *think*. She was in the stone grave of Kalt Hasa again, facing Salvotor, his hands covering hers over the knife, his eyes craving her blood, coveting all of her enslaved to all of him, bound by his will and intentions.

Like she'd just bound herself to his own *son* with that Name.

Bile surged up her throat; she folded onto the stone, destroyed by the shaking that knocked her teeth together, biting back vomit at this thing she'd just chosen, this act she'd done without thinking. The choice she never should have made.

Thorne was before her, falling so hard to his knees they cracked on the rock, no more in control of himself than she was. He took her shoulders and squeezed tightly. "Cistine! Tell me what you need!"

She didn't want him to hold her. She didn't want him to leave. Her skin burned under his touch, but she knew if he let go, she would start falling and never stop.

Either you stand alone, or you fall together.

She buckled over, vomiting and sobbing, and Thorne wrapped an arm around her middle and slipped behind her. He held her hair back and propped her up while she retched again, watering eyes turning The City of a Thousand Stars to a wash of lavender lightning.

Look at you, Wildheart.

In the dark caverns of her sprit, Salvotor's shadow settled in and made a home for himself, basking against the bleeding walls, smirking and content.

His work was done.

EPILOGUE

THE GOLDEN GHOSTLAMP glow bathed Thorne's face as he propped his shoulder against the closet doorframe, staring at the bed. Cistine stretched across it, tracing one finger over the cream-and-copper bedspread, her gaze a thousand miles absent. Thorne's heart hurt, a true, physical *ache* in his sternum, and he balled his fresh shirt between his fists.

He cursed himself for not realizing this was coming. Her time in that mountain had changed her, and he'd watched her cram away the damage so she could focus on the mission to bring Salvotor to his knees. But now that was behind them, and everything was free to crash down.

"Do you want to come sit?" Cistine asked.

"Do you want me to?"

When she nodded, he mussed his hair and tugged on his shirt, falling cross-legged beside her. She laid her hand on his knee. "This was *not* your fault, Thorne. I'm not mad at you. Maybe I shouldn't have had so much to drink...maybe that affected my dream somehow."

He brushed his knuckles along her arm. "Do you want to tell me what you saw?" Curiosity scratched desperately at his heart—to know what his grandmother said to her in that vision, and Julian, though he wasn't certain he'd like what he learned.

It was almost a relief when Cistine shook her head. "Not yet. I'm afraid it will make me sick again." She shuddered. "I've never felt so out of control. Not even when wielding augments."

Thorne stretched out beside her, folding his arms behind his head. "What do you need?"

She closed her eyes. "Can you talk to me until I fall asleep?"

He swallowed the harsh scrape of tears from the back of his throat. "Let me see if I remember the story of the Starchaser."

The tale came with the memory of a dark hall and a scarlet door, but those were not the parts he let himself dwell on. Instead, he dug up every memory of Baba Kallah from those days, the smell of freesia and powdered cosmetics gathered in the lapels of her fine shirt while he rested his head on her chest; her strong, veined hands stroking his hair when she held him against her and told him this same story from memory, the rasp of her voice turning the words to a lullaby.

He told it the same way now, just as quietly, stumbling now and again over the parts he'd forgotten since childhood; but Cistine never corrected him or interrupted, and when he reached the story's end, his voice husky with tears that refused to fall, she let out a soft snore.

Carefully, Thorne tamed a snarled lock of hair behind her ear.

This night's terror was Salvotor's doing, and scarlet doors and dark halls be damned, he wanted to visit that secluded apartment and give him a reason to have nightmares of his own. But this was just as much his own fault. He'd let her talk him into the House of Visions despite his reservations, and true to his nature, he failed the ritual somehow, revealing wounds from his father that ran deeper than her ravaged ear and healed knuckles. Like their cabal, she had nightmares waking and asleep now.

Just like Thorne himself.

He shifted uneasily, pulse quickening with memories. The burn of that dagger six times across his chest; the sting of the whip; the agony in his overtaxed muscles when they forced him to kneel in his cage until every twitch of flanks and shoulders and haunches was like a blade to the legs.

A gentle knock at the door interrupted his thoughts, and he looked sharply across the room, meeting Maleck's wide eyes as they skipped between him and Cistine, then moved to the doors of Thorne's private balcony. Sighing, he eased from the bed and padded to the doors, letting himself outside.

Quill, Ariadne, and Tatiana leaned against the balcony railing. Aden reclined beside the doors, Ashe beside him, dragging a stone pendant along its chain around her neck. Something about that stone struck Thorne as familiar, but he couldn't remember why—and he was too exhausted and upset to care.

"Where's Cistine?" Quill asked. "Finally asleep?"

Thorne checked over his shoulder for any whisper of movement in his room, but there was none. "Yes. I took her to the House of Visions tonight."

He straightened with a grin as Maleck slipped over form the adjacent balcony to join them. "You're serious? She's one of us?"

"I told her all the reasons she could reconsider, but none of them swayed her." He leaned against the door, folding his hands around his neck. "Something went wrong. She didn't come out of it like all of you...she went deeper. And afterward she had some sort of fit. Shaking. Weeping. Sick."

Ashe lurched taller, dropping the stone to sway on its chain. "Poison?"

"Panic," Maleck murmured.

"I knew it." Tatiana snagged a hand in her curls. "As soon as she had her third drink tonight, I knew something was coming. I just didn't think it would happen this soon."

Thorne looked around at their solemn faces, choking on the same urgency that sent him running to his grandmother for guidance over the years; but she was gone, and they were here. "How do I help her?"

Ashe averted her gaze. "I wish I knew. I've helped her through plenty of things, but...I can't anymore."

Tatiana stood back from the railing, wrapping her hands around its iron edge and looking out across the city. "Then we walk through the darkness with her. She's done it for all of us, now it's our turn."

Quill nodded. "As far as she goes, for as long as it takes."

The weight on Thorne's chest lessened slightly. Even if he couldn't help her with all his shortcomings and failures, they could; together, they *would*. "Thank you. All of you. Not just for this, but for everything you've done. We wouldn't be standing here today without all of us together."

"Let's hope that's enough for what's coming," Tatiana sighed. "Salvotor won't go without a fight. We have to be ready for whatever that looks like."

"We will be," Ariadne said. "This cabal will not be driven out again."

"Not after all this time." Aden lifted his eyes to the last stars gulped down by the pale spread of dawn and chuckled darkly. "The gods must have some plan for us."

Thorne glanced through the balcony doors again.

He already knew the plan, the right path before him. He knew his future...she was sleeping on the other side of that door. And he would fight for that future, for her life, for both their kingdoms.

It was not a matter of whether they were ready to face the challenges and dangers of Stornhaz; it was a question of whether he City of a Thousand Stars was ready to face *them*—whether it was truly prepared for all the change that was coming at the hands of Chancellor Thorne, Princess Cistine, and their starchasers.

End

A GUIDE
TO OLD VALGARDAN

Words:

Allatok – Heathen

Slynar – Bitch (roughly)

Bandayo – Bastard (roughly)

Nahdar – Uncle

Allet – Brother

Malat – Sister

Tajall - Infant

Storfir – Big One

Stornjor – Great Love

Yani – Sweet

Sillakove - Starchaser

Selvenar – Blended hearts

Valenar – Blended blood

Creatures:

Zabeka (AMPHIBIAN)

ACKNOWLEDGEMENTS

HERE WE ARE, three books in, at the turning point. This was the installment where the series became infinitely harder for me, the one I wrote in a dash during NaNoWriMo in November 2017, then promptly started over from scratch in December. The one where the hardest growth—for me and Cistine—truly began.

First, thanks to God. For two dreams in two nights that made me feel like I could keep going, and especially for the one about Maleck and Cistine. When I ask, You answer. Every. Single. Time. I'll never stop being grateful for that.

To Danny: For loving me through the absolute curveballs of this book and teaching me what it means to love with my whole heart, for my whole life. You are the one I waited for. <3

To my family: For supporting, for believing, for asking how it's going, for giving me up to the computer and reeling me out for the important things like Christmas Day and movie nights. To Dustin and Mom for reading every ridiculous draft and loving the final product, and Dad for telling me to JUST DO IT. Welp, I did it!!

To Cassidy and Miranda: For meeting me face-to-face right smack in the middle of editing this book and changing the course of this series and my life forever. For sneaking peeks over my shoulders and asking, "WHO ARE YOU TORTURING NOW?" Yes, I still have the Snap of your faces when I sent you the snippet about the blood—and yes, that was the moment I fell in love with our friendship forever. This book is better with both your hands in it. I owe Kristoff's side of the story to your vision and questions. I owe you so much more than that, but words fail me. Just know I love you, forever and always. <3

To Atty, Chief, Joy, Holly, and Jen, who were there for that first torturous version and the crash-rewrite, who never told me how bad it was to begin with (you loved me too much!) but let me shovel in the sand so I could build the sandcastle. <3

To Maja Kopunovic: For being not just my cover artist, but my friend, and for going through so many versions of this cover until we got it PERFECT. Love you, Partner in Crime! <3

To Maggie and Lana: For getting excited about every story from *Faceless* to *Nightwing* and beyond. Your cheerleader strength in my life at 17 is the reason this book exists at 27. Thank you for keeping me strong for a decade and more and reminding me mir-ackles do come true. <3

To all the Dreamers who started this journey and those who've joined along the way. To Savannah, the Katies, Meaghan, Christina, Elsie, Lina, Sydney, Dani, the Brittanys, Leeva, Piper, Maverick, Tiffany, Savannah, Hannah, Holly, Heather, Becca, Bethany, Annelisa, Meagan, Allie, Stephanie, and everyone else—you made the dream *real*. I will never stop being thankful for what you've given me: hope and vision and a family of writers to belong with. <3

And to you, my reader. Three books you've been with the cabal now, and the adventure has only just begun. I'm so thankful for every bit of support I receive that reminds me why I do this crazy thing I do. I can never find enough words to express my gratitude; just know you help keep me going, one foot after the other. Just one more step.

See you in the next one! <3

Read On For a Sneak Peek at

THE STARCHASER SAGA
BOOK IV

CHAPTER ONE

THOUGH AUTUMN STILL reigned in the Northern Kingdom of Valgard, ice already crowned the upper passes of the Vaszaj Range, and Princess Cistine Novacek shivered in her piled-on furs every step she followed her friends up the mountain. Snow sucked at her boots, though she walked in the others' footprints: Aden in the lead, Quill at his heels, Tatiana on his. Quill's mischievous smirk held the secret of why he ripped them all from their private apartments in the courthouse and gave them wind augments to cross the distance, camping the night on this mountain's southern face and beginning this perilous ascent before dawn.

She paused, sweating despite the cold, gripping a hardy mountain shrub for balance while she sucked in lungfuls of air so frigid it stabbed her throat. It felt good in a way, a distraction from another night of restless sleep, the heaviness in her chest, the somberness that clung to her spirit, and the strange, sick sensation in her stomach.

All her life, there was a call inside her, a sweet and urgent song growing stronger after she came to Valgard. But when she first set foot on the great rune-slab lid over the well beneath the courthouse—one of the Doors to the Gods from which Valgard once harvested their mighty augments—the call went from shrill to sour. And now, deep in her core, it snarled.

Her fingertips rattled the leaves. She pushed off from the shrub, body singing with urgency, and the ice crust snagged her ankles. A gloved hand caught under her elbow, hoisting her back up when she stumbled.

"Careful," Thorne warned. "If you think you're cold now, I don't advise getting better acquainted with these drifts."

"So much for my plans to protest Quill's secrecy." She stabbed her feet more firmly into the footprints three-boots-deep ahead of her. "Ashe could tell you how effective my tantrums are."

But Asheila Kovar, her Warden since birth, wasn't here; nor was Maleck Darkwind, one of the cabal's most trusted warriors. They were in Talheim, Cistine's kingdom, where the weather was more seasonable and the world milder and full of light. She missed them, and her home, desperately.

"Princess Cistine Novacek, throwing tantrums? Surely not." Ariadne passed them breezily, throwing a one-sided smile back at her.

Thorne released Cistine's arm but didn't move away, and she risked a glance at him. His disheveled silver hair sparkled brighter than the icicles dripping from the mountain ledges, his concerned gaze searching her face. "Are you all right?"

She rubbed her arms and nodded. "Just wondering what Quill's scheming. But it's good to be out of the city for a bit."

He sighed a cold plume of breath and raised a tentative hand toward her face. "That it is." Cistine flinched at the motion, head humming with spectral sensations of a blow from a different hand, and Thorne recoiled. "I'm sorry, that—forgive me."

"There's nothing to forgive." But she couldn't draw in a full breath until she moved away from his voice and touch, from the memory stirred by his eyes and voice of an enemy more creature than man.

It was nearly sunhigh when they reached the treeline, a broad shelf of stone dropping perilously toward a thin river between the mountains, and Quill fanned out an arm. "We're here."

A lonely caw floated down from the trees; Faer, his trained attack raven, swooped from scouting to alight on his shoulder. Cistine wandered past them, brushing a hand down the bird's back and leaning over the ledge to peer at the water far below. Aden flung out an arm across her front, shaking his head. Tatiana whistled, high to low, folding her arms and cocking her weight on one hip.

"Impressive view, Featherbrain!"

"If the plan was to remind us of our nominal place in the vastness of Valgard, message received." Ariadne nudged Quill's ribs. "But couldn't this have waited?"

"The view, maybe. But not this." He plundered in his pocket and withdrew a glittering globe of godlike power—a fire flagon.

The taste of what lurked within that thin glass shell blew through Cistine sharper than any mountain wind. She didn't realize she'd taken a step toward Quill until Aden's deep voice halted her. "Why are we here?"

Quill's gaze fixed on Cistine, full of lively challenge. "Because I want to see what she can do."

As the Key.

The words hung unspoken and understood; they all must've been wondering it while they fought to rescue her from Chancellor Salvotor over the past two months. No one else like her existed in this kingdom, a girl forged of power in her father's bloodline before she was born—power that reached out to the flagon in Quill's hand.

Come. The familiar call thrummed in her chest. *Come and see.*

When she laid hold of the augment, Quill's three-fingered hand tightened over hers. "Only if you want to, Stranger."

She sucked air down deeply, filling the parts of her that went hollow during captivity in a dark mountain prison. "I want to."

She took the flagon and turned, catching Thorne's eye. He lingered farther off than the others, giving her a wide berth, but his attention was focused and intense, waiting for her to need him. That look, if not his touch, still made her heart race pleasantly. When he offered his hand, she slung off her pack and passed it to him. "What do you want me to do, Quill?"

A dart of his chin indicated a peak more than a mile away. "See that mountain? Try to hit it."

"That's all? You're not going to tell me how?"

"I think you already know how."

She opened her mouth to tell him that was absurd, it took weeks in sparring and swordplay before she started to feel the last bit competent, and this was no different—yet the augment trilled in her fist, and her spirit echoed it, a melody her untrained ears knew and loved.

"Stand back," Thorne warned as Cistine broke the flagon against her armored thigh. Panic lanced through her along with the fire that it might escape her control like the lightning in Kalt Hasa when she tried to set them free. But where that lightning was vibrant and volatile, this fire purred and hugged her contours, sliding into the reinforced armor that conducted it away from flesh it could otherwise melt, sinew and bone it could sunder in any body but hers.

And then it traveled deeper.

Frowning, she shut her eyes and dove after it.

This sensation was different from the blinding few moments of escape from Kalt Hasa when she embodied light, then lightning; the fire congealed at her very center, heat flowering into a sphere, and in her mind she could wrap her hands around it and mold it to her wishes. The more she concentrated, the stronger it felt—not only a fire augment, but the wild heart of fire for which she was Named. Her spirit sang to that which was like it, a portion crafted before her birth in a ritual known only to her father and the *visnprest* Order that came before, the making that would pass down to her descendants and their descendants. A trust as sacred as the throne Cistine was born to in the Middle Kingdom.

She reached the bottom of her breath, the door in her spirit where the fire shuddered to a halt. Then she opened her eyes, focused on that faraway peak, and unleashed a sickle of flame, blazing and bellowing like dragon's breath, blasting the cabal away with audible shouts.

Fire sheared into stone, booming like thunder. With a distant crack, droves of snow, ice, and rock gave way, and half the mountaintop plunged into the valley below.

It took far too long for the echo to fade, for Cistine's racing heart to slow and the embers to stop drifting from her fingertips. Behind her, Tatiana breathed, "Holy stars."

"*Logandir.*" The name was a helpless prayer on Ariadne's lips. Aden stared openmouthed. Quill folded his hands around the nape of his neck, gaping at the damage, and Cistine's cheeks heated like all the rest of the embers gathered beneath her skin.

Thorne cocked his head. "Why did you close your eyes?"

She swallowed. "It felt different from how I thought it would, so I followed the power and molded it into the shape I wanted...like how my mother molds clay in her sculpting classes."

Quill dropped his hands, looking swiftly at Tatiana.

"Is it...not like that for everyone else?" Cistine whispered.

"To us, the power simply *is*," Ariadne said. "We channel it, but we don't shape it."

Cistine hugged herself, cold all over again. "I wish it wasn't different for me."

Ariadne's angled eyes softened. "What we see as different, the gods often deem miraculous."

"Now, that," Quill said when another clot of rock shattered from an unstable ledge and hurtled into the valley, "is going to need a *lot* of molding."

"I'm ready whenever you are," Cistine vowed.

He turned his scorched-white wing of hair across his scalp. "Then we should probably start now."

When Thorne stepped up to Cistine's side, she didn't flinch this time. She desperately needed the solidarity of his presence in the silence that followed, beholding the destructive potential of her power.

ABOUT THE AUTHOR

Renee Dugan is an Indiana-based author who grew up reading fantasy books, chasing stray cats, and writing stories full of dashing heroes and evil masterminds. Now with over a decade of professional editing, administrative work, and writing every spare second under her belt, she has authored *THE CHAOS CIRCUS,* a portal fantasy novel, and *THE STARCHASER SAGA,* an epic high fantasy series. Living with her husband, son, and not-so-stray cats in the magical Midwest, she continues to explore new worlds and spends her time in this one encouraging and helping other writers on their journey to fulfilling their dreams.

Find Renee Dugan online at:
Reneeduganwriting.com

And on social media: **@reneeduganwriting**

www.ingramcontent.com/pod-product-compliance
Lightning Source LLC
Chambersburg PA
CBHW021326110726
47900CB00005B/1366